THE
BLOOD
RUNS COLD

CATHERINE MAIORISI

BELLA
B O O K S

2019

Bella Books, Inc.
P.O. Box 10543
Tallahassee, FL 32302

Printed in the United States of America on acid-free paper.

First Bella Books Edition 2019

Editor: Ann Roberts
Cover Designer: Judith Fellows

ISBN: 978-1-64247-026-0

Other Bella Books by Catherine Maiorisi

Matters of the Heart
No One But You

A Chiara Corelli Mystery Series
A Matter of Blood

Acknowledgments

The Blood Runs Cold, the second in my NYPD Detective Chiara Corelli mystery series, owes a lot to the people who made the first, *A Matter of Blood*, possible. But I won't bore you by repeating what I said about them.

As always, I'm grateful to my wife Sherry for her continued support and for accepting that I spend a lot of time in my head with strange characters. I particularly appreciate that she protects my writing time, even when it means less time together.

And to friends Lee Crespi and Judy Levitz who read early versions of this manuscript and provided invaluable feedback, I appreciate your willingness to read the same book multiple times.

A shoutout to my sister-in-law Barbara Felsinger for going above and beyond the requirements of sister-in-law-hood by sending copies of *A Matter of Blood* to many of her friends and then sharing their feedback with me. Hopefully, they'll buy their own copies of *The Blood Runs Cold*.

Thanks to Rachel Gold, Bella Books author of award-winning novels about transgender girls, for taking time to review my treatment of a transgender character. Hopefully, I got her right. I haven't read all of Rachel's books but I highly recommend *Being Emily* and *Just Girls*.

For answering my multitude of questions about police procedure, many thanks to Joseph L. Giacalone, a retired NYPD Sergeant and internationally recognized expert with an extensive background in criminal investigations. A professor in the Law, Police Science and Criminal Justice Administration Department of John Jay College of Criminal Justice, Joe is the author of *The Criminal Investigative Function: A Guide for New Investigators*.

And since I have so many questions about the New York police department, I also need to thank NYPD Lieutenant Bernard Whalen, co-author of *The NYPD's First Fifty Years: Politicians, Police Commissioners and Patrolmen*, for his willingness to help.

I also want to offer thanks to the bloggers and reviewers who support crime writers and their books. I know you do it because you love books and authors (most of the time). But I love you for doing it.

Once again, I was lucky to have Ann Roberts, an accomplished romance and mystery author, assigned as my editor. Although I'd read the manuscript of *The Blood Runs Cold* countless times, Ann found a number of incongruities (I call them gotcha items) and skillfully guided me to a stronger book. Thanks, my friend.

As always a huge thank you to Linda Hill for publishing *The Blood Runs Cold*. Linda, Jessica, and the other dedicated women behind the scenes at Bella Books do the hard work required to publish a book. I appreciate all you do, your good humor, and especially the patience you show when answering this anxious writer's questions.

And to my readers: *The Blood Runs Cold*, like *A Matter of Blood*, is set in New York City because it is *my* city and I love it. It also features NYPD detectives and, therefore, the New York City Police Department. Although I've spoken to many NYPD officers and detectives and asked many procedural questions, the police department portrayed is *my* fictional NYPD and any resemblance to the real NYPD is purely coincidental.

I love hearing from readers so please contact me through www.catherinemaiorisi.com. I hope you enjoy *The Blood Runs Cold*. And if you do, I encourage you to recommend it to friends, post about it on social media, and review it if you can. I'm truly grateful for your support.

About the Author

Catherine Maiorisi lives in New York City and often writes under the watchful eye of Edgar Allan Poe, in Edgar's Café near the apartment she shares with her wife Sherry.

While working in corporate technology then running her own technology consulting company, Catherine felt she was the only lesbian in New York City who wasn't creative, the only one without the imagination or the talent to write poetry or novels, play the guitar, act, or sing.

Years later, Catherine challenged herself to write a mystery but realized she didn't have the foggiest idea how to write a novel. So she spent the next nine months reading every book she could find about writing and tried again. When she sat down to write, Catherine's imagination came alive and four months later she had a draft of a detective/mystery novel.

Since then Catherine has published two NYPD Detective Chiara Corelli Mysteries, *The Blood Runs Cold* and *A Matter of Blood*. She has also published three mystery short stories in the *Murder New York Style* anthologies—"Justice for All" in *Fresh Slices*, "Murder Italian Style" in *Family Matters*, and "Love, Secrets, and Lies" in *Where Crime Never Sleeps.*

Catherine has also published two full-length romances — *Matters of the Heart* and *No One But You.* Her romance short stories include a standalone ebook, *Come as You Want to Be*, and "The Fan Club" in *The Best Lesbian Romances of 2014*, "All's Well that Ends Well" in *Conference Call* and "You Will See a Stranger" in *Happily Ever After.*

Writing is like meditating for Catherine and it is what she most loves to do. But she also reads voraciously, loves to cook, especially Italian, and enjoys hanging out with her wife and friends.

Catherine is a member of Sisters in Crime, Mystery Writers of America, Romance Writers of America, Rainbow Romance Writers, the Authors Guild, and the Guppies, an online chapter of Sisters in Crime.

Dedication

For my late parents, Helen and George Maiorisi: Although you never went beyond the eighth grade, you instilled a love of reading in me.

Although girls weren't supposed to be educated, you made sure I went to college.

Thank you.

CHAPTER ONE

Wednesday – 7 a.m.

Being ostracized was getting old fast. At least for NYPD Detective Chiara Corelli. And maybe for the press, since they hadn't shown up this morning. But from her vantage point in a car a block away from the station house, it was clear her colleagues were still in the game.

She hadn't missed this while Parker was away. And she wouldn't miss being tied to her desk now that Parker was back. "I've been going in alone for the last two weeks, Parker. No need to subject yourself to the gauntlet. You can follow later when it's safer."

"Damn you, Corelli, stop playing the martyr." Detective P.J. Parker made no attempt to hide her anger. "Watkins told me the captain escorted you in while I was away so there *was* no gauntlet. But I'm back and so is the gauntlet. And just because they haven't attempted to kill you up to now, doesn't mean they won't try today. So don't even think about going into that crowd or anywhere else without me."

"Kissin' my ass won't change my decision, Parker."

"Treating me like the enemy won't change mine. Besides, I'm anxious to get inside where I assume you'll let me in on your decision about my future."

Good. Parker isn't taking my shit. That thought caught Corelli by surprise. She couldn't remember ever treating anyone the way she'd treated Parker on the Winter case. Nasty wasn't her style, yet the words slipped out before she could stop them. Parker thought she had PTSD. Could she be right?

Parker got out of the car then leaned in before closing the door. "Better hurry, your fan club is getting restless."

As they approached, the crowd shuffled into two rows of uniforms back to back forming a gauntlet through which they had to pass to get to the station house. These were her colleagues. She used to trust them to watch her back. Now she had to trust Parker to protect her from them. And, this daily ritual of humiliation had replaced their respect. She hated it, but she'd known the consequences of going undercover to expose the ring of dirty cops. Each time she approached the mouth of the funnel, she remembered the video she'd seen of a snake swallowing a cow—whole. And each time she reminded herself that unlike the cow, she came out the other end a little battered but alive. She'd faced worse things in her life. And survived.

She popped two Maalox tablets, then elbowed Parker. "Here we go."

Parker rubbed her ribs. "Jeez, Corelli, I don't need black and blues from you."

"Oops, did I wrinkle your silk shirt?"

"Crazy bitch," Parker muttered.

"Could you speak up? I didn't hear that," Corelli yelled.

Shaking her head, Parker linked arms with Corelli and they plunged into the belly of the beast, elbowing the line to make space to walk side by side. With the temperature and the humidity both already in the nineties, the stench of sweating bodies, cloying colognes, scented soap, and stale booze was oppressive. And sickening. Although it would serve them right if she vomited all over them, she put a handkerchief over her nose. She stumbled over a leg. Parker steadied her. Corelli kicked the offender. Elbows smacked her arm, her stomach, her back. Only her quick reflexes protected her face and her eyes. She punched to the right, felt Parker punching to the left. Sweat stung her eyes and lips. She gasped for air as the two lines pressed closer, intensifying the heat.

Trailed by hissing and muttered insults—bitch, whore, traitor—they fought their way through the roiling mass of humanity.

She strained to see how far they had left to go but could only see the shoulders and heads of the uniforms sucking her forward, like that cow. Just when she thought she might pass out from the heat and the stink, they were at the door to the stationhouse. A uniform blocked it.

Corelli pushed him aside. "Move your fat ass, Donnelly."

"Bitch," he said. He raised his hand.

Before she could respond, Parker was nose to nose with him, her hands fisted at her sides. "Don't even think about it."

He dropped his hand. "Black bitch," he muttered and stepped away.

Corelli turned to go after him but Parker clasped her arm, and spoke softly. "I can fight my own battles."

Corelli nodded. Parker probably faced down the racism of cops and the rest of the world every day. She didn't need Corelli's protection. But maybe they needed to have a conversation about racism. Corelli continued forward. During most of her first month back on the job her colleagues had performed a coordinated ballet of standing, showing backs and hissing each time she passed them, but the action disrupted their work and the captain had prohibited it. Now they were confronted by a hostile silence and averted eyes as they made their way up the stairs to the squad and their desks.

The room was empty. Corelli threw her jacket on her desk, stood in front of the ancient air conditioner and raised her arms, trying to cool down and dry her silk blouse. After a minute she went to the water cooler, drank a cup, refilled it and drank that. She tossed the cup, dropped into the chair behind her desk, and rubbed her leg. "Damn gauntlet. Is it my imagination or are they getting rougher? My body is one big black and blue. They getting you too, Parker?"

Looking sweaty but still trim and neat in her navy suit and light blue silk shirt, Detective P.J. Parker ignored the question.

Corelli wiped her face with a handkerchief. "You know, Parker, my navy suit and lavender blouse look nice with what you're wearing. Maybe we should coordinate what we wear every day."

As if she hadn't heard, Parker walked to the cooler, downed a cup of water, and strode back. Placing her hands on the desk, she leaned in so she was eye-to-eye with Corelli. "No doubt about it. Either you're nuts or you have a serious case of PTSD." She straightened, breaking the contact, and took a deep breath. "If talking about coordinating our outfits means I'm staying, you could have told me in the car and made it easier."

"This might come as a shock, Parker, but making life easier for you isn't in my job description."

"So am I still working with you?"

The night they wrapped the Winter case, just over two weeks ago, Parker's father, US Senator Aloysius T. Parker, appeared on TV and used case information that was not public to accuse Corelli of being a dirty cop and a racist. When Parker called to deny being the source of the leak, Corelli was in a rage.

"Does this mean you don't want to work with me?" Parker asked.

"I don't know what it means," Corelli said and ended the call. After she cooled down and was thinking clearly, Corelli could see no reason for Parker to turn on her. Parker wanted homicide and she knew without Corelli she'd lose the opportunity. Besides, she had begun to trust Parker and believed her.

Then Parker hadn't picked her up the next morning and it wasn't until she'd fought her way through the gauntlet that she found out Parker had started a two-week detective training program that morning. She'd felt betrayed by Parker, but it turned out that Parker, along with Corelli and the captain, had been blindsided by whoever scheduled the training.

But she hadn't shared any of this with Parker in the car this morning. She tried not to think about why she enjoyed torturing Parker but she couldn't resist. "You sure you didn't give Senator Daddy any information?"

"That's. What. I. Said." Parker's words were clipped, as if she was trying to stay in control. "I distinctly remember telling you that I haven't talked to the senator in five years."

"And are you sure you didn't know in advance about the training?"

Parker rolled her eyes. "How many times do I have to say it? I didn't know until late the night before. I tried to call you but you were ignoring my calls after the senator's attack. I wasn't too worried because you're my superior and I assumed you knew and forgot to tell me. No, actually I assumed you purposefully didn't tell me just to keep me off balance."

Corelli couldn't fault Parker for expecting the worst of her. And as Parker's superior, she should have been involved in the scheduling of her training. Also because she wasn't allowed to work cases if Parker wasn't there as her bodyguard, the training dates should have been cleared with the captain. But the blue wall punishes however it can.

Corelli flashed a gotcha smile. "We don't assume, Parker, we work with facts. Didn't you learn anything during your two weeks of detective training?" She gazed at Parker, pretending to consider the issue. "Okay, since you didn't leak to Senator Daddy and you didn't know about the training in advance, you're staying. But your job description no longer says bodyguard and detective-in-training. You're now just a detective-in-training."

"Uh-uh." Parker's already tight jaw jutted out. "Until Captain Winfry or Chief Broderick tells me different, I'm watching your back."

"If you want to work with me, you do what I say. Got it?"

Parker's eyes sparked. Her face flushed. "Stop treating me like—"

"Corelli." Detective Ray Dietz appeared at the top of the steps. "Potential homicide on West Twelfth Street and the captain says it's yours."

"Jesus, Dietz, Parker just came back, how can we be up already?"

"Look around, Corelli." He waved his hand indicating the empty room. "We got ongoing investigations, we got vacations, we got sick leave, we got court appearances, and we got whatever. But we don't got any warm bodies except you and the kid here, so you're it."

The anger always just beneath Corelli's calm exterior bubbled up and nearly erupted before she caught herself. Screw the paperwork and the cold cases. Give her a homicide investigation any time. She grabbed her jacket. "I'm on it, Dietz." As she started down the stairs, she turned back. "You're with me, Parker. You can fill me in on what I can't treat you like later."

CHAPTER TWO

Wednesday – 9 a.m.

Even in death, Leonardo del Balzo was gorgeous. He lay on his back on the sofa, wearing only pajama bottoms, hands folded over his bare chest, a rosary entwined in his fingers. Except for the small hole Corelli knew was at the back of his head, he could have been sleeping. Of course, if he was sleeping, two NYPD detectives wouldn't be staring at him from the doorway of his living room.

The room was cool. The black glass beads of the rosary glittered in the dim light of the lamp on the end table near del Balzo's head. The scent of incense lingered in the air, and a Gregorian chant played softly in the background. The phrase "may your soul rest in peace" echoed in Corelli's mind along with the image of another beautiful young man, Luca, her adored older brother, in his casket with his confirmation missal and black-beaded rosary clasped in his hands. A sudden stab of loss took her breath away. Twenty years later and she still ached for Luca. She had been too young to find the man who killed him, but she would track down Leonardo del Balzo's murderer, whatever the cost.

Aware of Parker waiting for instructions, Corelli forced herself to focus. The killer had obviously taken care and spent time setting up the scene. What did it mean? A religious fetish? A funeral fetish? Did the killer bring the incense and music or did he just take advantage of what he found? Were they dealing with a serial killer? "Parker, ask Dietz to find out whether we've had other vics posed like this."

While Parker made a note, Corelli turned her attention to del Balzo, the "what" of him: curly sandy hair, tanned skin now drained of color, and a lean, muscular body, now flaccid, tall enough that his feet hung over the arm of the six-foot sofa. Like her, he had the blue-green eyes characteristic of Italians whose families carried the blood of the Norman conquerors of Southern Italy in their veins. The "who" of him they would learn by talking to family, friends, acquaintances, colleagues, neighbors, enemies—anyone who touched his life. And from those interviews, hopefully, they would identify the one person who wanted Leonardo del Balzo dead. A serial killer would be another story.

"Ready to go in?"

"Yes." Parker sounded tense. Recently promoted out of uniform after saving a family in Harlem, she still wasn't totally comfortable in her new role. And she was still wary of Corelli.

They donned the requisite protective gear, and placing their feet carefully, stepped into the living room. No sign of a struggle. No sign of a gun. A small incense burner filled with ash sat on the coffee table near an open bottle of San Pellegrino water and a half-empty glass. They circled the room slowly, touching nothing, observing everything.

When they stopped, Parker took out her pad and pen and started sketching the scene.

Corelli was pleased to see that Parker had learned the value of sketching as a tool to really seeing. "What do ya see?"

Parker chewed the top of her pen. "He's laid out as if in a funeral parlor, though the smell of incense and the religious music suggest a church. He's in his pajamas, let the killer get close enough to put a bullet in his head, and there's no sign of a struggle. So probably the vic, um, Mr. del Balzo knew his killer."

A burst of sound in the hall signaled the arrival of Detective Ron Watkins and other detectives who would work the case. The crime scene team crowded in behind them. The photographer greeted

Corelli as she moved into the room and began to photograph the scene.

Archie Blockman, the Medical Examiner, appeared in the doorway. As usual, Archie's clothes draped his elongated body perfectly. Today he wore a forest-green suit with a pale green shirt, a silk tie with green and brown and orange streaks and a matching handkerchief in the breast pocket of his jacket. "Ah, Chiara, I see I'm in the right place." He suited up and pulled on gloves.

When the photographer signaled she was done, Archie picked up his bag and moved to the body. He grunted as he lowered himself to his knees next to the sofa. Then he was silent, his focus on the body. Corelli had never asked and he had never said, but she had the impression he said a prayer before examining a victim, that the prayer and the extreme elegance in clothes and manners he affected were his way of distancing himself from the dehumanizing aspects of his job.

He examined del Balzo, then waved Corelli over to help turn del Balzo on his side, revealing the hole in the cerebellum the EMTs had reported when Corelli and Parker arrived. He muttered to himself as he stepped through the process. Then he sighed and pulled himself to his feet.

"So what do we have, Arch?"

He removed his gloves and pushed his manicured fingers through his rust-brown curls. "As EMS reported, a single shot to the cerebellum with a small-caliber gun. No exit wound. Probably killed him instantly. Off the cuff, I'd say TOD somewhere between nine last night and three this morning. Probably killed here. No apparent defense wounds. Can't say much more until we get him on the table. We'll take him now."

"When do you think—"

"Today, if I can, Chiara. If not, tomorrow morning for sure." He waved his team in from the hall to remove the body, his thoughts already somewhere else as he removed the protective gear. The CSU moved into the room, energizing it with their sense of purpose as they began performing their assigned roles.

She supervised for a while, then turned to Watkins, watching from the hall. "Parker and I are going to take a quick look in the bedroom. Keep an eye out for a phone, address book, appointment book, or a computer. Also, get a team out to canvas the neighborhood. Let's go, Parker."

"Got it," Ron said, opening his phone.

Corelli stopped in the doorway to the bedroom and Parker slammed into her.

Corelli threw up her hands. "Christ, Parker, I thought we already had the don't get up my ass discussion."

Parker staggered back. "Sorry, I didn't know you were going to stop."

"Don't you remember what I said? Bumping into me irritates me, breathing down my neck irritates me, but apologizing irritates me worst of all. Suck it up, Detective. Concentrate. Observe. A homicide investigation is not the place to daydream."

Corelli glanced over her shoulder. "And, don't just say fuck you to my back and ignore what I say. You should know by now I always stop before entering a room to get an overview, and so should you."

When she turned to survey the room, her eyes widened at the large crucifix hanging over the bed. Maybe it was the lack of a wedding ring, or something about the apartment, but she had assumed del Balzo was single. How did he have sex with that in the room? She could never do it. But then again, it wasn't an issue for her these days. She was still mourning Marnie. So, despite her attraction to a suspect on their last case, the job was her life, twenty-four-seven. *Some role model you are. You tell Parker not to daydream and here you are thinking about a woman instead of del Balzo.* She shook her head and focused on the room.

The bed was neatly made, so probably no sex in bed with the killer last night.

Parker was already at work. "Have you ever seen a closet like this?"

She joined her in front of the closet. Suits, shirts, ties, pants, and jackets, hung by type and color, sporty on the right, more formal on the left.

Corelli snorted. "Not in my apartment." She moved to the night table, opened the drawer and pulled out a wallet. "We can rule out robbery. His American Express, Master, and Visa cards are in his wallet along with nearly three hundred dollars. Driver's license indicates he's thirty-three, employee ID card indicates he works at the United Nations. Only other thing in the wallet is a business card for an attorney, Scott L. Sigler."

Parker checked the pockets and linings of all the garments, taking care not to disturb the arrangement. "Nothing here. Just some change, a couple of paper clips, and a napkin from the FruFru Club on Bleeker Street. Sounds gay."

"It is." Corelli bagged the wallet.

Parker examined each of the ten boxes on the shelves and found only shoes. "Nice soft leather," she said. "Italian, I guess. There's nothing in the clothes or the shoeboxes. And nothing but a cardboard box on the floor, not even dust bunnies."

Corelli searched the other night table. "Just some condoms, loose collar stays, and some change here."

Parker rifled through the contents of the box. "Magazines and newspapers, all in a foreign language."

Corelli took a look. "They're Italian. I'll check them later."

"I've heard you speak Italian but I figured it was because your parents didn't speak English when you were growing up. So you read too?"

"Yup. Gianna and I spent summers in Italy when we were kids and our cousins taught us to read and write. You impressed?"

Parker closed the box of magazines. "Let's just say I'm surprised."

"You think I'm just a dumb ass Italian from Brooklyn?" Corelli moved to the large dresser.

Parker spoke to Corelli's back. "You used those words to describe yourself, not me."

Corelli glanced over her shoulder. "Touché." She turned her attention to the dresser. Like everything else, it was neat. A comb and brush, a bottle of cologne, and what looked like a family picture. A striking older woman, maybe his mother, a man who looked like him, probably his father, and two young women with del Balzo between them, maybe his sisters.

Corelli started going through the drawers. "You think his closet is neat, wait until you see his drawers."

Parker started on the other column of drawers, whistled again at the neatly folded clothing separated by type—underwear, T-shirts, socks, shorts, handkerchiefs.

They moved back into the living room. Corelli stopped to talk to Ron. "We're done in the bedroom. Nothing there except his wallet. Any luck with a phone or computer?"

"Not so far," Ron said.

"We'll be out back questioning the witness."

On the way to the kitchen, they passed a small room set up for exercise with a Bowflex Home Gym, an elliptical trainer, a treadmill, a punching bag, and hanging on a wall, skis, rollerblades, and a mountain bike. Mr. del Balzo worked at looking good.

The sliding glass door in the kitchen opened out to the backyard where Officer Williams waited with the cleaning woman who had found the body. As she stepped into the sunlit yard, Corelli slipped on her sunglasses, then inhaled deeply, replacing the smell of death with the smell of newly cut grass and the fragrance of nearby flowering bushes. The backyard was quiet except for the drone of an electric saw somewhere in the neighborhood and the songs of the birds that seemed to be enjoying the late August morning.

Miranda Foxworth slumped in a chair at the picnic table, knees pressed tightly together, head in her large hands, a waterfall of long blond hair sheltering her face. She wore a tropical-looking yellow and coral blouse tucked into a solid peach skirt, and sandals with laces that crisscrossed her toned calves. Her nails were coral and looked recently done. She looked too dressed up to clean, but maybe she carried a change of clothing in the enormous bag on her lap.

Corelli sat at the table. "Ms. Foxworth."

Miranda Foxworth looked up. She brushed the hair off her face. Lips quivering, red eyes brimming with tears, she hunched into herself. She clamped her shaking hands on the purse. She looked poised to run.

Was it finding del Balzo dead? Or fear? As Corelli studied the woman, the small pink, white and blue enamel pin on the strap of her purse caught her eye. She recognized the transgender flag. A trans woman? She wouldn't have high expectations for any interaction with the police and many would have run rather than get involved.

Corelli removed her sunglasses, looked in Foxworth's eyes, and smiled. "Thank you for calling this in and waiting to talk to us. I'm sure it wasn't easy." She tilted her head toward the purse. "Nice pin."

Foxworth's eyebrows shot up. "Um, thanks." She seemed to relax at the acknowledgment.

"You clean for Mr. del Balzo?"

"Every Wednesday for the last two years."

"Tell me about this morning."

"I got here at eight thirty, same as always, and used my keys to get in. The alarm was off, the top was unlocked, and the bottom was locked but not double-locked. I didn't think anything of it because he's often late getting out and sometimes he forgets to lock up. But I was surprised to see him lying on the sofa when I walked past the living room door. At first I thought he was asleep, maybe hung over or sick, but then he looked…" She shrugged. "Not right. So I got closer. And I knew."

"Did you touch anything?"

"No. I couldn't breathe so I ran outside. Then I used my cell to call 911. Thank god Officer Williams got here so fast." She smiled at the officer, who pretended not to notice.

Corelli turned to Williams. He didn't wait to be asked.

"When we got here EMS was already with the victim—"

"Mr. del Balzo, Officer."

He flushed. "EMS verified Mr. del Balzo was dead so me and Santiago checked the house to be sure the killer was gone. Then Santiago went out front to wait for the detectives, for you, and I took…um, the witness, um, Ms. Foxworth, back here so we wouldn't contaminate the scene."

"Good work," Corelli said. "Was the sliding door locked when you came out here?"

Williams flushed again and glanced at the door. He cleared his throat. "I…I don't remember."

"It was locked." All eyes shifted to Foxworth. "He fumbled with the lock. I was surprised he was nervous too."

"Excuse us." Corelli stepped away from the table, signaling Parker and Williams to follow. She spoke softly to Williams. "Is this your first murder scene?"

He nodded.

"I appreciate your honesty. Whether or not the door was locked is an important detail for our investigation. Make sure your report says you checked the door and found it locked. In the future, be more careful and more observant."

He nodded. "Thanks."

She stepped back to the table and sat across from Foxworth. Parker and Williams followed. The conference seemed to make Foxworth anxious again; her face glistened with sweat and she was gnawing her cuticles.

"Ms. Foxworth, you told the officers Mr. del Balzo was the son of an ambassador at the United Nations. Are you sure?"

She tossed her hair and looked up at the tree. "Um. He never said, but you know, gossip around the clubs. And there were stories in the newspapers this week about the ambassador and the man in the newspaper was the same man in that picture on his dresser. Anyway, same name and Nardo was a dead ringer for him...oh, sorry, uh, spitting image."

Corelli had also recognized the name and the face in the photograph. Last week Ambassador del Balzo was named as a possible replacement for Italy's prime minister and the New York papers had been running stories about him. An angle to be considered. Could be the murder was politically motivated. Maybe a warning to Ambassador del Balzo? "He's called Nardo?"

"Yeah. Short for, you know, Leonardo."

"Do you know if Nardo had a cell phone or a computer?"

"Um, yes, an iPhone. I know because he advised me to get one." She dug in her bag and pulled out her iPhone. "I have his number if you need it."

Corelli nodded. Parker wrote the number Foxworth read from her phone.

"What about a computer?"

Foxworth hesitated. "He had a laptop." She closed her eyes. "A MacBook, I think."

"How did you come to work for him?"

"I only take referrals. A client must have given him my name."

"Which client?"

She closed her eyes and pressed her fingers to her temples. "I'm sorry, it's been two years. I can't remember. Maybe later?"

Corelli handed Miranda a card. "Call me as soon as you remember. Did Nardo keep valuables or money in the house?"

"Not since he was robbed about six months ago. The robbery really freaked him. That was when he installed the alarm and bought a gun."

Human nature. Install the alarm after the robbery. "Do you know where he kept the gun?"

"In the table next to his bed. He told me where it was in case someone broke in while I was cleaning." She shuddered. "As if I could shoot someone."

"Did you ever notice a prayer book or a rosary?"

"You mean like what was in his hands? I never look in my clients' drawers and I never saw anything like that lying around." Miranda pushed the hair out of her eyes. "There's a cross in his bedroom."

"Where were you last night?"

Her eyes filled with fear. "Me? Um, at the QueensBartique, a bar in Queens, until about eleven and then home with my partner. We live near there."

Parker asked her to spell the name of the bar and her partner's name. Miranda licked her lips and cleared her throat before responding. She watched Parker write it down.

"I didn't kill him. Nardo treated me with respect. He didn't care that I was his cleaning lady. He always introduced me to his friends and invited me to join them when we ran into each other at a bar or someplace. I could never hurt him." Tears streamed down her face. "I swear," she said, her voice husky, her palms up, pleading for understanding.

"It sounds like you traveled in the same circles. Did Nardo have any enemies?"

Foxworth pulled a tissue out of her pocket, dabbed at the tears in her eyes, then blew her nose. "Not the same circles. But once in a while we ran into each other at a bar. He was always a real gentleman. Everybody liked him."

"Was Mr. de Balzo transgender?"

Parker sucked in her breath. Williams was suddenly interested in the birds on the lawn.

Miranda didn't seem fazed. "No. But, um, I don't know. I guess it's okay. I mean he's dead…He's gay, um, was gay." She rubbed her eyes, blinked rapidly, and looked down with great interest at her fingers plucking threads from the handbag in her lap.

Gay. And he had a crucifix over his bed. How did he reconcile his homosexuality with religion? Many people believed they were mutually exclusive. She still didn't know where she stood on the issue. Not that she was religious, but she had gone to church every Sunday until she'd left home at eighteen, and in her experience the indoctrination of those early years was not easily erased. If the cross was any indication, he still believed. *Snap to it Corelli. Your mind is wandering again.*

Corelli sensed Foxworth hesitating to share something. "Is there something else, Ms. Foxworth? Please don't hold back. Something you know could help us find the murderer."

Miranda chewed her lip. "Well, like I said, as far as I know he wasn't trans or a cross-dresser, just a vanilla gay guy." She looked at Corelli. "But he called me in a rage Monday night. He said, 'It's payback time. I need you help.'"

"Who was he paying back?"

Miranda squirmed. "He didn't say. And I didn't ask."

"And why did he call you about this?"

"He wanted me to dress him like a woman—you know, clothes, makeup, wig, spiked heels, everything. We're about the same height so he thought my clothing would fit him. Said he was having a coming out party at the end of the week."

CHAPTER THREE

Wednesday – 12 p.m.

Corelli and Parker hesitated inside the outer door to del Balzo's apartment and listened to the activity on the street. Judging by the low rumble reporters and their cameramen were focused on recording what they knew so far—a reported homicide—not watching for Corelli.

Corelli pointed to the door, and using her fingers, did a countdown. On three, they bolted out the door, ran down the steps, and jumped into their vehicle before any of the reporters realized what was happening.

"Hey, there's Corelli," someone yelled as they pulled away.

Parker glanced in the rearview mirror. "Looks like somebody's on our side. Williams's partner stopped traffic and the media can't get through."

Corelli shifted to look back. "Well, well. It's nice to know not all cops hate me. Peer pressure forces the support underground, but it's there. Sometimes."

"Where to?"

"First Avenue. United Nations. I'd like to notify the ambassador before he hears it from a reporter."

Parker slowed as they neared the familiar slab of the thirty-nine-story Secretariat tower looming over the other three UN buildings like a gigantic gravestone. "There." Corelli pointed to the line of people shuffling into the building at 46th Street and then resumed her phone call with Detective Ron Watkins. Parker pulled over.

Corelli had asked Watkins to locate where in the huge UN complex they would find the ambassador, and now she was doodling in the notebook on her lap and uttering an occasional uh-huh. In the glare of the midday sunlight, she looked pale and shaky, and her hollowed-out, red-rimmed eyes accented by dark shadows underneath hinted at sleepless nights. When Corelli smashed her hand during the Winter case, she'd asked Parker to retrieve her gun from the bedroom and help buckle the holster. From her several forays into the bedroom, Parker deduced Corelli slept with her gun on the pillow next to her. Not too surprising. Tours in Iraq and Afghanistan followed by three months undercover investigating a ring of dirty cops could do that to a person. Being ostracized didn't help.

Parker hadn't known Corelli before they started working together a little more than a month ago, so she didn't know how she looked or what her temperament was like before Iraq and Afghanistan, or before going undercover. She did know that Corelli worked herself hard, in the office by seven every morning unless she was out at a crime scene, and following up on the case at night until it was too late to see witnesses.

And Parker knew, rather she believed, Corelli had PTSD. So far, Corelli seemed able to hide it from everyone but her. In the short time they'd worked together, she'd seen Corelli freaked by sudden flashes of light and loud noises, been at the mercy of her mood swings, anger, and nasty needling, and had watched Corelli deliberately put her life in danger. Yet in that time, Corelli had successfully dealt with threats to her life, her job, and her family while solving a complicated murder and bringing down the higher-ups in the gang of dirty cops she'd gone undercover to investigate. Corelli's mood swings and occasional nastiness made her difficult to work with, but she was giving Parker the education in homicide investigations she wanted, so it was worth it. Actually, what they taught in the two-week intensive detective training didn't come close to what she'd learned working just one case with Corelli.

"The ambassador isn't at the UN today," Corelli said. "He and his wife are being interviewed at home for Italian television. They live in a brownstone on East Fifty-Fifth Street between York and Sutton. Let's go."

A crone answered the doorbell. Dressed in black from head to toe, she was old, very old, and small, with sparse white hair tied back in a bun. Her eyes swept them like a metal detector. She shook her head when Corelli asked to see the ambassador. "Busy. No can see now," she said in broken English. "You come back."

She started to close the door but Corelli moved into the hall. "We'll wait, thank you," she replied in Italian. She displayed her shield and ID but the crone just waved it away.

The crone shifted to Italian. "They're on television so they'll be talking a long time."

Corelli nodded and responded in Italian. "We'll wait."

The old woman shrugged, pointed to the chairs in the large entry hall, and left.

Corelli took the opportunity to touch base with the team at the crime scene. They hadn't found the phone or the computer or anything else that might be helpful, but Watkins had come up with the address of the Italian delegation's offices. Apparently the delegations of all the UN's members had offices near the United Nations compound, but not in it. The Italian ambassador and his staff worked out of Three United Nations Plaza, a nearby office building.

"Hopefully, this means we won't have to deal with the UN's police force," Corelli said. "They get touchy when we're on their sovereign territory."

Corelli and Parker were reviewing the little they knew so far when the old woman beckoned them to follow her. They walked through the hall past an open door where they could see the formal living room filled with the TV crew packing up equipment, talking loudly in Italian, and laughing as they worked. They continued toward the back of the house into a sunroom overlooking a garden. Tall, handsome, well built like his son, and with the elegance and polish of the career diplomat, the ambassador stood with a drink in his hand and stared out into the garden. His wife sat in an easy chair with a drink in her hand, face dark and brooding, eyes riveted to his back, as if willing him to turn. Cocktails at noon? A little early in Corelli's book.

Corelli cleared her throat as she positioned herself so she could face the ambassador and still see his wife. Parker followed.

Mrs. del Balzo sat with her legs crossed. Her impeccable grooming, fashionable dress, and dark beauty were striking. Her sophisticated style complemented her husband. She showed no awareness of their presence so when she removed her eyes from him in order to see what had attracted his interest, she gasped, then the brooding mask slid back into place. Strangely remote, she watched them as the audience watches actors on a stage.

"Sorry to intrude, Ambassador del Balzo. I'm Detective Corelli and this is Detective Parker."

He looked puzzled. "What is it, Detective?" His English was excellent.

"I'm sorry, sir. I have bad news. About your son, Nardo," she hesitated. "He was found dead in his apartment this morning."

He stared at her. If he felt anything, he hid it well.

Mrs. Del Balzo gasped. "Oh, no, my Nardo," she said in Italian. Her face retained its mask-like quality, but the shaking hand and the jumpy leg communicated intense feelings. It was quiet, except for the tinkle of the ice in her drink and the soft laughter drifting in from the film crew. She very carefully placed the glass on the table next to her. "Ask them what happened, *cara*," Mrs. Del Balzo said in Italian.

He cleared his throat. "What happened?"

"It appears to be murder. His cleaning person found him this morning."

"Was it one of his...friends?" He looked like he smelled something bad.

"It's still early in the investigation."

He glanced at his wife. She dabbed her eyes with a handkerchief, then cleared her throat. She spoke softly in English. "Did he... suffer?"

"No. He died instantly."

"That's a comfort. Thank you," she said, smoothing her hair. "When can we make the funeral?"

"I'll let you know when we can release him. It will be a few days. Someone will have to formally identify him."

"You should do it, Leonardo."

"I don't have time. I'll send someone from the office." He turned to Corelli. "Or, if you prefer a family member, my son-in-law Emilio will do it."

Carla del Balzo shook her head. "No, *cara*, I will go." She met Corelli's eyes. "You will let me know when and where?"

"Are you sure?" Corelli asked.

"Yes, of course." Her voice seemed to catch. "He's my son." She dabbed her eyes again.

"And, you also have a daughter?"

Her face softened. "Actually, two daughters. But only Flavia is here in New York, with her husband Emilio."

"How can I contact them?"

The ambassador held a hand up. "I don't think they can help you."

"With all due respect, sir, I'll decide that."

He sighed. "They both work. You will have to go at night," he said, as if that was some insurmountable problem.

"That's not a problem," Corelli said. "And I'd like the telephone number for your daughter in Italy as well."

"Why?" Not hearing a response, he shrugged. "Give it to them, Carla."

Parker looked up at Corelli when she finished writing the names, telephone numbers, and address dictated by Mrs. del Balzo.

The ambassador cleared his throat, smoothed back his coiffed hair, and puffed up his chest. "Are you aware that I'm under consideration to replace the prime minister of Italy?"

"Yes sir, I am."

"Then you'll understand why you must keep the investigation as low-key as possible, not mention, um, his homosexuality."

The look of distaste on his face eliminated any doubt about how he felt about his son's sexuality.

Did her father feel that way about her? He had a problem with her independence, doing a man's job, not being married. But he'd loved

Marnie. She'd hoped he'd eventually understand that she and Marnie were lovers and accept her life choices but with Marnie gone that was not to be. "We'll do our best, sir, but you know the press."

"We'd like to be alone now. Please keep us apprised." Having dismissed her, he turned to gaze at the garden again.

He had his agenda and Corelli had hers. And hers was the one that counted right now. "We need the names of Nardo's friends before we go."

"I have no idea. Carla?" He turned to his wife who seemed focused on her reflection in the glass wall. She shook her head.

Corelli glanced at the information from the business card she'd taken from Nardo's wallet. "Do you know a Scott Sigler?"

The del Balzos exchanged a glance but it was Carla who spoke. "Is this Nardo's friend?"

"I was hoping you could tell me. He's an attorney so maybe it was a business relationship."

"Scott Sigler," Carla repeated. "Is that S-i-g-l-e-r?"

"Yes. Do you know him?"

"I'm sorry I do not."

"Anything else?" The ambassador made no attempt to hide his impatience.

"Do you think the murder might be politically motivated? Someone trying to stop you?"

"Italy is a civilized democracy, not a barbaric third world country. Any idiot would know the only way to stop me would be to kill me, not a member of my family."

"We should consider it, *cara*. Maybe it was an attempt to keep you out of the election."

He stared into his drink. "We'll think about it and get back to you. Now please leave us."

"One more thing, Ambassador. Did Nardo work at the UN?"

"He was a member of the delegation's staff."

"Please inform your office we're coming to interview Nardo's colleagues."

A shadow of annoyance passed over his face, and his voice expressed his irritation. "Must you speak to the people at the delegation? Your time would be better spent looking for those friends of his."

"Standard procedure, sir."

He seemed agitated. She braced for an attack.

"I'll call as soon as you leave. Signorina Frascetti, my assistant, will introduce you. Now can you find your way out?"

"Yes. But we'll be back to talk to you and your wife again, after you've had some time."

As they left the room, the wife said something in Italian and the ambassador responded.

Parker unlocked the car and slid in. "How come you didn't speak to them in Italian?"

"Their English was good so I went with that. Good thing too. They had an interesting exchange as we left. Mrs. del Balzo said, 'Are you happy now?' And the loving father said, 'It's for the best. Now he can't spoil our chance to be prime minister.'"

"Are you kidding me?"

"I kid you not, Parker, I kid you not."

CHAPTER FOUR

Wednesday – 1:30 p.m.

A tearful Rosina Frascetti met them at the elevator. Wiping her eyes and blowing her nose, the ambassador's assistant struggled to introduce herself. Corelli held the distraught woman's hands and offered condolences in Italian, hoping to calm her. After a minute, Ms. Frascetti took a deep breath and led them to a conference room.

"Please forgive me," she said in Italian. "I'm heartbroken. Nardo was such a wonderful boy, full of laughter and joy, full of life…" Her mouth moved but words didn't come.

Corelli sent Parker to find some water, and after a few sips and more dabbing and blowing, Frascetti regained control and apologized again.

They all sat. Parker placed her notebook and pen on the table.

"Please speak English, signorina," Corelli said. "Detective Parker needs to take notes."

"I'm sorry. I fall into Italian when I'm upset," Frascetti said in perfect accented English.

"How long have you known Nardo?"

"Since I started working for the ambassador. Twenty-five years. Of course, he wasn't an ambassador then. And Nardo was a happy-go-lucky eight-year-old." She smiled. "A chatterbox, very outgoing, and so bright and interested in everything. He had a thousand questions."

"So he was always happy, full of life?" Corelli asked, trying to keep her talking.

"No. I didn't see him for a few years, until he was twelve or thirteen, I think. By then he was withdrawn, so serious and high-strung. He hardly spoke. Carla, Mrs. del Balzo, said that was not unusual for teenagers and I guess she was right, because when he came to work with us at the UN about six years ago, he was in his mid-twenties and back to being happy-go-lucky, always joking and smiling."

"Was there any resentment here, you know, the ambassador's son getting special treatment, that kind of thing?"

"He didn't get special treatment. In fact, if anything, the ambassador was harder on him, very critical."

"Have you noticed any change recently?"

Her gaze shifted from Corelli to the wall behind her. "No. Nardo was always sweet to me, and polite. A real gentleman." Corelli wondered what she was hiding.

Suddenly all business, Ms. Frascetti looked at Corelli again. "Now, how can I help you?"

"Tell me about the staff, anyone particularly friendly or unfriendly with Nardo?"

"Nardo was a senior staff member, one of eighteen, and he worked closely with the other senior staff on major issues and with other delegations." She took a deep breath. "Six people have been at a conference in Geneva for the last week and two others have been in Italy for ten days, so only seven others plus the ambassador and I are actually in the office. As far as I know, Nardo was friendly with everyone."

"Do they know he's dead?"

"No. I didn't have a chance…Everybody was out when Ambassador del Balzo called."

"I'll tell them. Please ask whoever is here now to come into the conference room." Corelli walked Ms. Frascetti to the door and opened it. A man, standing with his hand lifted to knock, stepped back, surprise on his face. He used his lifted hand to brush his hair back, out of his eyes. "You must be Detective Corelli." He peered over her shoulder. "And that must be Detective Parker. So happy to meet you." He moved closer, close enough for Corelli to get a whiff of his musky aftershave.

"And you are?" Corelli said. He looked like a romance-novel hero—tall, well-built, wavy black hair pulled back into a ponytail, pale skin, blue eyes, and straight white teeth. It was no accident, she was sure, that his black attire emphasized all his best features. He flashed a killer smile that probably reduced most women to a puddle of mush. But she wasn't most women and felt no need to respond.

"Oh, Andrea, I'm so sorry," Ms. Frascetti said. "I've been so upset that I forgot I was supposed to wait for you. Detective Corelli, this is Andrea Sansone, the UN Security Chief."

He made a half-bow, then extended his hand.

Corelli ignored the hand. "This building isn't part of the UN's sovereign territory."

"True. I have no official role, but the ambassador asked as a special favor if I would assist you with your inquiries. Perhaps you need help with the Italian?"

"Actually, I speak fluent Italian, so your offer is appreciated but not necessary."

He shrugged and smiled. "Ah, well, since I'm here, I'm sure you won't mind if I sit in. I don't want to disappoint Ambassador del Balzo."

She knew he was here to report to del Balzo. And the people they interviewed would know it as well, so they would get the party line. It would mean double work but better to go through the charade and re-interview them later, than to risk a power struggle and maybe a complaint from the ambassador.

She took her time answering.

"All right, you can observe but we'll do the questioning."

He bowed his head, signaling acquiescence.

"Are you referred to as Security Chief Sansone or just Chief Sansone?"

"Andrea will be fine. And how may I address you?"

"Detective or Detective Corelli will be fine. Please take a seat," she said, waving him into the conference room.

"*Certo*, certainly," he said as he moved past her into the room and pressed his full body against hers. She whirled, hands fisted, ready to sock him. He smiled innocently as he pulled a chair from the table.

Rosina Frascetti grabbed Corelli's fist and pulled her into the hall. "Ignore him," she whispered. "He does that all the time. He thinks it's sexy." Corelli nodded. Frascetti went to invite the troops into the conference room. Aware of Parker's amused gaze, Corelli sat at the table next to Sansone, with Parker on his other side. She leaned in close to the offensive prick. "Try that again and I'll squeeze your balls 'til you pass out."

The cocky smile was replaced by shock. "I…what?"

Coughing to cover her laugh, Parker interrupted. "Chief Sansone, I need some information from you."

He turned to Parker with a smile. "Of course. How can I help?" He pushed his chair back, put his feet on the edge of the table, and trained his eyes on the door.

"Please spell your name and give me your address and phone number."

He avoided looking at Corelli as he answered.

Three women and four men filed in, greeted the security chief by name, and then took seats. Ms. Frascetti introduced Corelli and Parker and left. Wary but not unfriendly, the group eyed the detectives.

"I have some bad news," Corelli said. Everyone sat up. There was some clearing of throats and coughing. "Nardo del Balzo was murdered last night."

One of the women moaned. Another started to cry softly. One of the men took out his handkerchief and wiped his face. A man said, "No, no, it can't be," and started to stand. An older man with tears in his eyes put out a hand to keep him seated. "Was it another robbery? Do Leonardo and Carla know?"

"Yes they know. We've just started to investigate so we don't have a lot of details. We need to get to know Nardo and we hope you'll help. We'll speak to each of you separately. And I'd appreciate it if you would not discuss our questions or anything about Nardo until we leave. Can you do that?"

Seven heads went up and down. She pointed to the crying woman. "We'll start with you, *Signora*." The others shuffled out.

The woman said, "It's *Signorina*, Miss Romano, but please call me Claudia. Oh my god, this is terrible. Poor Nardo."

"Please spell your name, and give me your address and telephone number," Parker said. When she had finished writing, Parker looked at Corelli.

"What was Nardo like?" Corelli asked.

"He was lovely. Sweet, lots of fun, always laughing and playing. I'm old enough to be his mother but he made me feel young and beautiful. He noticed everything and was always ready with a compliment or to say something nice, or to help. He was very giving." The tears welled in her eyes. "It's too bad his father…" She glanced at Chief Sansone and looked down.

"What about his father?" Corelli asked, aware of Sansone dropping his feet to the floor and shifting forward.

Claudia flushed, hesitated, then looked up. She cleared her throat. "Too bad he has to deal with this now, you know, when he's a candidate for prime minister."

Corelli had a strong urge to punch the smile off Sansone's face, but she continued questioning. "Did Nardo have any enemies?"

"As far as I know he got along with everyone."

"Thank you, Claudia. That will be all for now." Corelli handed her a business card. "If you think of anything, please call me."

Claudia examined the card as she stood up. "Ah, Key-are-ra, a beautiful name."

Parker escorted her out and returned with Giorgio Fontani.

He provided the information requested. He had just started working at the delegation a week ago Monday and hardly knew Nardo or anyone else for that matter. After a few simple questions, Parker walked him out and returned with Franco Ginocchioni, the young man who had cried out when he heard Nardo was dead. His eyes were red and puffy.

"Tell us about Nardo," Corelli asked after Parker had taken down his information.

He cast a defiant glance at Sansone and described Nardo in loving detail.

"Did you and Nardo have a relationship?"

"Not sexual. Nardo didn't want to bring his personal life into the office."

"Would you have liked to be more involved?"

He sniffed and looked down so that his jaw-length hair flopped forward, semi-covering his face. "I, uh, yes, but it couldn't be."

"Did you feel rejected by Nardo?"

His head jerked up. "No. Well, yes, at first. But then we became friends, you know, ate lunch together sometimes, or once in a while we had a drink after work. He didn't want what I wanted, but he was careful to include me in his life. He went out of his way to avoid hurting me."

"Where were you last night?"

He sat up straighter. "Home."

"All evening?"

"Yes."

"Anybody with you? Did you talk to anyone?"

He chewed his thumbnail and considered the question. "No. I was alone. No one called."

The next three interviews added little information.

Parker brought in the last of the seven, Mario Derosa, the older man, the one who had asked the questions. He sat with his hands folded on the table.

"I can't believe the boy is dead. He was so vibrant, so present. A truly wonderful young man who would have gone far. He was easy to work with, down to earth, very, very intelligent, and willing to do anything that needed to be done. No airs about *him*."

Sansone straightened. Derosa's eyes swiveled to him.

"Who has airs?" Corelli asked. *Other than Chief Sansone who's wearing cowboy boots.*

Derosa shifted to look at Corelli. "Sorry, I meant Nardo had no airs. He was down to earth."

"Did you know Nardo was gay?"

He scratched his head and pulled on his mustache. Then he shrugged. "Yes."

"How did people in the office react to him? Any problems?"

He looked Andrea in the eye. "No, no problems. He was so personable and charming and unassuming that everyone," he hesitated, "all his co-workers, accepted him for who he was. This is a very sad day," he said, wiping a tear from his eye. "I don't understand why anyone would want to hurt him."

"Thank you," Corelli said, handing him a business card. "Please call if something comes to mind."

They were silent as Derosa left the room.

"Any chance I can get a card, Detective Corelli?" Sansone smirked. "I'll give you mine, if you give me yours." He handed her his business card.

"Sure," she said, tossing her card on the table and pocketing his. "How well did you know Nardo?"

"As a matter of fact, I've been close to the del Balzos since I was a boy. I'm seven years older than Nardo so I was like an older brother when we were younger. And before you ask, yes, Ambassador del Balzo recommended me for the job of Security Chief."

Surprise, surprise. *What an arrogant creep.* "Where were you last night?"

"Me?" He sounded incredulous.

"Yes, Chief Sansone, you."

"Why would I, how could you think?" He stopped sputtering and smiled at her. "You make a joke, yes?"

She met his eyes. "No joke. Can you account for your time last night?" She was enjoying his discomfort. Too bad only she and Parker were seeing it.

"Well, I, uh, it's a private thing, you know." He seemed very interested in his fingernails. "With a woman. We had dinner and, uh, slept together."

He licked his lips and grinned as if to say, "I can't help it if I'm so attractive."

"Now that wasn't so hard was it? Please give Detective Parker her name, address and telephone number and we're done."

"Well, I don't really want to bring her into it. As one professional to another, I give you my word that I have no reason to kill Nardo."

Parker put her pen down and followed the discussion with a little smile on her face.

"As a professional, you must know that it's routine to verify everyone's whereabouts at the time of the murder. I wouldn't be doing my job if I made an exception for you. The information, please."

He pulled a small address book from the inside pocket of his jacket and made a show of thumbing through it. It appeared to her he was trying to decide which name to give. Finally, he looked up with a smirk and dictated the requested information.

"Thank you for your cooperation, Chief Sansone," Corelli said. "Since you're not the killer, perhaps you can tell us if you know of anyone who would want to kill Nardo?"

"You heard the testimony. Everyone loved him. This can't be the work of someone who knew him. It has to be a stranger, perhaps someone he picked up and brought home. You know these gays."

The derogatory tone of his voice screeched through her body, as if he had run his fingernails over a blackboard. She stood and leaned closer to him. He looked up smiling but the smile faded when he saw her face. "No, as a matter of fact, I don't have the remotest idea of what you're talking about."

"But I—" He stood, nearly clipping her chin.

"Forget it. Let's go Parker, I think we're finished. I've had all I can take."

"Wait. Let me explain."

"Explain it to your boss. He'll understand."

CHAPTER FIVE

Wednesday – 4:30 p.m.

Parker walked fast to keep up with Corelli. "I thought you were going to deck Mr. Blazing Teeth."

"I thought about it but he wasn't worth the trouble. Pain in the ass sure put a damper on things."

"You can't blame them for not talking in front of the boss's snitch."

"Some would say I shouldn't talk in front of you, Parker. Things could get back to Senator Daddy."

Parker grabbed Corelli's arm. "If you think I'm a snitch, why am I here?"

"Because I'm a pushover? Nah, just kidding, Parker. I'm almost sure, but not a hundred percent yet. I need more time." *Damn, I should be reassuring her, teaching her, not undermining her. When did I become this abusive person?*

Parker's face darkened. "Maybe, I should leave—"

"Forget it." *As much as I hate to say it, I need you with me.*

Parker dropped Corelli's arm and walked away. She slammed the car door and started the motor.

Corelli slid in next to her. "I tagged Claudia Romano, Franco Ginocchioni, Mario Derosa, and Rosina Frascetti, the ambassador's assistant, as hiding something. You see anybody else?"

Parker took a deep breath. "No."

Corelli pulled a notebook out of her pocket and peered at what she had copied from the business card in Nardo's wallet. "Next stop, Lexington Avenue and Fifty-Seventh Street. Maybe we can catch up with Scott Sigler, attorney."

They left the car in a loading zone and headed for Sigler's office building. As usual, Fifty-Seventh Street was teeming with people clutching shopping bags from Tiffany, Bergdorf, and other high fashion stores in the area, some strolling, some standing eyes up gaping at the skyscrapers, others trying to read guidebooks as they walked. All the while, impatient New Yorkers snarled and harrumphed as they zigzagged past, rushing to somewhere or other. Corelli noted conversations around them in at least six foreign languages. Tourists or new Americans? Hard to say.

The law offices of Isaacs, Greenbaum and Levitz were in a glass and stone skyscraper that filled the corner of Lexington and Fifty-Seventh. At the thirty-eighth floor they stepped off the elevator into a wood-paneled reception area and faced a receptionist sitting behind a high, ten-foot long wooden counter. An abstract canvas in shades of blue, green, white, and yellow filled the wall behind her. The five or six groupings of sofas, chairs, and low tables reflected the same color scheme. Despite the classical music playing softly in the background and the bright sunlight streaming through the wall of windows, the room felt cold and unwelcoming. They had clearly spent a lot of money, but somehow missed the mark.

Once Corelli explained they'd come to inform Sigler of the death of a friend, the receptionist's icy disinterest melted. She summoned Sigler, saying only that he had visitors. When he arrived, she shepherded the three of them to a small conference room right off the reception area.

Sigler followed them in and closed the door but didn't move into the room. His eyes went to the gold shield clipped to Corelli's jacket. "What is this about?"

"I'm Detective Corelli and this is Detective Parker. Please sit, Mr. Sigler. We have some bad news."

He moved to a chair but kept his eyes on them, as if he thought they might jump him.

"Has my apartment been robbed?"

"How do you know Nardo del Balzo?"

"He's a friend. Why?"

"I'm sorry to tell you that Mr. del Balzo was found dead in his apartment this morning."

He bolted out of the chair, knocking it over, and swayed as if he might pass out. Corelli put a hand on his shoulder to steady him. Parker righted the chair and Corelli guided him into it.

"I can't believe it." He put his hands over his face, his body shuddered as he struggled for control, but the tears came anyway.

"I just saw him last night."

"What time last night?"

"About seven. I had to work late so we met for a quick dinner at *Tre Fratelli*. It's around the corner. He walked me back about eight and said he was going home."

He hunched into himself, his shoulders shaking as he struggled with his feelings. There was something awful about men crying. They fought so hard to contain the sobs that it seemed like their bodies would implode. The sounds coming from Sigler in his effort to fight his tears were painful to hear. Corelli glanced at Parker. She looked ready to run. "Do you know of anyone who would want to harm Nardo?"

He shook his head. "Was it another robbery?" He pushed the words out between gulps of air.

"We believe he was murdered." Corelli watched for a reaction.

His eyes widened and the sobs erupted. When the sobs had softened to an occasional catch in his breathing, Corelli pushed a nearby pile of paper napkins to him. "Scott, we need your help. Can your pull yourself together?"

He wiped his eyes, blew his nose, then tossed the napkin in the wastebasket. "Sorry. How can I help?"

"What did you do after Nardo left you?"

"I signed in downstairs and came back to work. I left about three a.m."

"Why so late?"

He rubbed his temples. "I'm an associate. It's the job."

"How did you get home?"

"I walked. I live on East Sixty-Sixth Street, between Second and Third."

"A doorman building?"

"No."

"Is there anyone who can confirm the time you arrived home?"

He sat up straight.

"You think I mur...that I did it?"

"Just routine, Scott. We have to ask."

He twisted his wristwatch and focused inward, trying to remember. "I stopped for a pint of ice cream at the deli on Sixty-Sixth and Third Avenue. The guy might remember. And there was a guy on Sixty-Sixth walking a big black poodle. But I don't know him and I don't know if he would remember me. I didn't notice anyone else."

"Did Nardo seem worried about anything?"

"He was upset about an argument he'd had with his father the other day."

"Do you know what they argued about?"

"He didn't want to talk about it but he did say he'd decided to see a therapist to work out his side of it so he could get on with his life. Now he'll never..." The tears flowed again.

"Were you lovers?"

"About a week. Last night he asked me to go to Provincetown with him for a long weekend." He looked up. "You know, on Cape Cod, they have these special gay party weekends?"

Corelli nodded.

"I was really excited. Something really good was happening between us." He trembled, covered his face with his hands and began to sob.

"Scott, look at me."

He lowered his hands.

"Who would want to hurt Nardo?"

"I don't know."

"We need the names of Nardo's friends. Can you help?"

He moved his arm across his face, drying his eyes on his sleeve. "He mentioned some first names but I never met anybody. And now I never will."

"Did he mention someone named Franco?"

Scott began to hiccup. "I don't think so."

Corelli decided they would get nothing else from him. "Would you like us to drive you home? Or call someone for you?"

"No thanks. I need to be alone for a while."

They were at the door when Scott said, "Wait. Nardo did say something but I thought he was joking. He said the 'un-Christians' were stalking him, leaving phone messages."

"Un-Christians?"

"Yes. He said they're like the undead. They want gay blood."

CHAPTER SIX

Wednesday – 5:30 p.m.

"Use the lights and siren," Corelli said, as they sat in rush hour traffic. "Captain Winfry wants to see me before he goes home."

Parker pulled the light from under the dashboard, placed it on the roof, and headed west on Fifty-Seventh. A few shrieks, an illegal left onto Fifth Avenue and they headed downtown. The siren cleared the way to an extent, but as usual the streets were clogged and even those cars and taxis inclined to move to the right, were stuck. Once they passed Forty-Second Street, though, it was clear sailing back to the Village.

Eyes on the road, Parker said, "This "un-Christian" thing sounds weird. Like vampires or zombies. Do you think it's some kind of kinky sex thing?"

Corelli laughed. "The only thing I know for sure is that it's not vampires or zombies. But from Scott's description, it sounded more ominous than kinky sex. It's worth following up, though. A lot of men prey on gays."

"Speaking of bloodsucking creatures, the media is out in force again." Parker drove past the precinct, turned the corner, and stopped. "How are we going to get through?"

"Must be the del Balzo case. Somebody in the house probably tipped them off that we were coming back in." Corelli pulled on her braid. "They're behind barricades so we should be able to make a run for it."

"I'll drop you, then park."

"Good idea."

"Should I meet you in Winfry's office?" Parker asked as she put the car in drive.

"No. Contact the Hate Crimes Task Force and see if they know anything about this "un-christian" thing." Also, touch base with Watkins to see what we have so far. I'll meet you at your desk when I finish with the chief. We'll grab a bite and after that revisit the four from the Italian delegation. Let's see what we get without Andrea Sansone hanging on their every word."

"Here we go." Parker drove up on the sidewalk in front of the station, putting the car between the media and Corelli. As she entered, Corelli glanced across the street. The media pack was frantic, pushing at the barriers, pointing cameras, waving microphones, screaming questions. She smiled.

Corelli studied Captain Jedediah Winfry from the doorway, his face scrunched in concentration, so focused on the document in front of him that he hadn't heard her knock. She was a pariah in the department, shunned by every other commander, yet he had requested she join his team. At first she didn't know if she could trust him, but he'd backed her up all the way on the Winter case, and in the end she understood. Unbidden, the rage bubbled up, took her breath away. Righteous Partners had stolen something precious from him. And from her. She hated not trusting other cops.

He massaged his forehead with both hands, then leaned back and stretched, contemplating the ceiling. On his way back to the document he noticed her and smiled. "Detective Corelli, please come in. Have a seat." He waved her to a chair in front of his desk.

"Captain Winfry." She closed the door and moved to the chair.

"How's it going with your colleagues?"

Her military bearing already had her sitting straight and tall, but she stiffened. "Everything is fine, sir. I appreciate your prohibiting the back turning and hissing in the house."

He laughed. "Actually, I think everybody was relieved about not having to jump up and down and make funny noises every time you decided to take a piss or get a breath of air."

"You wanted to see me, sir?"

"Before I go there, I want to know if anybody gets rough."

"I can handle it, sir." *Need to work on that. I didn't mean to sound angry.*

He studied her face and she thought she saw the beginning of a smile. "Of course you can. And how are you dealing with the howling pack of reporters?"

Right after she'd aborted the undercover assignment it had been crazy but interest had faded quickly after she was suspended. But during her first case back on the job, the Winter investigation, it seemed as if someone was inciting them, and now it was as if she had stepped on a nest of red ants. They followed her everywhere, shouting questions, pushing microphones in her face, leaving messages on her home answering machine. And, the very public attack on her integrity by U.S. Senator Aloysius T. Parker a few weeks ago was feeding the fire of interest. The whole thing was exhausting. Would she ever get back to being just another detective?

"I ignore them." *Most of them. I'll figure out the senator's game, if it kills me.*

"It's only going to get worse now that you've caught the del Balzo case. Maybe you need to throw them a little something."

"With all due respect, sir, the last thing I need is publicity. It won't help regain the respect of my...of other police. If I don't give them anything, they'll get tired and go away."

"Quite the contrary. As long as they can't get you, they'll want you. Maybe you need to set up an interview."

When the river Styx freezes. "I'll give it some thought, sir."

"Don't give me lip service, Corelli. Figure it out."

Oops. Could he read her mind? "Yes sir."

"Now, where are you with the del Balzo case?"

"You're aware the ambassador is being touted as the next prime minister of Italy?"

"Yes. Between the press, the UN, the mayor, and Italian politics, you've caught a very hot potato, Corelli. Not good for either of us if you fail to close it quickly."

Did he want her off the case? She stood. "Sir, if you think—"

"Sit, Detective. And relax." He watched her settle. "I've no doubt you're up to it. What do you have so far?"

"I'm not sure what to do with it but I overheard the ambassador tell his wife that now they don't have to worry about their son interfering with him becoming prime minister. They were speaking Italian and didn't realize I'm fluent."

His eyebrows shot up. "I think you'd better keep that to yourself unless you get something concrete."

"Only Parker knows. But other than that, we have nothing. It's early yet, but we can't rule out some kind of political motivation, someone trying to send a message to Ambassador del Balzo. Then there's the gay angle. Leonardo, the son, was gay, and his boyfriend said something about him getting telephone calls from," she used her fingers to mime quotes, 'the un-Christians,' whatever that means, so we're looking in to that too. We've just scratched the surface, but so far everybody says he was a wonderful guy."

"What do you need from me?"

"Help. Besides me, Parker, and Watkins, I'd like Ray Dietz, and Heiki Kim, and anybody else you can free up. Also, a room to set up a murder board and meet. That's it for now but I reserve the right to come back to you." She smiled. "If that's okay, sir?"

"Send Dietz in when you leave. And I'd like a daily update on this one."

She stood. "Thank you, sir."

"One more thing. Are we clear about Parker?"

"Yes sir. She's mine and only mine until I decide her training is complete."

"And?"

"Sir, I believe a bodyguard is not necessary now that the Righteous Partners threat is gone."

"I seem to recall Parker was assigned to protect you from all other police, not just Righteous Partners. She remains your bodyguard until I decide you are not in danger. Got it?"

"Yes sir."

He stood. "Do I need to call her in here?"

"No sir. I'll take care of it."

He glanced at the window behind him. "Judging from the noise, the crowd outside has grown. When you're ready to leave I'll give them a statement. Use that as cover to slip out the rear door."

"Thank you, sir." She headed for the door but turned when he spoke again.

"And Corelli, I meant what I said. Figure out how to use the press to your advantage. Because if they turn on you it won't be pretty."

As Parker moved toward her desk, Dietz called out, "Hi ho, Parker, message for you." He waved a pink slip at her.

She veered to the right and sat in the chair alongside his desk.

"Hi ho? Is that the white man's version of yo?"

"Are you being a racist, Parker?"

"That for me?" she said, reaching for the message.

Dietz pulled it back, over his head. "Gimme a second, will ya." He glanced down at the paper. "This guy, calls himself Randall Young, came looking for you today. Says he's your daddy."

She jumped up, leaned in to his face, arm pulled back to strike. "Is this your idea of a joke, Dietz?"

He caught her arm. "Don't go ballistic, Parker. I'm just passing on what the guy said. It's no secret Senator Parker is your dad. Anyway, I looked him over and he seemed all right so I said I would give you his number and you would call if you wanted to talk to him. So here it is."

She stared at the paper but made no move toward it.

"Should I toss it?"

She bit her lip. "Did you tell him I already have a father?"

"Not my job."

She grabbed the message. "Did he say anything else?"

"Well, I asked him how he came to be your daddy, you know, just as a test, but—"

"You what?" All heads turned at the sound of her voice. Dietz stood up and yelled, "Whatcha looking at? Get back to work. We're just conversing here." He glared until everyone turned back to their conversations. Then he sat again and looked at her. "Don't get your braids in a knot, Parker. I was joking. Only thing he said was he'd like to talk to you, face-to-face."

"Probably just a nut case."

"He seemed okay. Big guy, well-dressed, neat, sounded educated, little bit of drawl like he's from the south. Might be worthwhile talking to him just to set him straight, get rid of him."

"Thanks Dietz. Sorry about—"

"Nah, it's me. I can't resist. You always bite. Let me know what you decide. I'm curious."

"Me too." She walked back to her desk and stared at the pink slip in her hand. Her mind was racing. Her original birth certificate said father unknown. Her drunken bitch of a grandmother always said her mother slept around so much it could have been anyone. Could it be...or was it some sort of scam? And why now after all these years?

CHAPTER SEVEN

Wednesday – 9 p.m.

Corelli pushed her plate aside. She knew she should force herself to eat, but after two or three bites of the grilled chicken sandwich, she'd lost interest. The only trouble Parker was having with her rare burger was keeping her hands clean as the blood oozed onto her plate. Feeling queasy, Corelli looked away from the pooling blood and once more scrutinized the door to the deck for reporters. As the captain suggested, they had used the rear door and made it to their car before the pack noticed. Parker had lost them easily, but Corelli feared some of them knew about Buonasola, her favorite restaurant at the South Street Seaport, and would come looking for her. She pulled the sandwich back and forced herself to take another bite.

She was aware of Parker sneaking glances at her. Parker was sensitive to her moods probably because Corelli dumped her rage on her more often than not and she never knew when she'd be attacked. But it was also true that Parker was insecure and probably assumed she and the captain had discussed getting rid of her. *Of course, I've given her good reason to be insecure.*

"So the good news is the chief is giving us some detectives and a space to work the del Balzo case. The bad news is, he wants you to continue to act as my bodyguard," Corelli said as they waited for their checks.

"You all right with that?"

"The help and the space, yes. But I don't need a babysitter. I told him I'd let you know. I thought this was over. But an order is an order."

"Can you...um, say no?"

"Not an option." Corelli cupped her hands over her eyes and massaged her forehead and temples. She felt Parker's gaze, but she was tired, so tired. Since the early months of her last deployment in Afghanistan, she rarely slept more than two consecutive hours because as soon as she fell into a deep sleep, the nightmares started.

"It's probably a good thing because of the PTSD."

"I've told you I don't have...." Corelli glared at Parker. "I hope you haven't shared your unprofessional diagnosis with anyone?"

"You don't have to get so nasty. I would never do that unless I felt you were a danger to yourself, or me."

"So your current diagnosis is that I'm not suicidal?"

"Except for your performance on your Harley when you were attacked on the Belt Parkway, you seem sound."

She couldn't argue with that. When she thought about it, after the high of facing death wore off, it did seem a little reckless. "Boy, I feel better now."

"So maybe I should start charging for the analysis." Parker said it with an almost smile but it made Corelli uncomfortable. Enough talk about her mental state. Time to change the subject. "And speaking of work, did you follow up with the Hate Crimes Unit like I asked?"

It took Parker a few seconds to change gears. "Um, I did. The calls that have been reported were all about saving the souls of the gay men. They haven't heard anything about threats or 'un-Christians' looking for blood, but they said they'd look into it."

"So nothing there for now." Corelli tossed some money on the table. "Pay our checks. I'm going to stop in the ladies' room. I'll meet you at the car."

She splashed cold water on her face, trying to avoid her reflection in the mirror, but it didn't matter. She knew how haggard she looked—dark shadows under sunken eyes, cheekbones made more prominent by her lack of appetite. She dried her face, did some yoga breathing to energize herself.

Parker was waiting in the car. Corelli climbed into the passenger seat. "Let's start with Claudia Romano on the Upper East Side, Eighty-Second and Park."

Parker turned toward the entrance to the FDR Drive. "So, do you think any detectives will be willing to work with us? What if they try—?"

"I'll kick their asses off the team. We're gonna be under intense scrutiny and pressure on this case. We can't do it alone, Parker. I promise you, anybody who can't make the case the priority, whose goal is to make sure I—we—fail, will regret it. But, in addition to fighting off the press, dodging people trying to kill me, and finding del Balzo's killer, you and I will need to be alert for sabotage. Okay?"

"Just another day on the job."

"You got it." Corelli smiled. Any small ray of humor from Parker was a happy surprise.

Rush hour traffic had dissipated and the FDR moved quickly to the Ninety-Sixth Street exit. The slight jerk of the car as Parker stopped at the light nudged Corelli out of her reverie.

"You okay, Parker? You seem withdrawn," Corelli asked. Of course, she was the one who was withdrawn.

"Thinking about fathers."

"What about them?"

"About fathers and their kids," she said, fingering the pink slip in her pocket.

"Any father in particular? Senator Daddy, maybe?"

"Not him. Fathers like del Balzo who hate their kids and fathers who walk away from their kids. But I guess there are worse things, like those religious fanatic fathers who kill their daughters because they want lives different from their parents. How weird is that?"

"Some fathers just can't accept their children for who they are, just can't tolerate their children choosing to live a different life from theirs. They seem to think it means something about them. Sometimes it's religion, sometimes it's control, sometimes it's holding on to old ways, to traditions." *And don't I know it.*

Claudia Romano's building was a new high-rise. The doorman buzzed Romano's apartment and after a brief discussion with the person at the other end of the intercom, directed them to the eighteenth floor.

Claudia was standing in the doorway of her apartment when they stepped off the elevator. She greeted them and waved them into her living room. "Is something wrong?"

"We have a few more questions," Corelli said.

"Will it take long? I…We're getting ready to go out for dinner," Claudia said, her gaze going to something or someone behind them.

Corelli turned but it was only an empty hallway. "We just need to clear up something you said this afternoon."

"Please sit," she said, pointing to the sofa. She perched on the arm of one of the easy chairs facing them.

"Claudia, you started to say something this afternoon, and Detective Parker and I thought you changed your mind because Andrea Sansone was in the room. Detective Parker will read the sentence we're referring to."

Claudia watched Parker thumb through her notes, then sighed. "It's all right. I know the sentence you're referring to, but I shouldn't have said anything. If she finds out she'll have me fired."

"Who? Mrs. Frascetti?"

"No, not Rosina. Carla. She does his dirty work and you're either for or against Leonardo, especially now with the election coming up."

"They'll only know if you reveal we talked again."

"I don't know."

"Please, for Nardo."

It was quiet except for the rasp of Claudia's breathing. Corelli experienced a moment of guilt for pressuring her, but then reminded herself she was trying to find a killer.

"I hope I don't live to regret this." Claudia took a deep breath. "The ambassador always seemed uncomfortable around Nardo. He was hypercritical and contemptuous of the boy. And to be honest, Nardo provoked him. He would, how do you say it, act like a girl, um, flounce? Is that the word? But when his father wasn't around he wasn't like that at all."

"Anything else?"

"The ambassador has been very tense this last week or two. You know he's in line to replace Berlusconi?"

Corelli nodded.

"I heard Nardo and the ambassador had a huge fight Monday. Apparently, they were screaming at each other in the ambassador's office, and then Nardo came out, slammed the door, and ran from the building. He didn't come to work yesterday."

"What was the argument about?"

Claudia shrugged. "*Chi sa?*"

Parker stopped writing. She coughed.

Corelli turned to Parker. "It means, who knows?"

Claudia said, "Sorry, I forgot."

"I'm almost ready, Claudia," a masculine voice sang out from the direction of the hall. Her gaze went to the hall behind them. She got to her feet. "Is that all?"

The detectives turned to see what she was looking at just as Mario Derosa, dressed but toweling his hair, walked through the door.

He flushed, a stricken look on his face. "Oh."

Seeing how embarrassed they both were, Corelli took control before they felt the need to explain. "Mr. Derosa, I'm so glad you're here. You've saved us a trip to your apartment in Queens. We have a few more questions. Please join us."

Derosa and Claudia exchanged glances. He cleared his throat. "Give me a minute to get rid of this towel. Anyone else want a drink? Detectives? Claudia?"

They refused but Claudia nodded. She sat down, studiously avoiding looking at them.

Corelli attempted to ease her obvious discomfort. "How do you like this neighborhood?"

Claudia glanced in their direction, seemed to decide they were friendly, and flashed a smile. "Oh, I like it a lot. It's convenient to the subway and a quick ride down to the office."

Derosa returned. He handed Claudia a glass and sat in the easy chair next to her.

"So what else can I tell you, Detective Corelli?"

"As I mentioned to Claudia, both Detective Parker and I sensed having Andrea Sansone in the room caused most people to censor what they said. We'd like to hear the truth."

"Very perceptive. Andrea is Carla's lapdog, so everyone is careful around him because even something said as a joke is repeated, or should I say reported."

"What did you mean when you said Nardo had no airs about *him*. Does the ambassador have airs?"

He thought about the question. Finally he said, "Let's say they have ambitions."

"They?"

"Carla and Leonardo."

"And?"

"And nothing or nobody else matters. Everything is about him, about his career. They used many people to get him where he is today."

Claudia reached over and touched his hand.

He smiled at her and sipped his drink. "Are you going to repeat what I say?"

"No one knows we're here. I won't use your name unless the information becomes critical to the case. Please help. The more we know about Nardo, the better."

He scratched his head and pulled on his mustache. He sipped again, put his drink down and patted Claudia's hand, smiling gently.

"Leonardo was repulsed by Nardo's gayness. He seemed to hate the boy and made no attempt to hide his feelings. Nardo responded by exaggerating his gayness and pretending to be a swishy queen, sticking it up Leonardo's nose constantly. A terrible situation for them and for those of us who watched it play out, knowing how badly Nardo wanted his father's love."

"Was Mrs. del Balzo aware of this dynamic?"

"Carla acted like it wasn't happening, even when she was in the same room with them. She never attempted to reconcile them, just put on lipstick or powdered her nose."

"Claudia mentioned an argument Monday. Do you know what it was about?"

He smoothed his mustache. "Leonardo came back from a meeting preening like a peacock over what people were saying about his replacing Berlusconi. He strutted into the office bragging, 'everybody knows how hard I've worked for this, how much I deserve the honor, and what a wonderful day it will be for Italy.' Nardo reacted like the proverbial bull seeing a red cape."

Derosa downed some of his drink. "Nardo followed Leonardo into his office and slammed the door. My office is right next to Leonardo's, but the door was closed for most of it. I could hear them shouting but I could only understand a word now and then."

"You have no idea what the argument was about?"

He stroked his chin with his thumb.

"Nardo came out of the office shouting, 'You'll never be prime minister. I'll make sure of it. The newspapers will love the story. We'll see how far you go after I talk to them.' He was crying when he stormed out."

Derosa was silent.

"Is that all?"

"Isn't that enough?"

"Yes, I guess it is. Thank you. Thank you both. And please forgive us for intruding." As they stood to leave, Corelli asked, "Where was Ms. Frascetti during the argument?"

He laughed. "Sitting at her desk with her mouth open, just like me."

CHAPTER EIGHT

Wednesday – 9:30 p.m.

They were each lost in thought on the way out of the building, but once they were settled in the car, Parker spoke. "Better to be abandoned by your father than to have him be repulsed by you, don't you think?"

"My, my, aren't we philosophical tonight." Corelli hadn't meant to be condescending, but she could hear it in her voice.

Parker ignored it. "Just reflecting."

The idea of fathers being repulsed by their child's sexuality hit too close to home for Corelli. She changed the subject. "I'm reflecting on what Mario Derosa told us about Nardo threatening to go to the media to embarrass the ambassador and tank his political ambitions. That's probably the coming out party Nardo mentioned when he asked Foxworth to dress him as a woman. Father and son were locked in an ugly dance. Why? We'll drop in on the del Balzos tomorrow, see if we can shake something loose." She glanced at her wristwatch. "Let's take a drive to Brooklyn to talk to Nardo's sister, and then on the way back we can hit Ginocchioni in the Village."

Nardo's brother-in-law, Emilio Ottaviano, answered the door with a question on his lips. "Is it necessary to do this now?"

His accent was thick. "It's late and we have just returned from comforting Carla and Leonardo. My wife is very upset." He looked solemn but not too broken up by the death.

Ottaviano was handsome if you liked the type—long brown hair, sexy brown eyes, and full lips packaged with a slight but muscular body encased in tight jeans and a fitted T-shirt. Her sister Patrizia would be filled with joy knowing Corelli was meeting all these good-looking Italian guys. Too bad their beauty left her cold.

"I'm sorry Mr. Ottaviano, but the faster we get our questions answered the faster we can find the person who murdered Nardo."

He glanced back into the apartment. "I suppose it's best to get it over with. But we didn't have much to do with Nardo, so I doubt we know anything that will help." He stepped aside. "Please come in."

A woman looked up from the sofa where she lay curled on her side, a wad of tissues in her hand, a table full of soggy tissues in front of her, her face puffy and swollen and streaked with mascara. So the whole family wasn't made of ice. She was a more human version of her mother—softer, sweeter, but with the same dark, sophisticated looks.

"My wife, Flavia." Emilio helped her sit up, then sat close. His hand brushed her hair gently. They were a striking couple: both slender, graceful, with creamy olive skin and sensuous features.

"I'm Detective Corelli and this is Detective Parker. We're so sorry for your loss, Mrs. Ottaviano."

"Thank you," she said, her voice catching.

"I'm sure this is a hard time for you, but I hope you'll answer a few questions about your brother."

"Yes, certainly, if I can. Please sit."

They settled into the two chairs facing the sofa. Parker opened her pad and placed it on the arm of her chair.

The clicking of Parker's pen triggered Corelli's questions. "Mrs. Ottaviano, are you older or younger than your brother?"

"I'm in the middle. Younger than Nardo, older than my sister, Antonia."

"Has anyone been in touch with your sister?"

"Yes. We talked to her this afternoon. She's flying in tomorrow."

"I see. Do you know Nardo's friends?"

She glanced at her husband. His jaw was tight.

"Emilio and Nardo don't get along. We haven't seen Nardo in about a year. And we've never socialized with him so I don't know any of his friends." She burst into tears.

"What was the problem, Mr. Ottaviano?"

He flushed. "It was his, you know, his being, how do you call it? A faggot? I wasn't comfortable with him, and I didn't like the way he treated my father-in-law, Ambassador del Balzo."

"Did you argue?"

"Yes."

"When was the last time you saw him?"

His eyes met Corelli's. "As Flavia said, about a year ago."

"What did you find offensive about Nardo's treatment of the ambassador?"

Flavia spoke up. "Nardo was angry with our father and ignored him when we were together. He wouldn't tell even me what it was about."

"What offended you, Mr. Ottaviano?"

He glanced at Flavia. "He rubbed the ambassador's nose in his disgusting life."

"Do either of you know what Nardo and the ambassador argued about on Monday?"

Flavia looked at Emilio. He shrugged. "I, we, didn't know they argued."

"Please let me know if you think of anything that might help us," Corelli said. She put her card on the coffee table. They stood and Emilio escorted them to the door.

In the car, Corelli said, "Ottaviano was lying about something."

"I thought so too."

Corelli sighed. "We'll have another go at him if we need to. Wouldn't life be peachy if everybody told the truth the first time?"

Parker grunted.

"Okay, give me Ginocchioni's telephone number. Let's see what he has to say for himself. Spurned love is a good motive for murder."

She hung up when Ginocchioni's answering machine picked up. "Not home. We'll check again before you drop me off later."

"You see Ginocchioni for it?"

"Him or somebody like him, someone who Nardo knew, didn't fear, and would let into his apartment wearing just pajama bottoms. Now that I think about it, the ambassador is a good fit too."

"And so is Mister Blazing Teeth."

"Hmm. You're right. We'll see him tomorrow too."

CHAPTER NINE

Wednesday – 11 p.m.

Parker stood by the car, hand on her gun, and watched until the elevator door closed on Corelli. Then she drove uptown to Hattie's Harlem Inn on 125th Street where she'd arranged to meet her friend and mentor, Captain Jesse Isaacs, for a drink. Jesse was there already, seated in a booth talking to a tall, good-looking man. Detective Ron Watkins in her hangout? Why was he crowding her when he knew she'd made it clear she didn't want to get involved with someone she worked with?

She stopped and struggled to gain control of the anger she could feel building. She needed to be cool. Watkins high-fived Jesse and walked over to the bandstand. He picked up a guitar. Three men joined him and they began to tune up. She remembered now; he'd mentioned the gig. When they started playing, she strolled over to join Jesse.

"Hey, P.J., see your boy up there?" He lifted his chin in the direction of the band.

"He's not my boy."

"Hmm. And I thought you invited me here as cover so you could come hear him play."

"I don't need cover. I forgot he was going to be here. That's not why I wanted to meet."

He waved the waitress over and she ordered a beer. He examined her. "If it's not Watkins, what is it?"

She gnawed the cuticle on her thumb but didn't say anything. The waitress put the bottle and the iced glass on the table and walked away without comment.

"Give me a second, Jesse." She filled her glass and drank some beer. She fingered the paper with the phone number, then related Dietz's encounter with Randall Young.

"I don't remember any mention of a man in the report of your mother's murder. They had a hard time figuring out who she was because there wasn't anything to identify her in the apartment—no letters, no diary, no wallet, but who knows?"

"You sure?"

He snorted. "Don't you think I would have hunted him down?"

"Yeah, I guess." She pushed her glass in circles.

"How did he find you?"

"Saw my picture on the front page of the *Daily World*." She poured the rest of the beer into the glass and drank. "You know, the thing with the Toricelli kid."

He tapped his fingers in time to the music. "I'd talk to the man. Why get crazy wondering? Hear what he has to say and then decide. If it's a scam, you'll be onto him pretty fast. Arrange to meet him here at Hattie's and I'll be here too in case he's trouble."

"I don't need a babysitter."

"I know, Ms. Prickly Pear, but you said he's a big guy, so unless you plan to shoot him, you might need backup if he gets rough. Let me know."

They sat in companionable silence listening to the music. When Parker spotted Detective Charleen Greene standing at the bar, she stood. "I'm tired, Jesse, I'm going home." *So is Watkins coming onto Greene now?*

"The set's almost over. Aren't you going to say hello to Ron?"

"I'll see him in the morning." *Wouldn't want to come between him and his date.*

She felt Jesse's eyes on her as she darted through the crowd, not looking right or left and not acknowledging Ron's smile and quick wave.

CHAPTER TEN

Wednesday – 11 p.m.

As Corelli hung up her jacket, the bell rang. She smiled, suspecting it was either Gianna or Simone. Her sisters sensed her aloneness and sadness and had taken to dropping in late at night. So far neither of them had pushed her to talk. Instead they came to comfort and support her and left it to her to decide what she wanted to tell them. She pressed the intercom button.

"Yes?"

"It's Andrea Sansone, I need to speak to you."

"I've had a long day and I'm off duty. Please come to the station house tomorrow."

"I must speak to you now."

Her inclination was to get rid of him. But she had threatened him today, not a good thing. It was going to be tough if it turned out del Balzo killed his son, so it would be better to avoid an international incident now over Sansone invading her privacy. She buzzed him in.

She slipped her boots back on and waited in front of the elevator in her shirtsleeves. She started to unbuckle her holster then decided to keep her gun on to emphasize this wasn't a social visit.

The elevator opened. He seemed surprised to see her standing there. Perhaps he had expected a traditional apartment where he would have been facing a hallway or maybe he thought she'd greet him in a sexy nightgown. He hesitated, then stepped into the small space between her and the elevator. He looked past her, surveying the ten-thousand-foot loft.

"*Che bella*." His voice was soft, full of wonder.

Corelli turned, seeing the loft through his eyes. It was beautiful. But it didn't matter that he thought so. She loved it. She had worked hard to make it a home, her kind of home, not one that required a man and children. The loft reflected the artistic side of her rather than the drab, all-business cop, and the colorful rugs, paintings, wall-hangings, and objects from all over the globe pulled the cavernous space together, making it warm and welcoming and comfortable.

She felt his breath on her neck, and fearing a sexual advance that would require decking him, she shifted to face him.

"*Mi piace*," he said in Italian, then in English. "I like it." He tore his eyes from the loft and looked at her. He seemed overwhelmed. "It is so inviting."

She suspected he had never been inside a converted industrial building and was used to the rigid formality of luxurious, designer apartments. But he got it and appreciated it. If she wasn't feeling so invaded by him, she might have been gracious and thanked him.

"Your uncle did very well by you. But I'm sure you're the one who decorated it, made it so welcoming."

If he expected a reaction to his knowing she owned the building, something very few people outside her family knew, he didn't get it. She kept her expression bland. "How did you get my home address?"

"I have friends."

Probably some helpful soul at her old precinct, where most of the detectives in Righteous Partners had worked, thought it might hurt to spread her personal life around.

"Now that you're here, what do you want?"

"May I come in?"

"I'm expecting someone so I'd rather not socialize. What do you want?"

"I'm afraid I offended you this afternoon. I'm sorry. Nardo was like my little brother and I'm sorry he's dead. And, I want you to know I don't have a problem with gay people. I spend time with Leonardo, and I pick up his attitude." He flashed the grin again, the one that probably caused women to swoon. He was trying, but she wasn't buying.

"Thank you for the apology, but in the future, please contact me at the station rather than at home."

The bell rang.

"Ah, your guest. I must apologize again, this time for intruding."

"Hi sweetie, it's Gianna." She buzzed her up.

"That must be your sister, no?"

"Let's get something straight, Chief Sansone. My private life is private. And my family is off-limits." She bared her teeth in an unfriendly smile. "So when the elevator door opens, please step in without attempting to charm my sister."

Gianna seemed taken aback to see Corelli standing there talking to a man. But reading the look on her sister's face, she offered no greeting.

"Chief Sansone was just leaving. Goodnight, chief."

He shrugged but managed to slip in a killer smile before the elevator doors slid closed.

"Well, well. He's very handsome. Are you keeping secrets?" Gianna asked.

"You know men, handsome or not, don't do it for me." Corelli stooped to kiss Gianna, and then arm and arm they went into the living room area. "He's just a bigoted hotshot trying to screw around with my investigation and invading my privacy in the bargain."

"You are a beautiful woman, Chiara. Maybe he's interested. But then again, if you just met, it's more likely something not so nice."

"I'd better get rid of my gun before I go after him and shoot him," Corelli said, shaking her head. "Want some wine or something?"

"Espresso would be good, thanks."

A few minutes later Corelli returned with a glass of *Avola de Nero*, an eggplant *parmigiana* sandwich for herself, and a decaf espresso for Gianna. Her sisters definitely coordinated these visits. Two nights ago Simone brought food and tonight Gianna showed up empty-handed, but they made sure she always had something to eat in the house when she got home late—usually every night.

She placed the wine, the sandwich, and the espresso on the coffee table and sat next to Gianna. Corelli took a bite of the sandwich but her anger at Sansone for coming here, knowing her business, choked her and made it hard to swallow. How dare he invade her privacy? Next time she saw him, she would tell him she was a lesbian and he shouldn't waste his charms on her. She stood up and walked to the window.

"It's dark. What are you looking at?"

She walked back and sat next to Gianna. *Would it shock her to know I'm dying for a glimpse of a woman who jogs along the river path? Would she think I'm crazy to believe I could recognize her from the eighth floor? In the dark?*

"Sorry, you know I can't sit still."

Gianna took her hand. "You look exhausted. Maybe I shouldn't have come so late. I'm a night owl and eleven is the only time I'm pretty sure to find you home, but you should get some sleep."

"I'm always happy to see you." And she meant it.

Gianna patted her hand. "I haven't seen you this unsettled since we lost the old Chiara."

"The old Chiara?"

Gianna put her arm around Corelli and pulled her close. "You probably don't even remember the wild one, the one always laughing and kidding around, focused on having fun."

"Well, I was much younger."

"You idolized Luca. We both did. But I've always felt we buried the young, exuberant Chiara with him."

Corelli thought back to the funeral. She'd been devastated. "And a depressed fifteen-year-old took her place. But didn't his death affect you that way?"

"I missed him, mourned him and still do. But you two had a special connection. Maybe because you looked alike, so different than Patrizia and me, maybe because you were so much alike."

"So you think I'm still depressed?"

"You didn't stay depressed. You changed. You became focused, serious, determined to save the world. The person you are today." Gianna stared into her espresso. "You were happy again with Marnie. But since she was killed, it's like you've been underwater, so difficult to reach. In fact, a few months ago I feared you'd given up on life."

"I didn't know I was so transparent." But she should have known. Gianna could always see into her heart and often understood her better than she understood herself.

"It broke my heart after Luca to see you so alone, so unable to connect with anyone or be comforted, even by me. And it breaks my heart even more now."

She put her arm around Gianna's waist and hugged her. "I'm sorry to make you sad."

"Don't apologize. I love and respect you for who you are today, but the old Chiara is a part of you too, and it would be wonderful if you could get some of her joie de vivre back. You had it with Marnie."

And then they'd volunteered to go to Afghanistan to train Afghani policemen. "I'm not exactly feeling jubilant right now."

"Oh, Chiara, I know losing Marnie was horrible. I'm sorry."

She stood. "Um, want some more espresso?" She moved toward the kitchen.

"Sit. That's an order," Gianna said, in her best deep, hard-boiled detective voice. "And, *mangia*," she said, pushing the sandwich toward Corelli. "Eat. You're getting too thin."

She sighed, plopped down next to Gianna, and took a bite. Gianna was still. Corelli squirmed as she always did when Gianna applied her silent interrogation technique. Gianna, eleven months older, had adopted Corelli as her own from the day Mama brought the new baby home from the hospital. And now thirty-five years later she was still mothering, and still as protective as she had always been. "What?"

"I'm worried about you, Chiara. You've gone away again. You seem so alone, so far away. I'm afraid I'm losing you."

Corelli cleared her throat. "I...It's hard." She wrapped her arms around herself.

Gianna pried one of Corelli's hands free and held it between hers. She shifted to the coffee table so they were facing each other. "Tell me. You'll feel better."

How to start? "I don't know who I am anymore. The job used to be enough but..."

"Because of Marnie? Iraq? Afghanistan?"

"All of the above, combined with the three months undercover, I think."

Gianna nodded and squeezed her hand, encouraging her to continue.

"Like the tours in Iraq, the last year in Afghanistan training the police was horrific—not knowing who to trust and who was going to try to kill you, having to kill, seeing your people get blown up, seeing Marnie die. Following that up with three months' undercover work investigating my friends and colleagues was more of the same, and in some ways, it was worse. At least in Iraq and Afghanistan I had Marnie with me for a while. Until she died." Her voice broke and she stopped to gain control. "Undercover, I was totally isolated. And in order to survive, I had to pretend to be like them, brutal, greedy, and immoral, because if I didn't stay in character, if I made a mistake, they wouldn't hesitate to kill me. I had to stay away from you and the family to maintain my undercover persona."

Gianna rubbed Corelli's hand. "And when it was over, you ended up on the other side of the famous blue wall with other police shunning you."

"That doesn't help."

"Oh, Chiara, honey, you put up such a good front that I never guessed you were still dealing with all that. How stupid? Mother of god, do you have PTSD? I'll bet you're not sleeping, jumping at loud noises, things like that?"

"How do you know about PTSD?"

"Well, I do read the newspapers. And the mother of one of Gabrielle's classmates has PTSD. It's been hard on the family since she got back from Afghanistan but she's in treatment now. Maybe you should—"

"I'll be all right. I feel better already just talking to you about it."

"Have you talked to anyone else? Parker? Or Watkins?"

"Parker knows but she and Watkins are my subordinates. I can't."

"Are you having nightmares? Tell me the truth."

"Yes."

"Oh, sweetie, maybe Simone and I could take turns sleeping here so you'd feel safe."

"Absolutely not. I sleep with my gun and if I mistake you for… someone else, I could hurt you."

"Promise me you'll get help."

"I promise I'll think about it."

Gianna pulled her close and hugged her. As usual, she knew just how far to push.

"Okay, but I won't drop this."

"I know."

Gianna retrieved a newspaper from her bag and flipped through the pages.

"To change the subject, I brought you Saturday's *Wall Street Journal*. There's an article about Brett Cummings, the woman involved in the Winter murder."

As if I could forget her. Corelli sighed. "Since when do you read the *Wall Street Journal*?"

"Marco brings it home. I recognized her name."

Corelli cleared her throat. "I read it."

"I might ask you the same question. Since when do *you* read the *Wall Street Journal*?"

"I saw her picture on the cover at the newsstand."

"Then you know she's an out lesbian. And you've seen the pictures, one with her brother, a priest. He's handsome but she's beautiful, actually gorgeous, but not in the self-conscious way of your Mr. Sansone. And she sounds like a kind person, someone I would like. Actually she reminded me of you."

"He's definitely not my Mr. Sansone. How does she remind you of me?"

"Well, you're both independent women, both kind, both beautiful, both strong, and both interested in outdoor stuff, you know, sports and jogging, that kind of thing. The article said she sails her own boat. Did you like her?"

God, how does Gianna…no, she can't. She's just trying to help. Wrong subject, though. She turned away from Gianna, toward the window.

"Yes, she's nice."

"Do you ever see people after an investigation?"

"No, why?"

"You and Brett have so much in common. You could be great friends. You need a friend, Chiara, somebody to do things with. It's not healthy, spending so much time working. And, Marnie wouldn't want you to mourn forever."

"It's less than two years, Gianna, not forever. And I'm not ready."

"I'm not suggesting a relationship, surely lesbians can be friends. Give her a call."

I'm not sure I can just be friends with her. "Maybe when I wrap up the del Balzo case."

CHAPTER ELEVEN

Thursday – 7 a.m.

As Corelli and Parker entered the conference room for the seven a.m. meeting with the full team assembled by Dietz, two detectives she didn't know turned their chairs to show her their backs. Now they were head to head, whispering. Not everyone was happy to be here. Dietz caught her eye and tilted his head toward the hostiles. She shook her head. She would handle it.

She stood at the head of the table. "Some of you have already started working on the case, but I'd like to officially welcome you all to the del Balzo investigation. And before we get into the details, anyone who is not willing to work with me is free to leave now, with no hard feelings. But, if you stay, you're stuck." The detective leaning back on two legs of his chair with his eyes trained on the window dropped the front legs to the floor and walked out with a smirk on his face. She looked around the room, giving them more time. The two hostiles hesitated, then grabbed their belongings and strolled out. "Is that it?" She eyed the group.

The sound of a chair falling over echoed through the tension in the room. She turned as a red-faced and sweaty Detective Justin Reilly, eyes down, scampered out. That one hurt. They'd been friends since they were both beat cops and she'd saved his life after he was buried under a ton of debris while they were rescuing people at the World Trade Center disaster. Dealing with the faceless mass of police ostracizing her was hard but being treated as a traitor by cops she'd considered friends, colleagues, and cops she'd socialized with, broke her heart.

A murmur passed through those remaining. "Anyone else? This case is a political hot potato and there's going to be a lot of pressure to solve it, so if you choose to stay, be prepared to give nothing less than your best. Make it easier on all of us. Be honest with yourself. Leave if you can't commit fully."

Heads nodded and whispers were exchanged, but nobody moved. She waited another minute. Only four. Not so bad. She made eye contact with everyone in the room, then relaxed. No more hostility. At least no overt hostility.

"Okay. Let's get started. Detective Dietz is going to be the inside point person for the team. Dietz please find us replacements for those four. And make sure they're willing."

"Gotcha." Dietz made a note.

She walked over to the bulletin board. "Here's what we have so far." She pointed to a picture. "Leonardo del Balzo, known as Nardo, found dead yesterday morning by his cleaning lady, Miranda Foxworth." She pointed to a picture of del Balzo's wound. "Del Balzo was shot once in the cerebellum, the back of the head, at close range with a small caliber bullet. The ME believes he died instantly. There was no sign of a struggle. He reportedly had purchased a gun after a robbery about six months ago, but we found no record of the purchase, no permit was granted and no gun was found in the apartment."

She pointed to a series of pictures. "When we arrived at the scene, Mr. del Balzo, wearing just pajama bottoms, was laid out on the sofa with a rosary in his hands and a CD of Gregorian chants playing on a repeat loop. Incense had been burned. According to Ms. Foxworth, the alarm was off, the top lock unlocked, and the bottom lock not double-locked. She said Nardo was gay, and though he wasn't trans or a cross-dresser, he called her in tears the night before his death to ask her to dress him like a woman because he was having a coming out party. We think he meant to rub his father's nose in his being gay."

Corelli looked around to see if everyone was following. "So far we've interviewed his parents and sister and brother-in-law, his coworkers at the UN, and Scott Sigler, a brand-new lover. Neither Sigler nor the family could give us the names of Nardo's friends, and his cell phone, address book, and computer, if he had them, are missing. We're trying to locate his phone company to get his phone records."

She looked up. Everyone was taking notes. "Here's the icing on the cake. Nardo was the son of the Italian ambassador to the United Nations, Leonardo del Balzo, known as Leonardo, and the ambassador is being touted as the next prime minister of Italy."

She looked around the room. "Detective Ron Watkins, Detective P.J. Parker and I are new to the oh-eight. Ron is still on restricted duty due to a shoot-out several months ago. Stand and take a bow, Ron. The autopsy is this afternoon at three. I'd like you to attend."

"Sure thing."

"Who checked out Scott Sigler's alibi?" she asked, looking around the conference table.

Detective Charleen Greene raised her hand. Corelli smiled. "What do you have?"

Greene shuffled some papers. "Based on time records in the office, the sign-out sheet, and the two guards in the lobby, we confirmed that Sigler left the office a little after three a.m. It seems that's a standard workday for young attorneys in these big firms. The staff at the restaurant knows him and confirmed he had dinner with a man fitting del Balzo's description. Waiter said they held hands most of the time and ordered champagne for some kind of toast. They walked out holding hands and looking happy." She coughed, took a sip of coffee. "Mohammed Hussein, the grocery clerk, couldn't say whether it was two or three that morning, but he knows Sigler because he often comes in around that time for a pint of ice cream."

She looked up. "And we got the dog walker too. Richard Smythe. Works three to eleven and usually walks his dog around three a.m. just before he goes to bed. He's seen Sigler before, but he remembers Tuesday morning because Sigler was eating a pint of ice cream with a plastic spoon and doing a little," she looked at her notes, "*Singing in the Rain* dance as he walked down the street."

"Good work. Sounds like we can eliminate Sigler. Who's following up on Ms. Foxworth?"

"That would be me," Ron said, opening his little black leather notebook. "Originally from Oklahoma, been in New York fifteen years. According to her, she's been cleaning houses about five years. Before that she worked as a payroll clerk for a small construction firm in Queens. She has about ten clients, mostly gay men, one lesbian, charges twenty dollars an hour. Neighbors say she and her partner are quiet, respectable, and friendly. No police record here, still waiting to hear from Oklahoma."

"Did you get a list of her clients?'

"Sure did. We'll be interviewing them today."

"Get somebody to help out with that. Any questions so far?" Nobody said anything. "Detective Parker and I are teamed up. Parker, please report on our interviews."

There was silence when Parker finished. Then Dietz said, "Geesh, the father was threatened, but murder his son? Sounds like a Greek tragedy."

The ambassador was Corelli's prime suspect but she needed to keep a lid on it for now so Parker didn't share the ambassador's comment about Nardo's death being for the best. Corelli put a hand up to stop the comments. "Don't get carried away, Dietz. There may be something there, but you know how family arguments go. Right now we just have the father's attitude and the argument, no real evidence. We need to tread carefully. Any hint of something like this could ruin the ambassador's career, for no reason." *And mine too.*

"I'd like someone to check out Andrea Sansone, he's Chief of Security at the UN and he seems to be in the ambassador's pocket— or maybe it's Carla del Balzo's pocket, but I get the feeling he does their dirty work. Who knows? Murdering their son might fall into that category."

"One more thing," Dietz said, speaking over the laughter. "We got a witness, one of the vic's neighbors. Forlini, you wanna report?"

"Yeah, sure."

Corelli smiled. "Forlini." According to Dietz, Detective Joey Forlini was one of the unsung heroes of the squad. He enjoyed the grunt work of canvassing to sniff out witnesses and the detailed preparation and analysis of the reports generated during an investigation to ferret out the few kernels of significance. People of all ages and economic and social status responded to his gentleness and compassion, and he often got information that others missed.

"Got a gay guy lives next door to Nardo. Said he was goin' down his steps Monday about seven and Nardo opened the door to a sexy guy in a suit. Said he was trying to look like he wasn't looking so he didn't see much. Described the visitor as slender, shorter than Nardo, with shoulder-length brown hair." He glanced down at his notes. "By the tone of Nardo's voice, he was surprised to see the guy. Guy's name was Emilio." He looked up. "That's all I got so far."

"Parker. What do we know about Emilio?

Parker cleared her throat. "Emilio Ottaviano is Nardo's brother-in-law. He told us he hadn't seen Nardo in a year."

Corelli exchanged a look with Parker. "Make a note to talk to him again."

"Good work, Forlini." She glanced at her watch. "If you leave right now, you might catch some of del Balzo's neighbors before they go to work."

"I'm on it," Forlini said. He gathered his papers and left the room.

"Okay, guys, we need to move quickly. Dietz, get somebody checking parking tickets Tuesday night around the area of del Balzo's apartment. And contact the taxi companies; let's see if anyone was dropped off near Nardo's apartment."

"Let me remind you," Corelli said, making eye contact with each detective in the room. "You were chosen for this case because you're damn good detectives, because you know how to handle people, and because you're discreet. Remember, it's not unusual for parents and children to argue, but they don't usually kill each other. We have a lot of digging to do before we seriously consider the ambassador. So any discussion of the argument and threat stays in this room. Right?"

Every head went up and down.

"I can't hear you."

A dutiful chorus of yeses brought a smile to her lips.

"One more thing. You may have noticed the crowd of reporters outside. I know it makes it difficult for all of you and I apologize."

The groan was louder than she expected.

"I'm with you on that. But let me remind you that being discreet is even more important with all those ears and mikes around. If you can, avoid the press totally. If they shove a mike in your face, no comment is the safest bet. Need I mention some of our brethren would like nothing more than to discredit me and the investigation, so please only discuss the case with the members of the team, in this room, with the door closed. Any leaks on this case may have disastrous consequences. Any questions?"

She stood.

"Charleen, sit in on the autopsy with Ron. Dietz, assign somebody to dig into Leonardo and Carla del Balzo. Also, let's trawl the gay bars again, see what we get."

The detectives began collecting their things, chatting with their neighbors.

"Parker and I are flying to Italy this afternoon," Corelli said in a loud voice.

"What?" Parker said, panic in her voice.

The room went silent. Everyone turned to look at Corelli.

"Just wanted to get your attention. I wasn't finished. Parker and I are going to verify the ambassador's story. See you all tomorrow morning, but please, let Dietz know the minute you think you have something. Parker, please brief Dietz on Sansone and give him the info on Sansone's alibi. Dietz, get someone on it right away. I'd like to confirm his alibi before we see him."

CHAPTER TWELVE

Thursday – 8 a.m.

Traffic was slow. Parker drummed her fingers on the steering wheel impatiently, her mind racing. Watkins and Greene looked pretty cozy this morning, probably got it on last night. He had the nerve to ask why she'd left so early. Does he expect her to fall all over him just because he plays in a band? Well he sure didn't waste a lot of time after she told him she wasn't ready for a relationship.

Corelli pulled out her cell phone and keyed in her password. Either the volume was up really high or she had it set for speakerphone, because Parker could hear Miranda Foxworth's breathy voice as clear as if her ear was to the phone.

"Sorry to call so early, detective. I thought and thought last night, and for the life of me I couldn't remember who referred me to Nardo, but this morning I was brushing my teeth and the name just popped into my head. It was Nelson Choi." Corelli jotted down the telephone number and address Miranda dictated, then keyed it in. The busy signal filled the car.

"Did you get that, Parker? Swing over to the Westside, Seventy-Fifth between Columbus and Central Park West. Let's see if we can catch Choi before he leaves for work."

"First east, now west, then back to the east side. This is crazy." She could feel the rage filling her. Corelli couldn't care less; she wasn't the one driving in all this traffic.

"Did I miss some special training at the academy that said we use traffic patterns to decide the order of interviews? Or is it my decision to see Choi first that you're questioning?"

"So where do you want me to turn?" Parker asked, not hiding her anger.

"You're the driver, you figure it out."

They rode the rest of the way in not-so-friendly silence. Parker felt bad about being crabby but then Corelli didn't hesitate to dump on her, and she was much nastier. She willed herself to relax as she double-parked in front of No. 23, a brownstone, similar to the other brownstones on the tree-lined street.

Corelli made no move to get out.

"Okay, Parker. What's going on?"

"Just the traffic."

"We've hit traffic before. You've been sullen and withdrawn this morning. What's bothering you?"

"I'm okay."

Corelli studied her, then shrugged. "Stay that way."

They walked up the curved stone staircase to the heavy wooden door and rang the bell. They waited, rang again. Nothing. Corelli hit redial on her cell. A machine picked up after one ring. "Hi, it's Nelson. I'm not in. Leave your name and number and I'll call you later."

She turned to Parker. "We missed him."

A woman maneuvered a stroller out of the neighboring brownstone. She paused to check them out, then started down the steps, struggling with the double, side-by-side baby stroller. Parker dashed down and over to help. Once on the sidewalk, the woman smiled and pushed her hair off her face. "Thanks. Can I help you?"

"Yes. We're looking for Nelson Choi," Parker said, displaying her shield. Corelli joined them and offered her identification.

The woman took her time. She compared their pictures to their faces, then dug into her bag, retrieved a pen and a small notebook, and copied their names and shield numbers before giving them her attention. *Smart lady.* "Has Nelson done something wrong?"

"No. We need his help. A friend of his has been killed."

The woman busied herself tucking in the blankets and cooing to the two blue-eyed, blond infants. Hard to tell if they were girls or boys since they were dressed in yellow and green.

"He's not home."

Corelli smiled. "Yes, we see. Do you know where he works?"

"Wall Street. But I don't know which firm. Anyway, he's probably not there. He flew to Chicago Saturday and he wasn't sure when he would be home because he planned to spend some time with his partner Jeremy in East Hampton." She smiled. "Sorry. I don't know Jeremy's last name or anything helpful."

Corelli thanked her, handed her a card, and got back in the car. While Parker drove down Central Park West to get to the Sixty-Fifth Street Transverse and cross to the East Side, Corelli called Miranda but she didn't pick up. She called Dietz.

"Dietz, Miranda Foxworth gave me Nelson Choi as the friend who referred del Balzo to her, but he's not at home. Find her and if she knows where Choi works, send someone to talk to him. If she doesn't know, put somebody on finding out ASAP. I think it's a Wall Street firm."

She listened for a minute. "Yes, I know. Get somebody. It's important."

CHAPTER THIRTEEN

Thursday – 9 a.m.

Parker turned the car onto East Fifty-Fifth Street, toward the del Balzo residence. This time the street was lined with TV vans and the sidewalks with reporters smiling brightly into cameras and speaking earnestly into microphones as if they had real news to report. The morning TV news in action.

"Here we go again," Parker said.

"The uniforms are keeping them behind barricades and they're all focused on their reports, so maybe we can get in before they notice us."

They ran up the stone steps. Corelli flashed her badge at the young officer stationed at the door. He rang the bell for them and stepped aside. Were the chimes so cheerful yesterday? Corelli hadn't noticed. Someone called her name. She remained facing the closed door and ignored the questions shouted at her back. She marveled at the lack of interest shown by the del Balzos' neighbors. Nine o'clock on a warm August morning in midtown New York City, every TV, radio, and print news organization camped out on their street, and not a person in any of the surrounding brownstones was peeking out the window or standing outside gaping. The del Balzo residence appeared to be uninhabited.

She was about to ring again when the door swung open. The look of irritation on Leonardo del Balzo's face passed quickly but made it clear they weren't welcome. "Now what? Can't this wait until tomorrow's official reception?"

"Sorry sir. It's important we talk to you and Mrs. del Balzo now." His reluctance made Corelli want to push.

He hesitated. "Can't you get rid of those…people?"

"Freedom of the press. All we can do is keep them behind barricades."

Good thing they weren't vampires, because without inviting them in, he turned and walked to the back of the house. "Make it quick. My wife, um, we're trying to deal with this tragedy."

They followed him to the same glass-enclosed room. Nardo's mother sat in the same chair, her face bathed in the early morning sunshine streaming through the wall of glass.

"It's those detectives again, Carla," he said, not hiding his annoyance. "They have questions that can't wait. They promised to be quick."

They had made no such promise, but Corelli didn't correct him.

He picked up his coffee and sat near his wife, facing the two standing detectives. As far as Corelli could see, neither of them looked particularly broken up, but she knew people reacted differently. She realized it would be harder to judge their expressions while towering over them. "You know, I think we will sit," she said, even though they hadn't been offered chairs. She pulled a chair around so she was eye to eye with them. Parker followed her lead.

He seemed fascinated by the contents of his cup, while his wife gazed at them with suspicion.

Corelli watched them while Parker readied her pad and pen, then remained silent for another minute, hoping to make them uncomfortable.

"Ambassador del Balzo, what did you and Nardo argue about Monday?"

He straightened, surprise on his face. "Who told…?" He caught himself and sipped his coffee, tamping his anger by tapping his fingers on the cup. After twenty seconds, the diplomat emerged, his face guileless as he smiled. "It was personal, Detective, not pertinent to your investigation."

Good try, but the anger seeped out and his tone warned her off.

He opened his mouth to continue, but his wife put her hand on his thigh, silencing him.

"Did Nardo threaten to derail your bid to replace Berlusconi?"

Carla leaned forward. "Why do you persist with these rude and disrespectful questions when we are mourning the death of our son?"

Leonardo ignored Carla. "Who said Nardo threatened me?"

"Was that it?" Corelli asked.

"He had some fantasy story, a pack of lies. No one would ever believe it."

"His friend said the argument really upset Nardo."

Mrs. del Balzo choked and straightened up.

"Are you all right?" he asked in Italian.

She nodded, then asked in Italian, "Which friend?"

He ignored his wife's question. "What did this...*friend* say?"

"I'd rather hear your version."

Carla repeated the question. "*Quale amico?*"

He waved her question aside. "As I told you, the argument is not relevant to your investigation." He stood. "Now is there anything else before you go?"

"Yes." She remained seated. "Tell me what you did Tuesday night. In detail, please."

He glared at her then picked up his coffee cup. He stared out the window, sipping his coffee. "I worked until about six thirty, came home, showered, changed into evening clothes, and had a drink with Mrs. del Balzo. Then my driver took me to the UN for a formal dinner meeting which ran until eleven thirty."

"We'll need the names of the people at the meeting."

Carla reached for his hand and said in Italian, "They think you killed him. That could be a problem."

He patted her hand and smiled. "My wife says you think I killed my son. Is that true?"

Carla's eyes drilled into her but Corelli didn't flinch. "Just routine, sir. We have to account for everyone in an investigation." She answered in what she hoped was a neutral non-threatening voice. No use upsetting them. Yet.

Carla switched her attention to the ambassador. "Well, I have nothing to hide," he said. "Ask my assistant about the meeting. She'll give you the details."

"That would be Ms. Frascetti?"

"Yes, of course."

"Did your driver wait for you?"

"No. I told him not to wait. It was a nice night, so I thought I'd walk. I got home about midnight."

"Was Mrs. del Balzo with you?"

"No. It was a business meeting. She was upstairs in bed when I got home. I fell asleep reading in here, and then about two I woke and went up. Carla woke up when I got into bed."

"So no one saw you between eleven thirty and two?"

"That's correct. Are you insinuating…?"

"No sir, as I said, just routine. And you, Mrs. del Balzo?"

"I…I was alone, here, all evening. You don't—"

Corelli smiled. "We have to account for everyone. We'll let ourselves out."

The tall, skinny officer tried to warn her as she brushed past him, but she was distracted. She stopped short and took an involuntary step back onto his foot at the sight of the pack of howling reporters. She pivoted. "Where the hell are the uniforms who are supposed to be managing the crowd?"

He pinked, coughed, and flicked his eyes to the right. Three of them leaned against a squad car, watching, smirking. "Get your asses over here," she yelled, trying to be heard over the racket. One of the cops cupped his ear as if he couldn't hear what she said. Bastards. She looked around. This time there was no backdoor so they had no choice but to make a run for their car.

"Let's go, Parker."

They locked arms and dove into the pack. But she had underestimated the size of the crowd and the intensity of the need. Bodies pressed in on them as they pushed toward the car. The pressure on their arms forced them apart and the crowd surged between them. Like a school of piranhas attacking their prey, they assaulted her, screaming questions, grabbing her where they could, and pushing microphones and cameras in her face. Her bag was torn from her shoulder along with the sleeve of her jacket. *Lights flashed. People screamed. Things exploded in her face. She tried to cover her ears and her eyes but she couldn't move her arms. She was hit, her blood sprayed. She tried to scream for Marnie to help but couldn't get the sound out. Pressure on her chest. She gasped for air but there was none.*

A sudden lessening of the pressure allowed Corelli to breathe and to notice her surroundings. She blinked. Not Afghanistan. *A flashback.* But she was trapped by a screaming mob pulling at her, poking her, shoving things in her face. She went down on her knees, put her hands over her face and tensed waiting to be trampled. A sudden wind at her back, then at her sides, and she was lifted to her feet. Somebody moving behind her propelled her forward. She turned to swing at whoever was there, but she saw only the blue-gold-buttoned chest of a uniform whose arms were flapping at her sides like some crazed angel clearing a path for her. The crowd parted and her angel herded her between beating wings to a car. One long blue arm pulled the door open, the other eased her in. She grabbed the dashboard to still her shaking. She took a deep breath, then another. She noticed the blood dripping, yanked a handful of tissues from the box near her, put her head back, and pressed the tissues against her nose to curtail the bleeding. She breathed deeply to still her heart and steady her hands.

Peering around the blue-clad legs standing guard at her door, she watched Parker knock reporters out of her way as she moved around to the car. Another uniform, an officer, moved through the crowd, ordering them to disperse, then stomped over to the patrol car. The media horde broke into a run toward the vans parked along the street.

A fresh-faced, curly-red-haired young woman who looked like her breakfast was reversing its course and Gerri Murray, the WNYN camerawoman, remained where they were, against the iron picket fence. Murray, nicknamed Bear because of her size and her reputation for growling and snapping, looked more like a shaggy brown mama bear today, one arm around the young woman's shoulder, a hand holding the young woman's hand, speaking into her ear. Interesting.

Parker slid into the car.

"You okay?' Corelli asked, trying to head off Parker's scrutiny.

"Whoa, what's all that blood? Somebody cut you?"

"A bloody nose. I'm a little shaken, but fine." She dabbed her nose with a clean tissue and showed it to Parker. "See, no blood."

"Who did it?" Parker said, looking ready to kill.

"Hard to tell. But really, I'm fine. Relax, it's not your fault."

"All that noise and the flashbulbs, did you have a flashback?"

"No," she lied, not wanting Parker on her case. "They pressed in on me, making it hard to breath."

"Jesus, they tore your shirt and jacket."

Corelli lowered the window to speak to her guardian angel, still standing next to the car. She cleared her throat. "Officer." The young blond, crew-cut officer who had been standing at the del Balzo's door got down on his knees so she could see him. "Good work."

"Sorry about this mess, ma'am. Are you okay?"

"Fine. Thanks to you. Remind me of your name, please."

He straightened his shoulders. "Officer Jamie Twilliger."

"I'll remember, Twilliger. Who's the other officer who helped you with the crowd?"

"Mallory. The duty sergeant. This is my first day on the job and he told me he would come by to see how I was doing. He musta come after the riot started."

Actually, she had seen him pull up just before she ran down the steps.

Twilliger glanced at the patrol car. "I think he's upset with those three."

"Would you retrieve my bag? It's there." She pointed. "And then tell that reporter by the fence I want to talk to her." Maybe Captain Winfry was right. Throw them a little something to distract them. Maybe a one-on-one with a TV reporter would do it. "And when Mallory is finished, ask him to come here."

Twilliger returned with her bag, spoke to Bear and headed back to his post. The camerawoman stomped to the car, fists at her side, lips tight. "Leave the kid alone, Corelli. She wasn't involved. In fact, this is her first time out and the whole scene scared the shit out of her. Child can't stop shaking."

"Me either. Bring her over, Murray."

Murray frowned.

"Come on. You know my report card always says, 'plays well with others.'"

"Yeah, and it always says, 'excels at kicking ass' too."

"I promise I won't hurt her."

"Don't even think about it." Murray waved the young woman over.

"Detective Corelli, Darla North, WNYN's newest reporter. Darla, this is the fabulous, incredible, infamous, Detective Chiara Corelli and her associate, Detective P.J. Parker."

The girl was pearly white and still shaking.

"Relax. I don't bite. Well sometimes I do, right Parker? But I'm not going to bite you, Darla."

"Sorry. I'm just overwhelmed. I've never seen anything like that, the way those reporters attacked you."

"I'm a little overwhelmed myself. I'd like to talk to you without my press entourage, get to know you a bit. Are you available for lunch?" She smirked. "I mean, have lunch with us, not be our lunch."

"Very funny, Corelli," Bear said.

"Parker and I will be eating at Café Buonasola at the South Street Seaport. You're both welcome to join us—off the record, of course."

Darla looked at Murray. The camerawoman nodded. "That would be wonderful, Detective Corelli."

"What's your cell number? We'll call you when we know about what time we'll be there. If we're not there when you arrive, tell the maitre d' that you're waiting for me. See you then. Make sure you're not followed. And don't waste your time following us now. I'm not giving anything."

"Thanks," Murray said. "Let's go, Darla."

"Wait. May we take a few frames of those bloody tissues?" Darla tipped her head toward the dashboard. "And your bloody shirt? It would be great if you could step out of the car and hold the tissues to your nose."

Corelli hesitated. "Sure, why not. Not too long, though."

Mallory strolled over as the reporters walked away. He was frowning. "They bothering you?"

"Not them. I asked them to come over."

He nodded. "Sorry about this morning. It won't happen again. Not on my watch. And I'll make sure every shift change understands the rules."

"What you do with those three is your business. But Twilliger saved my life. I'll write something for his file about him taking the initiative this morning. I hope you'll do the same. And thank you for your help as well."

"It shouldn't have happened. You let me know if any of my guys gives you any trouble," Mallory said, and headed for Twilliger who was back at his post on top of the steps.

Parker started the car. "This is getting really bad. I tried to stay close, keep them away. If it wasn't for that uniform, they would have crushed you. Can we get a restraining order or something? I mean somebody's going to get hurt if this keeps up."

"You need a course in arm flapping, Parker."

"I," she frowned, took in the amusement on Corelli's face, then glanced at the young officer now back to his post. "It would help to have arms like airplane wings. What is he? About six-five? Maybe I can get myself stretched."

Ah, Parker, finally you get a joke and joke back.

Corelli laughed. "If those three goons had been doing their job and keeping the crowd back, it wouldn't have happened. Let's go before the piranhas get curious."

As Parker pulled away, Corelli looked back. "Mallory blocked the street with his car. Let's go to my apartment so I can wash up and change out of these clothes."

"You're going to talk to that reporter?"

"We'll see how it goes later."

CHAPTER FOURTEEN

Thursday – 11 a.m.

Corelli called Rosina Frascetti to let her know they were stopping by for the names of everyone at the dinner the ambassador had attended the night his son was murdered. Frascetti directed them to the Swedish delegation, which had hosted the meeting. The list of well over a hundred names included the lead representative, multiple subordinates and staff people from twenty delegations, plus the doorman, waiters, and other worker-bees. After interviewing three Swedes, none of whom could say when del Balzo left the dinner, she folded and pocketed the list. "Let's go to lunch, Parker. Following up with all these people is going to take a lot more time than we have. I'll have Dietz assign a team to do the interviews."

The maitre d' at Buonasola had seated the reporter and the camerawoman at Corelli's favorite table out on the deck. They were facing the water, leaving Corelli and Parker their usual places facing the door. Once greetings were over and they had ordered, all eyes settled on Corelli.

"Is this where you hang out?" Murray said.

"The fact that you're here is a privilege, Bear." She smiled at the two women. "I have faith that you'll both respect our privacy and erase it from your memories the minute you leave."

Bear sipped her iced tea. "Since when do you trust anyone in the media?"

"My trust is limited to present company. Thus, the request for privacy."

The waiter arrived with their food. After a few bites, Corelli noticed Darla was just pushing her salad around on the plate. Must be too nervous to eat.

"So, Ms. North, you must be wondering why I asked you to lunch?"

Darla nodded, cleared her throat. "Call me Darla, please." She raised her eyes to meet Corelli's. "And, yes, I am curious. I gather it's not every day the reclusive Detective Corelli invites a reporter to lunch."

"I think we can help each other."

Darla shifted in her seat, glanced at Bear, then Parker. She sat up straighter and glared. "Let's get one thing straight, Detective. I report the truth as I see it. So if you think I'm so desperate for a story that you can use me, forget it. Let's go, Bear." She threw two twenties on the table and pushed her chair back. "By the way, by the time you noticed me shaking and cowering this morning, we had already taped a segment. Catch it on WNYN's six o'clock news."

Ah, she liked women with backbone. She touched Darla's arm. "I'm not interested in using you or anybody. That's not how I work. But I think our needs might coincide."

"What did you tape?" Parker asked.

Darla sat. "The feeding frenzy, with all the other reporters looking like wild beasts. Our producer was very happy. It was only after we taped it that I fell apart. Right, Bear?"

Bear beamed like a proud mama. Her baby had stood up to the ferocious Corelli. "Damn right. Damn good work," she said, then went back to her steak.

Darla picked up her fork. "I'm listening."

"Has Bear filled you in on my background?"

"I did a little research after we talked. I know a little about your career, about your serving in Iraq and Afghanistan, and a lot about your undercover assignment and the aftermath."

"Good. As you witnessed this morning, the media is stalking me. And I think it's going to get worse because of the del Balzo case. So I want to give you an exclusive now, and depending on how that goes, maybe other interviews later."

"Why me? Do you think you can manipulate me?"

Corelli thought for a moment. "When I saw the look on your face this morning, I knew you had empathy, that you understood what the quarry feels like, that you couldn't bring yourself to act like a rabid dog. I sensed strength and integrity, and I felt I could trust you to be fair and honest. You just confirmed the strength."

"You got all that from seeing me cowering like a frightened baby."

"You don't survive patrol in Iraq and Afghanistan or being undercover investigating cops if you can't read people and situations quickly." Corelli put her hand on Darla's arm. "You might have felt like a baby, but that's not what I saw. I'm not comparing the two situations, but you reminded me of soldiers when they first arrive in Iraq and see the horrors they have to deal with. It's hard to take it in. Want to think about it?"

Darla glanced at Corelli's hand, then at Murray and Parker. She smiled. "Are you kidding? I just need a little time to prepare. Can we do something for the ten o'clock news tonight?"

"Great. But let's set some ground rules. First, nothing personal, nothing about my family, nothing about my love life, real or imagined. Second, I won't answer questions about the del Balzo case so you can ask, but unless it's something I want to get out there, I won't comment. Third, we limit it to five minutes or less."

"Okay, how about this? I clear any questions about your family before we begin to tape and you decide whether we include them. Everything else is up for grabs, including any previous cases and the undercover assignment."

"That's fair. Except I can't give you too many actual details about the undercover work."

"I'm more interested in your feelings than the details."

"You can ask, but I may not answer."

"How about a series of three- to five-minute sketches over the next week or two? And you give me a heads-up on anything that's breaking on the del Balzo case."

"The series is fine but no promises on del Balzo. We'll have to see how things unfold. Do we have a deal?"

Darla's eyes were shining as she extended her hand. "Deal."

"I'm depending on you, Darla."

"Unless you're trying to use me, you'll be happy. I promise. You want to come to WNYN for the taping?"

"Not particularly."

"The police station? Your apartment?"

"Someplace neutral. Give me a second." As she picked up her cell phone she directed a question to Bear. "Downtown Brooklyn, Atlantic Avenue near Court Street okay for you?"

"Sure."

"If my friend doesn't object, I'll use her office." She pressed the speed dial number for her friend, private investigator Tess Cantrell. "Tess, can I use your office tonight for a TV interview?" She looked at Darla. "What time?"

Darla checked her watch. "We'll go back now and do the background. Seven?"

"Seven. See you." Corelli closed her phone. "Parker, give them Tess Cantrell's address."

CHAPTER FIFTEEN

Thursday – 2:30 p.m.

They went to the conference room. Corelli gathered the reports that had come in since the morning meeting and handed half to Parker. Detective Joey Forlini's report caught her eye as she thumbed through her pile. Forlini had managed to catch up with two more of Nardo's neighbors. The man directly across the street said he went to check the door and window locks before going to bed at eleven thirty and noticed a tall man dressed in black ringing the bell. Didn't see much since the man was wearing a hat and facing Nardo's door, but he had a lit cigarette. The door opened and a bare-chested Nardo hugged the man and let him in.

She handed the report to Parker. "Could be Leonardo was the tall man. On the other hand, it doesn't sound like father and son were on hugging terms." She shuffled through some reports and scanned the list of items forensics took from the scene. "The tall man had a lit cigarette when he went in but the forensics' list doesn't mention a butt in the apartment or outside. He must have flushed it or taken it with him."

She picked up Forlini's second report. The other neighbor, an older woman two doors down across the street from Nardo's apartment, noticed a young man sitting on her step watching Nardo's door. She had seen him on her step two or three times before. Last week she'd mentioned him to Nardo and he'd asked her to call him if she saw the guy again. So she did. She thought it was about ten thirty but Forlini was checking her phone records. Said the guy was slender, young, with straight chin-length dark hair, and she's pretty sure he wore glasses. After she talked to Nardo, he came out and called to the young man. They both went in the house. Nardo was bare-chested.

Corelli sat back. "Parker, look at this one."

"This sounds like what's his name, the teary guy from the delegation," Parker said, stretching.

"Ginocchioni. That's what I thought. Maybe he was crying when we interviewed him because he killed Nardo. He hasn't been in the office today and doesn't pick up his phone. How about we go to his apartment about six tomorrow morning and bring him in?"

"Nothing I'd rather do then get up at five and confront the little twerp."

And no problem for me since I never sleep. Corelli picked up another report.

Darla, Bear, and Tess were chatting like old buddies when she and Parker arrived. Corelli glared at them. "Nice. I turn my back and find you three schmoozing and talking about me. What did you tell her, Tess?"

Tess Cantrell laughed. "Watch out for her, Corelli. She's wicked, made me tell all your dirty secrets."

"Quick, Bear, get her on film." Darla giggled. "I want that evil look for the lead-in. Hey, you didn't say friends were off limits."

"I should have. Arrest them, Parker."

"What?" Parker tensed. Then, taking in the smiles, she realized it was a joke, and relaxed. "Okay, hands behind your backs."

"Sounds like fun," Darla said, "but y'all made a bargain with the devil so we'd better do the interview first."

"And you'd better double check everything Tess told you. PI's are disreputable liars."

Bear stood. "All right kiddies, playtime is over. If we're gonna air this at ten, we need to get started."

Corelli looked around. "Where do you want me?"

"That chair," Bear said, pointing to an easy chair positioned in front of the bookcases, next to a small table with a large arrangement of flowers.

"Thanks for the flowers, Tess."

"Thank WNYN," Tess said.

Bear studied Corelli. "Your cheek is purple, your nose is swollen, and your eye is black."

Corelli gingerly touched her face. "Can you cover it?"

Darla lifted Corelli's chin and eyed the bruises from several perspectives. "We'll be leading with the attack on you so I'd rather not cover the bruises. Unless you're self-conscious."

"I'm fine with leaving it."

Bear adjusted the lighting and checked various camera angles to get the best shot, while Darla fussed over Corelli, arranging her collar, straightening her jacket, and clipping on a mike. Finally, Darla sat facing Corelli. "We're going to go right into the question and answers, Detective Corelli. Bear and I will edit and fill in the intro and anything else we need back at the studio. All right?"

"Yes, but I thought we'd agreed you could call me Chiara?"

"I'll be more formal on camera." Darla addressed Parker and Tess. "If you want to stay, you need to be quiet. No comments, no giggling, no noise, or you'll ruin the take." She adjusted her clothes, turned to face Corelli, and nodded at Bear.

"Good evening. I'm Darla North and my guest this evening is Detective Chiara Corelli." Darla smiled. "It is truly my pleasure to meet you, Detective Corelli, I've heard so much about you." Her voice was strong and tinged with hints of the south.

Corelli smiled. "I'm sure you have, Ms. North."

"Detective Corelli, I understand you are currently leading the investigation into the murder of the son of Ambassador Leonardo del Balzo. Given that the ambassador is considered the likely successor to the current Prime Minister of Italy, I imagine this is a very sensitive case with a high priority."

"Every murder is a sensitive case for us and every murder is a high priority for us. NYPD doesn't discriminate on the basis of fame or fortune. Of course, the media often gives the rich and famous more coverage, and thus puts us under more pressure, but our goal in each and every case is to arrest the person or persons who took the life of the victim or victims, as quickly as we can."

"You've been on the police force for fifteen years and a detective for eight of those fifteen, but your service hasn't been limited to New York City. You served two tours in Iraq and not that long ago you returned from Afghanistan. How long were you there?"

"I was on a training mission for about a year."

"What was that like?"

"Difficult. Not being able to identify the enemy is…crazy. We were there to train the Afghani police but we didn't know who we could trust, who might lure us into a trap or who might show up shooting some morning. To say it was extremely stressful is an understatement. It's a terrible war, hard on the troops, many of them young, forced to live in hell for a year or more. The price we pay as a country is very high."

"Would you go back?"

"If I'm called, I'll go."

"And less than two weeks after you landed in New York City you were back on the job and starting an undercover investigation of a ring of cops suspected of working for drug dealers. How did you get involved in that?"

"I was asked."

"And of course you said yes. So you went from hell in Afghanistan to living a lie in New York City, investigating your friends, the people you depend on to watch your back. Sounds stressful, not being able to trust anyone, to confide in anyone, having to pretend to be somebody you're not. How did you deal with it?"

Corelli shrugged. Her smile showed her sadness. "You do what you have to do to survive, to do the job you're asked to do."

"You could have said no. Why didn't you?"

"Being undercover and investigating my friends and colleagues is one of the most difficult things I have ever done. It was harder than being in Iraq or Afghanistan. But I believe the NYPD is the greatest police department in the world. Most cops are honest and risk their lives every day to make New York safe for citizens and visitors. Dirty cops hurt us all, other police and the citizens we swear to protect."

"I'm sure that's true. But why you, Detective Corelli? Why take on an assignment no one else would do? Why put yourself in incredible danger?"

Corelli leaned forward. "I believe it's important to do the right thing regardless of the consequences, to live with integrity, to be the best that I can. In this case, I believed the right thing was to eliminate the small number of corrupt police in order to protect and defend the integrity of the police department."

"But instead of being thanked by your fellow police officers, they're ostracizing you. Being on the other side of that famous blue wall must feel terrible."

"It doesn't feel great, but my eyes were open when I accepted the assignment. I knew if I made it out alive, I would see a lot of blue backs during the rest of my career."

"If you made it out alive?"

"It's the risk every police officer takes every time they report for duty."

"You were undercover three months. Why did it end?"

"I was ordered to kill to prove my loyalty so I could move up to the next level in the criminal organization. Rather than kill, I aborted the operation. Unfortunately, that meant I never learned the names of the people running things."

"But you must have killed in Iraq and Afghanistan? Or on the job?"

"Yes, I did. It wasn't easy. But in war it's kill or be killed. I killed to protect myself or members of my group or civilians who were being threatened. I've never killed in cold blood."

Darla shuffled her papers, giving the viewers a few seconds to absorb the comment. "Detective Corelli, earlier you said you aborted the undercover investigation without learning the names of the upper echelon. So there are still police out there who were key members of Righteous Partners, as I think they called themselves. Does that mean you're in danger?"

"I believe we got all of them in a later operation. But, being a cop is dangerous. The fallout from the undercover assignment just enhances the danger somewhat."

"Are you afraid?"

"I'm watchful, but I don't let fear rule my life."

"Just a few more questions, Detective. How is it that you were assigned to the del Balzo investigation?"

"The luck of the draw. Detective P.J. Parker and I were the only detectives available when the call came in."

"Are you getting the cooperation you need from your colleagues?"

"Yes."

"And you wouldn't tell me if you weren't. Right?"

Corelli smiled but didn't respond.

"Speaking of danger, the media seems to be stalking you. As you know, WNYN did a brief segment earlier tonight showing a large number of our competitors in the New York City media attacking you. Viewers who haven't seen the clip may want to stay tuned to see it later in this hour."

Darla smiled. "Thank you so much, Detective Chiara Corelli, for taking the time out of what I can imagine is a very busy schedule, to talk with us tonight. I hope we can do it again." She leaned over and shook Corelli's hand.

"You're welcome, Ms. North." Corelli smiled and held Darla's eyes.

Bear held the camera on them for ten or so seconds before she stopped filming and turned the lights off. Tess clapped. Darla sat back. "You were terrific. Better than I expected and believe me I had high expectations. And thanks, Tess, for the use of your office. It was perfect."

"For Corelli, the office is yours anytime you need it. Just give me a call."

Darla turned to Corelli. "What about the series of interviews, Detective, um, Chiara?"

Corelli got to her feet. "Darla, Bear, you were wonderful. My par…My sisters will be proud. If we do another, Darla, I'd like to feature some of the people I work with, the ones working on the del Balzo investigation. Maybe do one of our meetings. I'd have to clear it first. What do you think?"

"Let me think about how to approach it," Darla said. "And I'll come up with some other ideas. Don't forget to watch tonight."

"How'd I do, Parker?" Corelli asked, after they were in the car.

Parker chewed her lip. "I saw a part of you I haven't seen before. Usually, you swagger, you're critical, impatient, angry, moody. You rarely show the gentle, sensitive, caring detective who loves the department and other police."

"You gonna tell Senator Daddy so he can go for my gentle, sensitive belly?"

Parker looked as if she had been punched but she recovered quickly. "Fuck you."

"Abusing a superior is not allowed, Parker." She really did enjoy pulling Parker's chain. "Now let's go see why Nardo's brother-in-law lied to us."

CHAPTER SIXTEEN

Thursday – 9 p.m.

Ottaviano's face darkened. "You again. Can't you leave us in peace?"

Corelli pushed past him. "I will when you tell us the truth."

"Who's there, Emilio?" Flavia asked in Italian from inside the apartment.

He replied in Italian. "The detectives have a few more questions. I'll take care of it." "Ask them in," Flavia said in English.

A not-very-happy Emilio led them into the living room.

Flavia's eyes were puffy and red, but she looked less fragile than she had on their last visit. "Please sit. What more can we tell you?"

Ottaviano sat next to his wife and draped his arm over her shoulders.

"Actually, it's Mr. Ottaviano who can help us. We have a witness who saw him go into Nardo's apartment Tuesday night and we'd like to know why he lied about it."

Flavia pulled away from her husband. "You saw Nardo and didn't tell me?"

He reached for her hand but Flavia shrank back. He flushed and looked down. "Leonardo was upset about a conversation he had with Nardo on Monday, so I went to Nardo's apartment to try to talk some sense into him."

"What time was that?"

"I don't know exactly. Around seven?"

"What did they argue about?"

He stiffened. "I only know Nardo threatened to destroy the ambassador's chance to be prime minister. I was trying to stop him from doing something that would embarrass us all."

"Did the ambassador ask you to speak to him?"

"No, Carla asked me to intervene."

"How did Nardo seem?"

"Surprised but pleased that I had come. But when I brought up the argument he got angry, told me to mind my own business. We had words and I left."

"What was he wearing?"

"Wearing?" He thought for a second. "Um, jeans and a T-shirt."

"Do you know where Nardo kept his gun?"

He looked puzzled. "I didn't know he had one."

"What did you do when you left Nardo's apartment?"

"I went to La Cucina Bella to meet Flavia. We had an eight o'clock dinner reservation."

"Did you speak to your in-laws?"

"Only Carla, when I called to tell her what happened."

"Was Mrs. del Balzo upset?"

"Of course. She felt pulled between Nardo and Leonardo. Afraid Nardo would do something stupid to interfere with Leonardo's chance of being prime minister."

"Why did you lie to us?"

He brushed his hair back, then glanced at Flavia. "I was afraid you would think I killed him."

He walked them to the door. Corelli moved in close, forcing him to look up at her. "Lying wastes my time and distracts me from tracking the killer. Do it again and I'll throw your ass in jail so fast you won't know what happened."

Corelli gave Parker directions to Gianna's house and stared out the passenger window as they drove.

Parker tapped the steering wheel. "You sounded like you wanted to kill Ottaviano."

Corelli's head swung back toward Parker. "I do. I could. I'm so freakin' tired of people lying and hiding things and playing games, complicating things that are already difficult." She cupped her hands over her eyes and rubbed her forehead. "And, you, Ms. Fancy-pants ADA? You think it's okay?"

Parker's hands tightened on the steering wheel. "I won't waste my breath answering that one."

They found parking right away on Gianna's block. Corelli knew she was on edge. Gianna would calm her, help her center so she could think clearly.

"What a surprise." Gianna hugged Corelli, then Parker. "Nice to see you again, P.J."

"We were in Brooklyn, so we thought we'd drop in for a cup of coffee and something good to eat." Corelli cocked her head. "But it sounds like you have company."

Gianna flushed. She took Corelli's hand. "Zia Marina and Patrizia."

Corelli made a face. Oh great, the dynamic duo: the sister who preached being a cop is no job for a woman and the aunt whose mantra was 'a real woman gets married and takes care of her family.' Her father, at least, just acted like she was invisible, but these two never stopped nagging and criticizing. And if that wasn't bad enough, Zia Marina's life work seemed to be finding a husband for Corelli. She always had some good man from Italy lined up. Corelli avoided any contact with her and no longer responded to her calls.

"Another candidate?"

"Um, yes. That guy from the UN."

The two detectives exchanged a look. "Sansone?" they said, in unison.

She nodded. "He was at Zia Marina's house last evening."

"He what?"

"She called me this morning, all excited. She said she needed my help on something important but she wouldn't tell me what." She lowered her voice. "They just got here a little while ago. Someone introduced him to her. Sansone told her he had met you and found you very attractive, but he wanted to do things the right way, so he was hoping for family approval and a formal introduction. Of course, Zia Marina was thrilled that an Italian man like Sansone was interested in you. She told him about Uncle Genaro leaving you the building and a lot of money, so he would be willing to put up with your stubbornness and unwomanly behavior."

Parker coughed. "I'll wait outside." She started toward the door.

Too late for that. "Stay. You already know most of it."

Corelli dropped Gianna's hand. "And you're going along with this?" Corelli's voice was hard. "I expect better of you, especially after our discussion last night."

"They just got here. I'm not going along with anything. I know how you feel about—"

"Go back to your company," Corelli said. "Let's get out of here, Parker." She pushed past Gianna and walked out the door.

"Sorry, Gianna, she's kind of on edge tonight." Parker ran to catch up to Corelli.

Corelli kept her eyes straight ahead as Parker climbed into the driver's seat and started the car. She was used to Patrizia and Zia Marina treating her like a pawn in their marriage game, but Gianna's betrayal hurt. And she would kill Sansone for violating her privacy. She could feel Parker's concern, but she needed a few minutes to get control before she could discuss this situation. Parker headed for the Belt Parkway.

Corelli broke the silence. "Now you know I own the building I live in."

Parker cleared her throat. "You told me in the airport in West Virginia, when your super was attacked."

"Right. I forgot." Corelli felt tension in her arms and realized both hands were fisted. "I'm ready to kill Mr. Blazing Teeth, worming his way into my life."

"Patrizia, I know. Who's this sea-ah person?"

"My father's oldest sister. The two of them won't be happy until I'm married and staying at home serving a husband and children." She grimaced. "Too bad it's never going to happen."

"How did he find her?"

"It sounds like he has ties in the Italian community. A few phone calls—and Zia Marina welcomes him with open arms. The real question is why would he drag my family into this?"

"Maybe he finds you attractive."

"And maybe he's trying to complicate the case, throw up a smokescreen. But I can't see the benefit of leveraging the Italian connection. Does he think he can seduce me and control the investigation or maybe get me thrown off the case?"

Patrizia and Zia Marina were too old fashioned to understand, but how could Gianna, her closest friend and confidant, the person in the world who knew her best, join the enemy? She closed her eyes, leaned her head against the seat, and didn't say another word until Parker pulled up to her building.

"Don't forget we're going after Ginocchioni tomorrow morning. Pick me up at six."

Damn, she'd let her exhaustion come through in her voice. Parker shifted to face her then glanced at the clock on the dashboard. The last thing she needed right now was a PTSD lecture from Parker. "We have a murder to solve, Parker, and that's our priority, not sleep." She sighed. "Don't wait for me to get in. It's late and the bad guys are all asleep."

"I'll wait."

They went through this every night. "Suit yourself."

At the door to her building, Corelli glanced back. Parker only considered her safe after she was in the elevator with the doors closed, so she was standing by the car, eyes scanning for danger. Why did she give Parker a hard time? It was her job, after all. Yet she, Corelli, had proved she could take care of herself, hadn't she? She didn't need anyone and resented having a babysitter. But, orders are orders. She shoved the key in the lock but pulled back at the sudden pricking in her calves. What the...? She grinned.

"Where did you guys come from?" She crouched to pet the two kittens attacking her.

Thwack.

"Shooter. Get down!" Parker shouted.

Luckily she was down already. The windows exploded. Glass bit at her face.

Thwack.

She drew her gun, grabbed the kittens, and rolled into the shrubbery, behind the tree. Her vision was blurred. She rubbed her eyes. Shit. Blood.

Thwack. Thwack. More shots. Bark exploded around her. She covered her eyes. Could he see her behind the tree? Night goggles. She crawled further, behind the garbage bins. With her gun clasped in two hands in front of her, she tried to locate the shooter to return fire. A flash from the building across the way. The shooter or someone putting on a light. She couldn't tell.

"Officer down, officer down!" Parker shouted.

Parker must be hurt and calling it in.

"Where are you, Parker?" she yelled, frantic to get to her. She blinked to clear her eyes, but she couldn't see her.

"Parker," she yelled again.

"Under the car."

"Are you hit?"

Thwack. Another shot. Where the hell is the shooter?

Sirens. Near. Police cars filled the street and suddenly the only noise was the staccato reports from the radios.

Parker slid out from under the car. No obvious wounds. Police gathered around her and she gesticulated toward the building across the street. Orders were given to search that building and others nearby and the police dispersed.

Corelli took some deep breaths, gearing up to deal with the fallout from the attack. Hopefully she wouldn't have to face the media. As her adrenaline settled, she became aware of the kittens wrestling on her back.

Parker crouched in front of her. "Where did he hit you?"

"I'm not hit. I thought you were."

"You sure? You're bleeding like a stuck pig," Parker said, dabbing Corelli's face with a clean white handkerchief. "And your hair is full of blood."

Corelli touched her head and looked at her fingers. "Must have been the glass when it shattered. Scalp wounds always bleed a lot."

"And what the hell is that?" Parker tilted her head at the kittens cavorting on Corelli's back. "Playing with kittens while somebody's trying to kill you?"

"Get them off me, please," Corelli said, crawling closer. The kittens' needle-sharp claws dug into her but she didn't want to hurt them by knocking them off. They must have thought she was playing when she rolled into the shrubbery.

Parker took the two fuzz-balls in one hand and extended her other hand to Corelli. Corelli crawled out of the shrubbery. She grabbed the hand Parker offered and pulled herself up. Suddenly lightheaded, she swayed. "Sorry, I'm a little dizzy."

Parker held on to her and handed her the kittens. She brushed Corelli off and waved over one of the EMS guys just arriving.

"Whoever it was did a job on my lobby," Corelli said. "All the windows are out."

"Where are you hit?" the EMS guy asked.

"I'm not hit. I was under there." She pointed to the glass scattered around the doorway to her building. "It must have cut my face and scalp when it shattered."

He took her arm. "Come sit in the ambulance. Let me take a look."

She sat, holding the now sleeping kittens. If it wasn't—

"Hey, Corelli, anything for a little attention, huh?"

She looked up. "Thanks for your concern, O'Malley. No, I wasn't hit by a bullet, just some flying glass."

"Well, your luck is holding. Be glad it's me here. Anybody else might have taken advantage of the situation and put a bullet in you." She turned to Parker. "And, you, I presume, are the babysitter, Detective P.J. Parker?"

Parker nodded.

"Detective Erin O'Malley," Corelli said, introducing them.

"Let's talk while he cleans you up." O'Malley rubbed the kittens. "You always carry your pets with you, Corelli?"

"These guys saved my life. If I hadn't crouched down to pet them, the first shot would have shattered my head instead of that window."

"Ah, I understand your attachment. Didn't the shooter follow you down?"

"I rolled into the shrubbery, there, near the entrance, and crawled behind the tree. There were more shots, a couple came close, but I don't think he could see me."

"Did you return the fire?"

"No. The glass nicked me and the blood blurred my vision. I held off because I couldn't track him. It happened really fast. I heard Parker shouting 'officer down' and right after that the sirens, then the shooting stopped and you guys arrived. When it was safe, naturally."

O'Malley ignored the dig. She turned to Parker. "You thought she was shot?"

"Yeah. It happened so fast. I heard the bullet, I shouted, and she went down, glass flying all over the place. I saw blood so I thought she was hit. But she crawled away so I knew she wasn't dead."

"What about you, Parker, did you return the fire?"

"By the time I figured which building it was coming from, there were people standing in a lot of the windows and I was afraid I'd hit a civilian. Then I heard the sirens close by, and I figured the shooter would hear them too."

"Neither of you fired a shot. That makes it easier."

The EMS bandaged the cuts on Corelli's forehead. "You're all right. Like you said glass cuts. I picked out as much as I could. Comb and wash your hair to get the rest out, but be careful. Dab with peroxide if you start to bleed."

"Did you check her back and the back of her legs?"

Corelli gave Parker a dirty look. "I'm fine."

"Let me take a look." He helped her get her jacket off and lifted her shirt. "Nothing. Good thing that glass is the kind that shatters into little pieces or you might have been stabbed."

"My legs are fine too." Corelli turned to Parker. "What about you?"

"Just a scrape on my hand when I rolled under the car." She held out her hand.

The EMS guy examined it, cleaned it, and put a bandage on. "Anybody else?"

"Just us," Corelli said, standing.

"Take good care of those kitties, Corelli, you owe them." O'Malley checked out the group of officers huddled in the street. "Don't go anywhere. I'm going to see if I can get this show on the road." She started to walk away.

Corelli spotted Karen, her building superintendent.

"Just a second, O'Malley. Send that blonde to me." Corelli pointed to a woman in the crowd of bystanders.

"Your wish is my command."

Karen ducked under the tape and ran to Corelli. "Holy shit. What happened?"

"Here." Corelli handed her the two kittens, one all gray, one all black. "These guys saved my life."

"They what?" Karen said, taking the sleeping kittens and cradling them in one arm.

"I'll explain later. Where's your wife?"

"Rosie is trying to find out what happened from a cop she knows." Karen indicated a cluster near the shattered door.

"I need you and Rosie to do a couple of things. Bring the kittens up to my apartment and put them in the gym. Then go around to the all-night market and buy some cat food, kitty litter, and a box to put it in. When the police are done, sweep up the broken glass and get someone to board up the broken windows for tonight. First thing tomorrow, call the glass people and have bulletproof glass installed."

"Sure thing, boss," Karen said. She reached over and picked some glass out of Corelli's hair. "Are you sure you're not hurt?"

"I'm fine, really."

Corelli and Parker leaned against the building watching the investigative team do its work. She'd thought it was over when they had jailed the upper echelon of Righteous Partners, but it looked like Captain Winfry was right about the threat still being out there. It made her angry. Had she missed someone or was this a disgruntled fellow officer who felt she had betrayed the unspoken pledge to the blue brotherhood? Why become a cop if you didn't believe that honesty and integrity were more important than misguided loyalty? She sighed. It was complicated. Cops need to know fellow officers will watch their backs, so when someone like her turns on other cops, she can't be depended on and is a danger. It doesn't matter that she risked her life for the department and for them. Some cops supported her but wouldn't acknowledge it openly for fear of repercussions.

The police were keeping civilians, including her tenants, to one side and herding the media together at the end of the street. Of course, distance didn't keep the media from calling out questions to get her attention. She was glad she didn't have to deal with them tonight.

Parker pushed away from the building to face her. "I think you should call Gian...someone to let them know you're okay. All these cameras and reporters, it'll be breaking news and even if they don't see it, someone will probably call them about it. They might worry."

Parker, who she was constantly baiting, was worried about her family. She struggled to suppress the smile threatening. "Thanks. You're right. And, they'll think the worst."

"Do you want me to call, Gianna?" Parker sounded tentative. She probably expected to get slapped down.

Ordinarily she would call Gianna, but she was still raw from the betrayal. Simone wasn't always dependable. "Yeah, that would be good. Tell her I'm okay but if she asks to speak to me, tell her I'm being interviewed about the incident."

Parker pulled out her phone and stepped to the side. She spoke for a few minutes, every once in a while looking at Corelli, then came back to stand with her. "All set."

As the investigation was winding down, Captain Winfry appeared. He must have come in from home. He spoke to O'Malley, then strode toward them.

"Are you two okay?" Captain Winfry's voice thundered.

"Yessir, just some cuts and bruises."

He looked them over. "Good work, Parker."

"It wasn't me, it was—"

"The kittens. I heard. But I was talking about you keeping your head, waiting it out rather than firing randomly and maybe hitting a civilian. That's excellent work in my book."

Parker blushed.

Corelli poked her.

Parker stood straighter. "Thank you, sir."

"They tell me the shots came from an empty apartment in that building," he pointed across the street, "but they found no evidence of the shooter. Of course, they'll be taking fingerprints, etcetera. You need some time off?"

They looked at each other. "No sir," they said in unison.

He smiled. "That's what I thought."

O'Malley approached. "Captain, we're ready to talk to the media. Corelli, you want in?"

"Only if I'm ordered to."

"Not necessary tonight," Winfry said.

"What about you, Detective Parker?" O'Malley said.

"No way," Parker said. "I said what I have to say in my statement."

O'Malley shrugged. She looked at Winfry. "It's just you and me, Captain. And you two are free to go."

"Come upstairs, Parker. Give the press time to leave."

They rode the elevator in silence for a few floors, then Corelli turned to Parker. "Thanks for thinking of my family and making the call to Gianna. I appreciate it."

"You're welcome."

Corelli turned on the lights in the apartment. "Help yourself. Beer in the fridge, booze in the cabinet by the stereo, glasses there too. I'm going to check to see whether my guests have destroyed the gym yet."

"Pour you something?" Parker said.

"A brandy, thanks."

She joined Parker on the sofa. "Looks like Karen went all out for the little darlings. They were snuggled up on a cat bed." She still felt jumpy inside so she lifted her glass carefully. Good. Hands steady.

"You going to keep them?"

Corelli sipped her brandy. "No. I'll take them to a shelter."

"They did save your life. Some shelters kill the animals they can't get rid of."

The kittens appeared, stared at Corelli, then jumped into her lap.

"Besides," Parker said, grinning, "they really seem to like you."

They watched the two kittens curl up together. "You think I should keep them?" Corelli rubbed their bellies, generating a low rumble.

"Keep the mice in check."

"What mice?"

"You know, in case."

"I'll think about it." There *was* something comforting about their weight and warmth in her lap but having pets meant responsibility.

She raised her glass to Parker. "You and Winfry were right. I'll try not to give you a hard time anymore."

"Thanks. But it would be better if we were wrong."

"And he was right-on about your control. It's no mean feat to keep your finger off the trigger when somebody is shooting at you. You were very clearheaded, holding your fire when you saw civilians in the windows."

Parker stood. "So, we still on for six a.m. tomorrow?"

Oops, too much praise.

CHAPTER SEVENTEEN

Friday – 6 a.m.

Parker pressed the button next to Ginocchioni's name and leaned on the door, ready to push it open as soon as he buzzed them in. But nothing happened. "He's not answering the phone or the doorbell. Maybe we have another body."

"If he doesn't answer in a couple of minutes we'll buzz the super."

Parker pressed again. Waited. Pressed.

Corelli called Ginocchioni's number, and figuring he was screening calls, spoke to his answering machine. "Mr. Ginocchioni, this is Detective Corelli. If you do not respond in two minutes, police officers will use a battering ram to knock down your front door and the door to your apartment."

A sleepy, accented voice came through the intercom. "I'm sleeping. Come back later."

Corelli spoke into the intercom. "Let us in NOW or we'll come in and get you."

The door buzzed and they pushed through into the hall and walked up the stairs to the second floor. Ginocchioni stood without his glasses, blinking, in the doorway, wearing pajama bottoms. Nice pecs and abs.

"What do you want?"

"We've been leaving messages for you so you know what we want. We can talk in the hallway or you can let us in."

He glanced back into the apartment. Maybe he wasn't alone.

"Could we talk outside after I shower and dress?"

"No." Corelli raised her voice. "Now. Here or in the apartment."

He tried to close the door but Parker shoved her shoulder against it, opening it wider. Corelli bared her teeth. "You know, Mr. Ginocchioni, we can arrest you and take you to the station in your pajama bottoms and then get a warrant to search your apartment. Be a lot easier if you invite us in and we talk here."

The door of the apartment across the way opened. An elderly woman stuck her head out. "Everything all right, Franco?"

"Um, yes, it's about my friend who was murdered." He stepped back. "Please come in. Can I make some coffee?"

"That would be nice," Corelli said, following him through the small, neat, modern living room to an even smaller kitchen. Also neat. He started spooning coffee into an espresso pot.

They needed to see the rest of the apartment to find out what he was trying to hide. Corelli dipped her head at Parker.

Parker frowned, then she got it. "Okay if I use the bathroom?"

Ginocchioni's hand hung in midair. He opened his mouth but nothing came out. His hand shook and the finely ground coffee drifted to the counter like mutant snowflakes.

He definitely had something to hide. "Is there a problem, Mr. Ginocchioni?"

He dropped the spoon and wrapped his arms around himself. He hung his head. "You might as well see it now."

"See what?"

Corelli followed him into the living room and down a short hall with two doors, both open, one the bathroom, one the bedroom. Parker was right behind. Corelli stared into the bedroom. The unmade bed was understandable. The bouquets of fresh flowers, flickering candles, and burning incense, were a surprise. As was the altar on which they were placed.

"Holy shit," Parker breathed in her ear.

Corelli switched on the light. Ginocchioni had constructed a memorial to Nardo del Balzo, a six-foot table with framed pictures of Nardo, a small stuffed bear, a white handkerchief, a half-filled glass, some cigarette butts, a book, a chewed wooden pencil, a theater ticket stub, and a note signed by Nardo. The wall behind the table was covered with pictures. In a poster-sized one a laughing Nardo stood with his arm over the shoulders of the shorter, grinning, Ginocchioni, in others Nardo posed with members of the Italian delegation, most were of Nardo alone and looked candid, taken when he was unaware. There was one of Nardo and Scott Sigler holding hands and smiling into each other's face in front of Tre Fratelli, the restaurant. Probably the night Nardo was killed.

She felt a pang of envy. Would anyone ever love her that much now that Marnie was dead? She looked from the altar to Ginocchioni. He was sick. And his love was a sick fantasy. What she and Marnie had shared was mutual. And, real. She shivered. Was she building an altar to Marnie in her heart and mind?

"So now you know." Ginocchioni sounded defiant but his body language, arms wrapped around his chest, indicated he was defensive.

Corelli took his arm. "Can you dress quickly? It would be better to talk at the precinct."

While he dressed they strategized about how to get him in the house without dragging him through the gauntlet with them. They agreed Parker would take him in, put him in an interview room, then come back to the car to walk the gauntlet with her. As it turned out, six-forty-five was too early for reporters and for her colleagues to form the walk of shame, so they strolled in and settled in the small interview room. A still teary Ginocchioni slumped in a chair, head drooping.

"May I call you Franco?" Corelli asked.

He didn't respond but his shoulder moved slightly.

"I'll take that as a yes. Sit up," she said, her voice firm. "Franco, look at me."

He raised his head and brushed his hair off his face.

"How long were you stalking Nardo?"

"Stalking? What does this mean?"

"How long were you following him, taking pictures without his knowledge, sitting outside his apartment, things like that? How long have you had an altar in your apartment?"

He flushed. "I loved him."

"How long?"

"A few months after I joined the delegation I realized I was in love with him. He was very sweet to me but he wasn't interested. To understand his life, to learn how to get him to love me, I started following him. He was—"

"How long, Franco?" She was losing patience.

"Maybe fifteen months?"

"And the altar?"

He picked at the cuticle on his thumb. "It just grew. He was so beautiful. I wanted his face to be the last thing I saw at night and the first thing in the morning, so I made the picture of the two of us into a poster and taped it on the wall facing the bed. I liked it so I added flowers and candles and incense, then things that reminded me of him, things he touched, things to honor him. I bought a camera so I could take pictures of him."

"You were outside Tre Fratelli Tuesday night?"

"Yes. I followed him. He was holding hands with a guy when he came out."

"Did you follow them after they left the restaurant?"

"Of course. I needed to know where they went. Maybe get the guy's address. But they went to an office building and he kissed Nardo goodbye."

"It must have made you angry to see him with another man."

"I cried."

"Were you jealous?"

"Yes. It hurt," he said, anger pushing pathos out of his voice. "He was supposed to love me and he never even saw me. But then I realized it was the other guy's fault for coming between us. Nardo didn't want to kiss him, he was just being polite. Nardo wanted me."

"What did you do when they said goodbye?"

"I followed Nardo to his apartment. But I was hungry and I needed the bathroom so I went to The French Roast on Sixth Avenue and had a sandwich and a cup of coffee. Then I went back and sat on the steps across from his apartment and watched."

"What were you watching for?"

"I told you." He was impatient. "I wanted to know everything about his life. I wanted to know about the other men, who he was sleeping with."

"And did he have a lot of visitors?"

"No. That's why I knew we'd be together some day. He didn't have a man in his life."

"Did you see Nardo again Tuesday night?"

He smiled. "He came out and invited me into his apartment. I was excited because I'd never been there before. He was in pajamas." Ginocchioni looked as if that was some wonderful gift, and then he looked down, shading his face with his hair. "He yelled at me. He was angry because the *chiacciatra* across the street told him I sat on her steps and watched him sometimes."

Parker cleared her throat. "What does *chia*—"

"Gossip, chatterbox," Corelli said.

He sniffled. "He said I was sick. That if I continued to bother him he would call the police and they would send me back to Italy—or maybe to jail. That he wanted me to get out and leave him alone. I tried to explain but he pushed me. Hard."

"I'll bet you were really angry. Where did you get the gun?"

"What gun? I was crying and I ran out. He slammed the door behind me. I walked away, fast, crying. Then I went to a bar near my apartment and got drunk."

"I don't think so, Franco. I think you were so hurt and angry at his shabby treatment that you pulled out your gun and shot him. What did you do with the gun? Will we find it in your apartment?"

"I don't have a gun. I didn't kill him. He hurt me but I loved him. I knew someday he would really see me, that he would love me. I loved him so much. How could he not love me back? And now we'll never have a chance." He put his head on his arms on the table and sobbed.

They left him in the room. Parker rubbed her eyes. "He sounds crazy enough to have killed de Balzo for love."

Corelli yawned. Their late night was catching up to both of them. "We'll see what forensics turns up and we'll check his alibi at the bar. You might be right, he could be one of those sick bastards who say I love you so much but if I can't have you, I'll kill you so no one else can."

CHAPTER EIGHTEEN

Friday – 7:15 a.m.

"Okay people, sorry to be late. Let's get started," Corelli shouted, trying to be heard above the ear-shattering chatter in the conference room. She looked around. How could they make so much noise and still be chewing and drinking. She tried again. But no luck.

Dietz stood and yelled. "Shut up!" The room fell silent. "Our illustrious leader wishes to speak."

She tipped an imaginary hat to Dietz.

"You've all heard about the shooting, I presume?" She didn't remember any photographers last night, but somehow the front pages of all the morning papers had pictures of her sitting on the back of the ambulance holding the kittens and Parker standing next to her, looking worried. "And seen my picture with the three heroes of the night—Parker and the two kittens."

Laughter from the troops.

"All four of us are fine."

Detective Hei-kyoung Kim raised her hand. "Do you think it was one of us?"

The laughter stopped and tension filled the room.

"No evidence was found at the scene, Kim. I'd like to think not."

Kim was visibly upset. "Then who?"

"Your guess is as good as mine." Corelli made a mental note to speak to Kim later but now she needed to ease the tension. "Let's talk about the important things. Did anybody see my debut on WNYN last night?"

The team laughed again. Better.

"Yeah, when do we get autographs?" Forlini said.

She flushed. "How did I do?"

"Made the department look good, I'd say," Forlini said.

Kim raised two fingers to her temple in salute. "Made me proud."

"Quite a lineup on WNYN," Watkins said. "They led off with the shooting, replayed the media attack, and closed with the interview. It was very effective. Most of the other channels just had the shooting."

"I'm taking bets the TV guys and gals will be all over you trying to outdo WNYN," Forlini said.

She let the comments fly for a few minutes, then raised her hand for silence. "Now that my fifteen minutes of fame are over, you're up, Watkins. Results of the autopsy and anything else you have."

"Sure thing. But first, have you named the kittens?"

"Not yet. I'm not sure I'm keeping them."

"That's like throwing away your lucky rabbit's foot. You gotta keep them," Dietz said. "You should have a naming contest."

"I'll take it under consideration, Dietz."

Watkins took a quick swig of his soda, pushed it and his fried egg sandwich to the side, wiped his hands, smoothed the sheaf of papers in front of him, and opened his black leather notebook. "Based on last meal, et cetera, time of death between nine p.m. and one a.m. No defensive wounds present, no wounds except the bullet, so he probably knew his killer. The bullet, a twenty-two caliber, lodged in his brain and killed him instantly. We haven't found any proof that he bought a gun, so if it was his, it was illegal. So far only Scott Sigler and Miranda Foxworth knew he had the gun and where he kept it."

"We've eliminated Scott. Have another go at Ms. Foxworth. Watkins, Greene, anything else?"

Greene took over. "We've started talking to Foxworth's clients, but we've only caught up with two of them. One didn't know del Balzo and the other had run into him at parties and bars but only knew him to say hello. Both had solid alibis. We've set up meetings for tonight or tomorrow with some of the others."

Watkins turned a page in his notebook. "Oklahoma police found no record for Miranda Foxworth."

Corelli turned to Dietz. "Did we track down Nelson Choi?"

"Got it," said Dietz. "He's a hotshot investment banker at Stillman, Friedberg, and Choi, a Wall Street firm. That's him in the name." He hesitated, as if waiting for comments.

"Dietz," Corelli said, "we're impressed. Now get on with it."

"Sorry. Anyway, the New York office said he was in Chicago, but Chicago said he had left for the day and would be flying back to New York tonight. Nobody knew when he would be back in the office. Chicago gave us his cell number, but when I called, it went directly to voice mail. I left your cell number and asked him to contact you as soon as he gets the message."

"What about Andrea Sansone and the del Balzo research?"

"We got sidetracked with Choi so we haven't done much. We'll get on it."

"Forlini, Parker and I read your reports on the neighbors last night. Good work. We brought Franco Ginocchioni in this morning. He had an altar dedicated to del Balzo in his apartment and he's admitted to stalking him. Your witness says Nardo was alive when Ginocchioni left, but he's given us permission to search his apartment. Get a team and check it out after the meeting. If you don't find the gun or something to link him to the murder, release him but take his passport."

"Will do. I spoke to another neighbor, a young lady who lives across the street from del Balzo. She was putting her garbage in the can in the front of her building and saw a guy ring del Balzo's bell Tuesday night." He glanced at his notes. "She said he was another spectacular specimen like del Balzo—tall, long wavy black hair, very handsome, dressed in black—and since she was pretending she wasn't looking, she happened to notice he was wearing cowboy boots. She thought maybe she'd seen him before, but couldn't be sure since," he made quote marks with his fingers, 'so many of those gay guys are hunks it's hard to tell them apart.' I still haven't gotten some people at home."

Corelli and Parker looked at each other. "Sansone?" they said, speaking at the same time.

"What?" Dietz said.

"Andrea Sansone, the guy I asked you to check out yesterday, has long black hair and wears cowboy boots. Check out his alibi, then maybe we'll bring him in for questioning."

"Okay guys. I'm getting desperate. We need something and we need it fast." She looked around the room, noting the nodding heads.

"I've got something," Kim said. "We got a report of a taxi drop in front of del Balzo's apartment at eleven Tuesday night. Pick up on Fifty-Seventh and Lexington Ave."

"That sounds like—"

"Scott Sigler." Kim waved a piece of paper. "He charged the fare to American Express."

"Good work, guys. Bring him in this afternoon. Sweat him a while and then Parker and I will take him."

Corelli turned to Dietz. "We need a canvass of the ambassador's neighbors to see if anyone saw him or his wife coming in late."

"His wife?" Dietz said. "You think she murdered her son?"

"She doesn't have an alibi and she seems as obsessed with being prime minister as the ambassador, so let's see if we can eliminate the two of them."

"Jeez, you really think both parents are suspects?"

"Didn't I teach you anything, Watkins?" She grinned softening the rebuke. "If we're not thorough, we can't be sure."

"Yeah, yeah, I know," Watkins said. "But it seems a little far-fetched."

Corelli scanned the group. "As I said, we're being thorough. But let me remind you, no mention of this outside this room. Also, be discreet when you talk to the neighbors."

She waited for the murmurs to die down then continued. "Parker and I started the follow-up on the guests at the dinner that the ambassador attended Tuesday night, but there are about a hundred people on the list and we need a team to talk to everyone."

A few seconds of silence before a collective groan as they realized how much grunt work was involved.

"Let's see if Dietz can get some cadets from the academy to help. You guys can supervise them and get it done faster." She waited for Dietz to jot it down. "Anybody have anything you need or want to say before you leave?"

Someone yelled, "Help," and everybody laughed.

"All right, let's get to work. See you tomorrow. Keep us posted." Corelli gathered her notes while chatting with Detectives Greene and Watkins about the TV interview. After they left Corelli and Parker were alone at the conference table.

"You know, Parker, I keep coming back to the idea that Nardo knew his killer. And the ambassador is my prime suspect."

"What about Carla? You really think she did it?"

"You've seen her. What do you think?"

Parker rubbed her forehead. "Yeah, I guess so. She's icy and she acts like becoming prime minister is the only thing that matters in the world. But that doesn't mean she's capable of murdering her son. Besides, she wasn't hysterical or anything but she did seem upset to hear Nardo was dead."

"The ambassador, on the other hand, didn't react at all when I told him his son was murdered. Actually, it seemed like it wasn't a surprise." Corelli was trying to follow the facts and not allow her dislike of the ambassador to lead her astray. "Also, he didn't hide his disgust at Nardo's being gay which would explain Nardo's desire to embarrass him by dressing as a woman and destroy his chance of being prime minister. Maybe Nardo knew something about a mistress or some financial misdeeds or even an association with the mafia. In any case, the ambassador appears to have the most to gain from Nardo's death. Was the threat to his political ambitions a compelling reason for him to murder his only son? Maybe. If Nardo did go public with something scandalous the ambassador stood to lose the election, probably his current job, and maybe even his wife.

"As for opportunity, he could still have done the murder even if he left the UN shindig at eleven. And, of course, if it was Nardo's gun, he could have known it was there. We need to push harder to find out what Nardo had on him."

"Those are my thoughts. Whatdoya think Ms. ADA?"

Parker rolled her eyes. "I think Dietz is right. What you're sketching here could be a Greek drama or a Shakespearian tragedy. The only thing missing is proof that it went down that way. I think we'd better continue to investigate."

Corelli sighed. "It would be a lot easier to be a playwright or an author making it up as you go along." She stood. "But we're detectives so let's get to work."

Dietz came back into the room just as they were getting ready to leave. "Captain Winfry would like a few minutes."

"Probably about the interview," Corelli said. "I'll pick you up later, Parker."

She knocked and entered. "Morning, Captain."

He looked up. "Corelli. Sit. Good interview. And what's her name, Darla North, did a great job showing that mob scene. Looked like a scary situation. Maybe they'll ease up a bit."

"It was scary. If that rookie officer, Twilliger, hadn't rescued me, I don't know…"

"I saw Sergeant Mallory's report. Twilliger will be commended. The others will be taken care of."

"Sir, Darla North wants to do a series of short interviews, and if you have no objection, I'd like the next one to highlight the team working on the del Balzo murder. Maybe invite her to sit in on a meeting, give some of the others a chance for screen time. She might also want a minute or two of your time."

He sat back, rubbed his chin, and eyed her. "They did say they wanted you to be nice to the press. But you can't give it all to her—"

She stood up. "Sir, I—"

"Privilege of rank, Corelli. I get to talk first, so sit down. I understand you don't want to feed the piranhas, so figure something out, a print interview or maybe a press conference when you have something to announce, but you can't give it all to WNYN. Bring North in to do the team thing, though. I think it will give people a boost."

She smiled. "Yessir."

"Remember, diversify." He stood up.

Corelli stood. "Sir, I thought Parker and I avoided the walk of shame this morning by getting in really early, but Dietz told me you've prohibited officers from congregating in front of the station in the morning and you've ordered the media contained away from the building. Thank you. Life is much easier when you don't start the day by running the gauntlet to get to your desk."

"Although only you two were forced through the gauntlet, the public and many of your colleagues complained that the huge crowd and the media circus made it difficult for them to get in and out of the station. Let me know if they try something else."

CHAPTER NINETEEN

Friday – 9 a.m.

The press corps came to life shouting questions, extending microphones, and pointing cameras, but since they were behind barricades on the other side of the street, Corelli and Parker ignored them and walked up the steps to the front door where Officer Twilliger was standing at attention.

"Morning," Twilliger said, leaning over to ring the bell for them. "Um, I heard about the shooting. I'm glad he missed. And thanks for puttin' in a good word to the boss."

Corelli smiled. "Good work always earns good words in my book."

"Yeah, well if there's ever anything I can do for you, on or off the job, you let me know."

"I'll remember."

Once again the crone answered the door, but today, with her face red and swollen and her eyes small slits, she looked even older. A rosary with ruby-red glass beads and a gold crucifix dangled from her hand, and she seemed to be muttering prayers.

"You."

"Yes, *Signora*, so sorry for your loss," Corelli said in Italian, touching the crone's shoulder.

"May his soul rest in peace." The crone made the sign of the cross then pulled a handkerchief from an apron pocket and mopped the tears making their way through the deep crevices in her face. She stepped back and pointed to the hall.

The hallway was dim, but the soft rumble of voices led them to the living room. Behind them, the doorbell chimed again. They stood in the doorway. Two days ago, laughing and joking TV people had filled this formal but tastefully decorated room. Today the crowd was somber, dressed in dark clothing, small groups talking in muted tones, sipping coffee from delicate china cups.

A wake, Corelli thought, no body, but it's still a wake. The del Balzos sat next to each other on two easy chairs. Carla, carefully made up. Both of them impeccably dressed and coiffed. Neither of them looked as if they had shed many tears, but was it professional control or cold hearts? On the other hand, Flavia, sitting to Carla's right, was sobbing, while Emilio, standing next to her, stared straight ahead, stone-faced. The doorbell chimed over and over. People streamed past Corelli and Parker and joined the line of mourners waiting to express condolences, and when they were face-to-face with the bereaved, leaned over them, kissed a cheek or the air near a cheek, took a hand, patted a shoulder, spoke softly, and then faded into the crowd.

Nardo's colleagues from the delegation clustered together off to the side, swollen eyes, red noses, comforting each other. No professional façade there. Franco Ginocchioni was not the only one sobbing openly; several of the women and even Mario Derosa broke down from time to time.

"There's our man Sansone, back to us," Parker said, tilting her head. Sansone held a beautiful young woman, patting her tenderly and speaking softly in her ear. She looked up at something he said and smiled through her tears. The resemblance to Nardo was striking. Most likely his sister, Antonia.

Corelli joined the line. "Wait here. I'll get del Balzo." When she reached Leonardo, she whispered that she would like to see him privately for a few minutes. Carla opened her mouth but Leonardo placed his hand on her arm and said something softly to her. She nodded. He rose and excused himself. Corelli and Parker followed him out to the glass-enclosed room. He walked to the window and turned.

"So what news do you have, Detective? I assume it's important or you wouldn't have interrupted us while we're mourning the loss of our son."

"It is important. I need to know what it was that you and Nardo argued about."

"I've already told you, that is none of your business. It has nothing to do with his death."

"With all due respect, sir, this is a murder investigation. Everything is my business. So you'll make your life and mine easier if you tell me."

He started toward the door. She thought he was going to leave them, but then he turned and walked back. Flushed and breathing heavy, he stared out the window, then shrugged. "Enough. Nardo had some crazy idea that I did something to him when he was a boy, but it was not true. I will not discuss it. Do you understand?"

"I do, sir. But unless we can find someone who can verify your story about when you left the dinner or what time you arrived at home, you are a prime suspect. Do you understand?"

The color drained from his face.

"How dare you accuse my husband of murdering our son." The barely controlled rage in Carla's voice was chilling. The three of them turned toward the door. Sansone stood behind her. "How dare you come into our home when we are mourning and make these filthy accusations. Get out. Now." Carla's voice was husky, deeper than normal and ice cold.

"Carla, please, they are only doing their job."

"You are too nice, Leonardo. They are insulting you."

She moved to the side and pointed at the door. "You are speaking to Ambassador Leonardo de Balzo who will soon be the Prime Minister of Italy. We will not tolerate such insults. Now go."

The media had its usual Pavlovian response to their appearance on the steps, but they were still cordoned off on the other side of the street and Corelli ignored them. She smiled at Twilliger. "Take care, Officer."

The gawky officer grinned and raised his fingers to his hat in salute. "You too, ma'am."

She put on her sunglasses. "That was productive," she said as they hit the sidewalk.

"What a piece of work. She's like a pit bull," said Parker. "Did you get the feeling we were supposed to salute and kiss the ambassador's ass?"

"Now that you mention it," Corelli said. "Too bad she came in. I think he was about to say something. It was a mistake to see him with her there; we need to get him alone." She sighed. "Let's go downtown and see if anybody has anything useful."

"*Aspetta*, wait."

Corelli spun around ready to punch whoever had grabbed her arm. "Chief Sansone."

"You are too far out of line. You accuse Leonardo, but he would never kill his son. I don't say it because of my love for him but because he is, uh, how do you say, too squeamish, too soft. And you have upset Carla. She adores Leonardo. They have worked very hard to get to this place and they have too much going on right now to be under this scrutiny."

"Do you know what Nardo and his father argued about?"

"I told you what I know. Nardo believed that Leonardo did something to him, something he didn't do. Really, it is no concern for you."

"Oh, but it is my concern. Everything is my concern until I find out who murdered Nardo. And if it was his father, I will find out. So if Leonardo has nothing to hide, I suggest that you encourage him to cooperate."

"You don't know who you are dealing with. Be careful, Detective, you might get hurt."

"Is that a threat, Chief Sansone? Maybe somebody will try to shoot me?"

His eyes narrowed. He smiled, but it wasn't the big smile. It was tighter and lacked the warmth and charm of those that had come before. "I don't know what you mean. I just want to remind you that the stakes are high. I'm sure you understand."

"You think del Balzo tried to shoot you?" Parker said as Sansone hurried away.

"Just fishin'."

CHAPTER TWENTY

Friday – 10 a.m.

A fidgety Scott Sigler stared at the two-way mirror, as if waiting for a movie to start. They watched him for a few minutes. He looked ten years older.

"Why don't you take him, Parker, I'm getting tired of doing all the work," Corelli said, slanting her eyes to the right to catch Parker's reaction.

Parker stared at Corelli for a few seconds. "Is this a trick?"

"Would I do that to you?" Corelli smiled. "Well, maybe, but not this time."

They walked out of the viewing room and into the interview room. Sigler jumped up. "Do I need a lawyer?"

"You tell me. *Do* you need a lawyer? Have you committed a crime?"

Sigler shifted his gaze to Parker. "No. I don't…I haven't done anything wrong. Why am I here?" He ran a hand through his already disheveled hair.

"Sit down, man," Parker said, sitting.

He followed orders and sat facing Parker but his attention was on Corelli, who stood leaning against the door.

"You left something out the last time we talked. We'd like to hear the full story now."

"As I said, I had dinner with Nardo then went back to work. Surely you checked the sign-out sheets in the lobby?" He looked from one to the other of the detectives.

"Surely, we did check and they corroborate your lie. And when we checked some more we found that you left the building and took a taxi to Nardo's apartment at about eleven o'clock Tuesday night."

He blanched. "How did you find out?" He rubbed his eyes. "Shit. I didn't think it was important because I didn't actually have contact with Nardo. While I was paying the taxi driver, a man rang Nardo's bell. He opened the door, they embraced and kissed, and walked in the house. I was stunned and rooted to the spot for a minute. Then I started walking uptown, fast. At Twenty-Third Street, I took the Lexington Avenue subway back to the office."

"What was he wearing?"

"Nardo or the man?"

"Nardo."

"He was bare-chested but I couldn't see what he was wearing on the bottom."

"What did the man who rang the bell look like?"

He closed his eyes. "Um, I only saw his back, but he was tall and dressed all in black. And, he was wearing a black hat."

"How did you feel, seeing Nardo embrace another man?"

"At first I was jealous. But by the time I got on the subway, I realized I was being stupid and possessive and jumping to conclusions. Nardo and I hadn't made any kind of a commitment to monogamy. And, after all, Nardo had invited me to go to Provincetown with him, not the mystery man. I decided I had a lot to be happy for and I would deal with the mystery man if he became an issue."

"Did anybody see you?"

"I thought I saw the curtain move in the house across the street as I turned away, but I was upset, so it might have been the tears in my eyes that made it seem to move."

"How did you get in and out of your office building without the guards seeing you?"

"Easy when you're friendly with the cleaning people. They let me out the freight entrance. I don't do it too often, but it comes in handy when I really need to get away. And you can check. I don't bill for the time I'm not there."

"We'll leave that to your conscience."

They dismissed him and went back to the team's conference room.

"Dietz, get Forlini back to the neighbor who saw the tall dark mystery man go into Nardo's apartment. Maybe he can confirm Sigler's story. And maybe the other neighbor saw Ginocchioni leave. She didn't say, but I'll bet she watched to see what was going to happen."

Corelli's phone rang, startling the three of them. "Corelli." She rolled her eyes. "Tell him we're on our way."

She stood up. "Come on, Parker. Chief Broderick wants to see us."

As Corelli and Parker left the conference room, an officer handed her some phone message slips.

"Thought you would want to see these before you go."

"Thanks." She thumbed through. "What do you think, Parker? Our friend Sansone wants to apologize and suggests that he and I have dinner tonight to discuss progress on the case. Why don't I call and ask him to meet me here later?"

"It would make your sister Patrizia happy if you had dinner with him. You know, a nice Italian guy with a good job."

"Maybe I should interview him and then have dinner?"

"You can't do that, Corelli. He's a suspect."

"Duh, thanks for reminding me."

Parker's face darkened. Ah, she's pissed off. Corelli put her hands in front of her. "Just kidding. Even if he weren't a suspect, I wouldn't have anything to do with him. Wait a second while I tell Dietz to expect him."

CHAPTER TWENTY-ONE

Friday – 12 p.m.

Chief Harry Broderick waved them into the chairs facing his desk and wasted no time with pleasantries. "I just got off the phone with the mayor, who, as we know, is no fan of yours, Detective Corelli."

Parker twitched.

Corelli didn't blink at his formality and the censure in his voice. Their friendship had been solid until the undercover investigation ended. His failure to speak out to prevent the department from smearing her reputation by intimating she was dirty, his failure to publically support her in the face of the ostracism, and his failure to fight the mayor to get him to allow her back from the leave she was forced to take, had shaken her trust in him, had convinced her he had become just another bureaucrat protecting his ass. She met his gaze, sure he could read her anger. And her disdain.

"His honor received an outraged call from Carla del Balzo." He glared at them. "According to Mrs. Del Balzo, you are harassing the ambassador, accusing him of killing his son. Is that true?"

Corelli didn't like the tone of his voice, the fact that they were tried and convicted based on the complaint of a suspect. "Right now, he's our prime suspect, but we don't have anything concrete yet. And to be frank, we don't have much else either."

"I know you're aware of the sensitivity here, with him about to become the prime minister, but she sounds vicious. Combining her venom with Mayor Matthews's vendetta can only lead to trouble for you, Corelli, for all of us. Bring me irrefutable proof, not just feelings. And, brief me every day."

"Yessir."

They stood up and moved toward the door.

"Wait."

They turned.

"I heard about the shooting. I'm glad you're both all right."

He held up a copy of *The Daily Post*, the one with her sitting on the back of the ambulance holding the two kittens. "I need the names of your kittens. I'm thinking about giving them a commendation for their life-saving effort last night." He grinned.

"Very funny. They don't have names. I'm probably going to give them away."

"Really, Corelli, you owe them. You should take care of them."

"I'll add your name to the list in favor of keeping them."

"You're getting to be quite a media personality. Very nice interview on WNYN last night. You got something going with Darla North?"

Was he implying a sexual relationship? She studied his face. *Maybe.* "Did you see her piece on the media feeding frenzy?"

"Yes. Very dramatic. Maybe it'll get you some sympathy from the del Balzo woman."

She raised her eyebrows. "Not likely. Carla is more cold fish than bleeding heart. Anyway, I spoke to North after she filmed the piece and she requested an interview. Since Captain Winfry has been on my ass about making nice with the press, I said yes."

"Winfry's right. We're getting pressure to put you out there."

"Probably Matthews trying to use me to save his campaign."

He looked surprised. "That's a positive way to spin it. Hanging out with the media is improving your outlook."

"You'll be happy, then. I've promised her a couple more, maybe a chance to sit in on the team meeting."

"Better spread yourself out or you'll be accused of being in bed with Darla North." He smirked.

"I can't win, can I?"

He raised his hands and shrugged his shoulders as if to say, "Don't blame me."

She gave him a dirty look and reached for the doorknob.

"Wait, I almost forgot. Kate Burke, the Speaker of the City Council, called just before you walked in. She knew del Balzo and would like a report on the investigation. She's tied up all day and this evening, but she'll make herself available whenever you can fit her in tomorrow."

She made a face.

"I'm sure it's not necessary to remind you we need all the allies we can get, but I will. We need any and all allies. Fit her in. *Capisce?*"

"Yessir. I understand. Actually, we haven't had much luck tracking down his friends. Maybe she'll be able to help us."

CHAPTER TWENTY-TWO

Friday – 6 p.m.

Dietz jumped up when they walked into the conference room. "Everything okay with the chief?"

"Just Carla del Balzo rattling his cage."

"Means you're on to something." He handed her a file. "Sansone's alibi didn't check out. He's in interview room one."

She glanced through the file. "Gotcha, Romeo. C'mon Parker, let's have some fun."

Andrea Sansone was pacing and ranting in Italian, when Corelli and Parker arrived. "This is outrageous," he said, waving his arms to indicate the interview room. "You keep me waiting in this small place for two hours. They take my cell phone and tell me I cannot leave until I see you. Explain, please, Chiara. I am not amused."

"Please sit, Mr. Sansone. And please speak English. We have a few questions for you." She sat at the table but Parker remained standing in front of the door.

He took a deep breath. "Questions? I called this morning to apologize for my meanness and then you called and agreed to have dinner." He had switched to English and he sounded hurt.

"No sir, I called and asked if you would meet me here. I didn't mention dinner. It would be inappropriate for me to have dinner with a person of interest in an investigation. I was trying to save you the embarrassment of being escorted out of your office, perhaps in handcuffs. Now, please sit." She pointed toward the chair on the opposite side of the table.

He placed his hands on the back of the chair. "What does this mean, person of interest?"

"It means you lied about the last time you saw Nardo. And it means you lied about your alibi. And it may mean you murdered Nardo. That's what we're here to determine. We can do this now or we can get more formal. It's up to you." She sat. Parker remained at the door.

His face reddened. He pulled the chair out and sat facing her with his hands folded in front of him.

"Please, I would like some water."

Parker stepped out. When she returned with the water, she took the chair next to Corelli.

"*Grazie*," he said, after drinking. Then, as if Parker had given him a magic potion, he was back, all smiles and oozing charm. "I'm sure there's been some mistake. Perhaps I will call the ambassador?"

"That's a good idea, Mr. Sansone, but first perhaps you could explain a couple of things."

"*Certo*," he said. He smiled, then looked at Parker. "This means certainly."

Mr. Blazing Teeth, as Parker had tagged him, was back.

"Mr. Sansone—"

"Andrea, please."

The oozing charm was back as well. Corelli thought she might vomit.

"Andrea, you said you spent the night with…" She glanced down at the papers in front of her. "Monique Von Huevendal. Is that correct?"

"Yes."

"And you said you spent the night at her apartment?"

"Oh, no, it was my apartment."

"I'm puzzled, either way. There is no Monique Von Huevendal at the address you gave us, or anywhere else in New York City for that matter. And neither your evening nor your night doorman saw you come in."

"The doorman was mistaken. The door was free when I arrived home. And this is the name and address she gave me. I can show you my address book."

"We also checked the security tapes in your building and you were nowhere to be seen."

He shrugged. "Maybe the camera didn't work."

"What restaurant did you eat at?"

He smiled ruefully. "I'm sorry, I can't remember."

"Was she a prostitute?"

He glared at her. "I do not need to pay for sex or female company."

"What were you doing at Nardo's apartment at ten p.m. Tuesday night?"

"I told you, I was not there. I was otherwise occupied." He smirked.

"That's interesting. We have a witness who saw you there."

"No, I wasn't there."

"Lies, lies, lies, Andrea. You're digging a hole for yourself. You say you were where we have proof you weren't, and you say you weren't where we have proof you were. Better to admit the truth."

He frowned. "What do you mean, 'digging a hole'?"

"Would you like an interpreter?"

"No. You explain, please."

"It means that every lie makes it clearer that you were there and makes us wonder why you're lying if you didn't kill him."

He paled but smiled his slimy smile. "I think I must have a lawyer."

"Do you want a public defender?"

"Who is this?"

"A lawyer paid for by New York City."

"No. I must call Leonardo. He will know what to do."

They left Sansone to make his phone call and went out for a sandwich at the deli near the precinct. They were at the register paying when her phone rang. "Sansone's lawyer is here. He would like to talk to you," said the voice at the other end.

"Give us a few minutes," she said.

The uniform standing outside the interview room stopped them. "You have a surprise waiting for you."

"What surprise?"

He grinned and made a zipper motion across his mouth, but his eyes were sparkling.

She glared at him, then shrugged.

He opened the door.

He was right. She clamped her mouth shut to keep her jaw from dropping. Standing over Sansone was Louden Warfield III, criminal defense attorney extraordinaire, every cop's, and for that matter, every prosecutor's, nightmare. She nodded Parker in and shut the door behind her, nearly catching the uniform's head, and not at all sorry about it.

Warfield straightened and pinned them with deep blue eyes the exact color of his crisp, long-sleeved shirt. He was tall and slender, and she knew he could charm a jury with a single smile of the kind he bestowed on them. She had never gone up against him in court, but he was known as a cop killer. Blond men often seemed insipid to her, but not Warfield. He was handsome and projected power and confidence.

Warfield quickly slipped into his jacket, as if embarrassed by his red suspenders, and extended his hand. "Louden Warfield," he said, his voice deep and mellifluous. "We haven't met before, Detective Corelli, but I'm an admirer, in awe of your integrity and bravery."

Corelli shook the offered hand. "Flattery will get you nowhere, Mr. Warfield." She smiled. "And I'm kind of in awe myself." No need to alienate him and make something she sensed was going to be difficult even more difficult.

Parker had already taken her seat, but he leaned over the table and offered his hand. "And you, Detective Parker, a hero, saving that boy in Brooklyn."

He'd done his homework.

Parker hesitated. Corelli held her breath and hoped Parker wasn't going to explain that Corelli had saved the boy. Parker glanced at Corelli, then clasped his hand. "Pleased to meet you, sir."

"I'm glad to see you both in good health after the shooting last night. Are you thinking it's related to this case?"

Ha. Trying to divert attention. "It's still under investigation," Corelli said.

She wondered if del Balzo had pulled strings to get Warfield, and just what strings would get him to come here so quickly. It was no secret Warfield was gay. Did the homophobic ambassador and the equally homophobic Sansone know, or didn't it matter when you needed the best to save your ass?

Sansone stood up. "Deni, um, Mr. Warfield is my—" He looked at Warfield.

"Attorney," Warfield said, sitting at the table. "We should be able to clear up this little misunderstanding quickly."

Deni? They must travel in the same upper-class circles.

"Before we start, is anyone there?" Warfield tilted his head toward the two-way mirror.

"No. It's just us," Corelli said. She took the chair next to Parker. "You wanted to talk to us, Mr. Sansone?"

"*Si*, er, yes." He avoided her eyes. "Andrea, please," he said, almost mechanically.

"Detective Corelli, Mr. Sansone tells me he's under arrest." Warfield removed a yellow legal pad and a big, fat, black fountain pen from his briefcase and placed them on the table.

"Not yet. He was brought in for questioning about inconsistencies in his answers to questions with regard to his whereabouts on the night Leonardo del Balzo was murdered."

He uncapped the pen and made a note on the legal pad. He looked at Sansone. "Andrea, I believe you want to explain."

Sansone glanced at Warfield and straightened. "You are correct. I did go to Nardo's apartment that night. Ambassador del Balzo asked me to try to talk some sense into Nardo, to keep him from doing anything to endanger his bid to be prime minister. We argued, Nardo called me a coward, and I walked out. But Nardo was alive when I left. I swear. He was my little brother. I could never hurt him."

Sansone flicked his eyes over to Warfield and was rewarded with a pat on the hand and a smile.

"Do you know what Nardo and the ambassador argued about? What he threatened the ambassador with?"

"No. He would never tell me why he was so angry with Leonardo, why he acted so, so girly when Leonardo was around. That was not how he was usually. That's what we argued about. After he accused me of being a coward, he cried and said he'd decided to be done with it. Then he threw me out."

"And what did you do then."

"I walked for a while to calm down, and then I called Leonardo at home, as he asked, but I got the machine so I left a message that Nardo wouldn't listen." He put his head in his hands.

Warfield patted Sansone's arm. "And then there's the matter of where he went afterward. Correct?"

"Correct."

They waited. Corelli stared at the men, one more gorgeous than the other, and felt not a glimmer of attraction to either. Did Parker?

"It would be best if you explained, Andrea," Warfield said.

Sansone flushed. He stared over her shoulder. "I…was with Deni…at his apartment. I…am a homosexual." His voice cracked and his face flushed.

Once again Corelli clamped her mouth shut and put on her bland interrogation face, but he had knocked her off balance. She kept her eyes on them, not daring to look at Parker.

"I went to Deni's apartment when I left Nardo and stayed the night there." Sansone took a deep breath. "I didn't tell you about Nardo because he was the only one who knew about me. We argued about my pretending to agree with the ambassador's, how do you say, homophobia. I was upset and I went to Deni."

"Detective Corelli, I can corroborate Andrea's story and the security cameras in my building will confirm what we're telling you. He lied to protect his privacy. He fears the ambassador will reject him just as he rejected Nardo. And he lied to protect me. But, as I'm sure you know, I'm far from closeted. Now, how can we protect Andrea's privacy?"

"Mr. Warfield—"

"Please call me Deni."

"Deni. First, Andrea is not off the hook for the murder. We're in the middle of the investigation and it may be a while before we can clear him. Now, if we can ask our questions and get honest answers, and if you both put your statements on the record, I have no need to publicize Andrea's homosexuality. I can't guarantee privacy but it won't become an issue unless he's guilty or someone tries to point the finger at him."

He looked at Sansone, who nodded. "Okay, we'll both go on the record. Andrea will answer all your questions and provide any help he can. It doesn't sound like you have any solid evidence. Would you be willing to release Andrea to me with my guarantee that should you find something that actually ties him to the murder, I will bring him in?"

Corelli rubbed her forehead. Warfield knew she didn't have enough to hold Sansone, so he was just being polite. "That would be fine, depending, of course, on how our questioning about his visit to Nardo goes."

Warfield smiled. "Let's get started then."

Corelli led Sansone through the events of that evening until she was satisfied they had the truth.

"Andrea, when we were leaving the del Balzos earlier today, you threatened me. You said, 'The stakes are high. You don't understand who you're dealing with. You could get hurt.' What did you mean?"

He shifted, coughed, and cleared his throat. "Carla and Leonardo have worked their whole lives to get to this place and now that they are so close, they will be ruthless about eliminating obstacles to Leonardo becoming the prime minister. Of course, I meant anything legal such as using political clout, going to the press, and demanding your job."

Corelli sat back and gazed at him, holding hands with his lover. She couldn't resist.

"One more question, Andrea. Why do you join in the ambassador's homophobia? Why not tell him?"

Sansone's eyes filled.

Warfield draped his arm over Sansone's shoulders. "I don't see how this is relevant but Andrea can answer, if we go off the record."

His eyes seemed to be scanning her brain to analyze why she needed to know. Lots of luck. She didn't know herself why she needed to know.

"You're right. It isn't relevant but I would like to understand."

"Are you willing to answer, Andrea?" Warfield asked, handing him a handkerchief.

Sansone nodded and wiped his eyes. "Leonardo is the only father I've ever known. He found me in the gutter when I was five, took me in, educated me, and treated me like a son. I love him. When Nardo was born, I feared he would forget me but he didn't. Always it is like I am a son. About the time Nardo started to act out about being gay, I was exploring my own, um, sexuality. When I saw Leonardo's reaction to Nardo, I felt he must never know, so I betrayed myself and Nardo, day after day. I was the good son. I lived in fear of losing my family."

"Thank you, Andrea," Corelli said. She stood and the other three did the same. Warfield hugged Sansone then turned to gather his papers.

"So Andrea, what was that drama you acted out with my aunt in Brooklyn the other night?"

"What drama?" Warfield asked.

Sansone coughed and glanced at the door. "Detective Corelli seemed to be focusing on Leonardo, so I, um, made a connection with her family to get information about her so I could," he flushed, "distract her. I told her aunt I was interested in marrying her."

"I should arrest you for that, for getting my aunt all riled up, for giving her hope I was finally going to toe the line," Corelli said. "For your penance, you may have to go back and tell her I'm a lost cause, and she should forget about ever marrying me off."

Sansone looked confused. Warfield laughed, then Sansone and Parker joined him.

"Sounds like justice to me," Warfield said.

CHAPTER TWENTY-THREE

Friday – 8 p.m.

They stepped out of the car, drew their weapons, and back-to-back scanned the street and the nearby buildings. "Clear here," Parker said, without turning.

Corelli walked briskly toward the building. "See you tomorrow." The windows and door to the lobby were still boarded up. Karen, her super, had called earlier to say the glass company would install the bulletproof glass tomorrow. She put the key in the door.

"Chiara?" The voice was tentative.

Corelli stiffened. Gianna stood in the shadows. Corelli spun to look at Parker, fearing she would mistake Gianna for someone wanting to hurt her.

Parker was watching with her gun in hand. "I see her."

Corelli flipped Parker a two-finger salute, then faced the door. Gianna spoke to her back. "Chiara, please, can we talk?"

She turned the key and pushed the door open.

"Please, you haven't responded to any of my messages. I can't stand it when you're mad at me. And I've been so worried since last night. Suppose you were killed and you were still mad at me? What would I do?"

The pain in Gianna's voice knifed through her. Gentle, loving Gianna would never purposefully hurt her. But she had. Corelli stepped aside. "Come in."

They were silent in the elevator, unable to look at each other.

In the loft Corelli headed for the bedroom to get rid of her weapon and wash up. "Pour me a glass of wine and help yourself to espresso or whatever." She let the kittens out of the gym and, as usual, they tumbled after her.

She splashed cold water on her face and looked in the mirror. *She's your sister and you love her. Your anger is hurting both of you. Don't be so hard on her.* She dried her face and went to the living room.

"Are these the kittens that saved your life?"

Corelli picked them up and sat next to Gianna on the sofa. "Yes."

"Are you keeping them?"

She rubbed them gently and was rewarded with stereophonic purrs. "I'm not sure I can be trusted to take care of them properly."

She shifted on the sofa so she could see Gianna's face. "I'm sorry," they said simultaneously.

Gianna put her arms around Corelli. "Forgive me. I never meant to hurt you. I had no idea what Patrizia and *Zia* Marina were up to when they came over. Besides, I know you're a lesbian and you're attracted to Brett Cummings not Sansone."

Corelli's jaw dropped. After thirty-five years she still underestimated Gianna.

"Oops." Gianna put her hand over her mouth. "Open mouth, insert foot."

Corelli struggled to keep her face bland.

"Don't deny it. You have feelings for her."

"What do you mean 'feelings'?"

"Chiara, you're not the President of the United States and you're not on trial here. I know it's true." Gianna reached out and touched Corelli's cheek. "It's all right, sweetie. Marnie would be happy for you."

She squeezed Gianna's hand. Why was this so hard? She loved Gianna and trusted her more than anybody else in the world. Why not get it out? Parker had witnessed…it. But what "it" was Corelli still hadn't worked out.

"You could say I have feelings." She flushed. "I've never felt such an intense attraction in my life. The first time I saw her, I almost passed out. I was electrified. I couldn't speak. I couldn't move. All I could do was stare. If it weren't for Parker, I'd probably still be standing there, gaping."

"And she?"

"The same, I think. We kept locking eyes and blushing. Then the next day we were alone in her office and she told me she had only felt that kind of attraction once before in her life, that we were soulmates and she wanted to get to know me. I told her to forget it but she said she was patient and would wait."

"Knows what she wants. So what happened?"

"She was a suspect and I was so intent on proving I was objective that I lost my objectivity. When the case was over she left a message telling me she understood and she forgave me. She asked me to call her to talk."

She'd listened to Brett's message hundreds of times and each time she felt the same surge of heat and an intense longing.

"So why haven't you called her?"

The anger burst out. "I've told you before, it's too soon. I can't forget Marnie."

"And, I've told you, you've been alone way too long. Marnie is dead. And she, of all people, would want you to live and love. You need someone. If you're attracted, I say go for it. At least call her. Go for a walk, have a cup of coffee, go to a movie. You don't have to get married, at least not right away."

"My emotions are out of control. Maybe it's just a passing thing."

Gianna laughed. "Let's see, on the one hand, you don't call her because you think it's too soon to have a relationship. On the other hand, you don't call her because you think it's just a passing thing. There's faulty logic in there somewhere."

Corelli rubbed the kittens' ears, felt them vibrate with pleasure. "I didn't choose to feel this attraction."

"So why fight it?"

"There are too many problems."

"My warrior sister running from problems? My little sister who faced down a Mafia boss at fifteen, who went to war, who stepped up to the undercover investigation from hell because it was the right thing to do? She who wears a gun and risks her life every day? I don't think so. The only problem I see is you. You're afraid to let yourself love again. In fact, you can't even commit to love the kittens."

"Gianna, I watched Marnie die. I can't go through that again."

"Oh, Chiara, honey, you were both at war. I don't want to minimize your experience; it was horrible, but people watch loved ones die every day. Husbands, wives, children, and parents die of cancer, heart attacks, murder, and many other terrible things. We have no control over death. But we do have control over our lives. Take a chance on your future, Chiara. Loving, finding your mate, is well worth the risk. Go for it, sweetie."

"You make it sound easy."

"It's not as hard as depriving yourself of love."

CHAPTER TWENTY-FOUR

Saturday – 7 a.m.

Parker stopped in front of the station house a few minutes before seven a.m., leaned on the steering wheel, and whistled softly. "Nice. Not a reporter or camera or microphone in sight. I know the captain said no gauntlet but what's going on with the media?"

"Maybe the press sleeps in on Saturdays. Or maybe there was some kind of national disaster they considered more important." Corelli checked her cell phone to see if anyone had notified her of a disaster. Oops. It was off. She turned it on. Something must have happened. She had twelve texts and three voice mails but before she could retrieve any of them, the phone rang.

"Darla North here. Have you seen the *Post*, this morning?"

"No."

"Take a look. You should rebut. I'll wait for your call." The phone went dead.

Rebut? That didn't sound good. Corelli turned her phone off. She didn't want any more calls until she knew what was going on.

"We need to find a copy of this morning's *Daily Post*, before the meeting," she said as they entered the station. No need to search. The headline on the paper the officer at the desk was reading brought her up short: "Detective Accuses Italian Ambassador of Murdering Son."

"Uh-oh," Parker said.

Corelli braced herself for the cold shoulder. "Can I borrow that, Hutchins?"

The uniform's eyes appeared as he lowered the paper and widened when he saw who it was. "Corelli." He stood, closed the paper, and folded it to hide the headline. "It's a lousy article. Are you sure you want to read it?"

Well, well, maybe I'm not ostracized on Saturdays. "Better to know your enemies, Hutchins."

"If you say so." He handed her the paper. "I haven't finished reading all the dirty details about you, so I'd like it back."

"Sure thing." She opened it, and with Parker peering over her shoulder, read the main article.

Detective Accuses Italian Ambassador of Murdering Son

Carla del Balzo, the bereaved mother of Leonardo del Balzo, the young man found murdered in his apartment Wednesday morning, took time out from grieving to speak to the *Daily Post*. Mrs. del Balzo was outraged that Detective Chiara Corelli accused her husband, Ambassador Leonardo del Balzo, of murdering their son. The ambassador is the frontrunner to replace Italian Prime Minister Silvio Berlusconi. Mrs. del Balzo said she was stunned and offended by the inconsiderate behavior of the detective at a time when they are mourning the loss of their only son. "This accusation is ludicrous. There is absolutely no evidence to indicate that my husband killed our son because it is a fiction of her imagination. Detective Corelli has not allowed us to grieve; instead she has repeatedly questioned us and hurled accusations. I understand Detective Corelli's own parents refuse to talk to her or acknowledge her existence, so perhaps she projects her father's murderous feelings onto my husband. Or, as has been suggested, perhaps Detective

Corelli is experiencing post traumatic stress problems, resulting from her investigation of her colleagues, most of whom consider her a traitor and want nothing to do with her."

The del Balzos have requested that the detective be removed from the case but say they have been ignored.

The article went on to discuss gossip and rumors about Corelli and to recapitulate the story of her undercover assignment, the accusations of fellow officers, and the attack by Senator Parker.

"With four New York newspapers, it's interesting she went to the *Daily Post*, the only paper to attack my ethics for going undercover to investigate other police. And it sounds like our friend Sansone may have fed her some information about my family."

She folded the paper and handed it back to Hutchins.

"Pretty lousy article, eh Corelli?" Hutchins took the paper and looked down at his desk. "You don't deserve it."

"Thanks, Hutchins. It is lousy but it makes me wonder what the ambassador is hiding. Let's get some air, Parker." They stepped outside.

"What are we going to do?" Parker asked.

"First we're going to call our friendly reporter back and see what she has in mind." She took out her phone. "Then we're going into the morning meeting so we can prove that del Balzo did it or find the person who did. That is, if they don't fire me first." She smiled. "Don't worry, Parker, it won't affect you."

"I'm not worried about myself," Parker said, blushing.

"What would Senator Daddy think, Parker?"

"He'd think Mrs. del Balzo was right about you suffering from PTSD."

"*Touché*."

Corelli speed-dialed Darla. "It's me. So what did you have in mind?"

They talked for a few minutes and agreed to meet at Tess's office after the morning meeting. "Darla is already working on a story to counter the *Post* article. She's done her research and is going to interview people on other cases I've investigated to get a more rounded picture. She mentioned the Winter case, plus some cops I've worked with, and I don't know who else. We'll meet with her later to give her a chance to ask me a few questions."

Before she could turn it off, her phone rang again. She checked the display before answering. "Sal. How are you?" Sal Cantrino, editor of *The New York Daily World*, was the younger brother of her best friend growing up. Corelli had changed his diapers, wiped his runny nose, and bought him ice cream more times than she could count. Now, he was a fierce ally.

"Hey, babe. I'm calling to save your ass. How about an exclusive to counteract that hatchet job in the *Post*? I noticed you're pretty chummy with the new reporter at WNYN. You haven't forgotten your old friend, have you?"

"I could never forget you, Sal. I—"

"You're not going to mention the diaper thing and my cute little ass, are you?"

"Would I hold a thing like that over your head? Actually, I was going to agree to the interview but questions about my harassing Carla and Ambassador del Balzo are off limits. Yes, and the interview is yours."

"You got it, Chi. At your place tonight?"

"Better let me call you later, Sal." She ended the call and turned the phone off. They want press contact she'd give them press contact.

The team seemed half-asleep when they walked into the conference room. Some of them, Corelli knew, had been trolling the gay bars until the wee hours for information about Nardo or the 'un-Christians.' Some of them, she was sure, were out late trolling the bars on their own time for their own purposes. Hopefully, it was exhaustion and not mass depression over the article.

She picked up Ron's copy of the paper and waved it. "Everybody see this?"

Some nodded, others waved their copies.

"What can we do?" Dietz asked.

"Our job. We're the good guys so let's track down the killer, whether it's the ambassador or someone else. For your information, I spoke to the chief last night and he mentioned nothing about removing me. But he asked for irrefutable evidence if we find the ambassador is guilty." *Of course, that was before the article appeared.*

The team cheered.

She swallowed and forced a smile. "Thanks. Now what do we have."

The gay bars had been a waste of time. No one wanted to talk to the detectives or be seen talking to them. She sighed. "Dietz, see if you can get some undercover guys who can pass, and try again tonight."

After Parker reviewed their discussion with Sigler, Corelli asked Forlini to follow up with the neighbors to see if the man who reported seeing the mystery man ringing Nardo's bell noticed a taxi discharging a young man, and whether the old woman noticed Ginocchioni leaving after Nardo called him into the apartment.

"Parker and I also interviewed Andrea Sansone and his attorney, Louden Warfield III last night—"

Somebody whistled.

"Yes, the Louden Warfield III. Sansone seems to be in the clear."

Now she had two reasons to murder Sansone, for getting her aunt and her sister all excited about his interest in marrying her and for using information about her family that he had come by dishonestly.

CHAPTER TWENTY-FIVE

Saturday – 8:30 a.m.

They drove to Tess's office to meet with Darla and Bear.

"Questions about the del Balzo accusation are out."

"No need to worry, honey. All the other stations will be going negative, but our story isn't about the accusation, it's about you. We just need to ask you a couple of general questions but our focus will be on what other people say about you."

Honey? "What other people?"

Darla smiled sweetly. "Trust me, darlin'."

"How come you sound more southern each time I see you?"

"'Cause I'm gettin' more comfortable with y'all."

"What are you smirking at, Parker?"

Parker put her hands up. "Just listenin' and learnin', honey."

"Wipe that smirk off your face. We'll see how you feel when these two get their hands on you."

When they'd completed the usual preparations, Darla settled into the chair facing Corelli. "Okay, Chiara, relax. Ready?"

Corelli took a deep breath and sat back. "Shoot."

The lights went on. The camera whirred.

"Detective Corelli, you have solved a large number of homicides, have you not?"

"Yes, I have."

"How do you do that?"

Corelli smiled. "There's no simple answer to that question. Every crime is different. Every victim's story is unique, as is his community. Every murderer has his own style. Every witness sees something different, every suspect has a different story and a different relationship to the victim. The truth is always elusive. But, generally, we start by looking at the crime and the victim, then follow the evidence—forensic evidence, if we find anything or other evidence like telephone records, witnesses, et cetera."

"What do you mean 'by looking at the crime?'"

"Where and how the person was murdered. Was it a drive-by shooting or a beating in an alley? If the victim was murdered at home, was it the result of a break-in or did the victim seem to know his killer? We consider the specific conditions in which the murder occurred."

"And how do you look at the victim?"

"We talk to the people close to him, try to find his enemies and identify anything in his life that might have resulted in his death, like a relationship gone bad or financial problems or involvement with criminals. That kind of thing."

"So what's involved in following the evidence?"

"Lots of tedious work—talking to potential witnesses, to family and friends, and then following up on anything that sounds suspicious or doesn't seem to fit. We spend a lot of time going back to people because they lie to us, and we know they're lying but we don't know what they're lying about. In most cases, the lies don't actually have anything to do with the murder. It may be something they want to cover up because it shows them in a bad light. But sometimes the liar is the murderer. We can't know which it is until we determine what the person is hiding, so we go back repeatedly to ask questions, sometimes the same question. The person probably feels like we're hounding them, but we're just trying to get a story that makes sense."

"I see. If someone seems to be covering up something, you will revisit them over and over, trying to figure out what they're hiding, and whether they are the murderer. Is that correct?"

"Absolutely."

"Thank you once again, Detective Corelli. I hope we'll talk again soon."

The camera stopped, the lights turned off.

Corelli frowned. "That's it?"

"Yes, ma'am. That was perfect. Thank you. We'll be on at ten o'clock tonight. Let me know what you think."

As they were crossing the Brooklyn Bridge into Manhattan, Corelli turned on her cell phone to retrieve messages and almost dropped the phone when *La Traviata*, her ring tone, blared.

"Corelli."

She could barely understand the words but she recognized the breathy voice. "Another body? Who? Slow down, Miranda. Take a deep breath. Now tell me. Who?" Parker's eyes flicked from the road to Corelli.

"Spencer Nickerson? Where?" Please repeat that. She glanced at Parker, rooted in her bag for a pen and paper and jotted down the information. "Stay there. Don't move. Don't touch anything. I'm on the way." She turned to Parker. "Sixty-Eighth between Lex and Park."

"Got it." As Parker swung onto the East River Drive, she extended her arm out the window to put the light on the roof.

Corelli called Dietz. "Foxworth has another body. Another client." She gave him the address. "I don't care about jurisdiction. Get everybody we need there." She put the phone in her bag and looked at Parker. "Hit it."

Parker switched on the siren and they sped uptown, weaving in and out of traffic.

CHAPTER TWENTY-SIX

Saturday – 10 a.m.

Miranda Foxworth huddled in the corner of the small vestibule, shaking, tears streaming. She shrank back when the door opened, then threw herself into Corelli's arms. Corelli patted her back, reassured her that she was safe and then held her at arm's length. This must be her cleaning outfit: sneakers, worn sweat suit that might have started out purple but was almost lavender now, and a purple cloth tied around her hair.

"What happened?"

Miranda sniffled and gulped, then took a deep breath.

Watkins and Greene pushed into the small hallway. Miranda screamed.

"Sorry, sorry, I'm so scared." The tears flowed again. "I can't believe it. I feel like I'm in that *Groundhog Day* movie where the same thing keeps happening every day."

Corelli squeezed Miranda's hand. "You're safe with us, Miranda. But we need to know about this morning. What time did you get here?"

She nodded, dried her eyes, and blew her nose. "About ten of eight. I let myself in and went straight back to the kitchen to put on a pot of coffee. I read my newspaper and drank my coffee. Then about ten after eight, I changed my clothes and pulled out everything I need to clean the house. I usually start upstairs, three bedrooms and his office, then do downstairs, living room first, then the dining room, the hallway, and last the kitchen."

She stopped.

Corelli said, "Go on, you're doing fine."

"When I finished upstairs, I went into the kitchen, turned the radio on, loud, so I could hear it in the living room and then I opened the door and went in." She gripped Corelli's arm. "And he was there. On the sofa. He looked like he was asleep, the same as Nardo, with the beads in his hand." She swallowed a sob. "What's going on?"

"You can't stay here, Miranda, but I need to ask you more questions. I'd like you to go to the station. You'll be more comfortable there. Okay?" Miranda nodded. Corelli glanced over her shoulder. "Greene, get Ms. Foxworth's things from the kitchen and then have a uniform drive her to the stationhouse and stay with her in case she needs anything before we get back."

She turned back to Miranda. "Try to relax. I'll be there in a couple of hours."

Miranda nodded. "Do you need the key to the house?"

"That would be helpful. Do you know anybody we could call about him?"

"I don't. He owns a computer business someplace, but I don't know where. Maybe his book, whatdoyacallit? Diary? Calendar? His office is upstairs. Maybe, there."

Miranda let go of Corelli's arm and dug into the bag Greene handed her. She came up with a key labeled *Nickerson* and gave it to Corelli.

Greene took Miranda's arm and escorted her out.

Corelli stared after them. Was Miranda capable of murder? She turned back to Parker and Watkins. "Think she killed them?"

"If she didn't, it's one hell of a coincidence," said Watkins. "And she'd better start getting next of kin information when she signs up a new client."

Parker ignored the joke. "What's the motive for killing two of them so close together? And, why call us if she did it?"

"Good questions." Corelli had asked herself the same questions. It didn't make sense. "Maybe she was blackmailing them and they started giving her problems. We'll look into their accounts and hers. But right now let's see what we have."

Donning gloves and booties, they stepped gingerly down the hall until they came to an open door. The living room. As Miranda said, the radio was blaring.

Corelli shook her head. "Assumptions, assumptions."

"What?" Parker said.

"I assumed Miranda listened to music while she cleaned but that's an NPR show. Watkins, please turn the radio off."

Sudden quiet, then Watkins reappeared.

"Thank you." Corelli tipped her head, listening to the murmur of what sounded like a Gregorian chant.

The three of them stepped into the room. The lights were on. Spencer Nickerson, if they were to believe Miranda, tall and handsome, with dark hair, pale skin, and blue eyes was stretched out on the sofa wearing casual but clearly expensive clothes. Like Nardo del Balzo, Nickerson lay with his hands folded on top of his body, a rosary clasped between his hands, the smell of incense in the air, and the Gregorian chant playing softly in the background. The small hole in the back of the head wasn't visible, but she had no doubt it was there. No sign of a struggle. Somebody he knew. A tray of cheese and crackers, two plates, two knives, but only one glass of red wine on the coffee table.

May he rest in peace. As always, the words reverberated in Corelli's head.

"Well girls and boys. Miranda Foxworth has a lot of explaining to do. We haven't released anything about the laying out of the body or the rosary, so it's probably not a copycat. Not only is she the connection between the two, but she's the only one who knows the details. The media is going to love this."

"How do you think it went down, Parker?"

Parker cleared her throat. "It could be one of us. The public doesn't know, but our whole team has seen pictures, the CSU team has been on the scene, and who knows who saw the pictures at the ME's office?"

Corelli considered the statement. Based on her undercover experience, she no longer discounted the likelihood of one of their own being the murderer. "You don't like Miranda for it?"

Parker met Corelli's eyes. "Not really. The only motive I can think of is the blackmail angle you mentioned, but I don't get that vibe from her. And, look at the scene. There's wine and a tray of cheese and crackers, two plates and two knives on the coffee table. Would Nickerson, or anyone, entertain their cleaning person that way? The way I see it, he and his guest are drinking wine and chatting. The guest gets up, maybe to use the bathroom, then comes back and shoots him up close in the back of the head. The killer lifts his feet and lays him out on the sofa. He's dead weight, I mean, too heavy to move, so his feet are on the arm of the sofa, not on the cushions."

"Plausible," said Watkins.

Corelli nodded. "My take exactly." Noise behind them pulled Corelli's attention away from the scene to the hallway. "Sounds like forensics has arrived." She stepped back and peered into the hallway. "Has the ME arrived yet?"

"Today you are privileged to have a Medical Legal Investigator, an MLI not an ME." A stately dark-skinned woman stepped out of the crowd in the vestibule. Exuding power and confidence, she extended her hand. "Gloria Ndep, I joined the ME's office a couple of weeks ago. And you are?"

Corelli introduced herself and the other two detectives. Ndep raised one eyebrow slightly when she heard Corelli's name but her smile was genuine and warm. The photographer went into action, snapping all angles and the additional shots Corelli requested, and then Corelli and Parker took over. Corelli snapped some pictures with her digital camera while Parker made a rough sketch. Lastly, they took a closer look at Nickerson's body. While they were working, Ndep was also recording the context of the death, studying the scene, making notes, taking the temperature in the room, and drawing her own diagram. When they were finished, Corelli nodded to the MLI. Ndep put her notebook and pen aside and picked up her bag. She knelt beside the sofa and took a minute to study the body before beginning the examination. When she found the victim's wallet in the inside pocket of his jacket, she handed it to Corelli. The driver's license confirmed Miranda's identification of Spencer Nickerson, III. Parker helped Ndep turn the body over. When she finished, Ndep stood and signaled the team in to remove the body.

Ndep stripped off her gloves. "Estimated TOD was somewhere between nine last night and four this morning, and cause was almost certainly the small-caliber gunshot to the cerebellum resulting in instant death. But as you know, the autopsy might provide more definitive information."

Ndep followed the body out and the CSU team streamed in.

The lead technician, Lou Bullard, moved next to Corelli, watching his team get to work. "Anything in particular you want, Corelli?"

"Yes. Our guy was set up for two," she pointed to the plates, "but there's only one wineglass. Keep an eye out for the second or see if you can determine whether one is missing."

Bullard made a note. "Gotcha."

Corelli left Ron and Greene observing the forensics team and went upstairs with Parker to Nickerson's office, not on the second floor in a small bedroom, as she had thought, but up another flight to the third floor which was one large room. The deep wine-red carpet that covered the space was plush, bouncy to walk on. The computers, printers, faxes, and related equipment seemed to be working, and the only sounds were the underlying hum of the equipment and the occasional whirring of printers and faxes turning on, followed by the whisper of paper moving through the mechanisms and dropping into baskets. The four computers, each on its own small table in the center of the room, faced the windows, which framed several trees. The huge desk, in front of the floor-to-ceiling windows, was cluttered but appeared organized. A tiny stand held a stack of business cards, his. *Spencer Nickerson III, Chairman, Nickerson, Wentworth Financial Software*. His date book, one of those two-pages-for-each-day books that really busy people use, lay in the center of the desk open to today, a pen in the crease. Books lined the three inside walls. In one corner a small conference table with four chairs held stacks of computer printouts. In another, a small sofa and an easy chair faced a home theater system with a huge flat-screen TV, a stereo, a DVD player and some other not-so-easily-identified electronic equipment. All in all, a well-equipped and comfortable place to work.

No appointments last night, according to the entries in the date book. Something at eight tonight. Somebody would have to go through the papers here, but nothing but the date book was of immediate interest. They went downstairs.

"Do we have anything?" Corelli asked the forensics people moving around the living room and kitchen.

Bullard answered. "Looks like a glass *is* missing. There are ten in the closet and one in the living room. Most likely he had twelve. Might be nothing. Might mean the killer took his glass with him."

"Thanks. Ron, get the door-to-door canvass going. Parker and I are going over to Nickerson's office. Hopefully, someone will be in on a Saturday. We'll be back."

Corelli's cell phone rang as they pulled up in front of the office building that housed Nickerson's office. She made a face and grumbled as she searched her bag. "Remember the good old days when we didn't have cell phones, when we could get some work done without being interrupted every five minutes?" She glanced at the screen then took the call. "What's up, Watkins?"

She listened. "I'll be right there. Be polite. Ask him to wait outside. Stay with him but keep everything going."

She flipped the phone closed. "Drive back to Nickerson's house. My favorite captain is there claiming the case for his precinct. He must see some glory to be grabbed."

"Captain Benson?" Parker asked as she pulled away from the curb.

"The very one. We're on his territory but the cases are linked so I'm claiming it."

Ten minutes later, Parker pulled over to the curb. "What a madhouse. This is as close as I can get."

They got out of the car and surveyed the street scene. Parker moved off to the side to get a better view, then came back. "The sidewalk is lined with police on both sides. We'll have to walk the gauntlet to get to the door."

Corelli shrugged. "So what else is new?" She should have expected something like this. Benson wanted to humiliate her.

Though he wasn't involved with Righteous Partners, most of the dirty cops worked out of his house and the scandal made him look bad. Either he was a sloppy manager who didn't know what was going on under his nose or he turned a blind eye to criminal activity.

Parker eyed Corelli. "Doesn't it bother you?"

"Benson is playing to the media. Looks like every car in the district is here with lights flashing, and every TV station in the metropolitan area is recording the action."

Parker raised her voice. "I asked if it bothers you."

"If it bothers you, Parker, stay here. No need for you to deal with this."

Parker put her hand on her holster. "You don't go anywhere without me."

"Suit yourself."

Corelli took a deep breath, put on her sunglasses and plastered a smile on her face. Always show the bastards your strength, never fear or weakness. "Let's do it then."

As they strode toward Nickerson's house, someone yelled her name and the police lineup shifted, so that she and Parker would only see their backs. A couple of reporters called out to her but as they linked arms and entered the gauntlet, the only sounds were the whirring of the TV cameras and the soft rumble of the TV people explaining the famous blue wall for their viewers. At least this group from her old precinct didn't get too violent or say really gross things. Was it because many of them were friends or colleagues with whom she'd worked closely? Or hadn't they gotten the instruction manual on ostracizing? She touched Parker's arm. "See, piece of cake. Thanks."

Parker nodded.

Then they were up the front steps. Watkins opened the door and they joined him and Benson in the vestibule. Corelli offered a bright smile. "Captain Benson. Great welcoming committee. Made me feel right at home. How can I help you?"

"To begin with, Detective, you can move your investigative team out of my crime scene and then you can turn over any information you've gathered so far to the detectives from the one-eight. Am I wrong or is Mr. Nickerson outside of the oh-eight's jurisdiction?"

"With all due respect, Captain, our prime witness in the del Balzo murder discovered the body and it appears to be the same killer. I'm sorry you troubled yourself to come here, but I believe Mr. Nickerson belongs to us."

"As usual, you're out of bounds, Corelli. You can't pick and choose your cases."

"I'm sorry you feel that way, Captain. But, if you don't mind, sir, we have work to do. I'll bet headquarters will be impressed that the one-eight has nothing better to do than put on a show for the media."

He opened his mouth to speak, then looked at Parker and Watkins, and closed it. "This isn't over, Corelli. Not everybody thinks you should have free run of the department."

She watched him walk down the steps and speak to one of the officers. As his car pulled out, the gauntlet collapsed and his officers drifted away.

"This means trouble. Finish up as quickly as you can, Watkins. But first, Parker and I are going to need help getting back to our car."

"Take my car, it's not blocked in. Give me your keys. I'll catch up and exchange later."

Parker put her hand out. "You trust me with the BMW?"

"I hear you're a pretty good driver."

"Yes, I am."

Corelli stepped between them. "You should be honored. That car is Watkins's honey." As they walked out, Corelli elbowed Parker. "I don't know which is worse, walking the gauntlet or running from the press, but now we get to dash down the steps to escape the reporters. What a fun day."

CHAPTER TWENTY-SEVEN

Saturday – 12:30 p.m.

"Nickerson Wentworth Financial Software, may I help you?"
The young man at the reception desk spoke into the telephone
but his focus went to Corelli and Parker as they stepped out of the
elevator. He waved them to the nearby comfortable-looking chairs
and continued to deal with the call. "Josh isn't available. Would you
like his voice mail?"

Unlike the reception area of the law office they'd visited
yesterday, this office projected calm and competence and
telegraphed success without being ostentatious. Corelli and Parker
ignored the invitation to sit.

The receptionist ended the call. "Sorry." He glanced at his
computer and frowned. "Do you have an appointment?"

"We'd like to see Mr. or Ms. Wentworth." Corelli displayed her
shield and ID.

He glanced at the shield, then back at her. "What is this in
reference to?"

"It's personal." No way would Corelli discuss this with anyone
but Nickerson's partner.

The receptionist picked up the telephone but seemed to think better of it. "Please have a seat. I'll be right with you." He slid a card into the slot next to the door behind him and walked through.

Thirty seconds later the door opened and the receptionist popped his head out. "She'll see you now."

Wentworth stood at one of the two massive cherry wood desks that faced each other in front of the windows, talking on the telephone. She signaled one minute with a finger, then hung up. She shook their hands. "I'm Hillary Wentworth. Let's sit." She walked them over to the sofa and chairs. "I just telephoned home and my nanny said my children and my husband are fine. So what's this about?" She examined the cards Corelli and Parker handed her. "Detectives?"

As agreed on the way over, Parker took the lead. "Do you always work Saturdays?"

"We have a huge project with penalties for not meeting deadlines, so for the next couple of months, we'll all be working weekends."

"And Mr. Nickerson?"

"He often works from home but it's quieter here for me. What's this about?"

Parker ignored the question. "You and Mr. Nickerson are partners?"

"We created the software and we own the business together. Why? Is there a problem?" Wentworth's voice betrayed her annoyance.

"What happens if one of you dies?"

"I'd like to know what's going on." She looked from one to the other of them and getting no answer sighed. "We have an insurance policy that pays an amount based on a predetermined formula into the estate of the one who dies, in effect, buying the business for the surviving partner." Her eyes widened. She leaned forward, a note of panic in her voice. "Has something happened to Spence?"

Parker relented. "I'm so sorry to have to tell you Mr. Nickerson was found dead at home this morning."

Wentworth paled and gripped the arms of her chair. "Oh, my God, Spence." She covered her face then with an anguished cry, doubled over sobbing.

Parker tensed as the woman's pain flooded the room. This was the hardest part of their job by far and it wasn't something Corelli could teach. Each detective performed a balancing act on a precarious personal tightrope, a struggle between being sympathetic and being sucked into the emotional whirlpool of the bereaved. Parker, like every cop, would learn by doing.

"We're very sorry for your loss, Mrs. Wentworth." Parker's voice was sympathetic but her body language gave away her discomfort. Her gaze settled over Wentworth's shoulder, her hands clasped and unclasped and her leg shook.

Corelli cleared her throat. As a former assistant district attorney Parker should be able to control her emotions and present a composed face, even in uncomfortable situations. Parker glanced at Corelli, then took several deep breaths. With her body relaxed, Parker put her hand on Wentworth's shoulder, a comforting gesture, and when she looked up, handed the grieving woman a tissue from the box on the coffee table.

Satisfied that Parker was no longer in the grip of her emotions, Corelli left the room and returned with a cup of water. Wentworth waved it away but Corelli placed it on the table in front of her.

Wentworth dabbed at her tears. "What happened?"

"Just a few more questions," Parker said. "When did you last see him?"

"Yesterday. He often worked at home but yesterday he was here. We're bidding on some new business and we worked on the proposal together." She dabbed at the tears running down her face. "Sorry for being so weepy. I'm having a hard time taking this in."

Corelli met Parker's gaze over the woman's bent head, signaling she would take over. "Mrs. Wentworth," Corelli said, touching her shoulder. "Mr. Nickerson was murdered and we need your help."

"Murdered?" Her eyes widened. "Oh my God. Spence told me Nardo was murdered. Is somebody killing gays, some crazy serial killer?"

"That's what we're trying to figure out. Did Mr. Nickerson mention any plans for last night?"

Wentworth sniffled. "Actually, he did. He was crying about Nardo. Then he remembered a funny story about something they did and we laughed. He was laughing when he left. He said he had a hot date."

Corelli jumped on the possibility of a name. Friend or lover, it didn't matter. "Did he tell you the name of his date or where they were meeting?"

"No. He hasn't dated much in the last few years so he knew I was curious but he liked to tease me so he promised to share all the lurid details next time we saw each other. His words."

"Were Spencer and Nardo lovers?"

"Just good friends. Spence's lover died about four years ago. He'd started dating again this year, but he hadn't found anyone. Nobody measured up, if you know what I mean."

I do know. But it's not that nobody measures up to Marnie. It's that I haven't even thought about it. Until now. Nickerson waited four years to start dating. It's been less than two years for me and I'm thinking about it. Does that make me unfaithful? How long is long enough?

Corelli looked up. She'd drifted off and Parker and Wentworth were staring at her. "What about his other friends?"

"My husband and I haven't socialized much since the triplets were born three years ago, but I've met some of Spencer's friends at parties. He had lots of friends, but other than Nardo, I haven't seen much of them. There's Nelson, Bill, Abby, and Andy, but I'm drawing a blank on last names." She stared into space. "And, Meg. She's a well-known painter."

Neither del Balzo nor Nickerson were closeted, so why were they having trouble getting the names of their friends. Corelli opened her mouth to ask another question but Wentworth held up a hand to stop her.

Wentworth spoke to Parker who had started taking notes. "Kate Burke, the new speaker of the City Council is—was—a friend too. Maybe she can give you some last names."

Burke's name kept coming up. It looked like she couldn't avoid bringing the politician into the investigation. "Did Spencer keep an appointment book in the office?"

"Our calendars are on the computer and can be updated here or from home."

"We'd like to see Mr. Nickerson's appointments for the last few weeks."

"We can take a quick look, and then I'll ask Henry to print out dates as far back as you want and messenger it to you. Is that okay?"

"Sounds good."

She walked them over to her desk. "Pull a couple of chairs over. Where do you want to start?"

"Yesterday, then back a week or two."

She pressed a few keys. "We were together here all day yesterday. But there are three entries for last night, call K, just a note, no time, lama at eight thirty, Bill at eight. Spencer and his friend Bill had a standing appointment to go to the theater every other week. Henry probably has both numbers."

She buzzed Henry. He thought K could be Kate or a Ken, Spencer's friends, but he didn't recognize the other name. He had Bill's office, home, and cell numbers. She instructed him to write them down and bring them in. While they waited, she scanned several previous weeks, but there didn't seem to be anything other than business meetings, conference calls, theater with Bill, and occasional meals with his parents and, based on his use of first names, friends.

Henry knocked, entered briskly, then slowed as he took in Hillary's tear-stained face.

"Is something wrong, Hil?" His voice was gentle.

Hillary burst into tears again, covered her face with her hands, and rocked back and forth.

Henry looked from Corelli to Parker. "What's—"

Corelli answered. "Mr. Nickerson has been murdered."

Henry paled. "Oh, my god." He reached out to steady himself on the conference table. He looked like he might throw up.

She needed to wrap this up. "Henry, unless you have information about who Mr. Nickerson was meeting last night, we'd like to finish up with Ms. Wentworth now. Someone will be here later to talk to you and the rest of the staff."

"He didn't confide any details. I only know what's in his calendar." He turned toward the door.

"Wait." Hillary stopped him. "Please don't mention this to anyone. I'd like to let the staff know all at one time. Can you do that for me?"

He nodded again and left.

They did a quick check of Spencer's desk but everything on or in it was business related.

Hillary looked like she was fading fast.

"Just a few more questions," Corelli said. "Where were you last night?"

"Interviewing private schools for the triplets. Between six and ten my husband and I visited three schools and then dragged ourselves out for a drink and a late dinner." She frowned, then seemed to gasp for air. "Spencer and I have been friends since we were babies. Our families are close. We started at the same nursery school the same day and were together right through college. We developed this business together and we've been very successful. I loved him like a brother. I would..." She sniffed. "I would hurt myself before I hurt him."

She seemed to want to say something, thought about it, then looked down at her hands and spoke softly. "And if you think money gives me a motive, you should know both Spencer and I have family trust funds. And my husband is independently wealthy as well. Spencer and I work because we love what we do, because it's fun to do it together. And now I don't know if I can..."

Corelli waited. After Hillary seemed back in control, she continued. "I know this is difficult. I'm sorry but it's important we get as much information as we can as early as we can in the investigation."

She looked into Corelli's eyes. "Please go on."

"Do you know of anyone who works for you, maybe someone you fired, or a business associate who had a grudge against Mr. Nickerson? Anyone with a motive for murder?"

"We've never fired anyone. And we've given very large payouts to the few people who have left."

"We need to notify Mr. Nickerson's next of kin. Who would that be?"

"His parents, Cornelia and Reggie. They live on Sutton Place. I'll come with you." She hesitated, running her fingers over the keyboard. "No, I need to be with the staff, help them deal with this, and then I need to notify our clients. I'll call Woody. He'll meet you there."

"Who is Woody?"

"My husband. Spence's older brother. I should have called him right away. He'll be devastated. They'll all be devastated."

"How far is he?"

"He's at home, a couple of blocks from here."

"Tell him to wait out front. We'll pick him up."

Unable to speak when her husband came on the phone, Hillary handed the phone to Corelli. After a minute of stunned silence, he whispered he would wait out front for them.

"I'll call Spence's sisters and his other brother when you leave. I'll go there as soon as I take care of things here."

She flopped back in her chair, exhausted, her face a crumpled mess. "You know, Spencer laughed about someone leaving messages on his machine saying that homosexuals are an affront to God and should be killed. Is it possible he wasn't joking?"

CHAPTER TWENTY-EIGHT

Saturday – 1:30 p.m.

A white-haired woman with sparkling blue eyes answered the door at the Upper East Side townhouse. Corelli assumed she wore the pale blue running suit for comfort rather than for exercise since not a hair was out of place and her makeup was impeccable.

"Woody, darling, what are you doing here in the middle of the day?" The warm and welcoming smile drifted away as she took in his subdued demeanor. "What's the—"

"Mom, let me introduce Detectives Corelli and Parker. Is Dad home?"

"Yes. Is everything all right?"

"Let's go see Dad and then we'll talk."

She looked uncertain but turned, looking back with a puzzled expression as she led them through a long hall to an elegantly but comfortably furnished living room.

"Reggie, we have company."

Eyes on his son, he put his book down on the table in front of the sofa and stood. "What's wrong?"

"Dad this is…" He struggled to introduce them.

The elder Nickerson took his son's arm. "Are Hillary and the triplets all right?"

Woody nodded but was unable to speak. Seeing the appeal in his eyes, Corelli stepped forward.

"Mr. and Mrs. Nickerson, there's no easy way to say this. I'm so sorry to have to tell you that your son Spencer was murdered last night. He was found at home this morning."

It wasn't clear whether the father or the mother screamed but the two parents clutched their son and the three hung on to each other, sobbing. Two minutes later, two women and a man ran into the room and the six of them formed a circle of mourning. This part of the job was always difficult, but the pain in this room was excruciating. Corelli forced herself to stay present, storing the pain as a camel stores water to fuel her search for the monster who killed these two young men. Then, trying to give the family a modicum of privacy, she lifted her eyes to the wall of windows behind them, and taking in the blue sky and the brilliant sunlight streaming gloriously into the room, she wondered, not for the first time, how awful things could happen on such a beautiful day, how one family is wretched with grief and pain while the rest of the universe spins quietly and happily about its business. Next to her, Parker rocked from her heels to the balls of her feet, her breathing raspy, as if she was running. Dealing with the raw pain of others was difficult for Parker, but dealing with this family's pain was difficult even for Corelli.

After a few minutes, the circle opened and the other son asked what had happened.

"Please sit," Corelli said.

The circle straightened and they sat together, the parents and the sisters on the sofa and the two sons on the arms, each leaning in with an arm over the shoulder of a parent. Each sister held the hand of the adjacent parent as well.

The two detectives took the chairs facing them.

Woody used his handkerchief to dry his eyes. "Detective Corelli and Detective Parker, these are my sisters Cordelia and Megan, and my brother Marshall."

The father blew his nose. "Spence was really broken up about Nardo. Was it the same person?"

"It's too soon to say, sir," Corelli said. "I know this is difficult but I need to ask some questions now."

Marshall stood up. "It would be better if you came back tomorrow or the day after. We need time."

Spencer's mother seemed to have aged twenty years, yet she was the one who spoke up. "Marshall, sweetheart, let's get it over with. Ask your questions, Detective."

Corelli respected her strength in the face of such heartbreak. "When did you last see Spencer?"

"Yesterday," the mother said. "He was so distraught about Nardo being murdered that we insisted he have breakfast with us. I couldn't console him and I felt so helpless." She broke down again.

"Did you know Spencer was gay?" Corelli felt Parker's eyes on her.

Tears welling, the dad squeezed his wife's hand, then answered. "Spencer came out to all of us when he was fifteen. We were surprised, of course, and we were afraid for him because it's not an easy life. But it was never an issue for us. He was comfortable with himself and we respect our children and don't feel the need to impose our own values or prejudices on them. We want them to be happy and healthy. And Spencer was, except, of course, when his partner passed away several years ago."

"Did Spencer mention any plans for last night?"

The parents exchanged a glance and the father answered again. "He hadn't slept much the night before, so he planned to go into the office to work on a proposal with Hillary, have an early dinner and try to get some sleep. We wanted him to stay here where we could comfort…" He broke down.

Corelli pushed aside her reluctance to continue to question them in the face of their pain. She had a job to do. "Did Spencer mention any problems, any threats to any of you?"

They looked at each other, then shook their heads. The brothers and sisters hadn't seen him for three or four days but all had talked to him about Nardo.

"Just a few more questions. Did Spencer have a will?"

Woody answered. "Yes, I drew it up myself after his partner Elliot died. Other than donations to gay organizations, charities having to do with children, and Yale, his alma mater, the bulk of his estate will go into a trust fund we've established for all our children."

"Do any of you know any of his friends besides Nardo?"

Again it was the mom who spoke. "Spencer has been withdrawn since his partner's death and it's only in the last year that he's started socializing again so we haven't met many of his friends. I've met Abby and Nelson but I don't remember any last names." She looked at her other children but only got headshakes.

Corelli thanked them, passed out cards in case anyone remembered something, and left them huddled together on the sofa, comforting each other.

Parker turned the key in the ignition to lower the windows but didn't turn the car on because traffic was backed up waiting for a city truck to finish picking up the garbage piled in front of an apartment building up the street. They sat watching the slow-motion ballet of the sanitation workers as they lifted and tossed the black-bagged garbage into the maw of the truck, the only sounds the growl of the truck chewing and swallowing the bags and the occasional honking of an impatient driver.

Corelli broke the silence. "Two families, two gay sons, two totally opposite reactions. But the del Balzos's coldness, their disgust and disdain, made it easier to break the news. The Nickersons's pain is so profound that you can't avoid absorbing it."

"That's the family I'd want, one where everybody loves each other, no matter what."

"Who wouldn't?" Corelli had no illusions about her parents. If Righteous Partners had managed to take her out, her father would react like Leonardo and her mother would trail obediently along. Maybe it was an Italian thing.

Hillary turned the corner, waved, and walked over to the car. "How are they?"

"It was hard for them," Corelli said, "but they're surrounded by their children and lots of other people who've arrived in the last fifteen minutes."

"I called my mom to rally the family friends. At least they'll have lots of support." She shuddered. "It's all so unreal. I can't believe it, I just can't believe it." She gulped. "I need to go in now; I need to be with my family."

Corelli sighed. "Let's find Spencer's friend Bill. After that we'll have another talk with Ms. Foxworth."

"Are you sure Ms. is the right form of address for her?"

Corelli thought back to the pin on Miranda's bag and the moment that had passed between them. "I think she would have said if she preferred something else. It's a complicated issue and I'm not sure I totally understand it but I do know you can always ask politely what pronouns they use. And, Parker, when you meet someone with a woman's name wearing a skirt and heels and makeup, I suggest you start with Ms., no matter what you think you know about that person."

Bill Francis answered the door in his pajamas and demanded to know how they had bypassed the doorman. A display of shields and he stepped back to admit them to his apartment. He closed the door softly behind them but didn't move further into the apartment.

"What is it," he said. "Why are you here?"

"Are you a friend of Spencer Nickerson?"

He peered up at Corelli, then glanced at Parker as if looking for a clue. "Is Spencer all right?"

They'd decided Corelli would handle this interview. "I'm sorry to tell you Mr. Nickerson was murdered last night."

"Murdered?' He reached for the wall but stumbled.

Parker grabbed him and propped him up.

He rubbed his eyes.

"I just spoke to him yesterday. We had plans to go to the theater last night but he called about six to cancel."

"Did he say why?"

"He said something had come up. When I joked about him tossing me aside for a hot date he laughed and said 'more like a cold fish. Believe me, you're way hotter.' We rescheduled for next week and said goodbye. Do the Nickersons know?"

"Yes."

"Was it a mugging or a robbery? I can't believe it. Can we go in and sit down? I feel dizzy."

They helped him into the living room, eased him onto the sofa, then sat facing him.

He wrapped his arms around a pillow. His eyes filled. "Where did it happen? Do you know who did it?"

Corelli ignored his questions. "We're in the early stages of the investigation and we need your help. Besides your name, he had 'lama' in his calendar for last night. Was that related to what you were doing?"

"We usually didn't plan ahead. Just took our chances at the TKTS Booth in Times Square and bought whatever sounded interesting."

"So it's not likely that he had purchased tickets ahead of time?"

"He could have. Occasionally, he surprised me with tickets to something that interested him, especially if the tickets weren't available at the Booth. But I haven't heard of it. Maybe it's Off Off Off Broadway and I just haven't come across it."

"So what did you do last night?" Corelli asked.

"Me?" He rubbed his head again. "I stayed home, had dinner, and read until I fell asleep around eleven, I think."

"Did you talk to anyone?"

"The doorman when my Thai food was delivered and the delivery guy when he brought it up. I think that was about seven thirty. But nobody else. I guess I don't have an alibi."

"Do you need one?"

"Doesn't everyone in these cases?"

Ah, yes, TV. "Why would you want Spencer dead?"

"I wouldn't. I don't. We've been friends since elementary school." He struggled to control the emotions welling up.

"Do you know of anyone who would want to kill Spencer?"

"No, no one." He grabbed a tissue out of the box on the coffee table. "Except those religious nuts, the ones making those crazy calls."

CHAPTER TWENTY-NINE

Saturday – 3:00 p.m.

Miranda Foxworth sat at the table in the interview room with her head cradled in her arms. Parker touched her lightly when they entered and she lifted her head. She looked groggy, and from the state of her eye makeup, like she'd cried herself to sleep. They sat across from her.

Corelli took the lead. "So, Ms. Foxworth, two of your clients murdered within days of each other. Quite a coincidence. Any thoughts that might help us track down the murderer?"

She brushed her hair out of her eyes. "Do you think I'm in danger?"

"What do you think?"

Foxworth fingered her hair. "Why would anyone want to kill me? And if they did, why kill my clients? It must be somebody after rich gay guys."

Corelli was impressed. Despite her nervousness, Foxworth had handled that question deftly. But was she the one killing her clients? "Where were you last night?"

"I knew it. I knew when they searched my purse you would blame me. I knew I should have called my lawyer. I'd like to do that now, please." She lifted her purse from the floor next to her chair into her lap, ready to go.

"We just want to ask you some questions. Calling your lawyer will drag things out but you can call if that's what you want."

Miranda thought for a few seconds. "I'll answer but if I feel like you're after me, I'm going to stop talking and call her."

Corelli did not want a lawyer involved so she'd tread softly. "Fair enough. So where were you last night?"

"I was home all night with my partner, but you won't believe that, will you?" She reached her hands out, palms up, besieging. "Why would I kill them? They were both kind and treated me with respect. I'm here talking to you without my attorney because I cared about them and I want to help you find the killer."

"Okay. Who could have done this?"

"I've been wracking my brain, but I can't think of anyone except that religious guy that's been calling and threatening gay guys."

The 'un-Christians' again. That got Corelli's attention. "Which religious guy?"

"I don't know his name, but I heard somebody talking about it at a club the other night, somebody sitting at the bar near me. He said he was interviewed on some TV show and the next day the calls started."

"Who did you tell about Nardo—about the rosary and how he was arranged?"

"Nobody. I swear. Not even John, my partner. You told me to keep quiet and I did. I want you to find this guy before he hurts somebody else."

Corelli studied Miranda, the tension in her body, the sweat on her forehead, the shaking hands. She didn't think Miranda was a killer, and she felt guilty for inspiring such fear. "You can go, Miranda, but don't go far."

Miranda rocketed up, knocking her chair over. "Oh, sorry." She righted the chair and dashed for the door.

"Miranda." Corelli's voice was a command.

She stopped, her back to them, her shoulders scrunched, as if expecting a blow.

"Don't forget what I told you. Under no circumstances are you to mention anything about what you've seen at the scene of the murders or anything else related to the murders, not to your lover, not to your friends, not to your clients, not to your mother, not in the bars, not anywhere, especially not to the press. Understand?"

"Okay."

"Wait a sec. Detective Parker will get a uniform to escort you out."

They watched Parker leave.

"And, Miranda, you have my number. If you hear talk about calls from this religious guy, get the name and number of the person receiving the calls and telephone me immediately. But no heroics, okay? You stay safe."

Keeping her eyes trained on the door, Miranda nodded, and when the uniform appeared, she ran out.

"I still can't see a motive," Corelli said as she and Parker walked toward the case conference room. "What's your esteemed opinion, Ms. ADA?"

"The same as earlier today." Parker ignored the condescension in Corelli's voice. "I don't think she's guilty. Quite the opposite, in fact."

Surprised she hadn't risen to the bait, Corelli glanced at Parker. *I really need to think about why I try to provoke her. It's not right.* "Until we figure this out, though, we'd better notify her clients to be careful. Maybe somebody has it in for her."

"Corelli," Dietz yelled as they entered the conference room, "the captain wants you and Parker in his office ASAP."

They pivoted and headed for Captain Winfry's office.

"Do you think Carla del Balzo called to complain again?"

"Don't worry Parker, it's more likely Captain Benson or Mayor Matthews coming for me."

Captain Winfry waved them in. "Nice article in the *Post*, Corelli. Handling the del Balzos with kid gloves, I see."

His tone was teasing. It was nice to have a boss who supported her. "Just asking the questions that need to be asked, sir. The ambassador was our prime suspect and though he's not totally off the hook, this second murder makes that less likely."

He looked her in the eye. "Do what you have to do, Corelli. Makes me think he has something to hide."

She nodded. "Me too. But is it the murder of his son he's hiding? And would he kill a second time to cloud the issue?"

"Interesting thought, but I'll caution you again to be very careful about sharing it outside this room until you have proof." He straightened the papers on his desk. "Chief Broderick called me earlier. He's not very happy with you. I tried to head him off, but I couldn't talk him out of it. I'm not sure whether he's more upset about the del Balzo article or Captain Benson's claim that you're muscling in on his case. How did you manage to step on Benson's toes?" His smile took the sting out of the words.

"Miranda Foxworth, the cleaning woman who found del Balzo, called me this morning from Spencer Nickerson's brownstone when she found him dead. Nickerson's brownstone is in Benson's district, but since it was another of her clients, I responded to her call. We were on our way to interview Nickerson's partner when Benson showed up and claimed the case. When we went back to speak to him, we found a large uncontained media presence and a wall of blue that we had to pass through to get into the brownstone."

"I'm sorry," Captain Winfry said.

"It was a surprise but I can't say I blame him."

Winfry's face darkened. "He was asleep at the wheel, Corelli. Not your fault. Nothing for you to feel guilty about."

Once again, Winfry had read her mind. Was her guilt that obvious or was he that good?

"In any case, Nickerson was shot and posed in the same way as del Balzo. We haven't released the details to the press but it looks like the same killer. Foxworth is the most likely suspect but Parker and I don't think it's her. The two cases need to be treated as one. And investigated by our team."

He put his face in his hands and rubbed his forehead. He probably had a headache from dealing with turf wars. "Somehow the mayor found out you're talking about a serial killer—"

"I'm sure Benson got him involved and used those words. I didn't."

He sighed. "Probably true, but Mayor Matthews doesn't want to hear the words, serial killer because—"

"It will cause problems for his reelection if the press finds out that we have a serial killer."

"Politics." He shook his head. "I hate to waste your time on this Corelli, but Chief Broderick wants to see the two of you down at headquarters, now. Are you all right with this, Parker?"

"Not with the politics. I'd rather not be attacked for doing our job, but I'm on board with the investigation and pushing to combine the cases."

Well, thank you, Detective Parker. Now that Parker had taken a stand, she might as well put her cards on the table so Winfry wouldn't be caught by surprise if Broderick fired her. "I'm going to push the chief for a single investigation, Captain. I hope you'll back me up."

"A single investigation is the proper way to handle this. I support you one hundred percent, but given the politics, I'm not sure how much good it will do." Winfry stood. "I'd be happy to come with you if you think it will make a difference."

Corelli and Parker stood. "Thank you, sir. No need to waste your time too." She put a hand out to stop Parker from leaving before she'd updated Winfry. "Just so you know, I did another interview with Darla North this morning. She wanted to do something positive in response to the del Balzo article, though it's not mentioned in the interview. It'll be aired at ten tonight."

"It's really strong," Parker said, surprising Corelli. "And, I think, positive for the department."

"Jeez, Corelli, I unleashed a monster. Soon you'll be too busy to do the job." He laughed. "Go for it. You and the department need all the positive attention we can get."

"One more thing, Captain. I was thinking this might be the right time for a press conference."

He leaned back in his chair and stared at the ceiling, then smiled, a broad, knowing smile of approval. "You're a fast learner, Corelli. Have Dietz set it up for later."

He didn't stand when they walked in. Not a good sign. And he definitely didn't look friendly. They had barely stepped into the room when he lashed out.

"What the hell do you think you're doing, Corelli?"

She touched Parker lightly on the arm, signaling her to stay behind, then strode to stand in front of his desk. She met his eyes but her face was a blank mask. She tried to keep the hostility out of her voice.

"My job. Sir."

Parker's intake of breath signaled that she hadn't managed to hide the disdain she felt.

He chose to ignore her tone and tempered his own. "Tell me how you ended up on Benson's turf? The del Balzo case not keeping you busy enough?"

"We have more than enough on our plate. Del Balzo's murderer brought us to Benson's turf. Miranda Foxworth, the cleaning person who found Nardo del Balzo, called me this morning. She found another client of hers, Spencer Nickerson, also gay, lying on a sofa, with a rosary in his hands, dead by a small bullet to the cerebellum. Sound familiar? I believe we have a killer targeting gays. We need a single investigation."

He broke eye contact. "Have you looked at Foxworth? Maybe he, er, she—"

"We're looking, but she seems to be a solid citizen and we haven't uncovered a motive. Hey, the good news is that Ambassador del Balzo may be off the hook. That should make Carla del Balzo happy. And now you and the mayor can relax and let me do my job."

"The fact that the ambassador is off the hook may save your job, Corelli, because now you can stop pressuring him."

It didn't escape Corelli that Broderick chose to hear that the ambassador is, rather than may be, off the hook because of the second murder. He could pretend all he wants but she'd continue to investigate Ambassador del Balzo until she proved his innocence or his guilt. "You believe the story in the *Post*? You know me better than that. When Parker and I were leaving after announcing their only son had been murdered, the ambassador said to his wife in Italian that she should be happy about their son's death because now he won't interfere with *them* becoming prime minister. Put that together with the fact that he and his son had a screaming argument the day before…Wouldn't you follow up?"

He frowned. "I would. But it sounds as if you're being confrontational. Tread lightly." So did he just give her permission to continue to investigate del Balzo? Better not to ask.

He stood and walked to the window, then back. A sure sign he was uncomfortable with what he was going to say. "The mayor doesn't want to see anything about a serial killer in the media."

She could pussyfoot with the best of them. "I haven't used those words. And, two murders do not make a serial killer."

He was back at the window now, staring down at something of great interest. "Call it what you want. Mathews wants these two cases investigated separately. Of course, you'll share whatever—"

"It's not just me. Captain Winfry agrees that we have one killer and we need a combined investigation." Pussyfooting didn't work maybe direct would.

"Captain Winfry is entitled to his opinion, as are you, but the decision is not yours or his to make. As I said, tomorrow you will turn the Nickerson case over to Benson. Understand?"

"Would you excuse us, Parker? I'd like a minute with the chief."

When the door closed, she turned. "What happened, Harry? Where's the fighter? The man who believed we stand for the victims. You've become a bureaucrat, fat and comfortable, taking the path of least resistance. If we're going to catch this guy before he kills again these cases need to be investigated together. You know it. But you're afraid, afraid to take a risk, afraid to do the right thing, afraid you'll lose your job. What about your self-respect, your—"

He strode over and stood so close she could smell the coffee on his breath. His eyes were hard. "That's enough. I'll assume that little speech came from my friend Chiara, because any subordinate who addressed me that way would be back walking a beat in a minute. Tomorrow morning you will turn this new case over to Benson. That is an order, Detective."

She stared at him. He looked away. She shook her head. "Yessir."

"Corelli." His voice had softened. "I'm really sorry Benson orchestrated the public display of the blue wall and invited the press. He's being reprimanded."

"I'll live." She had to get out of here. It was easier to deal with his anger than his pity. And she needed to hold on to her anger.

"Good. And lest you think you're immune to politics, Kate Burke called again last night. She was on her way to a retreat in the Catskills where there's no TV, radio, or telephones especially cells, and she asked me to let you know she's driving straight back tomorrow morning and will expect you in her office at eight. You can't avoid her, so I suggest you get your ass over to City Hall first thing. You don't need any more enemies, and the gay community has some clout. Who knows? Maybe she can get the mayor to change his mind."

"Politics, politics, politics," she grumbled as she left his office.

CHAPTER THIRTY

Saturday – 4:30 p.m.

They were alone in the conference room. "Is this a good idea? I mean he did say to turn the case over to Benson," Parker said as Corelli opened the door.

"He didn't say I couldn't do a press conference. Besides, I'm not going to mention Nickerson unless a member of the media brings him up."

"You know they will."

Corelli raised her hands as if to say, what can I do? "Then I guess I'll have to answer the questions." She glanced back at Parker, then stopped, pulled the door closed, and leaned against it. "I don't mean to be flip or make light of your concerns. I need to do this to feel that I've done everything I can to keep the cases together. Harry, the chief, knows me well enough to place the blame where it belongs. It won't affect you."

"It's not me I'm worried about," Parker said.

"Ah, the loyal sidekick." She put her hand over her heart. "Don't worry your pretty head about me, Parker. I'm willing to live with the consequences of doing the right thing."

Parker shook her head. "You are one crazy bitch."

Corelli smiled. "But I'm your bitch. And this might have a good outcome for you. If I get fired, you won't have to work with me." She started to leave, then stopped and stared at Parker. "You honestly think I should stand by while they take the case away from us, making it difficult to solve either, and wait for more murders, maybe some we could have prevented?"

Parker responded immediately. "No, I don't." She met Corelli's eyes. "Let's go do it."

The laughter and shouted conversations got louder and louder as they neared the room where the press corps was assembled. No doubt the piranhas were hungry, ready to chew her up and swallow her.

Parker touched her shoulder. "Knock 'em dead."

"If only," Corelli said, flashing her Mona Lisa smile. She thought of Darla. They're not all vultures; they're just trying to do their jobs, to stay on top. She could do this. She took a deep breath, reached inside for a smile, and stepped through the door, onto the platform where her team waited. The room went silent. All eyes followed Corelli. When they reached the podium, Parker took a step back. Captain Winfry appeared from nowhere to stand beside Corelli.

Corelli scanned the audience. Darla and Bear must have arrived early because Darla was sitting up front and Bear was in the first line of camera people. Behind Bear, gangly Officer Jamie Twilliger smiled broadly. He waved. She smiled, a real smile this time. Suddenly the lights started flashing. *Lights. Explosions. Gunfire. Fire. Get down.* She started to drop but an arm circled her waist, keeping her upright.

"Open your eyes. Look at me," Parker whispered in her ear. Corelli turned her head. "Good. You're safe. Nod. Smile at me like I just told you something you like."

On the other side, Winfry placed a hand on her arm. "Steady." He spoke so only she could hear.

The contact, Parker's arm, her reassurances, Winfry's warm hand, grounded her.

Parker leaned in to speak into her ear. "Breathe deeply and say something to me."

Corelli took a couple of breaths, then nodded. "Thanks, I've got it now."

Parker smiled and tipped her head. Corelli's flashbacks were a secret they shared. Hopefully, no one noticed.

She owed Parker for preventing a PR disaster. Parker stepped back and Corelli faced the podium. She couldn't bring herself to call it PTSD yet, but the flashbacks were unacceptable and she would have to address them…sometime soon.

Corelli flashed Winfry a grateful smile. Once again he had sensed what she was feeling.

"You okay?"

"Fine. Thank you, sir." She sipped the water placed there for her.

Captain Winfry turned on the mike. "Ladies and gentlemen, thank you for coming tonight on such short notice. Most of you know Detective Chiara Corelli." He waited for the laughter to subside. "Detective Corelli and her team are in the thick of the investigation we're here to discuss, so I'll let her take you through what's happening. Please hold your questions until the end. Detective Corelli." He stepped to the side. The team stepped forward, closer to her.

She took a minute to look around the room and make eye contact with as many members of the press as she could. Some smiled, others lowered their eyes, all were silent. Only Darla looked concerned. "As you know, I'm leading the investigation into the death of Leonardo del Balzo, known as Nardo, a young man found murdered in his apartment Wednesday morning. NYPD has put together an extensive team," she indicated those standing around her, "that has followed every lead and continues to follow the leads we have. Now, we need your help in getting Nardo's friends or anyone who has information that might be related to his death, to call our tip line, 1-800-TIP-COPS. We'll be giving out a flyer with his picture and the information at the end of this meeting." She stopped. "So. Any questions about the del Balzo case?"

"Is it true you accused Nardo's father of murdering him?" said Jodi Timmons, a reporter for WNYZ, a TV station.

She smiled and shook her head. "We're in the early stages of the investigation. And you all," she waved a hand at the reporters, "should know better. I would never accuse anyone unless I had conclusive proof, so the answer is no. The del Balzos are under extraordinary pressure related to his bid to become Prime Minister of Italy and now the death of their only son. I believe they misunderstood my questions and my intentions."

She called on Ed Wallace from the *New York Daily World*. "Are you focusing on any suspects at this time?"

"As I said, it's still early and we're casting a wide net."

"Is it true Nardo was gay?" said the reporter from NEWS 1.

"I can't confirm that."

"Do you think the murder is related to his father's bid to be Prime Minister of Italy?" said Jose Marti, the Channel Five reporter.

"That is definitely an avenue of inquiry, but at this point we have absolutely no evidence that indicates the murderer was motivated by politics."

As she answered, she scanned the crowd. Her nemesis, Philip Melnick, the reporter from the *Daily Post*, was in the back of the room. She could tell by the smirk on his face that he was ready to zap her. As soon as she finished he jumped up and shouted his question.

"Detective Corelli, is it true you're trying to grab the Nickerson murder case from your old precinct, the one-eight, where you accused your friends and colleagues of running an operation that stole from drug dealers? If taking money from drug deals can be called stealing. Are you building an empire, looking to grab the publicity and glory?"

The room went quiet. She smiled and gave him a second to enjoy his attempt to smear her. "Well, Philip, we're not here to talk about the murder of Mr. Nickerson, but…let me explain. The team working on the del Balzo murder has more than enough to do. In fact, we're busy fourteen to eighteen hours a day working to find the person who perpetrated this terrible murder, and we have no need to take on another investigation." She took a sip of water to drag it out a little bit. "But the individual who found Mr. Nickerson also found Mr. del Balzo, and she called me to report Mr. Nickerson's death. As you may know, I try to be a good citizen, so I didn't stop to think, 'this is not my job. Let me dump it on someone else.' Rather I responded to a distraught call from a citizen in need. As it turned out, the two cases have a lot in common besides the individual who discovered the bodies. You could see it as a grab or you could see it as an attempt to solve both murders as quickly as possible by combining the investigations."

Melnick smirked. "I hear that you think we have a serial killer in the city."

"Your information is better than mine. At this point, all I can say is the two murders appear to be related." She held his eyes. "And, Philip, just as a matter of record on a moral point. I believe taking money or belongings from another person is stealing no matter how that person originally obtained such objects or who the taker is. And killing is killing." His smirk faded. "In my police department, police serve and protect, they do not steal and murder." He looked away.

Her point made, she was ready to end the press conference but then decided to field a few more questions to see what turned up.

She called on Andrew Baron of Channel 43, one of the biggest vultures, always looking to stick it to the police and make a name for himself. "Detective Corelli. This morning we all again witnessed you walking through a line of your brother officers where they turned their backs on you. Are you being ostracized? Is this punishment for your undercover investigation?"

"Your questions are not related to either murder investigation, so I'll pass."

"How do you feel about it, walking the gauntlet?" Baron was not giving up.

"No comment."

Darla's hand shot up. "Are you now responsible for the Nickerson case as well as the del Balzo?"

"At this moment, I am." Damn, that little southern belle was really in tune with her.

Corelli pointed at Helen Duggin from Channel 29. "What are the similarities?"

"No comment."

Unfazed, Duggin pressed for more detail. "Is it true that it was the cleaning woman who worked for both men who found them?"

"No comment."

Winfry stepped forward. "Thank you for coming, ladies and gentlemen. We'll keep you posted." He flicked the mike off. "Corelli and Parker with me."

He led them to his office. "Nicely done, Corelli. But what the hell happened in there? Are you sick?"

She glanced at Parker. "Just lightheaded, sir. I haven't eaten much all day." If Parker contradicted her, she'd be off the case. "And, thanks to you and Parker, I managed to stay on my feet."

Winfry turned to Parker. "How did you know—"

"Corelli mentioned earlier that she was feeling off, and I was standing right behind her so I saw her start to sway."

"Hmm." He looked from one to the other. "Well, be sure you eat. It won't do for you to get sick."

Corelli asked Parker to hang out with her during the interview with *The New York Daily World* to provide another set of ears and eyes to make sure she didn't give the reporter too much. They were relaxing on the sofa, Corelli with mint tea and Parker with a beer, waiting for the reporter, when Corelli cleared her throat. "Thanks for your support during the press conference, Parker. And with Winfry."

Parker smiled and lifted her beer to acknowledge the acknowledgment. Then the bell rang and Corelli went to buzz the reporter up.

"Nice to see you, Sal," Corelli said as she ushered Sal Cantrino into her apartment and over to the sofa. "Sal, this is Detective P.J. Parker, Parker this is Sal Cantrino, editor of *The New York Daily World*."

"Have a seat." She gestured to the sofa. "But don't sit on the kittens. Something to drink?"

"Ah, the hero cats." He rubbed their heads. "A beer would be nice."

Corelli got him a beer and sat. "Since when does the editor do interviews?"

"I've decided we'll do an article first so we can say what we want without you being involved. After that runs, I'll send the reporter to interview you."

Corelli breathed deeply and smiled. "That's great, Sal. The last thing I feel like doing right now is giving an interview."

"But you have to promise you'll do an interview some other time."

"You say when." She stood and stretched. "I didn't realize how tired I am." She glanced at the clock. "Anybody want to watch the ten o'clock news?"

First up was the footage in front of Nickerson's house. The two of them standing straight, heads held high, striding toward and through the gauntlet, Darla's voice describing what was happening. Then an interview with some expert from John Jay College of Criminal Justice who explained the blue wall and why Corelli was being ostracized.

"You two look good," Sal said. "I don't know how you handle the pressure, Chi."

Corelli shrugged. "All in a day's work." She flipped through the other news channels, checking out their coverage. Most flashed them walking through with a quick comment about the police ostracizing one of their own for turning against other cops. She turned back to WYNY and they watched the press conference.

"So what do you think, Sal?"

"Great. You came across as a professional trying to do a job. No defensiveness, even with that ass Metnick, no soft shoe avoiding questions. You were loud and clear."

"Thanks. Let's hope the mayor gets the message."

Last thing up was the interview. Corelli stared at the composed, attractive, confident Darla North introducing her latest interview with Detective Chiara Corelli. Had she imagined the scared, shaking Darla she'd met at the media feeding frenzy? She leaned forward, anxious to see what Darla had that she thought would neutralize Carla del Balzo's attack.

Darla introduced the program then interspersed the interview they had filmed earlier with interviews with witnesses and suspects from previous cases including several from the Winter case. Darla deftly brought each and every one of the former suspects to admit they were angry at the time that Detective Corelli hounded them, but she was justified because they were lying to her. No, the lies didn't have anything to do with the murder, mostly they were personal things. And yes, Detective Corelli had solved the crime and brought the murderer to trial. In addition, Darla had managed to find several current and former NYPD detectives willing to speak positively about her, and all had given her rave reviews as a detective, as a colleague, and as a human being. Corelli was overwhelmed. And disappointed. She'd harbored a fantasy that Brett would rise to her defense. Maybe Brett hadn't forgiven her after all.

How did Darla find these people? Corelli glanced at Parker, who was totally absorbed and didn't look guilty. Tess? Maybe Watkins? She was sure Darla wouldn't give up her source but whoever it was had done a great job. And, so had Darla and Bear. She turned the TV off.

Parker grinned at her. "Little southern belle sure came through tonight."

Sal stood and stretched. "She's southern?"

"Only in private." Corelli laughed. "How did she find those people?"

"Don't look at me," said Parker. "I volunteered but she said I was too close to the del Balzo investigation."

"That was great, Chi. I couldn't have done better myself. Gives me an idea or two for our article. I'm going to take off." He leaned over and kissed Corelli's cheek. "Night, Parker. It's always nice to meet the people featured on our front pages." He pulled Corelli up. "C'mon, let me out."

When Corelli joined Parker on the sofa, the kittens immediately jumped into her lap. "Have you decided on names?"

"I don't want to name them if I'm not keeping them."

"Uh-huh." Parker looked skeptical. "So how did you get so friendly with the editor of the *World*"

"You playin' gotcha, Parker?" Corelli laughed. "Too bad you didn't ask when Sal was here so I could have done a number on him." She rubbed the kittens' heads. Their warmth and their weight in her lap had a strangely calming effect on her. "Sal's older sister, Angie, was my best friend growing up. After school and in the summer Angie had to take care of him so he went everywhere with us. That meant I, too, took care of him. I love to tease him about changing his diaper and wiping his nose. He's like family. Nothing nefarious. Call him later and confirm my story."

"That won't be necessary."

CHAPTER THIRTY-ONE

Sunday – 7 a.m.

One by one they dragged themselves into the meeting, some with caffeinated sodas, some with Starbucks or no-name coffee. Some sipped and stared into space, some nibbled and stared into space, and some nibbled and sipped and read the morning papers or stared into space. No conversation, no kidding around.

When most everyone was accounted for, Corelli's everyday voice easily penetrated the eerie silence. "Morning."

"Morning." Dietz stood. "If I may, Corelli, we all attended the press conference yesterday so nothing new there, but I'd like to start the meeting by showing a tape of your interview on WNYN last night. It's less than ten minutes. You okay with that?"

"Sure." Maybe it would wake them up.

When it ended, the team cheered and energetic chatter filled the room. She tipped an invisible hat to Dietz. Not only was he a good detective and a tireless worker, but he was always tuned in to the needs of the group. It was a lucky break for her that they'd ended up in the same station again, especially at a time when she was short of friends.

"Thanks, guys. While we're on the topic, Darla North has asked to talk to some of you. I suggested she cover one of our meetings and then talk to anyone who has something to say. We can't talk about the investigation, but she'll have some more general questions. If you're not all okay with that, we don't have to do it. It was just a suggestion. Think about it and let Dietz know if you object. I'm good either way."

She let them discuss it amongst themselves for a minute, then called for quiet.

"Anybody have something? Anything that connects Del Balzo and Nickerson?"

Forlini cleared his throat. "Yeah, I caught del Balzo's neighbors last night. At first the old man said he didn't see anybody else when the mystery man entered the house, but when I had him try to visualize as he repeated the story he recalled a slender young man with dark, curly hair wearing a business suit getting out of a taxi. The guy watched Nardo embrace the mystery man, and then he abruptly turned east and walked away."

"Sounds like Sigler told the truth, so maybe he's off the hook. Anything else, Forlini?"

"Yeah. The old woman confessed she was anxious about Nardo inviting the stalker into his apartment and she stood at the window so she could see when the man left. He was only there about ten minutes. Then the door opened, and the guy was framed in the doorway with his back to the street. She's not sure but she thought Nardo pushed him out and slammed the door in his face. The man stared at the door for a minute, then ran down the steps and went west toward Sixth Avenue."

"Unless we find something to prove that one of them went back, Ginocchioni and Sigler seem to be in the clear. What about the bars? Anything?"

"Nothin' we didn't already know," Dietz said. "The undercover guys hit the gay bars and turned up a rumor or two about gays getting phone calls and hang-ups. They'll try again tonight."

"Anybody got anything about Nickerson? Any witnesses, any enemies, anything?"

"We keeping Nickerson?" Watkins asked.

She was going to do her best but given the politics, they'd probably go with separate investigations. And given her intention to take a stand and go public, she'd probably be fired, suspended, or at least, be pulled off the del Balzo case. "Benson is putting pressure, but for now, he's ours. So let's get on it."

"Um, the only thing we have," said Watkins, "is a message on his machine about a picture being ready. The place that called was closed for the weekend so we'll check it out tomorrow."

"Anything else?" She gave it a minute before she filled them in on what she and Parker were pursuing. "Turns out Nardo was a friend of Speaker Burke at the City Council. Parker and I are meeting her at eight this morning. Hopefully, she'll give us something, maybe a list of his friends. Or better yet, a list of his enemies. See everyone at seven tonight. Bring me something."

"Ever been inside City Hall?" Corelli asked as she and Parker crossed Chambers Street. Corelli had always loved the nineteenth century building with its high ceilings, lovely rotunda, graceful sweeping staircase, and ornate decorations.

"Yes, when I was an ADA I had a number of meetings there with the mayor and council members and staff. Why?"

Corelli kept walking. Finally she commented. "I think it's beautiful."

Parker grinned. "Into old buildings, are you? I would have never guessed."

"You don't know anything about me, Parker. Architecture has been one of my favorite things since I was a kid and spent time in Sicily. You can learn a lot about a culture by studying their buildings."

"I totally agree on both counts. Since you've kept me at arm's length, I don't know the real you, but I've had a glimpse or two behind the curtain. And, without a doubt, architecture is important to understanding a culture."

They showed their ID, walked around the barricades, and climbed the outside steps. They were expected so they were escorted right to the office of Kate Burke, first woman and first openly lesbian Speaker of the New York City Council.

Burke had run to a quick meeting and would be back shortly. Her assistant ushered them into Burke's office and instructed them to make themselves comfortable. They turned down the coffee or tea she offered.

Too wired to sit, Corelli prowled the office scanning the framed pictures of Kate Burke with various celebrities and politicians on the walls. Damn Burke for keeping them waiting. What could be more important than solving two murders? Trying to distract herself she moved to examining the pictures on the credenza. These looked more personal, more like jubilant family and friends on the steps of City Hall, probably the day she became speaker. The last picture jolted her. The shock of recognition felt like a punch in the gut. Her gasp brought Parker to her side.

"What is it?" Parker gazed at the picture, then turned to Corelli. "It's—"

The door burst opened and an energetic pixie in a tailored pantsuit whooshed in, trailed by a not-so-energetic entourage of two men and a woman. The pixie stopped short at the sight of Parker and Corelli and came close to being the bottom in a pileup of the minions at her heels. She didn't seem to notice the balancing act behind her, or maybe she conserved her energy for the important things.

"Detective Corelli, Detective Parker. Thank you for coming." She turned to the huddled group behind her. "All right folks, I need to spend a little time with the detectives. Let's get back together in about forty-five minutes. And unless you have a burning desire to spend another night at another political dinner, you all have the night off. Jamie will go to the Waldorf with me tonight."

As the door closed, Burke's smile faded. She walked over to the two detectives and looked at the picture in Corelli's hand. "That was taken on the steps outside the day I was sworn in six weeks ago. Seems like years. We were all so happy. Little did we know a few weeks later Nardo would be dead." She choked up. She ran her finger over the photograph. "These are my closest friends, my gay and lesbian family."

"Who took the picture?"

"The photographer from the *Daily World*. It was on their front page the next day and Sal Cantrino, the editor, had it framed and sent it over as a gift. Why?"

"Did the story include names?"

"Yes, I think so."

"And what are their names?"

She took the picture from Corelli. "Nardo," she said, pointing, then moved her finger, naming them. "Nelson Choi, Gary Turner, Ellen Delgiorno, Meg Lerner, my partner Abigail Woo, Spencer Nickerson, and," she looked at Corelli, "you've met Brett Cummings."

The minute she'd spotted her in the picture, Corelli had been gripped by fear for Brett's safety. So much for a passing infatuation. "Are you in touch with everyone in the picture?" *Please God let Brett be safe.* And the others too, of course.

"Not on a daily basis. Abigail, my partner, is in Washington discussing a commission to design a building, but I called her about Nardo." Her face crumbled. "Sorry, it's so unreal and things have been so hectic around here that I haven't had a chance to mourn." She took a tissue from the box on the credenza and dabbed her eyes. "Anyway, I called Nelson about Nardo. He's been in Chicago but he came back last night and went out to South Hampton to spend a couple of days with his partner. Gary lives in Toronto and was just here for the day. Ellen is on a four-week Nordic cruise but I emailed her about Nardo. Spencer and I spoke Friday about four. He was devastated too. He's in the city, probably at home stuck in front of a computer. Brett's been in Tokyo on business for a few days, but she's on a late flight back tomorrow night. I didn't want to tell her while she's so far away. I'll go to her place to tell her tomorrow." She sighed. "The only other one I haven't told about Nardo is Meg because I haven't been able to reach her. But that's not unusual. She disappears into her painting and hardly eats or drinks or comes up for air until one of us remembers to drag her out." She shook her head. "She's hopeless. She starts a painting, forgets what day it is, and ignores the phone and the door. I have her key. I'll go over tonight when I leave the dinner at the Waldorf."

Burke's schedule is as bad as ours. How to tell her? "Let's sit." Corelli led her to the sofa.

"Have you seen the morning papers?"

"Not yet. They're probably on my desk, but I've been in meetings since six this morning trying to head off a disaster of a building project in Queens. Why? Is there another disgusting article about you and the del Balzos?"

Corelli cleared her throat. "There's no good way to say this, Speaker Burke. I'm so sorry. Spencer Nickerson was found dead yesterday, murdered."

She pitched forward and would have fallen, but Corelli grabbed her and held her while she tried to catch her breath. Over Burke's shoulder, Corelli watched Parker take her notebook from her bag and flip through the pages.

"What's going on? Is it just a coincidence? Or is somebody targeting gay men?"

"No coincidence. The MO was exactly the same." *And Lerner is unaccounted for.*

"Give me Meg Lerner's phone number and address and I'll send a patrol car to check on her."

Parker wrote down the information and moved to Burke's desk to call the precinct.

"Was there anything about Nardo and Spencer that would cause them to be targeted?"

Burke frowned. "You mean like S&M, or drugs, or picking up unsavory characters or…" Her voice trailed off. "No. They were ordinary guys, special but ordinary. You know what I mean?"

Parker stood. "Sorry to interrupt. Can I talk to you, Detective Corelli?" She walked to the door.

Corelli excused herself and walked over. They stepped out of the office. "What's up?"

Parker closed the door. "I called Meg Lerner's number and a Detective Wachinski answered. Lerner is dead. Shot in the back of the head, laid out with a rosary in her hands, incense burning, and church music playing, probably Gregorian chants but he didn't know what it was."

Corelli paled. She leaned against the door. "Has to be the same killer. None of this has been released."

"I called Watkins. Miranda didn't clean for Lerner."

"Serial killers generally stick to the same sex."

"It looks like someone's picking off the people in that picture," said Parker.

Just what she'd feared the minute she saw it. Corelli took out her cell phone and pressed the fast dial number for Captain Winfry. She spoke softly. "We have another one." She filled him in.

"Yes. We'll do it informally. Parker and I will leave for Brooklyn in a few minutes. Would you call Captain DiLea at the seven-four to let her know we're on the way and make sure they hold everything for us? Thanks."

She closed the phone, took a deep breath, and went back into the office. Burke was glaring at her.

"Speaker—"

"Call me Kate please. What was that about? Why do I feel you're holding something back?"

"Kate. It gets worse."

"What gets worse?"

"This story." No way to soften this. "Meg Lerner was found murdered this morning, at home, arranged in the same way as Spencer and Nardo."

"Oh, my God. I can't bear it." She sank onto the sofa and covered her face. She could hide her tears but she couldn't suppress the sound of her agonized sobs.

Corelli believed human touch comforted people isolated in their grief so she sat next to Burke and put a hand on her back. When she regained control, Burke looked up. "Please tell me what is going on?"

"Best guess right now is somebody is targeting the people in that picture." *And that means Brett is in danger too.*

"But why? Why us?" Sobbing again.

"I don't know but we need your help. We need to beef up your security and arrange protection for the others until we know who is doing this."

She wiped her eyes. "Tell me what to do."

"First, call Nelson, Abigail, and Gary and tell them what's happening. I want Abigail and Nelson to stay where they are for a couple of days until we figure this out. We'll arrange protection for all three of them just to be sure. Then give me Brett's arrival information. Someone will meet her plane, someone she knows, to explain what's going on and guard her as well. When that's done, we'll talk."

It took a while because Kate kept breaking down and had to repeat the story to Abigail, Nelson, and Gary several times before they could take it in. In each case, Corelli had to get on the phone to clarify the situation and get the information she needed to put protection in place. Burke was a mess when she finished, but she turned to Corelli and said, "Now what?"

"Since it looks like this started after you became speaker, let's begin with that. Do you have any political enemies, anyone who might want to hurt you?"

Burke blew her nose and stared into space. "Lots of enemies. But I can't imagine any of them would kill to get to me. John Collins, a councilman from Queens, thought he should have the speaker's job. He even threatened me in a way. When everybody was congratulating me, he shook my hand and leaned in as if he was offering congratulations, but instead he whispered he would make sure that I lived to regret taking his job from him. Now I'm pushing him on a development in his district so he's really not happy with me."

Burke watched Parker write down what she said. "He's angry. But I can't believe he would do this, something so vindictive, no, something so insane. And what does he gain, unless he kills me?" She shook her head. "Then again, maybe I'm next."

"Anyone else?" Corelli asked.

"Tony DiSilva, the political boss in Staten Island, backed his own candidate against me and wasn't too happy that I won. But we're not talking about the mafia here. These guys have been doing this kind of backroom stuff for years and they don't usually kill the other party if they lose. And Tony is already reaching out to repair our relationship. Nobody else comes to mind."

"What about the Irish group, the ones who try to keep gays and lesbians out of the St. Patrick's Day parade?" Corelli asked.

"Uh-uh. Those guys might be biased but they're not killers. This is beyond the pale."

Parker finished writing and looked up. "That reminds me. In some of those pictures," she pointed to the credenza, "there are people in the background with religious signs. What about them? Any religious guys pestering or threatening or anything?"

Burke shook her head. "These so-called Christians who preach hate are always around gay events, and since I've been speaker there's always someone outside City Hall quoting the Bible and saying terrible things about gays and lesbians. One guy carries a sign that says homosexuals are an abomination and should be killed. But I can't believe that even these hate-filled Christian weirdoes would do something like this. It has to be some real sicko."

Corelli considered how much to tell her. Burke was a politician. She knew how to keep a secret. And Corelli needed her help. "We're checking that out, but this MO is unusual for a serial killer; no extraneous violence, no mutilation, nothing sexual." She waited a minute to give Burke time to take it in.

Corelli wasn't ready to drop the religious angle. "We believe both Nardo and Spencer received threatening phone calls saying homosexuals should be killed. A friend of Nardo's said he referred to them as the 'un-Christians,' out for gay blood. Have you heard anything?"

"Nardo mentioned it, but he didn't seem worried. We deal with this kind of stuff all the time. Especially the gay men."

Some of these so-called Christian groups were fanatics and having spent a couple of years battling religious fanatics in Iraq and Afghanistan, Corelli pushed again. "It could be someone who sees himself as the hand of God, a missionary, doing God's work by getting rid of homosexuals. Maybe you and your friends are the target because you're visible, and you're all successful, wealthy, and attractive."

"But how did he find them? We all have unlisted phone numbers."

"Good question. Maybe the Internet."

"So how can I help?"

"Right now the priority is keeping all of you safe. So we'll take care of Brett. You go straight home tonight and try to get some rest. Are you in an apartment? Is there someone who can stay with you?"

"Yes, a doorman building in the village. My brother will come. But I can't go right home. I have to go to a dinner at the Waldorf."

"Go. Be careful. We'll talk to your security team before we leave. You make sure security stays close at all times, and on the way home pick up your brother. We'll instruct the doorman to keep everyone out and we'll have either your security or a police officer outside your apartment door all night. And tomorrow, make sure your security detail picks you up and stays close whenever you leave City Hall."

"Whatever you say," Burke said, seeming to shrink into exhaustion.

"Please, stay with us a little longer, Kate. There is something else. Mayor Matthews is complicating the investigation by insisting that Mr. Nickerson's case be investigated by the precinct in which he lived. And he'll probably do the same with Ms. Lerner's investigation. He doesn't want us to say the words serial killer. We need a single investigation if we're going to solve this quickly."

Burke sat up, transformed into official mode. "That bastard. Worried about his re-election. I'll take care of it. He can forget support from the gay and lesbian community if he tries to pretend this isn't happening."

"Thank you. And, just so you know, I'm proceeding as if we have a combined investigation."

"That's crazy. You'll jeopardize your job," Burke said.

"My job is important to me, but not as important as stopping this killer."

CHAPTER THIRTY-TWO

Sunday – 10 a.m.

Even with the siren and lots of zigzagging around traffic on Flatbush Avenue, it took almost an hour to get to Meg Lerner's house in Park Slope, Brooklyn. And then they didn't receive a particularly warm welcome from the troops standing around waiting to do their jobs. The MLI from the Medical Examiner's office was particularly outraged at having to wait outside. Wachinski and Santiago, the two detectives who caught the case, were borderline hostile, but they had followed the order to keep the scene intact for Corelli and Parker to examine before the MLI and CSU began to work.

They led Corelli and Parker into Meg Lerner's house, a four-story brownstone facing Prospect Park. Walking into the first-floor hallway they faced a restored wooden staircase on the right and a hallway with two doors on the left. The first room contained a desk and computer, bookcases, file cabinets, and a small table with four chairs, obviously her office. The white-tiled bathroom with a tub, shower, and closets was between the office and a large sunny bedroom with a king-sized bed. French doors opened to a backyard with a gigantic barbecue, picnic table, and lawn chairs in a well-tended garden. Corelli gave it all a quick look. She faced the two detectives. "I'm not here to do your job or get in your way. I'm only interested in the scene. "Where is she?"

Wachinski looked dubious. "Fourth floor, her studio." He and Santiago started up the stairs.

Corelli and Parked followed.

On the fourth floor, they stopped to put on protective gear. When Wachinski opened the door to the studio, they were blasted with sunlight, a wave of heat, and the ripe smell of death. Even with the air conditioner running, the sun had hastened the deterioration of the body. Corelli assessed the room: all four walls were brick up to about three feet, then glass to the ceiling, which had four skylights—north, south, east, and west. You couldn't get better light than this. Paintings in various stages of completion were mounted on the four easels scattered around the large room. Built into the lower walls were raw wood storage racks jammed with paintings that Corelli estimated would be valued in the multimillions based on the last time she'd priced a Lerner painting. Probably much, much more now that she was dead. Two large cabinets with narrow drawers she assumed contained more drawings and paintings not yet framed stood near the only place to sit in the room, a dilapidated sofa facing the easels. The copious paint splatters dotting everything in the room—the floor, the easels, the tables next to each easel, the cabinets, the sofa, and Meg Lerner—echoed the vitality in Lerner's art.

Corelli and Parker moved into the studio. Wachinski and Santiago watched from the doorway. She couldn't see the bullet hole in Lerner's cerebellum, but she had no doubt it was there. Lerner lay on the sofa under one of the skylights, posed in the same manner as her two good friends, rosary in her hands, the ashes of incense in a burner on the nearest table, and Gregorian chants playing on an endless loop. The clock radio CD player on the floor near an outlet was very different than the players in the other victims' homes. Lerner had on a T-shirt, jeans, and sneakers all splotched with paint as were her hands and arms. A glass of red wine was on a small table next to the sofa.

When she and Parker had studied, photographed, and diagrammed the scene, Corelli turned to the two local detectives. "Thanks. You can bring the CSU and the MLI up here now."

"I'll let them know." Santiago left the studio.

"Who found her?"

"A friend." Wachinski looked at his notes. "Um, Amelia Freestone."

"Is she still here?" Corelli asked Wachinski, who seemed to be the primary.

"In the living room."

"We'd like to talk to her."

"You can try," Wachinski said, "but she hasn't said a word since she called 911."

He led them down. A quick look on the third floor revealed two bedrooms separated by a bathroom. The second floor opened into the dining room and a table set with two plates, a platter of olives, grape leaves, and dried-up cheese, a tray of crackers, and a single glass of red wine. Like Spencer Nickerson, Lerner had expected her killer. In these narrow buildings the rooms were railroad style, one led to another, so they continued through the modern kitchen into the living room. The dark blue walls and the matching blue plush carpet were offset by the covers of the books lining two walls. A large sofa patterned with various shades of blue and a matching easy chair faced a huge HDTV. A set of French doors led out to a deck. The picture of Meg with her friends on the steps of City Hall was prominently displayed on the coffee table along with some large art books.

Corelli and Parker moved into the living room, past the female officer watching the woman. Santiago returned and he and Wachinski stood next to the uniform.

Amelia Freestone huddled in one corner of the sofa staring at the TV, but whatever she was seeing was in her head because the screen was blank. Grabbing the blue and gold chenille throw draped over the easy chair, Corelli covered Freestone and sat next to her on the sofa. Parker took the chair on Freestone's other side and waited. Corelli found Freestone's hand under the throw and enclosed it in her own hands, rubbing gently. She knew not to rush the woman who most likely was in shock, so she didn't speak. Parker followed her lead. The detectives and the officer standing behind them near the door whispered and shifted impatiently. Corelli shot a warning look over her shoulder. After a few minutes, Freestone turned to Corelli.

"How is Meg? Is she...?" Her breath hitched.

"Amelia," Corelli said, pressing her hand firmly, trying to hold her attention. "Meg is dead. I'm sorry."

"Why?"

Corelli spoke softly. "I don't know but we'll find out. What happened this morning?"

Freestone was motionless. Her eyes were closed. She didn't speak.

Parker threw a dirty look toward the doorway, a warning to stop the coughing and shifting and whispering. After almost five minutes, Freestone opened her eyes. "I stopped by with her food and stuff. I let myself in with my keys because Meg is usually in her studio and never hears the bell when she's painting. I put the things in the refrigerator and walked upstairs to the studio to see if she wanted to stop to have a cup of coffee and a bagel with me. As soon as I opened the door, I smelled something really bad, but sometimes she forgets food in the studio, and with all that sun, it rots. I started to scold her." Freestone looked like she was going to be sick. "Oh, god, she was on the sofa in the sunlight." She swallowed. "At first I thought she was sick. I mean, she never sits when she's in the studio and she was just lying there. I went over to see if she was awake and she looked...and the smell wasn't rotting food...I knew something was terribly wrong so I called 911." Freestone spoke in a monotone.

"Try not to think about it, Amelia." Corelli knew it would be a long time before the poor woman got that image out of her mind but she needed her to focus.

"Did you touch anything?"

She shook her head. "I was going to touch her shoulder to...to wake her, but I could see she was...It wasn't her anymore. I backed away to call 911."

"Was the front door locked when you came in?"

Her eyes clouded over and her lids fluttered. Corelli feared she'd lost her but then she responded.

"No. The dead bolt on the top wasn't locked. The bottom was locked but not double-locked. Meg was pretty careful about locking up, because, you know, she was like unconscious when she was painting, so if somebody came in she wouldn't even notice."

Corelli glanced at Wachinski to confirm they were taking notes. Satisfied, she turned back to Freestone. "You brought food?"

"Meg would starve to death if someone didn't think about food for her, so she pays me to shop and cook. Every Monday, Wednesday and Friday I bring her pre-cooked meals she can just heat, and wine and other necessities. Sunday mornings, I bring her bagels and lox and other stuff from the deli. I'm an artist too but I don't make money like she does. The arrangement helps her and gives me more than enough to live on so I can paint."

"When did you last see Meg?"

"Friday night. We eat together every Friday when I bring the food."

"What time did you leave?"

"About nine, I think. I have an early yoga class on Saturdays. And she locked the door after me when I left."

"Did she mention any threats or phone calls? Did she seem troubled?"

"No she seemed fine. Happy about finishing the last of a series of paintings. And excited about a show she was planning with her work and the work of unknown women artists she was mentoring. She asked me to be in the show. After I calmed down, we talked about the art scene in the city, the usual stuff."

"Were you lovers?"

"I'm not a lesbian. Meg and I have been friends since junior high school."

Corelli turned to Wachinski. "Do you have any questions?"

He exchanged a look with Santiago, who shook his head. "Nothing right now except name, address, and phone."

Freestone provided the information. "An officer will drive you home," Corelli said. "Is there someone we can call to meet you there?"

Freestone nodded. "My boyfriend, T.J. James." She handed her cell phone to Corelli who passed it to the female police officer. They left Freestone sitting there facing the blank TV.

Corelli briefed Wachinski and Santiago on the other two murders and asked them to meet with her team later. She had already cleared it with the precinct commander, but she knew it wouldn't work if she couldn't get them on board. They agreed warily.

CHAPTER THIRTY-THREE

Sunday – 7 p.m.

"Listen up people. We've got another one." She waited until the uproar died down. "A woman, Meg Lerner, in Park Slope, Brooklyn, but the MO is the same." She brought them up to date. "Detectives Wachinski and Santiago, standing near the door, from the seven-four will focus on Lerner."

Wachinski raised his hand. "Preliminary TOD is sometime after eleven Friday night.

The autopsy is on the schedule for tomorrow afternoon so we should have a better estimate then."

Watkins raised his hand. "Are we dropping the del Balzo angle and considering this a serial killer?"

"Yes. But if this is a serial killer, he's not run-of-the-mill." Corelli walked to the whiteboard. She drew a line across the top and then another line down the center to create two columns. She wrote on top of the left, Serial Killer, and on top of the right, Our Guy. "So what do we know about serial killers? Anyone?"

Hei-kyoung Kim, known affectionately as Heiki, put up her hand. "They take a long time between victims."

"As time goes by the time between victims decreases," said Charleen Greene.

"Often stalk victims for some time," said Dietz.

"Generally go for either men or women, not both," said Watkins.

"Use excessive violence," said Wachinski, "more than necessary to kill."

"Sexually motivated. And often they sexually mutilate the corpse," said Parker.

Corelli finished writing the characteristics in the Serial Killer column.

"Anything else?" Corelli asked, looking around the room for raised hands. "What about often poses the body?"

"Right," someone agreed.

"Okay. Let's see how our guy stacks up." She went down the list filling in the Our Guy column. Three victims in three days; doing both men and women; minimal, not excessive violence; nothing sexual; no mutilation; poses the bodies. She put the marker down and turned back to the group. We're checking to see whether this kind of ritual posing has occurred elsewhere, but if this is a serial killer, he hasn't read *Serial Killing for Dummies*."

While the team absorbed the information, Corelli picked up the photograph they'd taken from Burke's office. "Our guy has killed three people, but I'm going to go out on a limb and say I don't think we're dealing with a serial killer per se. These killings seem too personal to me. Our killer is picking off the close friends of Kate Burke, Speaker of the City Council, the first woman and lesbian to hold that position. We believe he's using this picture to identify the victims." She held the picture up, then handed it off to be passed around.

"Why?" a voice from the back.

Corelli shrugged. "If we knew why, we'd have our killer."

"Could be a hate crime," said Charleen Greene.

"Could be. But think about it. It doesn't appear to be robbery, though Nickerson and Lerner were wealthy. There was no sign of a struggle at any of the scenes and no defensive wounds on any of the vics. It looks like the three of them knew the killer, or at least had no reason to fear him. Nickerson and Lerner had prepared cheese and crackers and wine so they were probably expecting the visit. We think the killer is using Nardo's gun. But how did the killer know Nardo had a gun and where he kept it? Any ideas? Questions? Comments?"

The room was quiet except for the rustling of paper and scraping of chairs.

Watkins spoke. "Maybe the del Balzo murder was spur of the moment. The perp took advantage of what was there, and he liked it so much he decided to do it again. And again. Only now he brings the gun and the rosaries and the incense and the CD player."

"Yes, he brings those things. But why these vics? It's certainly not random." Corelli put her hand up to cut off the buzz of conversation.

"We do have a couple of leads. Both Councilman Collins from Queens and Tony DiSilvo, the Staten Island boss, actively opposed Speaker Burke. The councilman actually threatened her. We need to find out what they've been up to." She looked at Dietz, "Send somebody to Staten Island to question DiSilvo. Parker and I will meet with Collins at City Hall."

Corelli ran her fingers through her hair. "Also, Burke confirmed Nardo and Nickerson were getting calls from somebody quoting the Bible and threatening to kill them. Parker spotted a couple of guys waving Kill the Homo signs in the background of one of Burke's pictures and The *Daily World* has offered to pull photos and articles and send them over. We need to identify them and bring them in ASAP."

She looked around the room. "Couple more things. The vics' names appeared in the article but Burke says their telephone numbers are unlisted, so how did the killer find them? We need to check the Internet to see if that information is available. Also, the first rosary was expensive, had a gold crucifix and cut-glass beads and probably belonged to del Balzo. That confirms Ron's theory about spur of the moment because the other two were cheaper versions. The rosaries, the CD player, or CDs may lead us to him. If he's targeted everybody in the picture, he must have bought multiple rosaries, CDs, and players. Find out where he's getting them. Maybe a clerk will remember somebody buying that many, or god forbid, more."

Forlini raised his hand. "You can buy incense on the street so that's not traceable. And you can get those cheap clock radio CD players in any chain drugstore. Since there's about one store per block in the city, he could buy one at each store and nobody would notice."

"Probably true, but we have to try," Corelli said. "We need more volunteers to hit the gay bars later tonight, see if we pick up anything about this religious guy." No response. Homophobia or just fear of being labeled? "Come on guys, just a couple of drinks and chat. This is important. Don't make me decide because I'm sure to screw somebody's plans for the evening." She looked around. Three hands went up. "A couple more please. Good. Have a good time."

She stood and stretched.

"Hey Corelli, you and your brother getting any threats? I mean, you're in the picture too," Heiki asked.

"Which picture?"

Heiki walked over holding the picture Corelli had passed around. She put it on the table and placed a small magnifying glass on it.

Corelli stared at the picture. "Oh, my God." She dropped into her chair. "It's not me. That's my younger sister, Simone, and my nephew Nicky. The three of us look a lot alike. We were so focused on Burke's friends that we didn't examine the background. The steps of City Hall were reserved for VIPs. What the hell were they doing there?"

Corelli swiveled to Parker who was standing behind her and was surprised to see she looked as shaken as Corelli felt. "Parker, call Burke, see if she knows why they were there."

She took a deep breath. "Do you have the list of tasks, Dietz?" He waved his notebook. "I got it all, don't worry."

"Okay. In honor of our Brooklyn colleagues, I propose we have only one daily meeting, at seven p.m., unless there's an objection—"

"Oh, please, let's keep it at seven a.m. I love getting up at five," Forlini said.

Corelli laughed and held up her hand to still the roar of protests that followed.

"Suck it up, Forlini, we'll go with seven p.m. Wachinski, Santiago, Watkins, Greene, and Kim, with me. Everybody else see Dietz if you need an assignment. Thanks guys, see you tomorrow night."

Bedlam returned as the team moved around the room, discussing the case and cracking jokes. Wachinski and Santiago approached Corelli warily.

"You know what to do, so go do it. Let Dietz know if you need resources and keep us in the loop. See you seven tomorrow night." Two sets of shoulders relaxed. Probably feared she would micromanage them.

When the two detectives walked away, Kim, Watkins, and Greene approached. "Good catch, Heiki. Parker and I will follow up with those two. How far did you get with del Balzo's alibi for Tuesday night?"

"But he's in the clear now, right?" asked Heiki. "I mean if it's a serial or some other nut."

"Maybe. But I'm not ready to drop him as a suspect yet."

"A guy from the Turkish delegation said he looked all over for del Balzo before dessert, around ten, but he was nowhere to be found. Then I talked to a young woman, Francoise somebody from the French delegation, and she confirmed his alibi. But my gut tells me they have a thing going," Heiki said.

Was it worth wasting a resource on the ambassador? Corelli didn't feel comfortable letting it go yet. She hoped it wasn't just a reaction to his homophobia.

"Be discreet but see what you can dig up about that. And try to find out what the ambassador was doing Friday night between seven or eight and midnight. Ask Dietz when you're ready for something else."

"No problema," Heiki said, clicking her heels and saluting.

Laughing, Corelli speed-dialed Simone's cell as Heiki strolled away. She was shunted to voice mail. "Simone, this is Chiara. I want you and Nicky at my apartment tonight at ten, no ifs ands or buts. Just do it. It's critical that I speak to both of you. Plan to sleep over." She knew she sounded angry but it was the fear. At least their names weren't in the article.

She turned to speak to Watkins and Greene. Parker was already huddled with them. "Watkins—"

"Yes, boss. Parker told us Brett Cummings is flying into JFK from Tokyo tomorrow night. Brett, huh? I'll be darned. Like a bad penny. We'll get the flight number and time from her office and meet her."

"Don't be a wise guy. She knows you, so it may make it a little easier for her. I don't want her left alone. Take her to her apartment and stay with her until someone replaces you."

"Sure."

"And during the day tomorrow please follow up on the Nickerson autopsy. Ask Dietz for a couple of people to help you, and Greene check out the staff at Nickerson's office."

As they walked away, Parker said, "I spoke to Burke's office. Nicky and Simone were guests of Spencer Nickerson."

"Nickerson? How the—"

"Everything all right?" Dietz said.

"I hope so." She leaned in close to him. "I still want the research on the del Balzos. But the fewer who know about it, the better. Keep the articles locked in your desk until I ask for them."

"You got it," Dietz said. "I'll lock up what we find with the I-talian magazines we got outta del Balzo's place."

"Hey, Corelli, big homo demo in front of City Hall," a male voice called out.

Homo? We need to do some consciousness-raising here.

"If this is what I think it is, Burke is a magician. Let's get over to One Police Plaza, Parker. We can update the chief and have a front row seat for the demo."

When they arrived at his office, his door was open and Chief Harry Broderick stood at the window staring down. The murmur of a female voice pulled Corelli's attention to the far wall where the screen of a large TV twinkled with pinpoints of light. She knocked.

"Come in."

Corelli and Parker joined him at the windows. Below them thousands of candles flickered in the early dark as people gathered in City Hall Park and overflowed into the nearby streets. The chanting sounded gentle in the distance. It was mesmerizing.

Broderick turned to Corelli. "Is this Burke's work?"

"She said she would take care of the mayor, but I didn't expect a demonstration or anything so soon. And it looks like she got the media out too. That'll definitely get Matthew's attention."

"Nice ploy, that press conference, Corelli. Nevertheless, I expect you've turned Nickerson over to Benson?"

She cleared her throat. "Chief."

He turned from the window.

"You know that Meg Lerner, the artist, was murdered in Brooklyn, right?"

"What has that got to do with Nickerson?"

"Lerner, del Balzo, and Nickerson are three of Burke's closest friends and they were all murdered and then posed in exactly the same way." She hesitated, giving him time to take it in. "The three killings are definitely the work of one man."

"Shit."

She showed him the picture. "Now the other six are at risk, at least six that we know of, and we need to solve this quickly. I'm taking the other two cases, with or without the mayor's approval. Or yours."

"Don't be foolish. You're jeopardizing your job. Matthews will use it to get rid of you."

"And if he does, I'll go to the media. I won't let his political aspirations jeopardize the investigation. Besides, there's something else. It turns out my sister and nephew are also in that picture." She pointed to the two figures standing next to Spencer Nickerson. "Their names weren't in the article but…" She shrugged. "Anyway, I can't wait for any more people to be murdered, whether it's more gays and lesbians or my nephew or my sister. I'm not asking for your approval, Harry. This is a unilateral decision."

He glared at her. "Just a couple of months ago you were dying to get back to work. Now you're ready to risk your job?"

She shrugged and smiled. "You know me. I don't have a choice. Even if it wasn't personal, I couldn't stand by and watch the bodies mount up just to save myself."

"Sure. It's the right thing."

"Sarcasm doesn't become you, Harry," she said, echoing his comment to her several months ago.

He picked up the phone. "I'd better call the chief so he can warn the commissioner and the mayor. Even if we are ignoring his orders, it'll be better if he isn't caught with his pants down."

Corelli smirked. "I hear Matthews pulls them down every chance he gets." She was sure that was the real source of her problem with the mayor. He had hit on her and she had rebuffed him. She wasn't interested in men, especially married men. "And, not we, Harry. Not you. Not Parker. Only me."

Corelli stared at the flickering candles as the chief made the call. Was she just being provocative, or did she have to do this, in this way? Not provocative. A killer was picking off gays and lesbians and she wouldn't be able to live with herself if she let turf battles or egos or elections get in the way of neutralizing him before he could murder again.

"Corelli." Parker interrupted her thoughts. "Please don't speak for me."

She met Parker's eyes. "You're willing to jeopardize your career?"

"Are you?" Parker shot back.

"Yes, but—"

"But what? Do you think I'm a coward? Or maybe you think my career is more important to me than stopping some son of a bitch who is killing innocent people, some like Brett and Simone and Nicky, whom I know and care about?"

Parker surprises me again. "I'm sorry, I didn't mean to imply anything about you. I just didn't want to pull you into the leaky rowboat with me."

"I appreciate that. But I repeat, don't presume to speak for me." Parker held Corelli's eyes until Corelli offered a small smile and a two-finger salute. "Welcome aboard the SS Sinking Ship." Parker nodded. They both turned to the TV at the sound of Kate Burke's voice.

Burke stood at a podium facing the bright lights and a dozen or more microphones. Her eyes were puffy and she looked exhausted, but she stood straight and spoke with resolve. "We've gathered tonight to mourn three wonderful, giving, tax-paying citizens of New York City, three of my closest friends, two gay men and a lesbian murdered in their own homes in less than a week. The three murders were done in exactly the same manner, with the victims…" She took a deep breath. "…with each of them posed exactly the same. When I pressed her, Detective Chiara Corelli agreed the murders were very likely committed by the same person. But," she paused for effect, "but," she paused again and looked from person to person to person in the audience and then straight out to the cameras. "I was shocked to find out that her team is officially investigating only one of the cases. In fact, the eighteenth precinct where Spencer Nickerson, a brilliant software entrepreneur, lived, is taking control of that case. And the murder of lesbian artist Meg Lerner," she stopped to blink back the tears, "is being handled by the seventy-fourth precinct in Brooklyn. This is not to denigrate the detectives at the eighteenth or seventy-fourth precincts, but clearly these murders are not separate incidents, and common sense tells us a single investigation is absolutely necessary if this sick killer is to be found and stopped before he..." She brushed the tears from her eyes. "Before he kills another innocent victim." Now she raised her voice. "Gays and lesbians are being targeted. Everything that can be done to stop this vile deviant must be done. And a combined investigation is the most expeditious way to bring this murderer to justice. The gay community demands it. NOW!"

The crowd erupted in a chant, fists raised. "One investigation! Now!"

"At least Burke's on our side," Broderick said. "Let's see what kind of clout she really has." He moved toward his desk. "Shut that thing off, would you?"

"Wait. Look. Mayor Asshole." Mayor Ricky Matthews strutted out of City Hall and headed for the spotlight, in front of the microphones where Kate Burke was standing. He leaned over, his mouth close to her ear, and said something. She listened. A smile flashed. She nodded and handed him the microphone.

"Let me say how sorry I am that these three fine members of your community, of the New York community, have been murdered. I will do everything in my power to ensure that the murderer is hunted down and punished. Not ten minutes ago, I spoke with George Neil, the Commissioner of Police, about combining the investigations. Detective Chiara Corelli of the eighth precinct has already assumed responsibility for the three cases and she and her team will have my full support in solving these crimes."

Corelli smiled. Matthews was slick. He didn't lie but he made it sound like it was his idea. Oh well, now he couldn't fire her and Parker for doing it.

Kate Burke reached for the microphone, leaving him no option but to stop speaking and hand it over. She thanked him and everyone who attended the rally on such short notice, and she ended with brief prayers from a minister, a rabbi, a priest, and an Imam. *That's New York.*

CHAPTER THIRTY-FOUR

Sunday – 10 p.m.

They'd agreed in the car that Parker would take the lead with the kids to keep it more professional, less personal.

Corelli was already upset as they rode the elevator up to her apartment. "I'm going to kill that kid."

Parker gave her a weird look. "Is this the PTSD talking?"

"Give me a break, Parker. It's a figure of speech. But no matter how many times I remind Simone, she forgets to lock the elevator door. Anybody could walk in."

The music was blaring when they stepped into the loft, but Simone and Nicky were not there. She spotted the two of them asleep on the floor behind the sofa. The kittens were curled up on Simone's chest. Corelli strode to the stereo and shut it off.

Two heads popped up, eyes wide. "Shit, auntie, you scared me," Nicky said.

Corelli stood over them, hands on her hips. "You should be scared, Nicky."

"I guess we fell asleep." Simone gently moved the sleeping kittens to the floor and stood to hug Corelli and greet Parker. Nicky did the same.

"Mom sent some food and we've been waiting for you to eat." She pointed to the table set for four.

"Looks like a feast," Corelli said. "Let's eat and talk."

"You sounded angry, sis," Simone said, pulling out her chair. "Did we do something?"

Corelli took the picture out of her briefcase before pouring herself a glass of wine from the bottle the kids had opened. "Wine, Parker?"

"No thanks, I'll eat but I'm driving so I'll just take some water."

"Why should we be scared?" Nicky said, reaching for the wine.

Corelli hesitated, then gave him the bottle. They weren't going anywhere tonight. They were so innocent, these two nineteen-year-olds. She didn't want to frighten them, but they needed to know. She handed the picture to Simone who looked at it and passed it to Nicky.

"What were the two of you doing there, on the steps with the VIPs?"

They exchanged a glance. "We were invited," Simone said, "by someone we know."

"And who would that be?"

"Spencer Nickerson?" Simone said, her voice going up at the end of his name, making it a question.

"And how—"

"Auntie, don't yell at Simone. He's a friend of mine." He coughed. "I met him through a group I belong to at college, a, uh, a…" He flushed, "a gay group."

It took all her highly developed detective skills to keep her face blank and her voice even. "You're gay?" She took a sip of wine to cover her surprise.

He flushed again. "Yes."

Chiara looked at her sister. "Simone?"

Nicky jumped in. "No, she's not. She was just with me." Though Simone was his aunt, they were only months apart in age and were best friends.

She focused on Nicky. "Were you and Spencer lovers?"

"Are you kidding? He would never fool around with a kid like me. He works with gay kids at the college, you know, helping them to come to terms with it. He wanted us to meet role models so he invited a couple of us to City Hall and to the party to celebrate Kate becoming speaker. I asked if I could bring Simone since she's interested in politics."

Corelli downed her glass of wine and poured another. She was dumbstruck. Patrizia would go berserk when she found out. "Does anyone in the family know besides Simone?"

"No. My mom will probably kill me."

Both kids looked anxious.

Maybe it's in the blood. "It's okay, Nicky. You know she accepted me and Marnie. Well, sort of. If she hadn't met Marnie and liked her before she realized we were lovers, it would have been a lot harder. Then, when she figured it out, she decided Marnie was the lesbian, not me." She took his hand. "I agree, she'll probably go nuts. At first. Then she'll blame me. And, eventually, she'll realize you're still her loving son."

Parker cleared her throat and the two kids turned toward her. "Spencer, Nardo, and Meg have been murdered in the past couple of days. We think the killer is going after everyone in that picture, so we're afraid you two might be in danger."

Simone choked on her wine. Nicky paled and his eyes filled with tears. "Spencer was such a great guy."

"But why would *we* be in danger?" Simone asked, having recovered.

"We don't know," Parker said. "Did either of you give your name or address to anybody at the rally?"

"Just to Spencer so he could put us on the list. Right Nicky?" He nodded.

The list. If Kate's enemy Councilman Collins was the killer, he would have access to the list. And he knew she was checking on him. If he connected Simone to her… "Find out who has access to the list, Parker. See if you can get Burke on her cell."

Parker walked to the sofa to get some privacy while she made the call.

Corelli moved behind Nicky and put her arms around him. She kissed the top of his head. "How long have you known?"

He looked at Simone. "About three years?" She nodded.

"I'm sorry I haven't been more observant, but I love you, and I'm here to help. We'll deal with your mom later. Right now being gay is secondary to your safety. I'd like you to stay here in my apartment for the next few days, until we figure out what's going on. If you lock the elevator when you're here, you'll be safe. Is that okay?"

"No classes tomorrow, but we need our books and stuff for homework," said Nicky.

"Parker and I will drive you home to pick up some clothes and books tomorrow."

The teens exchanged a glance. "If you think that's best, auntie," Nicky said.

"I do." With their safety arranged, Corelli relaxed. "Did you talk to anyone at the party?"

Now that he could be open, Nicky couldn't stop grinning. "Yeah, it was funny. The mayor and Kate Burke and her friend Brett thought Simone was you at first. And they thought we were twins until I told them she's my auntie." He lightly punched Simone's arm. "Brett said something about you, Auntie Chi. Do you remember what it was, Simone?"

Simone threw a piece of bread at him. "She said she'd met you recently and you'd touched her heart. I thought that was sweet. She's definitely interested in you, sis. She was real nice, looked after us. I liked her a lot. You have my permission to date her." Simone grinned. "I also talked to Kate. She offered me an internship with her next summer if I'm interested, so I talked to some of the people who work for her, to find out about the work. We both talked to Abby and Nelson and Nardo and Meg and Spencer and some of the other kids from Nicky's group. Anybody else you can think of Nick?"

He shook his head. "You got them all."

Parker joined the group. "Burke says just her office and security had the list. But the night security guys didn't know anything about it. I'll have to call tomorrow morning."

"Let's eat and call it a day, Parker. Nicky and Simone are going to stay here for the next few days."

After Parker left and the kids had gone to their separate bedrooms, Corelli stood at the window thinking about what they'd said about Brett and her friends. It was unfortunate Simone and Nicky were in that picture and possibly targets, but the experience was positive for both of them. For some stupid reason, knowing Brett had taken care of her sister and her nephew made her happy. And hearing the others in the group were also considerate of the kids deepened her sadness at their loss. Although whoever was targeting this close-knit circle of friends was not a traditional serial killer, he had to be sick. She felt better knowing Nicky and Simone would be safe in her apartment but she worried about protecting Brett and her remaining friends.

She felt the needle prick of kitten claws on her legs and picked up the kittens to keep them from climbing up her legs. She sat with them on her lap and they immediately curled up. She ran her hands over them, smoothing their fur, fingering their delicate ears. "What am I going to do with you guys?" There was something comforting about the warmth of their bodies, their softness, and gentle rumble of their purring. They helped her center. She smiled at herself. Other veterans had service dogs but she had two service kitties and she wasn't even embarrassed. She was hooked and probably should name them before they got too much older. Maybe she could get Darla to do a news feature on them and solicit names.

Her mind went back to Brett. She didn't need Simone to tell her Brett was interested in her but it was nice to hear Brett was thinking of her. She shook her head. Maybe she was hooked there too.

CHAPTER THIRTY-FIVE

Sunday – 12 a.m.

Instead of calling it a day, Parker headed for 125th Street and Hattie's Harlem Inn. Earlier in the day she'd left a message for Randall Young, the man who claimed to be her father, telling him to meet her there at midnight.

Being in Corelli's loft tonight had made her realize how much she loved the bright colors, the warm, homey feel, and the sunlight that streamed in through the huge windows during the day. Maybe it was time to give up the dreary one-bedroom apartment she'd come to think of as her rat hole, a place to run and hide from life. She couldn't afford anything as big or as nice as Corelli's loft, but she would take her time and find a large one- or two-bedroom apartment, a place with light, that she could make into a home. She smiled. It was time she stopped waiting for something she couldn't define.

Now she sat in a booth at Hattie's facing the door, gnawing her cuticles, bouncing her foot, and glancing every now and then at Jesse seated on a stool at the bar. Although he seemed to be watching the band, each time she looked, he gave a sneaky little wave and lifted his glass to her. Her hands shook as she fixed the coffee the waitress dropped off. Damn. Why was she nervous? She hadn't spoken to Young, just left a voice mail. If he was her father, why show up now? As far as she knew he could be a drug dealer, or he may have murdered her mother. In any case, he was probably just a scammer. She'd meet him, hear what he had to say, and unless she learned something that led her to believe he murdered her mother, be done with him.

A tall, well-dressed man appeared in the entryway and surveyed the crowd. Her stomach clenched and the rancid taste of bile filled her mouth. Serve him right if she threw up on him. She smiled at the fantasy. He headed for her table. No hesitation. Knows what she looks like. She unsnapped her holster. She didn't expect any trouble in here, but just to be safe.

Then he was there looming over her.

"Detective Parker, I'm Randall Young. Thank you for meeting with me. May I sit?"

"Yes."

He folded himself into the booth, clasped his hands on the table and studied her. "It's strange for me to meet you. I can't imagine what it's like for you."

"What makes you think you're my father?" she asked, bypassing pleasantries.

"You look exactly like the woman I think is your mother." He reached into his jacket. She drew her weapon but kept it under the table. Jesse slipped off the stool and moved quickly toward them. Randall withdrew an envelope from his pocket and slid it across the table to her, then clasped his hands again. "She's younger than you in the pictures but you are the image of Tasha. When I saw your picture in the newspaper, I was pretty sure."

She slipped the gun back into the holster as Jesse veered away from the table. Her heart was pounding so hard she was sure it would escape her chest. Was it audible on the other side of the table? She looked at Young, then lowered her eyes to the envelope. Tasha was her mother's name. No one had ever told Parker she looked like her mother. And the only pictures of Tasha she'd ever seen were the ones in the murder book of her unsolved case, which showed a decomposing, bloated corpse with a face battered beyond recognition. She swallowed, glanced at Young again, then lifted the flap of the envelope and slid the pictures out. The girl in the first picture was sitting on a swing in a playground, smiling at someone. Aside from the hairstyle and the dress, it could have been Parker. Her hand shaking, she put the first picture aside. In the next picture, a younger version of Randall Young towered above the vibrant young woman and they smiled at each other like two people in love. In the third picture, the boy and the girl, both smiling broadly, stood side by side wearing caps and gowns and holding diplomas. Tasha was alone in the last picture, sitting on a park bench reading, a pile of books next to her. Parker felt light-headed.

Randall Young studied her. "Would you like a drink?"

She nodded. "Bourbon on the rocks." He went to the bar and returned with her drink and a beer for himself. He placed the bourbon in front of her, careful not to get the pictures wet.

She sipped her drink. "When were these pictures taken?" She slid them back into the envelope and pushed it toward him.

He pushed the envelope back toward her. "These copies are for you." He took a swig of beer. "June, thirty-one years ago, when we graduated from high school. When were you born?"

She didn't answer. She was born thirty years ago in May. Could it be true?

"Which high school?" Not that she knew her mother had gone to high school, or where.

"Holy Trinity in Harlem. We were eighteen and in love. I had no job and no prospects so I enlisted in the marines after graduation. I wanted to get married before I left, but Tasha wanted to wait until we could afford a real wedding. We agreed we'd save and get married when I finished boot camp." He lifted the bottle to drink but stared into space, as if remembering.

"So what happened?"

He drank. "We were both ambitious kids, intent on making our way in the world, and we had managed to avoid the mistake many of our friends made, until the month before I left. Maybe it was anxiety about the separation or maybe because we knew we were getting married. I don't know. But whatever the reason, we had sex. It was wonderful. We were so much in love. A month later I left for Quantico. We agreed to write every day."

"And?"

"And, I got a letter every day. Tasha found a job and had started buying things for our apartment. Then I got a letter telling me she was pregnant. She was really excited, and so was I. Then she stopped writing and my letters started coming back, addressee unknown. I tried to call but their phone was disconnected. I kept writing but never got an answer. I still have the letters. Anyway, I was angry. I figured she'd met somebody else. When basic training was over, I came back to find out." He seemed to go inward for a minute, as if picturing what he was about to describe.

"I don't know how she is now or whether she's even alive, but in those days, her mother, your grandmother, was a drunk and out of it much of the time. It took me almost a week to find her awake and semi-coherent, but she was positively glowing with spite and hatred when she told me Tasha had met a rich man and had gone away with him. I was devastated. I left town that night and didn't come back until a few months ago."

Well that sure sounded like her grandmother, but then again he could have found that out by talking to people in her old neighborhood.

"I made a career in the marines, married and had two daughters. We lived in Florida. My wife died two years ago. I retired in June as a major and had a hankering to come back to New York. I tried to look up Tasha, but I haven't been able to find her or anyone who knows what happened to her. I couldn't locate your grandmother, and your uncle Al hasn't returned any of my calls.

Good old Uncle Aloysius T. Parker. How much did he know and why keep it from her?

"Then, I saw your picture on the front of the *New York Daily World*. For a minute, I thought it was Tasha, but when I saw the age and the name I suspected you might be my daughter. She never mentioned me to you?"

"What do you want from me?"

"Nothing. I don't expect you to open your arms and say welcome home daddy. But I would appreciate your mother's address. I want to talk to her, try to understand what happened."

"My mother is dead. She was murdered when I was three. She was selling drugs." Parker couldn't hide her anger and the bitterness.

The color drained from his face. "I am so sorry. I didn't know." He signaled the waitress over. "A beer and a shot of Dewars for me. Anything for you, Detective?"

Parker shook her head.

Neither spoke until his drinks were placed in front of him and he had downed the shot. He leaned forward. "No way. Tasha wanted to be a lawyer; no way would she sell drugs. Unless she was desperate."

They stared at each other. He lowered his eyes. "I'm so sorry. Who brought you up?"

"My aunt Tiffany, the heroin addict, but she OD'd a year later, then my grandmother, the alcoholic, for a couple of years until Social Services decided she was unfit. Then, Uncle Aloysius and Aunt Mariah adopted me."

"Sweet Jesus. If I had known, there's no way I would have left any child of mine with your aunt or your grandmother. Sorry. I don't mean to insult—"

"No problem. You can't say anything worse than I've thought and said about them."

"I'm glad your uncle took you in. At least, you had a good upbringing."

Right. All the comforts of home, except when he wasn't ignoring me, he treated me like trash.

"I know you go by P.J., but do you mind my asking what your real name is?"

"You tell me. What do you think your beloved Tasha would have called her daughter, your daughter?"

His eyes went to the beer bottle he was rotating in his hands, and he didn't speak for a few minutes. She glanced over at Jesse, who was totally focused on them.

"Well, it's just a guess. I didn't think she would make it your legal name. When she told me she was pregnant, we were both so happy. She referred to you as our 'precious jewel.'"

Parker felt the blood drain out of her. She stared at him. Could it be? Or had he looked up her birth certificate? No, once she changed her name legally, the old birth certificate would have been destroyed. Wouldn't it?

"Looks like I'm correct," he said. "If we had our DNA tested, we'd know for sure."

"Why bother? I've lived my entire life without you. I don't need a father now."

"Proud. Just like your mother. Not that I blame you for being bitter. I can't undo the past, but maybe we could start from where we are and get to know each other. Think about it and call me if you change your mind." He put some money on the table and stood. "Thank you for your time, Detective Parker."

"Wait."

He stopped.

"How would you feel if I told you I was a lesbian?"

"I'd feel fine. You can check with my daughter Noreen, your half-sister. She's been out as a lesbian since she was sixteen. She's happy, I'm happy."

She nodded. "Thanks."

"The ball is in your court. Give me a call if you want to talk again." He walked away.

Jesse took his place at the table. "So?"

"I don't know." She pushed the envelope toward him.

He whistled. "She sure looks like you."

"He wants me to take a DNA test. But I need to track down my drunken bitch of a grandmother before I do anything else."

"I know where she is."

"You do?"

"I've kept track of her over the years."

She sat back. "Why?"

"Because, as awful as she is, she's your grandmother. I just wanted to make sure you could find her if you ever wanted to. Want to go now?"

"It's late." Then she laughed. "Sure. It's not like she's getting up for work in the morning."

"Prepare yourself, P.J. She's living in a pigsty. It makes the place she had when you lived with her look luxurious."

"Bet she misses that child support check she got from the city."

He pulled to the curb. "That's it." He pointed to a dilapidated building on the other side of the street. Except for a few lights in the cracked and dirty windows, it might have been abandoned. "First floor, back apartment. Want me to come?"

"Thanks, Jess. I've got to do this myself."

There was no lock on the door, and by the smell of it, the narrow hallway was used as the neighborhood latrine. The rancid smell of the garbage added to the atmosphere. She held her breath and picked her way through the litter. Maybe it was easier if you were drunk and not so squeamish about germs and bacteria. The door was ajar. Parker rapped on it and walked in. The apartment wasn't much better than the hall. A man lay on a dirty mattress. Parker checked for a pulse and was nearly knocked on her rear by the body odor and the stink of cheap wine and vomit that stained his clothes and the mattress. Sure different from the homes of the Nickersons and the del Balzos. She continued through the apartment and found her grandmother collapsed into a paint-speckled chair that tilted to one side. She looked like an ancient witch, her hair a wild bunch of Brillo, her few teeth yellowed and decayed, her clothes matted and dirty. She smelled as bad as her companion stretched out on the mattress in the other room. The old woman looked up and peered at her as if she was a shadow standing in the sunshine.

"Whatcha doin' here, Tasha? Come to give your old mama some money?" She cackled, her voice rusty. She wiped her nose on her sleeve.

"It's P.J., not Tasha. I need to talk to you."

"Who? You think your mama stupid? You ain't foolin' me. Lookin' for mail again? Well he ain't writing. Randall don't want you now you soiled. Not doin' so good by youself, miss high and mighty? You be by youself with your precious jewel. Some jewel. You a whore just like me, just like your sister. Just think you better than us, gonna raise that little jewel like a princess. He ain't comin' back for you. Never. How come all a sudden you mama good enuf to keep you junk? Can't pay the rent huh? Now get them boxes and get outta my sight."

So it was true. Randall was involved with her mother. Well that's what she wanted to know. Parker threw fifty dollars on the table. She knew most of it would go for drink, but maybe the old lady would get one meal out of it. She was almost out the door when she realized what the old bitch had said. She walked back to the kitchen.

"What boxes?"

"You always be acting so innocent. The ones you snuck in the back of that hall closet. Woulda tossed them but forgot they was there. Didn't notice them until we already carried them here. Ain't nothin' but some old papers, nothin' worth sellin'."

"Where are the boxes?"

"Under the bed. Now we even, money for boxes." She seemed to think this was hysterical.

There was no bed, but Parker looked through every room until she found three cardboard boxes with her mother's things in a closet in the kitchen. She carried two boxes out to the stoop and returned for the third.

She glanced back at the old woman as she carried the last box out of the kitchen. She realized she was no longer angry about the abuse and neglect she had suffered at those claw-like hands. It was another time. She was no longer that little girl desperate to be loved and praised and fed and taken care of. Her grandmother no longer had any power over her. She was just a wasted old drunk, who had nothing to do with the adult Penelope Jasmine Parker.

Jesse had already carried the first two boxes to the car and stowed them in the backseat. She slid the last box on top of the other two.

"How did it go?"

"She thought I was my mother and she sort of confirmed what…" She wasn't sure what to call him. "What Randall Young said. And it turned out these three boxes belonged to my mother. All these years and I never knew. I don't know why I never found them. I searched that damn house from top to bottom when I was a kid."

"But you were usually looking for food or money, so maybe you ignored them."

"True," she said, remembering all the times she had been hungry and frightened, how she had learned to hide food right after the social worker's visit when her grandmother always stocked up for show. How she had learned to steal from her grandmother or the man sleeping with her at the time, never a lot, just enough to buy a burger or a slice of pizza. And how after Patrolman Jesse Isaacs noticed her scavenging for food, he bought her lunch and/or dinner almost every day and kept her company while she ate, always encouraging her to study, go to school, make something of herself. That changed of course, when Uncle Aloysius came into the picture. But even though Uncle Al and Aunt Mariah fed and clothed her, it was an unpleasant duty, not love for them. Jesse had continued to be her emotional anchor. She glanced at Jesse in the dim light of the car as they drove back to Manhattan. He'd stood in for the father she didn't know she had, spending time with her on the weekends and sometimes after school. "Um, Jesse, I was wondering how you feel about gays and lesbians?"

"You trying to tell me something?"

She shrugged.

"You need to find somebody to love, and I don't care what sex as long as they're good people. But, you know as well as I, it's not easy being a gay cop."

It made her smile. "I'm not a lesbian, Jesse, but I think it's gotten easier. Corelli is a lesbian and that seems to be the least of her problems right now. Anyway, working with Corelli on this case, learning about those gay guys and that lesbian painter, meeting other lesbians and gays has turned my head around. Up 'til now, I've mainly met gays and lesbians as a cop or an ADA, so I had a skewed picture, know what I mean?"

He laughed. "Detective Parker, you are getting an education. Good for you. It's a big world out there and gay or straight, white, black, brown or yellow, there are good people and bad people. Up 'til now, you've spent too much time with the bad, that's all."

Jesse stopped in front of Hattie's so she could pick up her car, and then he followed her to her apartment house. She got out. He rolled down his window. "Want help with the boxes?"

There was no way she was going to bring boxes from that filthy, roach-infested place into her apartment.

"I'd like to leave the boxes out here, just take the stuff inside. Could you stay until I carry everything in?"

"There goes my beauty sleep," he said, smiling. "C'mon. Let's do it."

First, they removed the contents from the cartons and piled everything on the steps, then he tossed the empties on top of the garbage bags waiting on the curb for pickup. While he methodically shook each item to get rid of any roaches living in the paper, she made multiple trips to her apartment, stacking her mother's books and papers and letters in neat piles on her desk. When at last she stooped for the last pile, she straightened up and acted on a sudden impulse to hug Jesse, surprising both of them. Usually she just barely tolerated the physical contact when he hugged her.

"Thanks for being there for me, Jesse. Tonight. And back then."

Parker stood at the desk looking at the books and papers and unopened letters, her mother's books and papers and letters. She picked up one of the notebooks and ran her finger over the neat, round schoolgirl script on the inside cover where her mother had written her name, Tasha Parker. She'd never held anything her mother had held or seen anything her mother had written, or if truth be told, never really had proof that her mother had existed. Now she hoped she would finally know something of the woman who had loved her, had wanted her, and had thought of her as her precious jewel, a woman she'd already outlived by eight years.

But first she needed a shower to rid herself of the smell and creepy-crawly feeling of Thelma Parker's hovel. Afterward, she dried off and lay down with the notebook. She immediately fell asleep.

CHAPTER THIRTY-SIX

Monday – 6 a.m.

The alarm must have gone off, but Parker sure hadn't heard it. She jumped up, straightened the bed, and was in and out of the shower before the hot water could make it up from the basement. She pulled her tan suit and red shirt out of the closet while drying herself, then dressed, strapped on her gun, and checked the mirror. She hung the wet towel in the bathroom. Ready to go in eleven minutes. She hesitated in front of the desk, debating whether she could spend just a few minutes looking through her mother's papers, but duty called. Corelli might look drawn and exhausted, but she was always on time. The papers would have to wait.

She arrived at Corelli's apartment fifteen minutes later than the usual six thirty a.m. and rang the intercom.

"Be right down," Corelli's disembodied voice beamed down from the eighth floor.

A few minutes later Corelli smiled at Parker from the doorway of her building. "Morning," Corelli said, sliding into the car. She handed Parker an insulated cup. "Thought you might need something to get you started." She waved a tinfoil packet. "Brought you a bagel, too."

Expecting the kindness to be followed by an attack, Parker tensed. She took a sip. The industrial strength coffee careened through her bloodstream, knocking the fog out of her head and putting her body on alert. She sighed. Damn Corelli always had her off-balance. Why was she being so nice? "Thanks, I needed that." She started the car and pulled away from the curb. "Sorry to be late."

"How many times do I have to tell you that apologies irritate me?"

Parker steeled herself for a tirade.

"Relax. You didn't leave here until, what, eleven thirty? You deserve a little sleep."

Yeah, more than two hours. "I was afraid we might be late for the morning meeting."

"I shifted the meeting to seven p.m."

"Right," Parker said, hitting herself on the forehead.

They arrived at the station a few minutes before seven. Word about the meeting being rescheduled must have gotten out because there were only a few members of the press lounging behind the barricades and no sign of the police who, even though the gauntlet was prohibited, often arrived early enough to jeer them. Maybe things were starting to loosen up.

By seven fifteen, they were in the conference room. "Our appointment with Councilman Collins isn't until nine. Why don't you catch up on paperwork while I read through any reports I haven't seen? We'll leave for City Hall about eight thirty." Corelli examined Parker. "Heavy night last night? Maybe you should take a nap while it's still quiet."

A lot heavier than you imagine. But I'm not ready to discuss it with you.

"Yeah, I had a couple of drinks with Jesse after I left you. Your coffee should do the trick." She unwrapped the bagel Corelli had brought her and took a bite. "Good. Thanks."

"Looks like I have to have a talk with Captain Isaacs. Can't have him leading the troops astray," she said, smiling, as she turned to the stack of papers to be reviewed.

Parker wished she understood Corelli's moods. Why was she so cheerful this morning?

CHAPTER THIRTY-SEVEN

Monday – 9 a.m.

By the time Councilman Collins invited them into his office, Corelli was ready to arrest him. He'd kept them waiting twenty minutes, despite their appointment. That was totally unacceptable in her book unless he had an emergency. Their time was as valuable as his, especially when they were trying to solve three murders and head off a fourth.

His office was smaller than Kate Burke's but the pictures lining his walls were interchangeable with those on Burke's walls, except he was the one shaking the hands and receiving the awards. Today's *Daily Post* was open on his desk confirming her suspicion the delay was designed to put them in their place. He glanced at the cards they'd given his assistant. "What can I do for you, detectives?"

"We have a few questions, sir." Corelli made no effort to conceal her anger.

He remained seated at his desk. "Can my girl get you coffee, tea, or water?"

Girl? His secretary was a middle-aged woman. Now she was really irritated. "We're not here to socialize, Councilman." Corelli's voice was hard.

He pursed his lips. "Please sit." He waved them to the chairs facing the desk.

They remained standing, staring down at him. "Where were you Tuesday and Friday evenings of last week?"

He crossed his legs and leaned forward. "You're heading up the GALS investigation, right? What has that got to do with me?"

One of the newspapers had tagged the case Gay and Lesbian Shooter and the acronym GALS had quickly caught on with the press and the public.

"As I'm sure you've heard, several of Speaker Burke's friends have been murdered and one aspect of the investigation is looking into who would want to hurt Ms. Burke. Since you opposed her in the election, we need to eliminate you. So please answer the question so we can move on."

He straightened an already straight pile of papers, picked up his appointment book and turned a few pages. "Uh, right. I was in Washington, D.C. I left early Tuesday morning and got home last night about ten. I have the plane tickets and the boarding passes, if you would like to see them."

"Great. If you could have your assistant make copies of the tickets and boarding passes, the bills for hotels and meals, and a list of appointments while you were there, we'll be all set. I'll send someone over to pick them up this afternoon."

He glared at her. "You don't believe me? I'll show you the boarding passes right now."

"It's not a matter of believing you, sir. It's routine to confirm what you've told us."

"But I'm a goddamn New York City Councilman, an elected official. My word should be enough. What will my constituents think?"

Not my problem asshole. "No one outside of our team needs to know we've talked to you, but we must see the documents in order to eliminate you. I'm sure your assistant can pull the information together in an hour."

His face and neck turned red. "This is outrageous. Are you insinuating that I would kill three people over a job? You'll just have to take my word for it. I won't waste our time and the taxpayer's money."

She leaned over his desk, making sure she had his attention. "If you force us to subpoena you to get the information, it's very likely you'll end up with bad publicity, the very thing you say you're trying to avoid. I'll expect the documents by the end of the day today or tomorrow morning at the latest."

They left him looking slightly ill, staring into space.

As soon as they stepped out of City Hall, Corelli called Dietz. "I need somebody on Councilman Collins, immediately. He's hiding something and I want to be sure he doesn't do a runner. Send somebody who knows what he looks like. Parker and I are outside City Hall now. We'll wait to be relieved."

Twenty minutes later, Detective Charleen Greene showed up.

Corelli explained why they were watching the councilman. "Just stay on him today. I want to make sure he doesn't take off. Keep a record of where he goes. Call me if he does anything unusual. Somebody will relieve you tonight."

Greene nodded. "Will do."

CHAPTER THIRTY-EIGHT

Monday – 10:30 a.m.

Corelli's phone rang as they walked into the case conference room. "Yes, Chief. We're looking at him because he threatened Burke after she won the election." She listened for a minute. "All I did was request copies of his receipts and the names of the people he met with. Now he's threatening me. Clearly he's hiding something. Let him call the mayor but that won't stop me from getting the information I need." She listened again. "No, I can't play nice with someone who might be killing people to get even. Sorry." She ended the call.

Dietz stuck his head in the door. "We identified three of the religious fanatics from the stuff the *Daily World* sent over. We nailed one of them, a guy named Orrin Snape. He's in room three. Another one, name of Fred Wilpersett, is on the way. We're still looking for Luther Phelps. Snape's a little weird. Take a look before you go in."

Observing Snape through the two-way mirror, they watched him ping-pong between two walls, touching one then crossing the room to touch the other, all the while muttering. He was stick-like and colorless. Except for the black cover and gold trimmed pages of the small book clutched in his right hand, everything about him was gray, like charcoal burned to ash, his clean but crumpled and threadbare clothes, his complexion, his scraggly hair and beard, and even his eyes.

"You guys do anything to agitate him?"

"Nah." Dietz shook his head. "He has a file. He's been around for years, always at the Gay Pride Parade picketing, not really bothering anybody, but the last year or so, he seemed to lose it. At the demonstration the day of Burke's election, he actually got physical with one of the other demonstrators, a gay man, and they both were arrested for fighting. Could be he snapped."

"I'll take this one, Parker."

They entered the room but Snape seemed not to notice. He continued to walk and touch, walk and touch. Corelli moved into his path. He stopped short, stepped back, and looked up at her. He wasn't as old as he'd seemed, but up close he smelled musty and his skin was dry and flaky.

"Please have a seat, Mr. Snapes."

"It's Snape, one Snape, like snake."

Corelli stepped to the table. A little small talk might calm him. "Interesting name. Where does it come from?"

"It come from Mississippi with me."

Not a great thinker, our Mr. Snape. "I meant originally."

"Snape ain't nothin' but American."

So much for small talk. "Do you know why you're here, Mr. Snape?"

He glanced at Parker, then Corelli. "You faggot lovers always chasing me 'cause I try to save the faggots souls."

Corelli sat. "Detective Parker, please help Mr. Snape into a chair."

He didn't fight Parker when she took his elbow and escorted him to the table. Once he was seated he opened the black book he was holding.

Corelli waited for Parker to sit. "Mr. Snape?" His head popped up. "Your signs say 'Death to Homos' and 'God Wants Faggots Dead.' That doesn't sound like saving souls to me. Isn't God about love? Why would God want you to kill people you don't even know?"

"God has called me to set things right in his name. God says, 'Do not lie with a man as one lies with a woman; that is detestable.' Leviticus 18:22."

Burke was right about unchristian Christians. "How many homosexuals have you killed?"

He stared into space as if he hadn't heard.

"Did you know Leonardo del Balzo?"

"Yes. The faggot is dead. 'If a man lies with a man as one lies with a woman, both of them have done what is detestable. They must be put to death; their blood will be on their own heads.' Leviticus 20:13."

"How did you kill Mr. del Balzo?"

"The homos are bringing God's wrath down on all of us. They must be punished."

"Do you pray with a rosary?"

"Papist idolatry."

"Did you kill Spencer Nickerson, Nardo del Balzo, and Margaret Lerner?"

"They're everywhere. They haunt me."

"Why did you murder them?"

"'Because of this, God gave them over to their own shameful lusts. Even their women exchanging natural relations for unnatural ones. In the same way the men also abandoned natural relations with women and were inflamed with lust for one another. Men committed indecent acts with other men and received themselves the penalty for their perversion.' Romans 1:26-27."

"What about Luther Phelps or Fred Wilpersett? Did they murder them?"

"They are abominations. God commanded us to save them."

Corelli stood. "Let's go, Parker."

They walked to Dietz's desk. "Hold him. Check his record in Mississippi. Circulate his picture in the victims' neighborhoods, get a search warrant and see if the gun turns up or the rosaries or anything that links him to the killings. But to be honest, I can't see any of the victims inviting Snape into their homes for cheese and crackers, much less getting close enough for him to shoot them in the back of the head."

He nodded as he jotted down her instructions. "They lost Fred Wilpersett."

"Lost him?"

"Yeah, he asked to use the bathroom before leaving and went out the window onto the roof. They're still searching."

Parker cleared her throat. "Shouldn't we check to see if Snape made the threatening calls?"

"Good point. Add that to your list, Dietz."

Dietz made a note. "Speaking of phone calls, Parker, you get together with that guy says he's your daddy?"

"It's none of your business, Dietz. I told you to forget it." Her voice was loud and hard, and she moved toward him fists ready at her side.

Corelli clasped Parker's shoulder, hoping to end the scene before it began. Parker tried to shrug off her hand but Corelli held tight.

Dietz put his hands out, palms up. "C'mon, Parker, just raggin' you."

Corelli heard Parker suck in air and felt her shoulders drop. Then it was over. She nodded to Dietz and steered Parker to the conference room.

CHAPTER THIRTY-NINE

Monday – 10:30 a.m.

"What the hell was that about?"

"I don't like people poking in my business, that's all," Parker said, lowering her eyes.

Corelli sighed. "So is this the source of all the talk about fathers abandoning their children?"

Parker picked at her cuticle. *What do you know about not having a father; you've got that big Italian family. But then again, your father looks right through you, like you don't exist. Like the Senator did to me.*

Corelli probably wouldn't let it go. And she could easily get the details from Dietz. Might as well control the narrative. "Yeah, I guess. This guy Randall Young saw my picture on the front page of the *Daily World* after the Toricelli thing. Anyway, he showed up the other day and left a message with Dietz saying he thinks he's my father."

"What does Senator Daddy have to say about this?"

There was no sarcasm or nastiness in the question, just a request for information. The other would have been easier to handle. Tell or don't tell?

Parker shrugged. "Don't know."

"And you believe this Randall Young? A guy who walks off the street and says he's your father. Jesus, Parker, you don't think you should discuss this with your father? Or, at least your mother?"

"It's not Dietz's business. And it's not yours either, Corelli."

Corelli's voice was hard. "It is my goddamn business when it interferes with your doing your job, which, I might remind you, is to keep me alive. Mooning around about fathers like you've been these last few days and being so on edge you want to slug somebody, is distracting you from the case as well."

Parker turned, her voice accusing and angry. "Look who's talking about being on edge. Don't tell me you haven't studied my file looking for ways to dig into me? You've done nothing but harass me since day one."

Corelli stood stock-still, staring at Parker. "I make my own decisions about people. I've never opened your file so if there's something in there I should know please let me in on the secret."

"Why the fuck should I tell you anything. You'll just use it against me."

"Because we're partners, that's why."

"Partners? You treat me like I'm an annoying insect that's bothering you."

Corelli grinned. "Well, I'm just taming you and training you to obey me."

"Partners are equals."

"Yes but one partner has to be more equal than the other, especially in the beginning."

"You are one fucking fucked-up bitch, Corelli."

"Ah, I see I've finally managed to cut through your shit. Now tell me why you haven't spoken to Senator Daddy, or your mom about this guy."

Parker squirmed under the intensity of Corelli's stare. She looked away. Was she ready to share the story of her life with this strange woman? Maybe. After all, not only had Corelli invited her into her family, she also trusted her with her life every day.

Parker looked Corelli in the eye. "Senator Daddy is my uncle, my mother...Anyway, he and my aunt adopted me when I was about seven. I don't remember my mother and I was led to believe no one knew who my father was."

"Well, I'm happy for you. I mean, that the senator is not your father. I'm just sorry you had to grow up with him. Have you checked this Young guy out?"

Understanding. Not the taunts Parker expected. She relaxed. "I met him at Hattie's last night. Jessie was there in case he turned out to be a nut."

"And?"

"He seems all right. He said except for the hairstyle, I could be Tasha, the girl he got pregnant and would have married when he got back from boot camp if she hadn't disappeared. He had some pictures of a young girl who looked exactly like me and he sounded like he was telling the truth, so Jesse and I went and found my grandmother."

Parker hesitated, not sure how much to reveal, not sure if it would turn Corelli off. Then Parker realized Corelli hadn't read her file because she didn't want to be influenced by other people's opinions, and there was no way Corelli would judge her for her grandmother's behavior.

"She's a drunk, has been as long as I remember. I haven't seen her since I went to live with the senator. She's living in some shithole in the Bronx. She thought I was my mother, called me Tasha. Turns out she had three boxes of my mother's stuff and never once mentioned them when I was growing up and asking about my mother." Her voice caught.

"What about Randall Young?"

"My grandmother's drunken jabbering confirmed what he said. And it looks like a younger him in the pictures." Parker removed the envelope from her pocket and handed it to Corelli.

Corelli studied the four pictures contained in the envelope. "She does look exactly like a younger you. And he resembles the boy?"

"Yeah, older, heavier, but you could see the boy in him. I didn't have time to go through her stuff, but there were letters to her from him so he's probably telling the truth. He asked if I would do a DNA test."

"And?"

She shrugged. "I'm not sure I need a father now."

"Might be nice to know, especially since I gather you and Senator Daddy aren't close."

Parker shrugged. "I've done all right without him. What if I don't like him? And he has two daughters, one's a lesbian."

Corelli laughed. "You mind having a lesbian half-sister? How did that come up, anyway?"

Parker felt sheepish. "You know, seeing how families feel about their gay and lesbian kids made me think. I asked him how he would feel if I was a lesbian, just to get his reaction, to learn something about him."

"And?"

"He told me about his other daughters and said he just wanted his kids to be healthy and happy."

"He passed the first test so why not do the DNA test and be sure?"

Parker looked down. "I'm thinking."

"Take your time. There's no need to rush into anything after all these years. Are you all right, Parker?"

Parker considered. Yes, she was okay and she felt relaxed with Corelli in a way she hadn't before. "Yes, I'm fine."

"Good. And, speaking about parents dealing with gay children, let's pick up Simone and Nicky and go to Brooklyn. I might as well face Patrizia and get it over with." Corelli made a face when she mentioned her oldest sister.

Parker had seen Corelli's older sister in action so she was sympathetic to Corelli's desire to avoid an attack by her. Not only did Patrizia feel that being a cop wasn't a proper job for a woman, she felt a woman's only job was to have children and to spend her life serving her husband and their offspring as she did, and their ancestors had done for centuries. Corelli was the rogue in the family, and therefore, responsible for any disturbance of the family tradition. Corelli was a lesbian, ergo, Patrizia would hold her responsible for Nicky being gay.

Corelli appeared exhausted and Parker wasn't sure Corelli had the strength to stand up to an attack today. Parker knew Patrizia would not air family problems in front of her, a virtual stranger, so she felt comfortable taking Nicky home to get his things without Corelli. "I could drive them myself if you want to stay here and work."

Corelli didn't hesitate. Parker knew she'd promised Nicky she would be there to support him, and no matter what she was feeling, his needs would take precedence over hers. Besides, she'd mentioned earlier that she feared Patrizia would try to bully Nicky into staying home and given the situation, she couldn't let that happen. "Thanks, but I need to be there to support Nicky," Corelli said. "Let's go pick them up."

Nicky talked nonstop and fidgeted during the drive out to Bensonhurst. Everyone else was quiet, spaced out, letting him fill the car with his chatter but not attempting to engage. As they pulled up in front of his house, Corelli turned to face him. "Nicky, I think we should wait to tell your mother about your being gay. I don't have the time to deal with her today and I want to be there to support you for as long as necessary when you do tell her. How about we pick up your stuff and tell her the three of us are going to hang out this week?"

The look on his face said it all, but he gave a casual, if that's how you want it shrug. "Sure, no problem," he said, as if he was doing her a favor.

To everybody's relief, Patrizia was out. Nicky rushed about gathering his books and notebooks and throwing clothes into a small bag. He wrote a note and tossed it on the table. "Let's get out of here before my mom gets back and we have to answer a thousand questions."

They picked up Simone's things and stopped at the restaurant so she could tell her parents she and Nicky were spending the week with Corelli. After fifteen minutes, Corelli was fuming. "Go drag her out, Nick." But before he could respond, Simone staggered out of the restaurant weighed down by two huge shopping bags.

Nicky jumped out and helped Simone into the car.

"Okay, Parker, let's go," Corelli said. She turned to Simone. "I guess they're afraid I'll starve the two of you."

"That's not it," Simone said. "You know Mama always sends all your favorites."

Her father's rejection was bad enough, but it pained her that her mother followed his lead blindly, acted as if she wasn't a person in her own right, never voiced her own opinion, and resorted to using food to show her love. If ever Corelli doubted her commitment to her career and a non-traditional relationship, she reminded herself of her mother's subservient second-class status. Her parents worked as equals in the restaurant, but at home her mother catered to her husband's every need or whim and served him like a slave. It irked her to see her mother jump at his every command. "Get me a glass of water, get me wine, cut my meat, get me the salt." She knew at an early age, even before she knew she was a lesbian, that catering to a man was not for her. Later, of course, Gianna and Marco had demonstrated that marriage did not have to be like that.

Conversation was more animated as they drove back, probably the relief of not having to deal with Patrizia. Corelli's phone rang.

"We've got Fred Wilpersett," Dietz said. "He's dying to meet you two."

"Then he won't mind waiting a little longer. After we get the kids settled we'll come in."

An hour and a half later, with Simone and Nicky safely ensconced in her apartment, they headed back to interview Fred Wilpersett.

"How do you think Patrizia will react when she hears Nicky is gay?"

Corelli snorted. "Badly. Very badly. She's one of those people who makes everything about her. You know, how could you do this to me? As if the kid had a choice or set out to be different. Maybe it comes from being the second child, when the first is adored by everyone."

"I thought she was the oldest," Parker said.

"Our brother Luca was older. He was handsome, smart, and kind. Everyone adored him. Patrizia was a year and a half younger, but old before her time, like you see her now. She craved attention and got it by being the antithesis of Luca—whiny, rigid, mean-spirited, and controlling."

"Luca was a mafia hit, right?"

Corelli hesitated. She trusted Parker with her life. Why keep her family history secret?

Sensitive, as always, Parker picked up her hesitation. "Sorry, I didn't mean to be nosy."

Corelli opted to trust. "He was killed by a bullet through each eye, mafia style, when he was nineteen. For years I blamed Toricelli but I recently found out it was a dirty cop and not the mafia. Luca was collateral damage, an innocent bystander who saw something he shouldn't have."

"Sorry," Parker said.

"Thanks. It was a long time ago."

"Poor Nicky, having to face Patrizia."

"Yeah. Patrizia is tough. But she loves Nicky and I don't think she'll chance losing him. She'll bounce back after the initial shock. Nicky's father, Joseph, may have a harder time with it, but if the rest of the family backs Nicky, he should be fine."

"I hope so. He seems like a good kid."

CHAPTER FORTY

Monday – 2:30 p.m.

Before entering the interview room to interrogate the religious fanatic who had gone out a bathroom window to avoid being questioned by the police, Corelli and Parker observed him through the two-way mirror.

Gawky, with pointy rat-like features, Fred Wilpersett was younger and not agitated like his roommate Orrin Snape, but he had that same clean, down-at-the-heels, underfed look as Snape. As they watched, Wilpersett removed his wallet from the back pocket of his pants and counted the bills, raising a question in Parker's mind. "It looks like these fanatics don't spend much on food and their clothes appear to come from a charity bin, but even apartments in run-down neighborhoods like theirs are expensive in New York City, as are utilities and transportation. How do they support themselves?"

Corelli glanced at her. "According to Dietz, one of the hate-mongering churches funds them."

They observed him for a few minutes more. At first glance he appeared relaxed but his eyes flicking to the two-way mirror and his leg beating a steady rhythm, telegraphed his tension. Parker tried to fathom why Wilpersett was so filled with hatred for gays and lesbians, but there was nothing she could see; he looked normal. Well, relatively normal.

"What do you think, Parker?"

"I can't see him being invited in for wine and cheese."

"I agree, but maybe he has a more acceptable looking sidekick who gets them in. And who knows, schweetheart, maybe we can get him to confess." Parker shook her head at Corelli's Humphrey Bogart imitation. Corelli really was crazy. She would never understand the woman.

"You take this one, Parker. I'll back you up."

When the door opened, he sprang from the chair, backed into a corner, and raised his hands defensively.

Parker extended her hands in an attempt to calm the man. "Whoa, we're not going to hurt you, Mr. Wilpersett," Parker said. "Have a seat."

He sidled over and lowered himself into a chair facing them. His eyes danced from one to the other and then settled in the space between, staring into the two-way mirror.

Parker wondered if anyone had been beating on him, he seemed like a…She couldn't help it, like a scared rat. "Mr. Wilpersett can you explain why you snuck out the bathroom window rather than come here to talk to us?"

"Uh, no."

"Could you expand on that?"

He remained silent and continued staring over their shoulders.

Parker turned to Corelli. "Should we read him his rights and book him for murder?"

"Murder?" Wilpersett sounded alarmed. "What murder?"

"Actually, it's three murders. Leonardo del Balzo, Spencer—"

"You mean them three faggots? You're crazy. Why would I kill them?"

"I can't imagine, but you are known to carry signs that say, 'Kill all the Homos' and 'Stamp out Faggots.' Kinda gives the impression you want to kill all gay men and lesbians. And escaping out the bathroom window and climbing over rooftops to avoid questioning might indicate you have something to hide."

Sweat appeared on his upper lip. "I'm trying to save their souls. Scripture says—"

"Spare us the quotations. Where were you Tuesday and Friday and Saturday nights?"

"I was…home. Me and Orrin stayed in those nights."

"Why those nights?"

"We had the flu."

"A three-day flu and not consecutive days? Interesting. And you didn't go out at all?"

He hesitated. "No."

"What about the threatening phone calls you've been making?"

"How do you—? I don't know what you're talking about. We don't even have a telephone."

"Why do you hate gays and lesbians so much?"

"We're doing God's work. Their evil behavior is bringing his wrath down on this country. Innocent people are dying because of them. The Bible—"

"What about love? I thought God was about love and forgiveness. You know love thy neighbor, do unto others, that kind of stuff."

"Evil must be punished. It poisons us all."

"Isn't murder evil? Why kill del Balzo, Lerner, and Nickerson?"

"I saw their pictures. The filth must be punished."

"What picture was that?" Parker sensed Corelli shift forward.

"All the pictures in the newspapers this week."

"So you read the newspapers. What other pictures of them did you see before you started killing them?"

"They were all together the day that abomination got elected."

"Are you referring to Speaker Burke?"

"The lesbian."

"How do you know they were together that day?"

"Saw them with my own eyes, laughing and hugging, while God watched and wept. I tried to stop it but the police are on the side of the sinners."

"How did you get their names and addresses?"

"God knows where they live, not me."

"And did God tell you to kill them?"

"You're trying to trick me. I didn't kill them. But they deserved to die. God killed them."

"If you didn't kill them, why did you run away?"

"Because you're constantly harassing us. The GALS killer is doing God's work, not me."

"Are you out for gay and lesbian blood?"

"Why would I suck the blood of such filth?"

Dietz was waiting when they left the room. "Good work, Parker."

"Thanks, but I didn't get much from him." She looked at Corelli.

"You shook him about the phone threats," Corelli said. "Dietz, send somebody out with pictures of Snape and Wilpersett and have someone check the pay phones in the area around their apartment. Hold him while we check for outstandings. Any sign of the third one? Phelps?"

"No. But he does have a sheet." Dietz opened the folder he was carrying. "Multiple assaults of gay men, attempted murder of a gay guy in St. Louis and another in Missouri. I would guess he's on the run." He handed the file to Corelli. She whistled. "This may be our guy. Blond, blue eyes, six feet, good-looking, the opposite of the other two." She looked at the pictures, then passed them to Parker. "I could see a gay guy inviting him home. Send someone to show the picture to Kate Burke, Miranda Foxworth, the neighbors of the victims, and the gay bars. Also, let's get his picture to the media. Someone must have seen him."

CHAPTER FORTY-ONE

Monday – 7 p.m.

Corelli strode in. She stood silently and waited for the group to quiet. "Anybody have anything?"

"Yeah," Dietz said. "I took a call from a guy a little while ago. He's been out of town for a few days and only heard about Nickerson's murder this afternoon. Said he was sitting outside at the restaurant across the street from Nickerson's townhouse Friday night and saw a tall, slender man dressed all in black with his hat pulled down, smoking. He didn't think anything of it until the guy put his cigarette out on the railing and stashed the butt in his pocket. What struck him as really odd was the guy put gloves on before ringing the bell. He couldn't see his face and didn't notice when he came out. He chalked it up to another weird New Yorker."

"It sounds like the mystery man outside Nardo's apartment," Corelli said. "What else?"

"We've got a guy like that near Meg Lerner's house," Wachinski said. "A witness, a mystery writer, passed a man going in the direction of Lerner's house when she was walking her dog. Said she noticed the guy because he looked like a character in a noir mystery. His clothing, including a slouch hat pulled over his eyes, was black. He was wearing sunglasses even though it was dark, and he had a cigarette dangling out his mouth. She said the Macy's shopping bag he was carrying seemed out of place. When her dog stopped to sniff something interesting, she turned back to look and saw the guy put the cigarette out on a telephone pole and pocket the butt. She thought she could use that in a book."

"Sounds like the same guy at all three scenes. Now we just have to identify him," Corelli said. "The shopping bag probably held the CD player and the other things required to pose the body."

"The autopsy confirmed Lerner died Saturday night between eleven and one a.m.," Wachinski said.

"I've been checking out the rosaries," said Detective Deke Simmons. "They're nothin' special, sold in religious stores around the city as well as the gift shop in St. Patrick's Cathedral. None of the clerks we talked to remembered selling them in any quantity and not one could remember a nervous or suspicious-looking customer."

"No luck with the CD player brought to Lerner's either," Forlini said.

"We got the results of the Nickerson autopsy," Watkins said. "The ME confirmed the time of death and the fact he was killed with a bullet to the cerebellum. We also got confirmation that the bullets used to kill del Balzo and Nickerson came from the same gun. Forensics is still examining the evidence picked up at each scene, but so far they have nothing significant to report."

"Thanks, guys," Corelli said. "We've secured the remaining targets, at least those we think are the targets, based on our theory that the picture on the front page of the *Daily World* is the source of the killer's victims. That includes my younger sister and my nephew, who were invited to City Hall by Spencer Nickerson. Watkins and Greene will be meeting Brett Cummings at the airport later and we'll put a twenty-four-hour guard on her.

"We do have someone who looks good for this. Dietz is passing out some info on him." Corelli held up a flyer. "Take one and pass them along." She waited until everyone had a copy and had a chance to read it. "Luther Phelps, an ex-con with multiple convictions for assaulting gay men and two open charges of attempting to murder them, is a member of the religious group harassing gay men. We believe the victims knew the killer or at least welcomed him in their houses, so that ruled out the other two religious guys. But this guy could pass for gay and might be invited in. He's disappeared but we're distributing his picture and description to the media so hopefully he'll turn up."

The silence was deafening. They had one suspect they couldn't identify and one they couldn't find, no other leads. Forlini suddenly woke up. "Hey, maybe he's the mystery guy in black?"

"Good thought, Forlini. Let's find him and we'll check his wardrobe."

The energy level was dangerously low. The troops needed a break. "Just a couple more things." She made eye contact with the team. "I can see you're all exhausted so take the rest of the night off and start fresh tomorrow. Continue what you're doing, and if you need something else, contact Dietz. Let's touch base again tomorrow night at seven. Have a good evening."

The room emptied quickly. Ron and Charleen stopped to say they had called the airline and Brett's flight was on time so they were going to have dinner and then head out to meet her plane.

Parker lingered.

She knew Parker wouldn't leave without her. "I'll work at home so you can drop me and get some rest."

"I'd rather review the case with you, if that's okay."

Corelli had planned to work out in her home gym, then soak in the tub for a while before reviewing the case in her bedroom. That wouldn't work with Parker there. "The kids are having a couple of friends over so it'll probably be noisy. Let's work here."

After a couple of hours Parker stood and stretched. "I need to move. I'm going to walk around the block. I'll be back in fifteen or twenty minutes."

Corelli went to the ladies' room and threw some cold water on her face. When she got back she stubbed her toe on a box next to the table. It was the box of Italian magazines and newspapers they'd taken from del Balzo's apartment. Since she was the only one who could read Italian, Dietz had it moved it into the conference room so she could look through it whenever she had a few minutes. She thumbed through a few of the magazines. The ambassador was no longer a suspect, but she was curious about the del Balzos, especially their attitude toward their homosexual son whom everyone, but them, seemed to love.

Back from her walk, Parker slid into the chair facing Corelli's desk. Corelli finished the article she was reading and put it aside. "Find anything?" Parker asked.

"Not really. But now that the ambassador isn't a suspect, I wasn't looking for anything, just satisfying my ghoulish interest. The del Balzos are so cold about losing their son, it's un-Italian. Anyway, most of the articles are just gossip, about them and their daughters, especially the single one. Strange that there's nothing about Nardo. Surely the press would have picked up something about his being gay or at least written about him as an eligible bachelor. It's almost as if he was dead before he was murdered. Anyway, there are a couple of stories proclaiming Carla as the power behind the throne, a few hints about the ambassador having affairs, a story about their hunting big game in Africa, pro and con discussions about his becoming prime minister and a lot of weird stories and candid photos, the kind you see on the front pages of the scandal sheets at the supermarket. You know how Carla always looks so perfect, sleek and pulled together like a fashion model? Take a look at these."

Parker thumbed through the pages. "What's this headline say?"

"Who really wears the pants in this family?"

"Good question. Wow, she looks like she's on a bender—sloppy and puffy. Do you think she's a drunk? In these she looks so butch she and the ambassador could be brothers. Jeez, look at these. She looks like, um, a queen or a fairy princess, all sparkly and gorgeous. And here she looks like she's been out picking up garbage. Are these for real? Man, she must be schizo."

"These rags often retouch the photos to make the people look horrible. And maybe they're just disguises to avoid the paparazzi that must be on top of them all the time. Anyway, it's nice to see she's human."

They worked another hour, then Corelli yawned. "Let's pack it in."

"I could use some sleep, but I need to make a pit stop before we go. Meet you at the elevator." Parker pulled her stuff together and headed out to the ladies' room.

CHAPTER FORTY-TWO

Monday – 11:30 p.m.

"Boss, we have a problem," Watkins said when Corelli answered her cell. "Brett Cummings wasn't on the plane. I had them check the passenger list and it looks like she changed to an earlier flight when she arrived in Houston, one scheduled to arrive at 9:05 instead of 11:14. She should be home already. We're about to get into the car but even at eleven thirty it's going to take a while for us to reach Battery Park City. You'd better get somebody over there ASAP."

"Will do. Thanks, Watkins."

Corelli ran to catch Parker.

"Watkins called. Brett took an earlier flight. Hopefully she went straight home. We need to get to her place. Now."

"I hope she didn't tell anybody about the change," Parker said, as they jogged to the car.

"So do I."

"Is Ms. Cummings home?" Corelli pushed her shield and ID in the doorman's face.

"I don't know."

She clamped her hand on his shoulder. "What do you mean you don't know?"

"My shift just started fifteen minutes ago. She hasn't come in since then." He glared at her. "You're hurting me."

"What about that limo parked in front without a driver?"

"It was here when I came on. I haven't seen the driver."

"Shit."

"Should I call up to her apartment?"

"Yes."

"Does she know what this is in reference—"

"Just call."

He shook off her hand, keyed something into his computer, and picked up the phone. He dialed the number, and they could hear the phone ringing.

"Sorry to bother you so late, Ms. Cummings, but Detective Corelli is here to see you." He waited. "Ms. Cummings, are you there?" He eyed Parker. "No, another detective. Should I send them away?" Corelli reached for the phone, but he jerked it back out of her reach.

"It's all right, you can go up. Middle elevator. Thirty-third floor, apartment A."

"Don't let anybody else up unless you clear it with me. Got that?"

"It's so late I don't think—"

"I didn't ask for your thoughts. Do you understand?"

She could hear the harshness in her voice, felt Parker stiffen, and acknowledged to herself she was dumping her anxiety on him, but she couldn't let it go. He reacted as if she had slapped him, and keeping his eyes on her, nodded. They moved into the elevator.

Neither spoke. Corelli rocked on the balls of her feet, aware Parker was picking up her tension and anxiety.

"I'm sorry Parker. I'm worried."

"Got that."

The elevator door opened, but Corelli didn't move.

"This is it."

"Sorry. Write a note saying, 'shake your head if you're not alone.'" Corelli removed her gun and held it at her side.

"I don't think…" Parker started, then seeing Corelli's face she wrote the note and handed it to her.

Parker took her weapon from the holster, then rang the bell. Brett answered, wearing pajamas and a robe. Corelli put her fingers to her lips and handed Brett the note.

Brett read the note, and taking in the guns in their hands, glared at them. "Is this some kind of sadistic cop game? Yes, I'm alone. Who were you expecting, a murderer?"

Corelli and Parker exchanged glances.

Brett sighed. "Please put those guns away and come in. Needless to say this is quite a surprise." She half turned to lead them into the apartment, then stopped. She looked from one to the other. "Is there a problem? My brother? My sister?"

"As far as we know, your brother and sister are fine. Can we go inside?" Corelli pointed to the living room.

"Of course. I'm sorry for being a grouch. I just got back from Tokyo. I've been traveling an entire day, so I'm tired. And a little freaked since my visitors don't usually arrive with guns in hand."

"We expected you to be on the 11:14 flight," Corelli said, as they followed her into the living room.

Brett turned and glared at Corelli. "Sorry, I didn't know you were interested in my travel arrangements or I would certainly have let you know I changed to an earlier flight when we landed in Houston." She pointed to the sofa. "You might as well sit. Would you like coffee or something else to drink?"

"Coffee would be great," Corelli said. Parker nodded.

"I'll be right back." Brett left the room.

Corelli let out her breath in a whoosh.

"She doesn't seem too happy to see us."

"Very perceptive, Detective," Corelli said. "I guess it was a little weird but better embarrassed than sorry."

The soft blues and greens of the room suited Brett, as did the bold accents of the six Meg Lerner paintings hanging on the one solid wall. Her stomach flipped, remembering she had to tell Brett that not one, not two, but three of her close friends had been murdered. "Nice view," Corelli said, turning away from the paintings to look at the Statue of Liberty, tall and bright in the darkness. The photographs displayed on top of the lustrous, black, baby grand piano standing in front of the windows caught her eye. She walked closer and picked up a picture she'd seen in Brett's office the day they met. She flushed, experiencing again the sadness and longing she'd felt the first time. Then, she hadn't known any of the people, had even expected Brett to be the man in the picture. This time, looking at the picture of Brett on her boat with her brother the priest, and her friends, she recognized Nardo, Kate, Spencer, and Meg. Putting that picture down, she picked up another she'd seen before, a family portrait of a preteen Brett with her mother, father, and younger brother and sister, then moving along the piano she examined several other less formal family snapshots and more pictures of groups of friends, including the *Daily World*'s picture of all of them on the steps of City Hall. In the last photograph in a simple silver frame, Brett and an attractive dark-haired woman embraced, smiling and gazing into each other's eyes, obviously deeply in love. As she read the inscription, 'To my darling Brett, together always, all my love, Em,' Corelli's stomach lurched and waves of disappointment and sadness washed through her. She glanced back at the other pictures but this Em wasn't in any of them. New then.

Her first thought was Brett hadn't let any grass grow under her feet. But even the beautiful Brett Cummings couldn't work so fast. Could she? It was just weeks ago she was flirting and telling Corelli she thought they were soul mates and she would wait for Corelli to be ready. And now this picture. Maybe Em was the first great love she'd mentioned. But if she was, what had happened to "together always"?

Corelli put the picture down and started toward the sofa. Brett stood in the doorway, watching her. Their eyes locked. Brett opened her mouth as if to say something then seemed to change her mind and carried the tray to the coffee table.

"Please help yourself." Brett had put out cheese and crackers, bagels, and croissants. "Don't worry, it's fresh. I had the refrigerator stocked this morning so I would have something to eat when I got in tonight and something for breakfast tomorrow."

Brett smeared brie on several crackers then sat on the easy chair facing them. She pulled her feet up under her. "So?" She kept her eyes on Parker.

Parker smeared cream cheese on a bagel. Corelli poured herself some coffee, sipped it, and sat back. "Have you been in touch with anyone while you've been away?"

"Just my office."

"That's it."

"Oh, and Nardo, a friend."

"About what?"

"Don't you dare play games with me, Detective Corelli," Brett lashed out. "What are you accusing me of now?"

Brett's anger traveled through Corelli's body like an electric shock.

"It's late and I'm really tired. I'd like an explanation before you interrogate me." Her tone implied they might begin to pull out her fingernails. "You tell me why you're here. Then I'll answer your questions." Having delivered her defiant message, she smiled, but there was no warmth in it.

Corelli sipped her coffee and nibbled a cracker, taking time to think before answering. "We think you're in danger."

Brett shifted, placing her feet on the floor and leaning in. "What kind of danger?"

"Ms. Cummings—"

"Brett, damn it, call me Brett. What's wrong?"

Corelli paled. "There's no good way to say this. I—"

"Just say it, spit it out. It can't be any worse than the thoughts running through my mind as you hem and haw."

"Several of your friends are dead."

"Dead?" She jumped up. "Who? Who's dead?"

Parker put a hand out to steady the tray.

"Not Em," she said, pointing to the picture, thinking she would make her feel better.

"Em has been dead for five years." Her voice was like a finely honed steel blade. "Who? Which friends?"

Corelli stood up and moved closer. "Nardo del Balzo, Spencer Nickerson, and Meg Lerner."

"My god."

Corelli caught Brett before she hit the floor. "Get some water, Parker."

She held Brett, breathing in the freshly showered smell of her, and wondering at how naturally they fit together. And given the circumstances, she felt ridiculously happy Em was dead. "I'm so sorry, so very sorry." She touched Brett's hair, her back, and felt her body responding to Brett without her permission. She tightened her embrace.

When Parker returned with the water she loosened her grip so Brett could sip from the glass Parker held. Brett whimpered. Her tears soaked Corelli's neck.

Parker stood, observing and waiting with more water.

Much too soon for Corelli, Brett took a deep breath and pulled away. She tried a smile but it didn't get past the pain on her tear-stained face.

"Thank you, Detect...Chiara. I didn't mean to, I mean that wasn't intentional, you know, throwing myself into your arms like that."

"It's all right. Why don't you sit?"

"Three of them. An accident?" she said, trying to understand. "But you're Homicide. Why would you...? Why do you think I'm in danger?"

"It wasn't an accident, Brett. They were murdered, shot in their homes by what appears to be a serial killer. We think the killer is trying to get to Kate Burke because she's a lesbian. And you and Nelson Choi and Abigail Woo and the others were identified as friends of Ms. Burke's in that picture printed in the *Daily World* the day Ms. Burke became the speaker."

"Murdered." She covered her face. "I can't believe it," she sobbed. "I can't believe it."

Corelli and Parker were silent, giving Brett time to absorb the horrific news and take in the fact she was in danger. Minutes passed before her sobs turned to sniffs. She dropped her hands and stared blankly at the windows, seeming distant and weighed down with sadness. Shaking her head, she walked to the piano, picked up the picture taken on the steps of City Hall, and stared at it. After a while, she replaced the picture and turned back to them, her hands in front of her, her sadness replaced by rage. "What kind of sick bastard kills innocent people, good people, just because they're different? On a day-to-day basis you forget that being a lesbian, being gay or trans, you're not like everybody else, that you're different. You live your life, working hard, paying taxes, trying to be productive, looking for love and happiness like everybody else, and then something like this happens and you're forced to confront the fact that you're a target, that people who don't know you or anything about you hate you and want to harm you." She lowered her hands. "Murder. How horrible. It's harder than losing someone you love to cancer or war."

She heard Parker's quick intake of breath. Corelli froze. *Marnie*. Feelings of guilt swept over her. How could she give in to her attraction to Brett? Her fear for Brett had opened her to the feelings she'd been pushing back. She'd made herself vulnerable, holding Brett and breathing her in, and now she felt herself close down. She needed more time to mourn Marnie.

"Oh, god, I'm so sorry." The tears streamed down Brett's face, glittering like the lights across the river in New Jersey. "I didn't mean…It's just hard to deal with, no warning, no way to explain it."

Brett had collapsed in a chair, sobbing. Corelli wanted to comfort her, but she couldn't. Parker, completely out of character, moved to Brett and took her hand.

The intensity of Chiara's feelings for Brett petrified her. But why? She'd risked her career and her life to do what she felt was right, yet she cringed in the face of lust, but of course she knew it was more than lust. Lust would be simple. This could be love. What if she let herself love Brett and something happened to her? She sat stiff with misery, staring at Brett and Parker. Normally she was the one who touched people in pain to offer human comfort, but she was afraid of contact with Brett. And she felt so alone.

Brett leaned into Parker, seeking comfort. Parker looked uncomfortable but then awkwardly moved her other hand to Brett's shoulder. Corelli felt a shiver of jealousy and looked away.

"Thanks," Brett said, and started to get up. "I need tissues."

Parker pushed her down gently. "I'll get them. Tell me where."

"Bathroom," she sniffed. "The end of the hall."

"Sure," Parker said, and walked out of the room.

Brett waited until she heard the bathroom door close. "Please forgive me, Chiara. The last thing I want to do is hurt you."

"Don't worry. I'm not made of porcelain."

"No, I think you're much softer than that."

Parker was taking her sweet time getting back. Corelli shifted uncomfortably, then forced herself to speak. "I'm sorry I said that about Em. I didn't know."

"How could you know? You haven't called me to talk." There was no accusation, just hurt.

"I, um, I've been busy and I'm not sure…" What was it that made her feel and sound like a tongue-tied fifteen-year-old whenever she was near Brett?

"Relax. Talking doesn't mean we have to get married. If I survive this…" Her eyes filled, but her voice was strong. "If the killer doesn't get me, I'm coming after you. Just to talk. Since you know I'm not a murderer, surely you can trust me enough to meet and talk?"

Corelli winced. *But could she trust herself.* "I deserved that. We'll see when this is all over."

Brett sniffed. "Definitely. We'll see each other."

Brett must be taking lessons from Gianna.

Suddenly aware of Brett's dripping nose, Corelli reached into her pocket for one of the extra handkerchiefs she carried for just these situations. She wasn't thinking clearly. Brett's remark, followed by Parker's holding Brett, had thrown her off balance. She handed the handkerchief to Brett. "Sorry, I forgot I had an extra."

"Thanks." Brett smiled. She wiped her eyes and blew her nose. "Now you'll have to meet with me so I can return the handkerchief."

Corelli fought back the urge to wrap Brett in her arms.

Parker strolled in. "Sorry to take so long. I needed to use the john." She handed Brett the box of tissues, a trace of smile flickering at the corners of her mouth.

Corelli realized the delay had been on purpose and glowered at her. Parker seemed not to notice.

"It's all right. Detective Corelli gave me her handkerchief," Brett said, showing Parker the crumpled white cloth in her hand.

Brett put the box of tissues on the table and stared at it as if it was a crystal ball. Then she looked at Corelli. "I can't take this in. My mind won't accept it. My friends. They're my family. How could they be dead?" She broke down again, sobbed for a while, then regained control.

"You think I'm next? What do I do?"

"We'll set up around-the-clock protection. Do you have to go to the office or can you work from here?"

"Um, I need to go to the office tomorrow, but after that I could work here at least a few days, if you think it's necessary. Will you and Detective Parker stay with me?"

"We can't. We're the lead investigators on the case." *Although if I could, I'd tuck you away in my pocket close to my heart, so I could protect you.* Where was this stuff coming from? *Next thing I'll be spouting poetry.* No daydreaming, no mooning around, no swooning, until you get this guy. "Watkins and another detective will be here soon to relieve us. They'll stay the night if that's all right?"

Brett nodded. "I need to see Kate and Abby and Nelson."

"Right now only Kate is in the city. Nelson and Abby are out of town and we've asked them to stay away for a few more days. But we'll arrange for Kate to come here. She may even show up later."

"Thank you," Brett sniffled. "Would it be all right, I mean could we go out and walk along the river while we wait for your replacements to come? I'd like to get some air."

"Sure, I could use a stretch myself."

"I'll be a minute. Let me throw some clothes on."

"This could be dangerous," Parker said, after Brett left the room.

"I know."

Brett led them out to the Esplanade, the path along the Hudson River, and headed south. The night was humid and the river misty. Except for a few dog walkers, the Esplanade was quiet. Brett followed the winding path onto a wooden pier that extended over the water and offered a view of the Statue of Liberty proudly holding her torch. Brett stopped, took a breath, and leaned on the railing facing the shore. "This is South Cove, my favorite place to sit and read in the day, to talk and dream in the evening. Ever been here?"

"Yes, often."

It was a little oasis in the city. On the water but connected to the city, the breeze was refreshing and the sound of the water gently flowing over rocks relaxing. Corelli glanced back. Parker was standing a little way off, her hand inside her jacket, scanning the path and the woods for danger. Either she was giving them privacy or she feared an attack. Probably both. Corelli stood next to Brett and enjoyed the feel of their arms brushing, the closeness. But they had work to do.

"Can you tell me about your conversation with Nardo?" Corelli asked.

Brett blew her nose then dried her eyes. "He called me in Tokyo, Tuesday night. He had had a terrible argument with his father, which really unsettled him. He recognized it was time for him to let go of old stuff with his father and get on with his life. He asked for my therapist's number. It was the middle of the night in Tokyo, and when he realized he had gotten me out of bed, he apologized profusely and said he wanted to talk about the argument, but it could wait until I got back. We agreed I'd call and set up a time to get together after I got home." Her eyes glistened. Then the tears spilled out. "He was so loving and such a wonderful friend. It's hard to believe he's gone."

"Did he say what the argument was about?"

"No. Just that it made him realize he wanted something from his father he would never get, and it was time to move on."

"Did he mention any threats?"

"Not that day but when we talked a few days before I left for Tokyo he said he had been getting calls from the 'un-Christians' as we call them. You know the religious fanatics who preach hate and carry signs saying, 'Kill the faggots.' Oh my God, do you think they're doing this?"

"It's something we're pursuing. Do you think any of your friends would invite the 'un-Christians' in for cheese and crackers or a drink?"

Brett laughed, a harsh sound that surprised Corelli. "Would you invite that Mafioso Toricelli into your house for cheese and crackers?"

Corelli felt Brett shift to look at her, but she didn't answer.

"Did Nardo feel threatened by his father?"

"You can't...hmm, nothing specific, but he was terrified of his father for some reason he never was able to talk about."

CHAPTER FORTY-THREE

Monday – 1:30 a.m.

It was late and Parker was exhausted. She'd wondered whether Corelli had gotten together with Brett. Tonight confirmed they hadn't. She'd never thought much about lesbians before, certainly never thought anything positive, but she'd seen the sparks fly between them from the minute she'd escorted Brett into the interview room, the first time they met. She respected both of them and it had forced her to rethink her prejudices. And seeing them together tonight confirmed in her mind they were well matched. Watching Corelli fight her feelings was almost as painful as watching Brett's anguish at losing her friends.

Jesse had told her Corelli and her girlfriend had been in Iraq together and Corelli had been there when her girlfriend was killed. Maybe that's why Corelli seemed to be trying to fight her attraction to Brett. She smiled. Her money was on Brett, one smart lady who clearly had no ambivalence about wanting Corelli.

She got ready for bed and sat at her desk, determined to stay awake long enough to start examining her mother's things. She ran her hand over the books and papers, hoping to feel something, but nothing happened. She reached for Tasha's journal but changed her mind and went for a large envelope jutting out from the bottom of one of the piles. She moved the books covering the envelope to the floor, then picked up the envelope which had "miscellaneous" written on it. Weird to think it was probably her mother's handwriting. She sat on the bed holding the envelope. She shivered even in the heat of the room, afraid to open it, afraid to know, then deciding knowing was better than the limbo she had lived in her entire life. She pried the metal clips apart and spilled the contents onto the bed.

She picked up an envelope addressed to Randall Young, but clearly never sent, examined it, inhaled the musty smell of old paper, and pulled out the contents. Tears stung her eyes as she gazed at a studio photograph of Tasha with a baby on her lap. Both faced the camera but Tasha's head tilted down to look at the baby dressed in a frilly pink dress with tiny white socks and shoes, her expression soft and filled with love. The inscription said, "To Randall, with love from Tasha and your Precious Jewel." Tears tumbled out of Parker's eyes, and it took her a minute to realize the strange noise was the sound of her sobs.

She brushed the tears with the back of her hand and smiled. The police reports said she appeared well cared for and loved when they found her at three years old sitting next to her mother's body, and now she knew for certain it was true. She was loved. Tomorrow she would buy a frame for the photo so she could put it out, look at it, but right now she needed to get some sleep. She now knew for sure her mother had loved her dearly and almost for sure Randall Young was her father. She could wait to know the rest.

CHAPTER FORTY-FOUR

Tuesday – 6:30 a.m.

In the elevator on the way up to her apartment last night, Corelli remembered Simone and Nicky were there so she rubbed her temples, did a couple of bends from the waist and breathed deeply to relax. Her exhaustion, her worries about protecting Brett and the others, and her conflict about letting go of Marnie, made it difficult to deal with Nicky's sexuality. But it pained her to see her sweet, vulnerable nephew struggling to deal with the loss of Spencer and the fear of losing his parents. She loved all her nieces and nephews, but she had a special affinity for Nicky, her oldest nephew. She'd always thought it was because he looked so much like Luca. But maybe it was because they were both gay. It didn't matter. He needed her love and support and acceptance to deal with his sexuality and his parents. The elevator door slid open. Steeling herself for the assault by youthful exuberance, she stepped into the loft and reveled in the glorious quiet. They must be asleep downstairs in the guest rooms. She crept into the bathroom, lit some candles, and crawled into a hot bath to unwind.

Marnie. Her thoughts drifted to the few intense days they'd spent in Provincetown right before they'd deployed. They'd acknowledged the very real possibility of one of them dying in Afghanistan and every touch, every kiss, every meeting of eyes said I love you, I cherish you, you will be in my heart forever. Marnie had insisted they grant each other the freedom to live should the other die. They clung to each other and cried as each of them repeated the promise: "I will mourn, but not forever; I will not forget, but I will let myself love again without guilt."

Easier said than done. But seeing Brett alive and well, holding her and talking to her had broken through the wall of anxiety she'd built, flooding her with the feelings she'd been fighting. She would always love Marnie, but maybe she was ready to open her heart. She ducked her head, letting the bathwater mingle with her tears, letting her guilt wash away. Marnie would laugh at her for making her attraction to Brett into such a big deal that she couldn't think straight. Once this case was over, she would call Brett to talk. Maybe if they spent a little time together her feelings for Brett would evaporate as quickly as they had appeared. Or not.

The kittens had trained her to leave her bedroom door open. If they couldn't get in to sleep with her they would scream bloody murder, scratch, and throw themselves at the door until she opened it. She put her gun in the drawer so she wouldn't accidentally shoot them or one of the kids overnight. She drifted, half asleep, half awake, and when she did fall asleep she had a nightmare, but this time it was about Brett. Someone was trying to kill Brett in the next room and she couldn't find the door to get in to save her. She woke covered in sweat and listened for the kids, but either she hadn't screamed, or they were in the deep sleep of untroubled teenagers. As if they sensed her terror, the kittens strolled in, jumped on the bed, and snuggled on her chest. Comforted by their warmth and soft snores she dozed off.

By six a.m. when Nicky stumbled out of bed, she had already been out to the all-night bagel place around the corner on Fourteenth Street and was at the table reading the papers, drinking coffee, eating an everything bagel, and fighting off the kittens, who were having a grand time climbing up and down her legs.

"Morning, Auntie." He helped himself to coffee and a bagel and joined her at the table. "We tried to wait up but we were both zonked. I guess you got in really late."

The cats switched to climbing up his legs. Jeans were much better for climbing.

"About one thirty. Parker and I were with Brett Cummings until we could get a police officer to stay with her."

"Is she okay? I mean, how horrible to hear your best friends have been…" He looked down at the kittens, took a deep breath, then looked at her, "…have been murdered."

Chiara felt protective of him and of Brett's privacy so she went with the short answer. No need to share Brett's anguish. "It was a shock. I'm sure it will take some time before Brett and Kate and the others are okay. But Kate arrived just as we were leaving. They're both strong women and they'll support each other."

He pulled the kittens into his lap and took a bite of his bagel before speaking again. "Brett's dynamite. Do you know she speaks really good Italian? We chatted with her and Nardo for a long time. She couldn't get over how much we both look like you. Spencer—" He looked away.

Corelli reached for his hand. "He was your friend, Nick. Crying is allowed."

He nodded and sniffled. "It's just hard to believe." He turned to her, a pained smile on his face, patted her hand, and picked up his bagel. "Anyway, Spencer bragged on Brett, said she's a super sailor, a super woman, and a super successful stockbroker. She offered me the opportunity to intern with her this summer, you know, learn the stock market. Cool, huh?"

Corelli's lips twitched. *Busy woman that Brett Cummings, seducing my sister and my nephew. Even speaks Italian. As if it wasn't hard enough to resist her.*

"What are you smiling about, Auntie?"

"Speaking of Spencer. Are you involved with anyone?"

He blushed, tears filled his eyes. "No. I had a crush on Spencer but, you know, he said he was still mourning his lover, and anyway it would be better for me to be with someone more my age, that I should be patient, that I would meet somebody special."

She hesitated to ask, this was her nephew for god's sake, but she needed to be sure. "You know about safe sex, right?"

He looked amused. "Yes, Auntie. Spencer made sure the whole group knew about it."

She sipped her coffee and peered at him over the rim of her cup. "So how did you know you were gay? How could you be sure?"

"I didn't know. I always had lots of girls as friends, but not, like, you know, girlfriends. But my friends and I went out in a group, guys and girls, not paired up in couples, and I didn't give it a second thought. I was only sixteen and I told myself I just hadn't met the right girl, that there was plenty of time for dating. But then I met this high-voltage guy and I knew I was in love. But we just had a brief fling and he moved on." He shrugged. "When I thought about it, I realized I had always had crushes on my friends and male teachers. I just hadn't noticed."

"How do you feel about it? About being gay?"

"I'm okay with Simone and my friends, but when I'm home or with the family, I feel anxious they'll hate me." He shrugged and looked embarrassed.

She reached over and took both his hands. When he looked at her his eyes filled. "I'm afraid to tell them. I think Auntie Gianna and Uncle Marco will be okay, like you, but my mom and dad and Grandma and Grandpa, maybe they'll disown me. Grandpa disowned you just for being a cop before he even knew you were a lesbian." He sniffed.

She squeezed his hands. "It's hard to be different, isn't it? And you're right, they will be very upset for a while, but they love you and with time they'll accept you for who you are. And if they don't, you'll still have family, like I do. It's painful to be rejected just for who you love but if you're ever going to be happy, Nicky, you can only be who you are."

"Thanks, I know I'll be okay. I just forget sometimes."

"Take your time. When you're ready to tell your parents, I'll come with you and so will Gianna and Marco." *And, who knows, by that time, maybe Brett will be there too.*

CHAPTER FORTY-FIVE

Tuesday – 8:30 a.m.

Parker rang Corelli's bell at eight thirty. When Corelli came down a few minutes later, Parker was sitting in the car with an easy listening station on the radio. She looked tired but relaxed, and there was something different about her, hard to put a finger on it, though. She wasn't smiling but she seemed to be enjoying a memory or a thought. She almost glowed, like she had a secret. Maybe she had met someone after they'd left Brett's apartment last night, even though it was so late.

"Good morning, Parker, get some sleep last night?"

"Fair amount," she said, with a dreamy smile on her face.

Not sharing, so that must be a sexual glow. Nice to see Parker looking so relaxed. Almost happy. Made her realize how tense Parker was most of the time.

Corelli sat back, closed her eyes, and let the music flow over her during the short drive to the stationhouse. Maybe some of the good vibe would rub off on her. But soon enough they were at the house and a howling media mob waited to devour them, or at least her. Had something happened? Or were they frantic because she arrived much later than usual?

Since the captain had decreed that whether at the precinct or at a crime scene, the media was to be restrained behind barricades in order to allow free, unobstructed access to all personnel, it had been easier to ignore them. But the distance didn't stop the mad dog press. Either they were optimistic or desperate because nearly every morning they lay in wait behind the barricades. They didn't seem to get that as long as they were a mob, she would refuse to talk to them.

Well, maybe it was her lucky day after all. Only twenty or thirty police were outside waiting for her. Whatever. She and Parker were getting to be old hands at this.

Parker took a deep breath. "The usual?"

"I wouldn't have it any other way."

They got out of the car and strode toward the door shoulder to shoulder. As she expected, the police turned their backs and a few hissed. The press, however, kept howling, screaming her name and questions she couldn't even hear over the din.

She relaxed as the door closed.

They took a minute to observe Councilman Collins through the two-way mirror. He was sitting with his elbows on the table, head cradled in his hands. Hard to tell whether he was hung over, upset, or feeling sorry for himself, but like any politician faced with his public, he pulled himself together when he heard the knob turn and they stepped in.

"I'll have your job for this."

Right. She smiled, a feral smile. For once she was dealing with someone even higher on the mayor's "shit list" than her, but even without that, she had Kate Burke on her side, so he could stuff it.

"Be that as it may, Councilman Collins, you'll have to answer a few questions first."

"Detective Parker, please read the councilman his rights."

He jumped up. "Wait just a minute here." His voice was tinged with fear. "I already told you I have nothing to do with the GALS killings."

Corelli circled him. "Yes, you did. But I'm not convinced. Why were you boarding a plane for Washington this morning?"

His head spun trying to follow her. "I often go to Washington on city business."

"And what business was so critical that you ignored the request not to leave the city?"

He bit his lip but didn't respond.

"I see. Maybe you can explain why we haven't received the documents we requested from last week's trip to Washington, the receipts and the list of the people you saw?"

"I told you, it's not relevant to the GALS investigation."

"Maybe you could explain why you needed a copy of the guest list the day of Speaker Burke's election?"

"Stop circling me. You're making me dizzy."

"Your obfuscation makes me dizzy. Answer, please."

She inched toward him, totally focused, as if he were prey. He stepped back. She resumed circling.

"Could we sit?"

"It was your idea to stand." She waved him to the table, but remained standing, leaning against the wall, facing him. He averted his eyes.

"I don't have a lot of time, Councilman, and I'm getting impatient, so if you're not ready to answer my questions, we'll go off and do other things while you think about it. And later tonight or tomorrow morning when we're back in the office, we'll check to see if you're ready."

He paled. "You have no right—"

"Oh, but I do." That feral smile was back. She moved toward the door. Parker followed.

"Wait. Anything I say must stay in this room."

She put her hand on the doorknob.

He reached an arm toward her as if to hold her back. "Wait," he said through clenched teeth. "I planned to use the list for fundraising when Burke fucked up. But I swear I never saw it. Security sent it to my assistant and she put it in the fundraising file."

Corelli stepped out of the room and a minute later Dietz appeared. "Check with security and his assistant to see if he's telling the truth."

Corelli stepped back in and went back to the wall.

Collins removed a neatly folded white handkerchief from his back pocket and swabbed the perspiration from his face. Clutching the damp cloth, he met her eyes.

"I've answered your question. I'd like to leave now."

"Ah, but we're just beginning. You haven't provided the requested documentation for your trip to Washington—names of people you met with and receipts for hotels and meals, et cetera. So why don't you tell us where you were Tuesday, Wednesday, Thursday, and Friday nights and give us the documents later."

He leaned back, passed the handkerchief over his face again. "I told you. It's not relevant to your investigation."

"I'll decide what's relevant."

Parker stood. "He's wasting our time."

"You want to book him, Parker? I thought we'd give him another chance." She stretched her legs and leaned back. "But my patience is running out too. What about it, Councilman?"

Parker sat again.

He looked from one to the other. "Good cop, bad cop. I get it."

Corelli straightened. "No, sir, you don't get it. If I don't hear an explanation in the next couple of minutes, we will hold you and get a warrant to search your office. How will that look to your constituents?"

"You can't." His voice was defiant.

"I can and I will." She locked on his eyes. "Your decision. How do you want to handle it?"

He stood. Parker bounced up and moved between him and the door. He ignored her and paced in the small space, pulling at his neatly coiffed hair.

"This will ruin me if it gets out. Promise you won't mention it."

"Councilman, you're going to have to take my word that I have no interest in ruining you or anyone. All I want to do is eliminate you as a suspect."

He glanced at the mirror. "Who's watching? I'll tell you two but no one else can hear."

"There's no one there." He seemed unaware everything he said would be included in their written report.

He sat again, put his face in his hands, rubbed his eyes and face, and took a deep breath. "All expenses for the trip were paid for by Longford Development Associates. I have no receipts."

"And they are?"

"They're bidding on a big development project in my district."

"Would that be the billion dollar project opposed by your constituents?"

"Yes. I…They wanted me to spend a few days with them so they could help me see the benefits of the project."

"In Washington?"

"No, Puerto Rico. My wife and I flew on their private jet and they wined and dined us."

"And do you see the benefits now?"

He flushed.

"Why were you taking the shuttle to Washington?"

"I wanted to get them to fake some receipts or something, to avoid this, my having to tell you I—"

"Took a bribe?"

He stared at his hands.

"We need some names so we can corroborate your story and once we do you're free to go on the condition you tell Kate Burke about this when she gets here in a little while."

"You promised," he moaned like a kid denied his ice cream cone.

"No sir, I said I have no interest in ruining you, which I don't, but I do have a strong interest in honesty and integrity. It will be easier for you if you confess. Maybe if your wife stands next to you while you apologize publicly, you'll get to keep your job."

CHAPTER FORTY-SIX

Wednesday – 9 a.m.

Corelli positioned herself at the top of the steps near the main entrance to St. Patrick's Cathedral and reviewed, for the hundredth time, all the precautions they had put in place to protect Brett, Kate Burke, Abby Wong, and Nelson Choi. When the del Balzo family had opted not to have a wake with an open coffin, Corelli arranged for the four friends to spend a short while with Nardo's body late one night at the morgue, hoping that would satisfy their need to say goodbye to their friend. As the person responsible for their safety, she argued against their presence at Nardo del Balzo's funeral today.

But the four were adamant, saying they would attend the funeral with or without her permission and with or without her protection. Nardo was their close friend, the first of their three close friends to be buried, and they would show their love and respect by attending his funeral. He would do no less for them. In her heart she knew if it were her friend, she would do the same. She was confident, or at least as confident as one could be when dealing with an obviously deranged killer, that he wouldn't try to kill any of them at the funeral. He liked privacy and time to arrange the body, so a public killing didn't fit his pattern. Yet, these murders were so personal, she assumed he would attend the funeral and she had planned for the possibility of an attack on the survivors. She had arranged extra security for each of them amidst the heavy security provided for Ambassador del Balzo, his family, and other dignitaries.

Now she and the numerous other detectives and uniformed officers spread along the top step of St. Patrick's Cathedral scanned the faces of mourners, checked hands and the bulkiness of clothing, and attempted to identify anyone who appeared out of place. Shoulder-to-shoulder uniforms with their backs to the cathedral faced the spectators lining the sidewalk behind the metal gates used for crowd control. The officers struggled to maintain a clear path from the curb to the cathedral entrance while scrutinizing the crowd for danger. Contained on one side of the entrance, newscasters pushed forward, shouted questions, and tried to stick their microphones and cameras in the faces of the guests arriving for the funeral. She spotted Bear, towering over some of the others. The del Balzos had approved one camera in the church to be shared by all networks, and Corelli had allowed newscasters who could be trusted to take notes but not broadcast, to attend the service in the cathedral. Darla was probably inside already.

Cars and limousines lined up for blocks. A police team checked the identification of the passengers in each car before releasing it to dispense its occupants at the cathedral's entrance. The Secretary General of the UN, a number of UN ambassadors, the governor, two senators, several representatives, the mayor, the chief of police, and other high level politicians had already entered when a voice in Corelli's earpiece informed her the next car at the curb would be Speaker Kate Burke and her partner Abby Wong, with their security detail.

Burke stepped out of the car, glanced at the crowd, but as a mourner today, not a politician, she ignored the press and made no move to greet anyone. Security enveloped her and Wong and the group moved up the stairs. At the top, just before they entered, Burke acknowledged Corelli with a brief nod.

A checkpoint for mourners arriving on foot was set up to the side of the entrance. A picture ID was required to pass through. Nardo's coworkers from the Italian delegation were amongst those who entered that way. They acknowledged Corelli as they moved up the steps. Men, alone or in pairs, drifted in. Scott Sigler arrived with a friend on either side and seemed not to see her when he walked past. It took her a minute but she did recognize a dressed-up Miranda Foxworth, looking beautiful, on the arm of a man Corelli assumed was her partner, John.

"Detective Corelli." Miranda spoke softly enough that no one standing nearby could overhear.

"Ms. Foxworth." Corelli nodded.

The next car announced contained Ms. Simone Corelli and Mr. Nicolas Gianelli and their bodyguards. Nicky got out first and reached in to help Simone. They seemed stunned to be in the spotlight. As soon as their guards gave the word, they hurried up the steps into the cathedral. Nicky gave a little wave when he spotted Chiara and whispered into Simone's ear as they stepped inside.

Then the voice in her ear whispered: "Ms. Brett Cummings and Mr. Nelson Choi." She tensed as the limousine drew to the curb and waited as Detective Forlini, the driver, came around to open the door. First out was Parker, followed by Charleen Greene. The three detectives scanned the crowd and then Parker leaned in to help Brett out of the car. She looked pale and lovely and dignified in black. If she was frightened, she didn't show it. She searched the crowd and finding Corelli, held her eyes for a few seconds before saying something to Parker, who nodded to Greene, standing at Brett's left. The three of them moved up the steps into the cathedral. Corelli let out the breath she was holding and watched Nelson Choi and his partner Jeremy, accompanied by Ron Watkins and another detective, follow Brett up the steps.

Finally, the last limousine arrived. Somehow the crowd knew it was the del Balzos, even though the windows were tinted so it was impossible to see inside. Conversations stopped and the crowd surged forward. Except for the swoosh of buses and cars on Fifth, the whirl of cameras, and the murmur of voices speaking softly into microphones in several languages, it was quiet, like a collective holding of breath. The chauffeur moved around to the passenger side and opened the front door.

Andrea Sansone, dressed totally in black but without his cowboy boots, jumped out of the front seat of the extra-long limo, faced the cameras, and then donned a black hat. Sansone opened the back-passenger door and helped Nardo's sister Antonia out. She took his arm. Nardo's brother-in-law Emilio followed and reached back for his wife, Flavia. Like everyone else in front of the cathedral, the four of them stared at the front passenger door of the limo. Carla del Balzo, looking very glamorous in black with a large black hat and a black veil covering her face, assisted by Sansone, exited as gracefully as one can from a limousine.

Last, the very distinguished and handsome Ambassador Leonardo del Balzo emerged, brushed his pants, and murmured something. Traffic seemed to slow. Cameras flashed and the crowd surged forward. The police line held and pushed back as the four younger people started up the steps. Sansone's eyes settled on Corelli, and while he didn't acknowledge her, she thought she detected the beginning of a smirk. She disengaged and moved her eyes to Nardo's parents, the ambassador with his hand at Carla's elbow, escorting her slowly up the steps behind Sansone and their daughters and son-in-law. The ambassador looked straight ahead, but it was impossible to know where Carla looked with her face behind the thick black veil. Corelli followed them into the cathedral.

The dimness, the smell of incense, the coughing and nose blowing, and the gentle whisper of conversation in the cathedral were familiar and comforting to Corelli. Heads turned as the del Balzos moved slowly toward the front pew and sat. She scanned the crowd again and noticed Darla and several other members of the media standing off to the side, speaking quietly into phones or small recorders. After a minute or so, the organ began to play. The *Ave Maria* soared. The mourners stood, faced the rear, and watched the priests greet the beautiful rosewood casket, sprinkle it with holy water, and chant as they followed the coffin down the aisle.

At the front of the church, the priests walked around the coffin swinging the censer or incense burner. Corelli moved down the side aisle and leaned against a giant column with a clear view of her five charges and their guards. With her hand on her gun, she scanned the crowd again. Brett whispered in Parker's ear. Parker nodded but never stopped surveying the area around them. The Mass started. And lulled by the music, the incense, the dimness, and the sleeplessness of last night, Corelli struggled to stay alert. She forced herself to breathe deeply, and she paced until the adrenaline kicked in again when the mourners lined up in the aisles on the way to the altar to take communion. She panicked; she couldn't see the seven and their guards behind the communion takers. She moved quickly toward them and shoved her way through the double line to the pews that held them. Everyone looked up. She apologized to the people she had pushed aside, smiled weakly at the guards and the guarded, but remained standing near the two pews while the line curved around her. She was thankful none of the five took communion. At last everyone was seated again and she moved back to her post.

Finally, it was over, and the coffin rolled toward the rear of the church, followed by the ambassador and Mrs. del Balzo, their daughters, son-in-law, and Andrea Sansone.

The crowd was huge but orderly and, as usual, the pews emptied into the aisles from front to back, allowing the people sitting up front the opportunity to exit first. Corelli stood to the side then fell into place behind the group of friends as their row moved into the aisle. Nardo's body was being flown to Italy for burial, so once they were out of the church her detectives would whisk the five friends away to Brett's place and Corelli would breathe again. But the line inched forward and Corelli became more and more agitated. "What's going on out there? Why are we moving so slowly?" she whispered into her mouthpiece.

"It's the del Balzos," the voice in her ear replied. "They're doing a receiving line in the vestibule so everyone is stopping to talk to them."

"Oh, great."

When they reached the vestibule she stepped to the entrance, trying to keep an eye on what was happening outside, stay away from the del Balzos, and still keep a close eye on everyone. Finally, the seven, with their guards standing close, were at the front of the line. Corelli said, "Bring their cars around. They'll be out in a minute."

Simone and Nicky stopped briefly to offer condolences in Italian. Corelli was amused to see both the del Balzos frown, probably trying to figure how they knew these two youngsters who looked enough like her to be taken for her twins.

Kate and Abby hugged Nardo's sisters, squeezed the hands of both parents and murmured something, then walked out, followed by their security detail. Nelson and Jeremy also hugged and spoke to the sisters, but when they reached the ambassador, he flushed and nodded, then turned away from them; neither del Balzo offered them a hand. The two men hesitated and moved out with Ron and his associate on either side. The prejudiced bastard couldn't even control himself at the funeral. It probably never even entered their little minds that Kate and Abby were lesbians, but they got it about Nelson and Jeremy. Brett hugged Antonia and whispered something that made the young woman sob. She grasped Flavia's hands and kissed her cheek. Flavia dabbed at her eyes when Brett moved on to the parents, who were waiting and watching her with interest. Brett's voice was soft so Corelli couldn't hear what she said, but it sounded as if she were speaking in Italian. Corelli edged closer.

"Nardo and I were very close friends," Brett said. Tears streamed down her face. "I can't believe it. I just spoke to him Tuesday night."

The del Balzos responded in Italian. Carla took Brett's hand in hers and leaned in close to say something Corelli couldn't hear. Brett removed a pen and a card from her bag and wrote something on the card before handing it to Carla. They hugged and Brett moved on. Neither of the del Balzos seemed to have noticed Parker standing just past them waiting for Brett. She smiled. Darla had somehow managed to be right behind Brett. The del Balzos turned as Darla offered her condolences. Corelli spotted Spencer Nickerson's parents and Hillary, his business partner, farther back in the line. She wished she could stay to watch that interaction, but this wasn't the time to feed her idle curiosity.

Standing on the curb, she breathed a sigh of relief when Parker handed Brett into the limousine and slid into the seat facing her. All safe, she felt the tension start to leak away. One down, two to go. But she couldn't relax with the killer still out there. She focused on the crowd filing out of the cathedral hoping to spot someone who raised the hair on her arms.

"Detective Corelli." Brett's throaty voice, made rougher by all the crying, pulled her attention back to the limo.

"Yes?" She crouched at the window to hear Brett over the noise of the crowd.

"I expect to see you at my apartment with the rest of the team. Simone and Nicky are coming too."

That was a command not a question. Brett definitely must be studying with Gianna. "Probably not. I'll be here for a while and then I have a lot to do at the office."

"You have to eat. Just come for lunch. Please." Brett smiled through her tears. "Don't worry, I'm too sad to attack you. You'll be safe," she said softly.

Corelli found herself smiling. "Well, if you promise." Might as well. She felt drained and she had to eat. Besides, she'd probably spend the time thinking about Brett anyway.

CHAPTER FORTY-SEVEN

Wednesday – 1:30 p.m.

Corelli groaned. She had expected a small gathering, just the five friends, her sister and nephew, and the detectives guarding them, but it looked like Brett had invited half the people who'd attended the funeral at St. Patrick's, including Darla North. So much for security. She searched the crowd for her people and felt a little better. Although they were eating like everyone else, they were on duty, spread out around the room, eyes vigilant, jackets open, ready for action.

"It can't be that bad, Detective." Brett appeared out of the crowd, Parker and Greene behind her but with enough distance to give them privacy. She put a hand on Corelli's arm. Her eyes were swollen and red, her nose dripping and red, her face pale and drawn, and still she looked beautiful. "I'm glad you felt safe enough to come," she said, her voice gently mocking.

"You promised to behave, there's plenty of police protection and I have my gun, so I thought I'd take a chance."

"Aha, do I detect a sense of humor under all that seriousness?"

Corelli's lips quirked. "No way. I'm always serious, especially when I'm on duty. And speaking about duty, who are all these people? How can we protect you all in this crowd?"

"Our friends, Nardo's friends, Spencer's family, other families. Calm down. I didn't invite the murderer. At least I don't think I did." Her voice broke and the tears flowed. "Sorry. I'm on an emotional roller coaster. One minute I remember my friends are dead and the pain and sadness overwhelm me, and then something like your being here makes me happy and I get all silly and playful and outrageous." She sniffed and smiled.

Corelli smiled back and instead of giving in to the impulse to wrap her arms around Brett, she handed her one of the clean white handkerchiefs she bought by the dozen. Their hands lingered a few seconds longer than necessary to make the exchange. Then Brett looked into her eyes and kissed the white cloth before applying it to her now sparkling and mischievous eyes. "See what I mean," she said. "I can't help myself."

She moved to Corelli's side so they both faced the room. "Anyway, don't worry so much. Your guys are on alert. P.J., um, Detectives Parker and Greene try to stay close." She raised her voice. "I'm a slippery character. Right, Detective Parker?"

"Yes. But between us, we have you on our radar," Parker said. She looked at Corelli. "Can we leave Ms. Cummings with you while we get something else to eat?"

Parker looked innocent enough so why did Corelli feel like she was conspiring with Brett? "Sure, take a break."

"I really haven't given them much time to relax." As Parker and Greene melted into the crowd, Brett moved closer to Corelli. "You look exhausted, Chiara. Come in and relax while I make you a plate." She put a finger on Corelli's lips to still the protest. "Don't worry, I won't put my secret love potion in the food." She removed her finger.

Corelli didn't fight it. She *was* exhausted and the easing of the tension at the funeral had left her feeling light-headed. "I'd love it, but I'll be circulating. You'll have to find me."

Brett squeezed her arm. "Rest assured, my dear detective, you won't lose me so easily. I'll find you wherever you are."

Brett walked in the direction of the table and Parker materialized out of the crowd and followed.

Corelli touched her lips. A love potion might just be the thing, take away her volition.

A waiter appeared and handed her a drink. "Ms. Cummings said you needed a glass of San Pellegrino water."

"Thanks." *She reads minds too.*

Corelli moved around the room, making eye contact with her people, listening in on conversations, nodding at the people she recognized. She stopped to confirm Darla was off the record, just a guest, then lightly touched Simone and Nicky on their arms as she passed them standing in a group with Nelson Choi, his partner Jeremy, and Spencer's parents. She overheard Spencer's mother say Nardo's parents bristled when she introduced herself and almost pushed her along. Nelson commiserated, saying they had been rude to him and Jeremy. No wonder Nardo hated them. She moved on. A group that included Meg Lerner's friend Amelia Freestone, Kate Burke, and Abby Wong was discussing Meg.

"Her paintings are worth a fortune. What will happen to them now?" asked a woman Corelli didn't recognize.

"Ask Brett. She's the executor of Meg's will," Burke said.

Brett appeared with a plate piled high, took Corelli's hand, and led her to a quiet space near the windows. She took an olive as she handed the dish to Corelli. For a second Corelli thought Brett was going to try to feed her and was relieved when she popped it into her own mouth.

She dug in. She hadn't realized she was hungry. She and Brett stood side by side, bodies touching lightly. Corelli felt her body heat up and wondered if Brett felt it. She wanted to touch her, comfort her. She swallowed. "I heard Kate say you're Meg's executor. From what you've all said about Meg, I'm surprised she had a will."

"Meg might have been absentminded and out-of-touch when she was painting, but she was no airhead. She knew the value of her paintings and worried about her legacy. Even though she didn't expect to die so young, she took steps to ensure her artwork would be managed properly after her death. She also wanted to make sure her alcoholic and abusive mother, father, and brothers didn't get a dime. You'll probably get to see the four of them at the funeral. They've already contacted her attorney about her will. I'm sure they'll challenge it."

"Who inherits then?"

Brett scrutinized her face. "Me. At least most of the paintings. Friends of hers like Kate, Abby, Nelson, Nardo, Spencer, Amelia Freestone whom I believe you've met, and other friends whom you probably haven't met will have the opportunity to choose a painting, or in some cases several paintings." Her eyes filled with tears.

Corelli nodded. "Most of these," she nodded at the paintings on the wall, "look like her early work. Gifts, or did you buy them?"

"My, my, you're familiar enough with her work to recognize it's early?" She smiled through her tears. "You are full of contradictions, my dearest detective. Years ago I met Meg at a studio she shared with another artist. I had gone to see the other artist's collages, but the minute I saw Meg's paintings, I lost all interest in the other artist. Meg was unknown, struggling to make ends meet, and so hungry to sell, for the money, of course, but also for the recognition, that she considerably underpriced the work. I bought the three big ones on the wall and paid her much, much, more than she asked. She was stunned and we became friends. She gave me the two small ones some time later because she thought of them as one piece with the three I purchased. Over the years I bought her work; occasionally she gave me a painting she thought I should have. Some of her later paintings are in the bedrooms and the study here, a couple are in my new office at Winter Brokerage, and the others you'll see when you spend the weekend at my place in Sag Harbor." Her eyes met Corelli's. "You will, won't you?"

"We'll see." Corelli cleared her throat. "She's given you quite a gift. And quite a responsibility, guarding her legacy."

"Yes," she said, staring into space. "And since Nardo and Spencer predeceased her, my first decision is what to do about the paintings she wanted them to have. I'll give Spencer's to his parents, but Nardo was so angry at his parents that I'll probably give it to his sister Antonia, whom he adored." She shrugged and said with a mischievous smile and a voice that seemed right out of *Gone with the Wind*, "I'll think about it tomorrow."

Corelli had eaten more today than she had in quite a while. Perhaps Brett had added an appetite potion to it. Or maybe she responded to personal care from a woman with a beautiful spirit. She handed the now nearly empty plate to a passing waiter. "Speaking of Nardo's parents, had you met them before today?"

Brett shoulder bumped her. "Am I to have no secrets from you? No, I'd never met either of them."

"Mrs. del Balzo seemed very interested in what you were saying."

"I told her Nardo and I were good friends and that I had spoken to him Tuesday night. She said she didn't know any of his friends and asked if we could get together soon to talk about him. I said I would call in a few weeks. That's it."

Corelli nodded. "Thank you for feeding me. I need to get back to work. Detectives Parker and Green will stay until all the guests and the catering people leave and Detective Kim arrives."

"I'd love for you to come back after work?"

Corelli liked that idea, but of course, she wouldn't in the middle of an investigation. "It'll be late. And it's not a good idea right now when you have my detectives hanging around. You be good."

Brett snorted. "You've made sure of that. Detective Kim and I have a lot of laughs, but I don't think she's a lesbian. Besides, I want what I want."

Corelli blushed. "Sorry, I should have said, be safe." She waved Parker closer.

"I'm shameless, aren't I?" Brett grinned, not looking sorry at all. She slipped her arm through Parker's and listened while Corelli issued orders.

"I'll walk you to the door, Detective."

Corelli stopped to speak to her people on the way to the door. Brett's two guards hung back, giving them privacy.

Brett spoke for Corelli's ears only. "I love it when you give orders."

"You're right," Corelli said, smiling. "You are shameless."

CHAPTER FORTY-EIGHT

Thursday – 8 p.m.

She longed for a hot shower, a reheated dinner courtesy of Gianna, and a glass of wine, but she settled for washing her face in the ladies' room and pizza and San Pellegrino sparkling water from the joint a few blocks away. While Parker went to the desk to retrieve their dinner, Corelli organized the reports into neat piles on the conference room table—del Balzo, Nickerson, Lerman, general—to facilitate their analysis of the cases.

She started to toss the copy of today's *Daily World* that someone had left on the table, but the picture of the del Balzos coming down the steps of St. Patrick's caught her eye. Carla's veil was up. She probably had forgotten to lower it after the reception line in the vestibule. They both looked distraught, as one would expect for a couple whose only son was being buried.

But something about the picture didn't sit right with her. Was she getting cynical? It seemed so posed. Each time she and Parker had talked to them, the ambassador had made no effort to hide his disgust for his son, and his wife had seemed distant and indifferent, only interested in protecting her husband's career. Yet, she remembered, Luca's death had seemed unreal, like a cruel joke until she had actually seen him lying in the casket at the funeral home. The del Balzos had had a family-only viewing at the funeral home before the service at St. Patrick's Cathedral, and that may have made it real for them—their son was dead. Perhaps that was why Carla wanted to talk to Brett about Nardo. Maybe the del Balzos were like her parents. Maybe Carla had followed Leonardo's lead and now that her son was dead, she felt a need to know more about him, about his life. Would her mother want to know about her life from her friends—well, her colleagues? Not much to know, actually. She was painfully aware she had disconnected after Marnie was killed, that Gianna and Simone were her only close relationships, and that while she loved the job, it was no longer enough. She wanted more.

The kick at the conference room door interrupted her musing. She opened the door and Parker staggered in juggling a large pizza, a bottle of San Pellegrino, a can of soda, and a container with a salad. "Ah, dinner, I'm starving," Corelli said, taking the pizza and the salad and placing them on the table. "Let's eat and work." She poured herself a glass of San Pellegrino. Parker popped the tab on the can of soda, and poured herself a cup.

Corelli read a report as she chewed her pizza and picked at her salad. Parker took a slice of pizza and opened today's *Daily World* to catch up on the news. They ate in silence.

Parker carried the remaining half a pizza and salad up to the squad where it would surely be eaten and returned with coffee for each of them.

Corelli sipped her coffee. "Let's start with Nardo. We'll go through your notes and the reports, and then we'll move on to Spencer and Meg." She pulled a new yellow pad from the pile. "I'm going to make a chart so we can see the commonalities and the differences."

"Sounds good," Parker said.

Corelli set up four columns: the leftmost for *Information* and the other three for the victims, *Nardo, Spencer, Meg*. As Parker read through her notes she filled in the rest. The first heading under information was *Method*. Under method she listed single shot to the cerebellum, small-caliber bullet. The second heading was *Crime Scene*, under which she listed rosary clasped in hands, incense,

Gregorian chants playing in a loop, bottle of San Pellegrino, wearing pajamas. They skimmed all the reports for Nardo and added a heading for *Suspects*, under which they listed the sightings by neighbors of Andrea Sansone, Emilio Ottaviano, Scott Sigler, and Franco Ginocchioni. Although no one had seen him she added Luther Phelps, the religious guy, who might be the tall man in black wearing a hat and sunglasses. They had pretty much eliminated all of them except the man in black because Nardo had spoken to Brett after Sansone, Ottaviano, Sigler, and Ginocchioni had all left the apartment. The gay bar canvas had turned up nothing, and his friends and family couldn't offer any help.

"Let's create a *Missing* heading and note Nardo's things that we didn't find— his gun, his iPhone with his address book and calendar, his laptop, and the picture of all the friends on the steps of City Hall. His cleaning woman said he had all of them. Kate and Brett confirmed the iPhone and the computer. As for the picture, Kate gave copies to Nardo, Spencer, Brett, Gary, Meg, Ellen, and Nelson. None of his best friends knew he had a gun. There was no sign of a struggle, and unless Nardo entertained in his pajamas, it seems likely he knew his killer. Could be a friend or maybe someone he picked up and brought home for sex. But that scenario doesn't quite fit with Meg being a victim. And of course we have the man in black."

"Let's do the same for Spencer."

When they had gone through Parker's notes and all of the information gathered on Spencer Nickerson, they stopped to discuss what they had and filled in the appropriate columns.

"The cheese and cracker spread indicates Spencer was expecting someone, probably his killer. There's no evidence his killer ate or drank, except a wineglass appears to be missing from Spencer's set of twelve. The cleaning woman said the full set was there when she cleaned two days before. She knows because she washed and dried a glass by hand and put it in the cabinet and there were no other spaces. All the others were there. His cell phone was found under the sofa and there were no suspicious calls, but there were a number of hang-ups on his home machine. His calendar was on his computer, on paper in his home office, and in his phone. Although his copy of the picture wasn't found during the search, it turned out he had sent his copy of the picture out to be framed professionally. By the time they knew it existed, they had already seen Burke's copy. He had an appointment to go to the theater with his friend, Bill, but he'd scratched it out and scrawled 'lama'. They'd discussed whether it was something to do with the Dalai Lama but apparently he wasn't in town, and Spencer hadn't been into any religion. They hadn't come up with anything else. The witness had described a tall man dressed in black wearing a hat and sunglasses.

"Meg is different again. Her phone, which contained her calendar, and the copy of the picture were all in the house where one would expect them. Her only appointment for the week was two days earlier with a gallery owner about the show of women artists they were planning. She had jotted notes on the pad next to the telephone: 'afbanchers,' 'redblucanturp,' 'narsmahere' and 'invtersho.' The only one that seemed to make sense was red and blue paint, canvas, and turpentine. Although she was dressed for work in her paint-spotted jeans, she also was expecting someone. She had a glass of wine on the table near her on the sofa and there was another glass, a bottle of wine, and some grape leaves, olives, and cheese on the table in the dining room. But apparently her guest was only interested in killing, not eating or drinking.

The dog walker described a man similar to the one who went into Nardo's apartment and the one seen going into Spencer's house, dressed in black, wearing sunglasses and a slouch hat pulled down to hide his features."

Corelli stood and paced as she summarized. "Both men mentioned the 'un-Christians' but as far as we know, Meg had not received any threats. Our theory about Luther Phelps, the religious guy, being the mystery man in black doesn't hold up since we have no evidence he had a desire to kill lesbians. I'm thinking we should eliminate him as a suspect for any of these murders." She looked at Parker. "What do you think?"

Parker chewed on her pen. "You're right. He doesn't fit."

Corelli nodded and continued. "Nardo's rosary was cut-glass, fairly expensive, probably his, probably from Italy. Neither of the other two was religious, so it looks like the killer purchased cheap rosaries somewhere and brought them with him. Nardo's sound system was playing the CD, which very likely was his. The killer brought a cheap CD player and the same CD to the house of each of the other two vics. So far, we haven't found where the killer is buying the players and CDs."

Corelli poured herself another cup of sparkling water and sat. "The thing that troubles me about the serial killer theory is that Nardo's killing seems opportunistic, that the killer didn't plan to kill him, but when something triggered the desire to kill, he used what he found—Nardo's gun, his rosary, the Gregorian chants— then lovingly laid him out. The other two appear premeditated. The killer went with the intention of killing them and brought the gun and the rosaries and the CDs and the players. Why these victims? Was it because the killer was able to reach them? Kate Burke, Nelson Choi, and Brett all had repeated hang-ups on their answering machines. Spencer's machine had a couple of hang-ups before he picked up, but the message cut off. Meg's machine was off and Nardo's machine had no hang-ups. If the picture was the source, why does it appear that the killer hadn't planned to kill Nardo? The fact that Simone and Nicky didn't have missed calls on their cells leads me to believe the killer is using Nardo's address book and not the list. But why?

"Nardo is the source. I'm starting to think about the ambassador again, but while I can imagine him killing Nardo in a fit of rage, I can't see him cold-bloodedly going after Nardo's friends to cover it up. On the other hand, being prime minister is very important to him and his wife."

"Yeah," Parker said, "I like him too. But don't forget he had an alibi for Nardo and for Spencer, unless his sweet young thing is in it with him. I doubt she'd lie to cover two murders."

"Maybe you and I need to have a go at her. Make sure she understands the stakes here."

Parker nodded. "Now?"

Corelli glanced at her watch. Eleven o'clock. "How about tomorrow morning early? Let's call it a night." She yawned. She knew she wouldn't sleep more than a couple of hours, but Parker might as well be fresh tomorrow.

Parker stood and stretched. "I need to make a pit stop. Meet you at the elevator in ten?" Parker asked.

"Perfect."

Corelli absentmindedly aligned the GALS case files on her desk. Something important was hovering in her mind, just outside her reach. A few rounds with the punching bag followed by a long hot bath when she got home might bring it out of her consciousness.

Her eye fell on the Italian magazine article about the del Balzos, her attention caught by the photograph of them dressed identically: in black suits, black shirts, black boots, and sunglasses. She picked it up and reread the text. "Who Wears the Pants, Carla or Leonardo? No Valentine chocolates for this ambitious lady. Her only passions are pistachio nuts and her husband's career. Most people who eat so many nuts would get fat, but not the mysterious Carla del Balzo, the power behind the throne. She burns lots of calories running interference for her husband's career. Some say she's left a trail of wounded and bleeding behind as she cleared the way for Leonardo's climb up the ladder. Now the pinnacle is in sight and rumor has it that The Carla will do anything to ensure she is Madame Prime Minister."

Corelli put the article down, one phrase reverberating in her mind: *The Carla will do anything to ensure she is Madame Prime Minister.* Sansone said the ambassador was "too squeamish, too soft" to kill his son. She skimmed her notes. Spencer said, "not a hot date, a cold fish." Lama. She rubbed her eyes. Could it be? Was that short for La Mama? And Meg's Narsmahere. Was that Nardo's mama coming here? It all fit. Nardo was going to expose his father's secret and said he had told his friends. Was Carla using his contact list to hunt down his friends, one by one?

She should have seen it; the woman was cold as ice. But could she prove it? Carla's DNA at Nardo's could be explained and she would bet they wouldn't find any at the other two crime scenes.

A trap. Corelli would have to set a trap. It would be hard to get the chief on board. Right now everyone was safe. She would think about it tonight, explore it tomorrow. Carla had asked to see Brett. She needed to warn Brett and let the officers assigned to guard her know Carla was not to be allowed into the apartment under any circumstances.

She speeddialed Brett's number and tapped her fingers, waiting impatiently. No answer. The machine finally picked up. Brett's voice. "Brett it's Detec, um, Chiara, pick up. It's important. I need to talk to you and I'm not hanging up until you answer." She repeated the message, fighting to keep the panic out of her voice. She hung up and dialed Officer McClusky's cell phone. It rang but she ended up in voice mail. She dialed the number for the concierge at the desk in Brett's lobby.

"Harborview—"

"This is Detective Corelli. Did anyone go up to Ms. Cummings's apartment?"

"No—"

"Did you send a woman up there?"

"If you'd just let me talk, Detective, the officer and Ms. Cummings just went out a few minutes ago, for a walk along the water."

"Was anybody else with them?"

"Not that I saw."

She closed her phone.

"I thought we were going to meet—" Corelli looked ready to throw up. "What's going on?"

Corelli shot out of her seat. "Let's go. Carla del Balzo is the killer and I'm afraid she convinced Brett to meet her outside."

Parker's mouth dropped but she didn't hesitate. They dashed out of the station and jumped into the car. Corelli called for backup, then shouted an explanation to Parker over the siren as she blasted down the West Side Highway.

"Isn't McClusky with her tonight?" Parker asked, keeping her eyes on the road.

"Yes, but she's not answering either. Damn, they're not supposed to leave the apartment."

Traffic at eleven o'clock was minimal, but it seemed like an eternity before they pulled up to Brett's condo. Leaving the car door open, Corelli sprinted into the lobby, Parker right behind. "Has Ms. Cummings come back?"

"Not yet."

"Do you know which way she went?"

"Sorry, I was distracted by another tenant who came in as she walked through the door so I didn't notice."

"I'll go to South Cove, you go north on the Esplanade," Corelli said, slipping into the vest Parker handed her.

"What if I see them?"

"Text me. But if Carla is with them, do what you need to do to keep Brett safe. I'll do the same."

They reached the path along the water and drew their guns before separating. Corelli jogged toward South Cove, Brett's favorite spot, and although Corelli hadn't said when they'd walked there the other night, one of her favorites too. She loved the peacefulness of it with its view of the statue and the sense of being enclosed by the water. The Hudson River smelled particularly fishy tonight and it seemed louder than usual, crashing against the pilings and the seawall. A light sprinkle hit her face. She hadn't noticed, but a boat must have passed, creating a wake. She was nearing the walkway, the best place to sit. She hesitated, listening. Was that the murmur of voices underneath the roar of the water, or her imagination? Voices. She was sure. She slowed down and stepped carefully. She could see Brett, but no one else. She put her phone on vibrate, and texted Parker. *B here. Send bk up to South.* She pocketed the phone, hesitated. If she were mistaken, Brett would be in a rage at her overprotectiveness. So be it. She crept closer.

Brett was kneeling beside someone on the ground. She couldn't see McClusky so it probably was her. Maybe she'd fallen? Corelli inched forward. Carla or someone dressed in black was pointing a gun at Brett who seemed to be trying to reason with her. Where the hell was the backup?

Suddenly Parker was next to her.

Corelli whispered in Parker's ear. "Go along the upper path and get behind Carla."

"Shouldn't we confront her together?" Parker whispered back.

Corelli shook her head and signaled her to move. When Parker was in place, Corelli inched closer. Now she could hear Carla speaking in Italian.

"Sorry Brett, but I have to kill you. If only Nardo hadn't told his friends the story about his father. I could have stopped with him. I do hate killing, you know."

"What story?"

Carla laughed. "Don't play games. Why else would he call you in Japan?"

"What story could be so terrible that you'd murder your son and others to keep it quiet?" Smart lady, that Brett. Responding in Italian would probably make her more real to Carla.

Carla snorted. "You know the saddest part about this whole thing is that Nardo was wrong about his father. It was me. Leonardo is too soft, too nice. He wouldn't have gotten anywhere without me. So you can see it wasn't fair Nardo was going to ruin his father's career, ruin our chance to be prime minister. After all, I got rid of that piece of shit as soon as we no longer needed him."

"My god, Carla, I don't know what you're talking about. Nardo never told anyone why he was so angry with Leonardo. In fact when I last talked to him, he had decided it was time for him to move on, forget about what his father had done to him. He was planning to stay in New York when you went back to Italy as prime minister. We were going to meet to talk about a job in my company."

"You're lying. I know he told his friends. And that bitch Corelli is trying to find out what it was. I guess he didn't tell her."

"But Detective Corelli wasn't Nardo's friend."

"You think I'm stupid? I saw her in the picture. I tried to shoot the bitch but she ducked. Well, when everyone is dead she'll never find out."

Corelli raised her gun and moved into the circle of light so Carla could see her.

"It's over, Carla. Give me the gun." She moved closer, maneuvering herself between Carla and Brett. She checked out Carla's gun. Oops, not the small caliber she'd been using.

"It's too late to stop." Carla laughed, a harsh, ragged, crazy sound.

"I've told her Nardo never told me anything about his father," Brett said.

Corelli glanced at the officer sprawled on the boardwalk. Her hair was soaked with blood and a wet, dark circle covered the ground around her head. The large rock nearby glistened.

"She's alive," Brett said. "Carla hit her on the head with that rock."

Corelli spoke to Carla in Italian. "Let me call an ambulance for the officer. My team knows it's you, so it won't do you any good to kill us. And if you do, you still will never be the prime minister's wife. Put your gun down and I'll tell the court you cooperated."

They were at a standoff, guns pointed at each other. Carla moved closer. Another couple of feet and Corelli could grab her.

"We have you surrounded, Carla. Give me the gun."

Her head swiveled.

"You lie," Carla said, pulling the trigger. Corelli felt a sting in her right shoulder, but she managed to push Brett away as Carla shot again and again. Corelli went down, blood spurting. More shots. Her head filled with the sounds of Brett's screams, the water lapping against the retaining wall, her own ragged breathing, and the drumming of her heart.

"Officer down! Officer down!" Parker screamed into her phone. She gave their location, then pushing Brett aside she knelt next to Corelli, who was still breathing but bleeding profusely from her head, left shoulder, and left leg. Brett was on her knees, sobbing. Parker assessed the situation. The head wound looked superficial but it and the shoulder were bleeding heavily. The leg was spurting blood as if an artery had been nicked. She grabbed Brett. "We have to slow the bleeding or she'll bleed to death." Parker removed her belt and used it to tourniquet Corelli's leg. She checked the tourniquet to be sure the blood had slowed, then removed her jacket and placed it on the shoulder wound and pressed. "Put your hand on top of mine and when I pull my hand out, press down hard."

Brett snapped to it. She pushed her hair aside and slid her hands over Parker's. "Like this?"

"Yes, that's good. Keep pressing." Parker removed her hand, then reached into Corelli's jacket pocket, removed a clean white handkerchief, and pressed it to the head wound.

"I shouldn't have waited. I should have shot Carla before she did any damage."

"Carla? Where's Carla?" Brett asked, fear in her voice. Her head swiveled but didn't move her hands.

"I shot her and took her gun. She's cuffed to a bench."

Parker looked up at the sound of running feet and voices. She hoped it was the EMTs. "Over here, two officers down."

Brett put her weight on Chiara's shoulder. "Don't die, Chiara. Please don't die."

CHAPTER FORTY-NINE

Saturday – 3 a.m.

She floated to awareness but lay with her eyes closed. Her mind heavy, foggy, tried to make sense of the heavy scent of flowers mixed with a chemical odor and frigid air. A funeral parlor?

"Am I dead?" She spoke aloud without meaning to, then realized if she were dead no one could hear her. Her throat felt dry and scratchy. *Do you feel things if you're dead?*

"No, sweetie, thank God, you're very much alive." Something warm touched her face, a hand, no lips. Gianna. Alive. She wanted to ask Gianna if she were sure and struggled to open her eyes, but it was too hard. She fell back into darkness.

The next time she came to consciousness, her mind felt sharper. She remembered Gianna had said she was alive. Not wanting to find Gianna was a figment of her imagination, she lay with her eyes closed, trying to remember what had happened. It was quiet except for the steady beep, beep, beep. Ah, a monitor. A hospital. Why?

Her eyes popped open. "Brett?" She tried to get up.

A hand pushed her down gently.

"Brett's fine. She's right outside waiting to see you."

She focused. Gianna was smiling. "Welcome back."

"Parker?"

"Fine too. She's been so worried. She barely eaten anything and I don't think she's stopped pacing since they brought you in. She called me on the way to the hospital."

Corelli tried to nod and winced.

Gianna brushed her cheek. "Easy sweetie, it's too soon to be athletic."

Corelli tried to smile but wasn't sure it worked.

"Drink?"

Gianna put a straw in Corelli's mouth. "Just a sip."

"Time?" What did they do to her throat?

"Three in the morning. It's Saturday. You've been out since Thursday night."

Gianna was smiling and crying at the same time.

"Don't cry."

"I'm crying because I'm happy. Better get used to it. Simone and Patrizia and Nicky are outside with Brett and Parker. We've all been waiting for you to wake up. Momma and Papa too, until we sent them home about eleven p.m. Do you want to see Brett?"

"First sisters and Nicky, then Brett and Parker."

Gianna left the room and returned with Simone and Patrizia who were also smiling and crying. She tried to smile back as they stood on either side of her bed, kissing and stroking her. Nicky held back awkwardly.

She reached a hand out to each sister and groaned at the pain that shot through her left shoulder. There was a collective intake of breath.

"Sorry, Chiara, I should have warned you not to move your left arm and shoulder. Or your head. One of the bullets hit your left shoulder and another hit the artery in your left thigh. They rushed you to the OR, gave you blood and repaired the artery, but they've kept you sedated to keep you still, so please don't try to move around. Let Patrizia take that hand. You just lie quietly," Gianna said.

"Hey, big sis, you're a hero again. You're making me the most popular girl in college. Everybody wants to know about you. Your picture was on the front page of all the papers. Of course, the first pictures when they were rushing you to the hospital weren't so hot, but the pictures from the file looked fab. Some people thought it was me," Simone said, grinning.

"Glad…to…help."

Patrizia picked up Corelli's left hand gently and brought it to her lips. "Stop being so silly, Simone. We've been so worried. Father Giovanni was here and Father Bart, the brother of that lovely Brett whose life you saved. And Parker. So many people were worried about you, cops, the mayor, the police chief, Kate Burke the speaker of the City Council, that reporter Darla North and her camera person, and others I didn't meet. We all prayed for you."

Corelli felt her lips quirk and hoped Patrizia wouldn't notice. At least Patrizia approved of Brett and her brother the priest.

"Need to sleep. Go home. Come…tomorrow."

Patrizia and Simone kissed her cheek.

"As Patrizia and Simone headed for the door, Nicky lingered.

"Nicky. We have…date…talk," she said softly, so only he could hear.

"Sure thing. When you're better."

"Go, Gianna. Rest."

"Are you sure, sweetie? I can sleep here again."

"No…come…morning."

Gianna kissed Corelli's cheek. "I'll be here early. Want anything?"

"You."

Gianna held the door for Brett and Parker. Brett was smiling and teary. Parker looked guilty, ill at ease. They moved closer to the bed. Brett covered Corelli's hand with her own, moved her face close, and locked eyes with Corelli.

"Chiara, I'm so sorry. It was stupid of me. None of this would have happened if I wasn't so pig-headed. I almost got you killed."

"Not…your…fault. Nobody…suspected. If she…came…to apartment. Might…have been…too…late."

Her eyes moved to Parker. "McClusky?"

"Fine. Lots of blood, but just a concussion. She went home last night."

"How did it…" She stopped to catch her breath, "…go down, Brett?"

"Carla called me. She said she was having trouble sleeping and would I see her? She sounded so distraught. I told her to come right over. She said she'd come to South Cove to get some air and could I meet her there now? I agreed without thinking. Officer McClusky tried to talk me out of it, but," she blushed, "I insisted. I invited her to join me as long as she gave me a little privacy. She called you but she couldn't get a signal in the elevator. She tried again as we walked toward South Cove, but your line was busy so she left a message. Then suddenly, Officer McClusky fell down."

She let go of Corelli's hand to brush her tears away. "I didn't understand what had happened so I knelt down to help her. It wasn't until I looked up and saw the gun pointing at me that I sort of got it, but not really. So I asked. That's where things were when you showed up."

Brett looked at Parker.

"Carla knocked McClusky out with a rock. She didn't shoot her because she was afraid the gunshot would attract people before she was ready to kill Brett, but she would have finished McClusky after Brett. We arrived before she could do either. She got off five shots at you and Brett, but you pushed Brett aside and took four bullets. Your vest must have slipped because one hit your left shoulder, though luckily it didn't hit the artery or any nerves. One nicked the artery in your left leg and it was touch-and-go as to whether or not they could repair it but they did. The third bullet grazed your head. The fourth hit your chest. The vest protected you but you'll be black and blue and sore for a while.

"You hit Carla's arm and stomach. I got her in the chest and shoulder. She's down the hall under guard. She bragged that she had outsmarted the NYPD and confessed to all the killings."

"Why?"

"Leonardo's boss started sexually abusing Nardo when he was eight years old. Nardo thought it was his father looking in the door the first time his boss raped him, but it was Carla and she allowed him to use Nardo whenever he felt like it. Nardo thought his father furthered his career by letting his boss abuse him but it was Carla. She let it go on for about five years, until Leonardo no longer needed the boss to advance. Then she killed the boss. When Nardo threatened to make the abuse public, she went to see him to convince him not to ruin his father's chances. She told Nardo it was her, not Leonardo, who had allowed the abuse, but he didn't believe her. He thought she was covering for Leonardo."

"Gun?"

"She gave Nardo the gun after the burglary. That's why we couldn't find any record of his getting it. She had a lot of guns, none licensed, including the rifle she used to shoot at you the other night. She and Leonardo are hunters so she's a good shot. As we thought, she was using the photograph to decide whom to kill. She thought Simone was you, that you were Nardo's friend and that you knew the story and were baiting Leonardo to get him to confess."

"She's crazy."

"Yep. But cool as a cucumber. Said she had no choice but to kill Nardo to protect their becoming prime minister. She knew where he kept the gun, so she excused herself to go to the bathroom, but she got the gun and walked up behind him and pulled the trigger. She said it was quick and painless; he never knew what happened. But Leonardo told her Nardo said his friends knew all about it, so she took Nardo's copy of the picture, so she could kill all his friends. Took his phone and computer and called the people in the picture, called until somebody answered."

"The ambassador?"

"He's devastated. Had no idea what she had done to their son. He's withdrawn himself from consideration for prime minister. He'd like to talk to you when you're up to it."

They were silent for a minute. Parker said, "Sorry, I should have shot faster to protect you."

"Parker." She extended her right hand. "Please."

Parker hesitated then took Corelli's hand. She brushed her eyes with her arm.

"You...get a medal." Corelli tried to smile. "Don't beat... yourself. Followed orders. My fault. I had no idea how crazy she was...I thought I could talk...her out of it. I'll be fine. Please...not your fault. I need...you to be...okay."

Parker cleared her throat. "Thanks. I..." She looked from Corelli to Brett and back. "The captain and the chief have been here. And hundreds of cops from all over the city have been waiting outside."

"To show backs?"

Parker shook her head. "To show respect. Even your favorite mayor made an appearance." She smiled. "Of course, he spent most of the time in front of the cameras taking full credit for everything. Darla and Bear spent a lot of time sitting with us waiting to see if you would make it. And, um, Gil Gilardi, a department shrink we have to see, stopped by to see how we were doing. I start seeing her Monday; you, when you feel better."

"Don't forget your dad spent the night with us as well, P.J.," Brett said.

"My dad?" She looked down. "Randall. Yes, he came to support me."

"Randall…sounds…good…man."

Brett took Parker's hand. "The EMTs said P.J. saved your life. If she hadn't applied a tourniquet to your leg and put pressure on your wounds, you would have bled out by the time they found us."

Corelli tried to lift her left arm and gasped and grimaced in pain. "What…will…Senator …Daddy…think?"

Brett frowned. "Senator Daddy?"

Parker smiled at Brett. "A private joke." She looked at Corelli. "He's pissed. I imagine."

"I'll…bet. He…say…anything…about it?"

"Nothing so far."

Brett put her fingers on Corelli's lips. "I think you need to rest, Chiara."

Parker nodded. "They took our guns, and you know, they're investigating, so I have lots of free time. I'll come by tomorrow, if that's all right with you?"

"Yes, come." Corelli tried a smile and hoped it wasn't a grimace. "Bring newspapers. And, you."

Parker's face lit up like the sun blasting out from behind the moon at the end of an eclipse. "Sure. Well, Brett's right. You should rest. I'll see you tomorrow. Brett, I'll wait and give you a lift home."

Brett smiled. "You go get some sleep, P.J. I'll stay with Chiara while she sleeps."

Parker grinned. "See you in the morning."

After Parker walked out, Brett clasped Chiara's right hand. "You and I have a lot to discuss, my lovely detective. I plan to do it while you're too weak to fight me off, but I'll wait until you're rested and alert."

"Just friends?"

"Until you say different, just friends."

Chiara squeezed Brett's hand and gently pulled her toward the bed.

Brett raised her eyebrows. "You want me on the bed?"

"Yes."

Brett kicked off her shoes, climbed onto the right side of the bed, and inched as close to Chiara as she dared. "Is this all right?"

As always when near Brett, Chiara felt the heat, the butterflies in her head, and the feeling of feathers brushing her skin. She turned to face Brett, gazed into those emerald green eyes, and sighed. "Perfect."